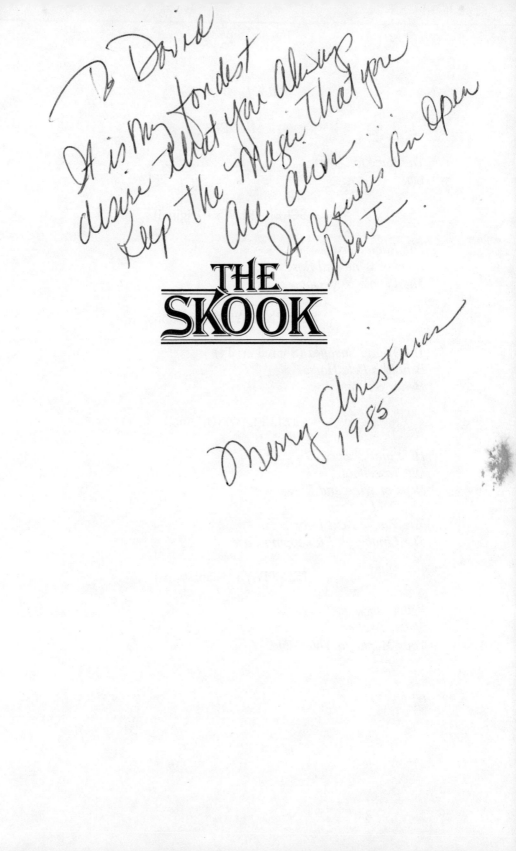

To David
It is my fondest
desire that you always
keep the magic that you
are alive ...
All alive ...
It requires an open
heart.

THE SKOOK

Merry Christmas
1985—

THE SKOOK

A NOVEL BY

JP Miller

WARNER BOOKS

A Warner Communications Company

Printed in the United States of America
First printing: August 1984
10 9 8 7 6 5 4 3 2 1

Designed by Giorgetta Bell McRee

Library of Congress Cataloging in Publication Data

Miller, J. P. (James Pinckney), 1919–
    The skook.

    I. Title.
PS3563.I397S58   1984   813'.54   84–2389
ISBN 0–446–51296–6

For Jace, Jack, Monty, Lia, Anthony, and Sophie

I had a dream, which was not all a dream.
LORD BYRON

THE SKOOK

Prologue

Everybody in the Lambert-ville–New Hope area remembers the big explosion of 1971. It broke windows as far away as Stockton. At first no one could figure out exactly what had blown up, or where. Finally a witness on the Bucks County side reported seeing a great flash on the bank of the river on the New Jersey side, and then having his eardrums almost broken by the blast. With this clue state troopers were able to find the spot where the whole side of a hill rising up from the river had been dislodged and had slid right down to the water's edge. It wasn't until the next day that word got around that Spanish Barrman had been buried alive.

A shudder went through the community. It was a horrible way to die, people said. Poor old Span. Hell of a nice guy. What a way to go. And after so much sadness in his life, what with the scandal and the divorce and all. And then that second wife, Yovi. What a saint he'd had to be to bear that burden.

There was a routine memorial service, attended by the young

widow Yovi in a black veil, and after that the event dimmed quickly. Span Barrman's departure had left no great vacancy in the community. He was replaced by another small businessman the way a broken cup is replaced on the shelf in a diner. Barrman Home Improvements, a siding and insulation company, was quickly sold by the widow to Barrman's installation foreman, Bobby Harris, who had been, along with Barrman himself, one of the three salesmen. Commissions owed served as the down payment, the bereft Mrs. Barrman took back the note at a few dollars a month, the name was changed to Harris Home Improvements, and the current of life in the Lambertville–New Hope region of the Delaware Valley flowed on its normal way.

It was not until almost a year later that the name of Barrman got into the papers again. This was on the occasion of the disappearance and probable death of the widow Yowa Pellegrini Spiegel Barrman, known as Yovi, along with Jerry Odessa, her lover-fiancé—or new husband (no one at the time knew which)—in the Gulf of Mexico. Their borrowed yacht, with no one on board, had run aground on a barren cay a hundred miles off the coast of the Yucatán.

The local papers, having no foreign correspondents, carried what little was said about the mystery in the New York *Times* and the Philadelphia *Inquirer,* rephrased, along with photos of Yovi and her companion, and then dropped the subject.

The people of the region—who had long been intrigued by the lurid, mysterious, and tragic history of Jerry Odessa and the Barrmans—now accepted the presumed deaths of the three principals as the end of the story. It was not until eight and a half years later that a traveler discovered that what had actually happened was quite different from what had been rumored, surmised, or reported in the press.

It was Span Barrman's custom to go fishing in the Delaware River on Sunday mornings. He usually stayed until sundown or later, and came home in a state of quiet drunkenness, the result of having sipped vodka all day long. He seldom caught fish; if he did, he gave them away before coming home, as neither he nor his wife liked to clean them, cook them, or eat them. He always went alone, without a radio or any companionship except his own thoughts and a fifth of Phillips vodka, and he always chose the same location, which was only a few minutes from his home.

This Sunday morning was rainy, and the river was up. It was not to be a good day for fishermen. Still, Span Barrman, being not a real fisherman but only a man who went fishing, saw nothing wrong with the day. He made his customary preparations, got his equipment together, including his vodka, and waited for Yovi to return with his car. Her own car, a six-month-old aquamarine Alfa Romeo, had refused to start because she had left the lights on all night. It was now almost noon, well past his normal departure time. He had been waiting, ready, and trying not to let himself get hostile, since ten. She was, after all, always late, and if you could not accept her failings, of which this was not the greatest, you could not be part of her life. There were times when not being part of her life seemed, to Span, an acceptable alternative to the waiting and the other things. He poured himself a vodka to help him wait.

He imagined her trying to gun around a sharp turn in his old station wagon with its loose shocks and bucking off the road and into a ditch. She always drove her own car well over the limit with the top down and her long blond hair whipping out behind her. She was especially fond of testing the little roadster's cornering ability. It gave her, she said, that roller-coaster rush.

She got home at half past noon. The infinitely changing green of her eyes and her soft kiss of apology melted his annoyance. He felt—and resented—an overwhelming surge of love. She was, after all, a wildflower, immune to moral laws.

She sat on his lap. "I'm sorry, darling. I stopped at Doris's for a cognac. You know how she runs on." She leaned close, rounded her mouth, and wafted alcohol fumes directly at his nose. Her lips were swollen, her eyes shiny. He fancied he had got a whiff of a musky lotion, too, but decided it wasn't likely. She was the cleanest person he'd ever known. The last thing she did before slipping in that soft, graceful way of hers into a bed was bathe. And then, just before dressing to go home, she bathed again. He knew this from his own experience, and he was sure she had not changed since she had become his wife. She went through the same routine even when she lay with him in their own bed. Although they had been married almost five years her day purse still bulged with a hair dryer, brush, comb, perfume (L'Air du Temps in an antique dispenser, a gift of Papa Pellegrini), skin lotion, toothbrush, toothpaste, and, in a secret compartment he was not supposed to know about, her diaphragm and jelly. She had a horror of the Pill, of all pills.

He tried not to love her. He tried not to hate her. On this particular Sunday he could not stop himself from doing either. He helped her bring the shopping out of the car, letting her walk ahead of him so he could watch her boneless gait, a marvel he never tired of witnessing. Her blondness made the light green cotton dress appear to glow; modest, high-necked, loosely draped, it flowed around her, molding and hinting. Beneath this chaste-looking garment, Span knew, there was only Yovi.

She was saying that she had been followed by a motorcycle gang on the river road, and that it had made her nervous. They had trailed her for a while, then roared within inches of her back bumper for a mile or so. Then they had pulled off into a side road by the quarry.

"Span, don't go today. Stay with me."

When she wore green her eyes were green; when blue, blue; when any other color, blue-green. She always wore pastels, Mediterranean colors. Now she wanted him to stay with her. She wanted him. Or someone. And he was there. She could be empty one minute, burned-out, then glow again the next. She loved him, he knew, in her way, but her way made him lonely. He could not handle the concept of making love to her while she still had Jerry's fingerprints on her, atoms of Jerry's blatant musk-oil cologne—he was sure of it now—in her hair.

"At least have a drink with me before you go," she pleaded.

She got a split of champagne out of the refrigerator. It was Piper-Heidsieck. She bought it in six-packs, like ginger ale. Span poured some vodka over two cubes of ice. He sat across from her. Her overwhelming sexuality made him talk defensively, compulsively.

"Tailgaters. God, how my dad hated tailgaters. He wanted to kill them. Something about him seemed to attract them, he thought. Probably he was just hypersensitive to people driving close behind him. He thought they were closer than they were. Anyhow, he finally put a big trailer hitch on the rear of his car—cast iron—and one day this tailgater was riding up close to his tail pipe and Dad slammed on his brakes and the guy plowed into him and ripped open his radiator and smashed the whole front end of his car. Dad drove away laughing. The other guy couldn't move. When my dad told the story, he always said the tailgater was 'a big black buck.' But he wasn't. He was white. I was there, and the guy was definitely white. I was so scared

I'll never forget. But my father hated black guys as much as he hated tailgaters, so I guess he just dreamed one up so that he could kill two birds with one stone. Damn. Why do I always speak of him in the past tense?"

"Span, you are the sweetest man I know." She got up and moved to the chair next to his.

"I guess that must be the hundredth time I've told you that story. I'm sorry."

"I don't mind. You feel your daddy slipping away so you can't stop thinking of him, even though you used to think you didn't love him."

"I don't know if I love him or not. I think maybe I'm just trying to."

She leaned over and stopped his hand, and took the unlit cigarette from his fingers and put it back in the pack. It was a gesture that meant he didn't have to smoke himself to death just because his father had done so. He got up and planted a thank-you kiss on her hair, smelling the musk again, and went out, pointedly leaving the cigarettes on the table. He had two packs in his tackle box.

Yovi poured what was left of her champagne into her glass and kicked off her sandals and went to the window and looked down at Span as he lit a cigarette before driving away. She waited, wanting to wave to him, but he did not look up. She watched until he disappeared, then she let her eyes drift back to the cars parked in front of the building. Two cars away from her little convertible with its dead battery, Archy Morse was carefully washing his red Corvette. He wore tight swim trunks and flexed his bunchy shoulder muscles and posed as though he knew he had an audience. Yovi pulled the curtain shut, finished her glass, and set it carefully on the table. She unzipped her dress and let it fall to the rug. She stepped away and posed in front of the full-length mirror, wearing nothing but her wedding ring and her rose-gold anklet. She smiled and sent herself a kiss of approval. Then, exhilarated, she walked lightly back to the kitchen, carrying her empty glass. She rinsed it and dried it carefully and put it in its special place. It was tall, fluted,

Baccarat. Span, always on the lookout for special gifts just right for her, had found it in a flea market, its pedigree unrecognized under a thick layer of dust, a bargain. It was a beautiful object to look at, and sensual to the touch. She picked it up again and held it, so solid, so regal, a sort of practical jewel. Yet, to be truly fulfilled, she thought, you must be filled full. She got another split out of the refrigerator, noting with surprise there were only two left. Oh, yes, she'd had one for breakfast. Mustn't forget to get more tomorrow. Tomorrow! God, tomorrow had a distant sound. Here she was, naked, gloriously free—and alone. It was a form of death, these times between; worse, actually. In death you felt nothing, but in this deep valley time you felt excruciating and unrelenting boredom. If only Span had stayed. Why did he always leave her on Sundays, the deadliest day of the week, when everyone she counted on was unavailable? During the week it was understandable that he should leave her to go to work. She had learned to manage then; she had the means—un-heart-touching means, with sad and unenduring results, but means to survive till the one day of the week when love—love, as opposed to the other—could be made with Span, all day, if only he wanted it as much as she, if only he wanted her more than he wanted the river. Oh, Span, Span, if you were home with me now I would make love to you, love, so that you would never forget, never.

She saw *The Songs of Bilitis* lying open on her bedside table. But reading was boring too. If only Bilitis lived in the apartment next door. She stretched out on the bed, leaned up on one elbow, and finished her champagne. Then she put one pillow between her legs and hugged another to her breasts and closed her eyes. She would think about love-moments, some of the special times. She would enjoy them again in memory. No. Impossible. If she had to stay alone today she would die. She could not call Jerry from the apartment because he lived across the river and she did not want his number to show up on the phone bill. He had told her this morning when he kissed her good-bye that he had to work the rest of the day and probably late tonight on his opening argument in a murder trial. Good, he'd be home. He'd just have to take a break for gallantry's sake. Damsel in distress. She called A. A. A. Emergency Road Service and told them her car wouldn't start. She told them it was an emergency.

2

Span turned right, crossed the old bridge by the quarry, and drove down the dirt road to the river. The road dipped steeply toward the water, then came to a dead end at the moldering shell of an old flood-wrecked summer house. He parked in his usual spot, with his front wheels against an algae-green foundation stone. Then he inched his way along the wet path under the cliff to his secret spot, where the river had worn the bank away at the curve, leaving a rooflike overhang with natural rock ribs coming down to the water on both sides. This was Span Barrman's private niche in the world. He unfolded his chair and sat down with a groaning sigh. He opened his tackle box and took out his vodka and treated himself to a long drink. He lit a cigarette and leaned back in his chair and puffed, staring out at the river. Old, like me, he thought. Gray and swollen, like me. Trapped in a big ditch, moving downhill, helpless and all wet, like me. The river, within its limits, does its thing, just like me. Like I. *As* I. Only it doesn't give a good God-damn for anything or anybody. That's what I have got to work my way into. Somehow. I've got it now, right this minute, so all I have to do is learn how to keep it. Just me and the river. Alone. Surely in the whole world there is no feeling as good as the feeling of being alone. No telephone. No business. No old ladies calling up to say their walls are sweating and my insulation did it. No salesman asking for an advance on commissions. No foreman calling in to say his wife is drunk again and he can't go to the job till he gets somebody to stay with her. No emotional attachment to any human thing. No dying father. No smug daughters who agree with their mother that their father's a louse. No ex-wife. No present wife. No smell of musk.

He breathed deeply of the river air, not quite fresh but wild and stimulating still. He took another drink and said aloud: "Yum yum. A bologna sandwich, a jug of vod, and no thou." He was in no hurry to fish. He flipped his cigarette stub out into the water and leaned back and closed his eyes.

His father had brought him to this river to fish forty years ago, when he was barely eight. It was the first time Orville Barrman had ever made an effort to relate to his son, and one of the last. The boy was physically weak. A scrawny five-pounder at birth, his prunelike skin had made Orville, never a diplomat, turn his back on the nursery window, convinced he had been saddled with one of God's errors. He had refused to look at the baby for two months and had taken no part in his christening, except to say "Name him whatever you want, Ida, but not Orville junior." So Ida Spanish Barrman had decided in a rare moment of rebellion to give her son her family name, presenting Orville with yet another reason to look askance at what his wife had birthed.

Span grew up terrified of his father, who seemed to him to be the most dangerous man in the world. He would not have been able to say why, because Orville had never physically punished him, nor ever threatened him. And he did not beat his wife. The nearest to violence Span thought he ever came were the times when, in the middle of the night, Orville would roar in a drunken voice that literally shook the house: "God dammit,

Ida!" After that outburst the boy would lie awake, shaking, waiting for the end of the world, although all he would hear after that would be his father holding his voice down for the neighbors' sake as he explained his point of view—which was the only one—to the woman he had come to believe was of subnormal intelligence. Without wanting to, Ida communicated her fear to her son. So the boy's terror of his father was real and constant.

Finally Orville decided he would quit discussing the boy with his wife and take matters into his own hands. The fishing trip was the first step. When Orville suddenly began to explain fishing to him, Span's fear and desire to please were near panic levels, making learning difficult. Orville decided his son had not only got his mother's weak body and timid disposition but her brain as well. All Span would remember from that fishing trip— besides his father's impatient sighs—were the scales of curling dead skin that caught the sun on the huge man's permanently sunburned nose. The rest was a memory of misery, and Span did not go near a fishing pole for thirty-five years after that day.

Orville worked for the state. He was a construction boss. He feared those above him, who had the power to cause him to lose his job and his pension, and he made sure that those below him, whose jobs and pensions were in his power, also feared him. He was proud of his physical strength, and he used it to impress his men. He could lift one end of an I beam and carry it while two ordinary workers staggered along with the other end. Orville laughed at them. This characterization of himself was the center of his life, so that having a weak son was like having a leper in the family. He wanted to hide him, to deny his existence. He ignored him. Discipline was left to Ida, who preferred to manage the boy with a quiet word.

Span was a loner who hung around the house and constructed a fantasy world that did not require the presence of other children. When Orville got home from work, having got off at four-thirty and spent several hours in the nearest bar, filling his great belly with beer, the boy was usually in bed, faking sleep. One night about two years after the fishing trip Span heard his father come in and start talking urgently to his mother. He got out of bed and pressed his ear to the wall and listened. His father was saying that the boy had been an embarrassment to him for a long time and that he had decided to do something about it. He had been forced into making the decision because his supervisor, Mr. DiBlasio, had brought up the subject of the annual picnic and asked if his ten-year-old kid would be on the softball team.

"Try to unnerstan how I felt, for God's sake, Ida, when I had to tell the man my boy didn't play baseball. I mean, Mr. DiBlasio is my supervisor, for God's sake. He says to me, with this kind of funny look in his eyes, he says, 'A ten-year-old boy doesn't play baseball?' And then he says, 'Oh, I'm sorry, Orville, I guess the boy's got some kind of a physical disability.' So then I said no, he didn't have. And the whole thing came out. Well, look, Ida, Mr. DiBlasio is my supervisor, for God's sake, and he's a smart man, so he offered to talk to me about it. 'I raised three boys myself,' he says. So we went to a bar and we talked about it. You know, when your supervisor invites you to a bar, you go. Anyhow, the upshot of it was that he said the boy spends too much time with his mama, too much time with a female—you know—role model, he says, and the whole thing is just going to keep on getting worse unless I take the bull by the horns. Ignoring the situation, which is what I've been doing, is wrong. The boy needs a daddy, and I'm not going to run from the job anymore. I see what I have got to do. Mr. DiBlasio came right out and asked me if Span even knew what kind of work I do, if he ever saw me at my work. He says, 'Orville, does the boy know how you earn your bread, the bread he eats? Does the boy know how to appreciate what goes into a slice of fried bacon on the table?' He says, 'Orville, you're his daddy. If you don't teach him what it means to be a man, who's gonna?' And you know what, Ida, he's right. The man's right. He's a smart man. He didn't get to be supervisor by being a dummy. So tomorrow morning the boy gets up when I get up, he eats when I eat, and he goes to the job with me, and he watches what happens when men—men, I'm talking about!—get in there with bare knucks and battle for what to eat, what to wear, and a roof to keep out the rain. Okay, Ida? Don't answer, because that's the way it is. This stuff is cold, for God's sake, Ida!"

There was a moment of silence, and Span, already terrified at what he had heard, had a feeling that his mother was about to tell his father that the food was cold because he had been talking instead of eating. But then he heard her say in her low completely subjugated tone: "I'm sorry. I'll warm it up."

He got back in bed, shaking. He could not sleep. At five o'clock his mother came in to wake him up. He made believe he was asleep, and when she said with a hopeful smile (she always tried to see the best side of everything) that she had a big treat for him, a big surprise—his daddy had decided to let him come to work with him for the whole day—he reacted the way he was expected to, with a grateful smile. He got out of bed and hurried to dress, the picture of a boy being honored by the company of his dad.

That day in the hundred-degree heat, as he watched the tank truck spray asphalt on the roadbed, he fainted and wet his pants. His father had to turn the job over to his foreman and put him in the car and drive forty miles to give him back to his mother. On the way home Span threw up on the backseat.

From that day forward Orville and his son were polite strangers. Span became a reader and a good student. At school he gained some self-confidence, and he suddenly sprouted up and filled out and discovered he was not at all bad in sports. When this happened the elder Barrman made overtures of friendship, of acceptance, but the boy had long since decided his father was not his kind of a person, and he gently rejected him. While Span changed, Orville seemed to remain the same. He still had a raw nose with ever-present flakes of dead skin catching the light, and he still sat all day Saturdays in his undershirt, listening to the ball game and drinking beer and picking the sun-blistered skin off the back of his hands, and all day Sunday fishing alone in the Delaware. It was not until five years ago, when the old man was stricken with a heart attack, that Span went to the hospital and looked at him with different eyes and saw that the big sun-reddened, dangerous man he had known all his life was not immutable. By then Span was an English teacher at a prep school, unhappily married to the person he now referred to as the Cow, and the father of two daughters with whom he could not communicate. This in itself made him more understanding and forgiving of old Orville. At least old Orville had made one marriage do him for his whole life, Span thought, and it looked very much as though his boy was not going to be able to duplicate that record of endurance. As a matter of fact Span's affair with twenty-one-year-old Mrs. Abraham Spiegel was, at the moment of Orville's attack, in full flower and getting more reckless by the day. On his first visit to the hospital Span only stayed a few minutes because he was using Orville's illness as a cover for his tryst with Yovi Spiegel at a motel on Route 202. He had expected the time with his father to be embarrassing, and it was, but for a reason different from the one he expected. He had anticipated awkwardness and long silences; instead he found an old man anxious to talk and reveal his long-repressed thoughts. Span was ashamed to cut him off and leave, but he promised to come back the next day and have a long talk. He did. The old man told him that his life was about over, and two of the things he was sorry for were that he had never got to know his own son, and that he had never done anything really brave or noteworthy in his life, anything that would set him aside from the herd. Span cried. He was sitting close to the bed, and the old man reached out and patted him comfortingly on the shoulder. It was then that he told Span that he shouldn't tell his mama what he was about to hear, but that the doctors in giving him the usual tests after a heart attack had found cancer in both lungs.

The following week Span had given Yovi the excuse that he was visiting his dad, and his dad the excuse that he had to figure a big siding and insulation job in Hopewell (he was moonlighting as a salesman for Freddy's Home Improvements to augment his teaching salary), and he had gone fishing alone for the first time in his life. He thought he was doing it to help him understand his father and forgive him for all the long years of alienation. He found that he not only accomplished something of this goal, but that he found a certain kind of peace within himself, something he had never known. He tried it again the following Sunday, and liked it even better; soon the Sunday trips alone to the banks of the Delaware became a part of his life, not to be displaced for long by any event, no matter how important or traumatic, not even by Abe Spiegel's having caught him making love to Mrs. Spiegel in the king-size bed in the Spiegel master bedroom and letting the two Doberman pinscher guard dogs hold him at bay, naked and humiliated, till the police came and took note of the details for legal purposes. Span's shame was heightened by the fact that he actually told Abe Spiegel he was sorry, and his voice broke while he was saying it, at the same time that he huddled in the corner of the bedroom, covering his panic-shriveled private parts with both hands, afraid to make the slightest move for fear of causing the two slavering dogs to attack, and Yovi went sullenly about putting on her clothes in the same room, brazenly walking about and ignoring the dogs (which were, after all, her own), and apparently so completely unrepentant that when Span stammered out his regret she threw him a look of scorn.

It was, up to that time, the worst moment of his life. His wife Deena Jane moved out with their two daughters the following day. The day after that, which was Sunday, he went fishing and consumed an entire quart of vodka. It was to be the best eight hours he was to have for some time.

The divorces followed. The Cow got everything, including not only the custody of Bicky and Sticky, who were fifteen and seventeen and would soon be on their own, but more alimony than Span could afford. Abe Spiegel, a moderately wealthy dealer in gold and precious stones, cast Yovi out without a cent, even forcing her to return the thirty thousand dollars' worth of jewelry he had given her in the two years they had been man and wife. He left her nothing but the rose-gold anklet, which he had ceremoniously put on her left ankle for a special reason known only to himself and Yovi. The anklet had no catch, no open link. He had closed the last link with a soldering tool. Judge Walter Youngford had ruled that the anklet could not be removed by ordinary means and therefore belonged to the lady.

After the divorces came Span's dismissal from Lockatong Preparatory School for moral turpitude, his purchase of Freddy's Home Improvements for no cash down when it was providentially discovered at exactly the right time that Freddy's blood pressure was so high he would have to retire, and Span's marriage to Yovi. Through this entire period of scandal and crisis there were two strange constants: Yovi Pellegrini Spiegel did not once indicate in any way that she was ashamed or regretful of what had happened, and Span did not miss a single Sunday of fishing in the Delaware. The first day he missed was the one weekend they spent on their honeymoon, in Bermuda.

Orville Barrman was sent home from the hospital to wait for death. He liked Yovi, showed some spark when she was around, and seemed to be proud of Span for having got himself into a scandal and come out of it with a pretty wife twenty-two years his junior and a business of his own. Orville had never liked the Cow, anyway. Too officious for a woman, he always said. Too bossy. And raising up those girls to treat their daddy like he was a fool. No wonder Span had jumped the fence and looked for greener pastures.

Ida, ever the dutiful wife, sat by silently and listened to Orville's opinions without offering any of her own. Although he was so weak he could hardly draw breath, and had to pause and gasp between sentences, she still dreaded his disapproval.

Span regretted that his father had had to get sick before they could get to know each other, even a little. He wished they could go fishing just one time together before the old man died, to wipe out the other time. But it was too late for that.

He took another drink and baited his hook with a cheese ball and tossed it out into the stream. Before he could settle back in his chair he got a strike, and he saw that it was an eel. It sped upstream, staying close to the surface, then downstream, then out toward midstream, then back, leaving a long silver wake. Then, as suddenly as it had started, it stopped. Span reeled it in, a dead weight, resigned, passive as a rubber snake. Span's installation foreman, Bobby Harris, loved smoked eel. This would be a little gift for him.

He dipped up some river water in his plastic bucket and dropped the eel in it. A strange sound accompanied the splash of the eel. At first he thought it was an echo or an auditory phenomenon, but then:

"Mr. Barrman?"

The voice was soft, almost effete, and near. It added gently: "Look up, Mr. Barrman."

Span looked up, directly over his head, and saw a face. The angle of his vision, the unexpected distortions of his own perception—due to his leaning back in his chair and looking straight up at a head that was pointed in the opposite direction, looking down—and the unique ugliness of the face itself caused him to fall over backward. He heard high laughter. He scrambled to his feet and looked up again, moving as close to the water as possible so that he could get a better look at the face on the rock overhang.

It was large and round and deep pink, like a cartoon piglet, with small, almost hidden eyes and a button nose and a wide grinning mouth featuring two enormous buck teeth with a gap between them. "You are Mr. Spanish Barrman, aren't you?"

The face was so grotesque, Span thought at first it was a mask. The voice was husky, breathy, androgynous: "Spanish Barrman, born April eighteenth, 1923, Trenton, New Jersey, at one-thirty-one A. M. Born at home. I do not recall the address, and it's not written on my paper here, but we've got it. Did you know you were an Aries native with Capricorn rising and a Taurus moon? Did you know you have a Grand Water Trine, Span, baby?"

Span's neck was hurting from looking straight up, and he was annoyed at the man's attitude and his voice, which made Span think of toadstools. "What do you want, fella? I don't think I know you."

"My public name is Larry."

"Your public name? What the hell do you want? What are you doing with all these statistics about me?"

"What we want, Span, is to talk to you about something real important."

"Like what?"

"Well, it's gonna take awhile, so maybe we all ought to meet up at your car, where we can be comfortable."

Looking up was blinding Span and making him dizzy. The vodka seemed to stir in his belly. A series of nauseous contractions undulated upward to the back of his tongue. He looked down and cleared his throat. "Look, fella," he said, "I came here to do a little fishing. If you want to talk to me, call me tomorrow at my business. It's—"

"We know. Barrman Home Improvements. I have the number. But tomorrow's too late. We want you now. We'll wait at your car."

Span looked up, squinting and frowning. "Who's 'we'?"

Larry spoke to someone behind him, repeating Span's question mockingly. Span heard a giggle and another face appeared beside Larry's. It was a picture of depravity, scarred, thin, and chalk white. It grinned with yellow teeth. "'We' is us, schmuck. Space Angels."

The name sent a chill through Span. The Space Angels were a motorcycle gang who practiced witchcraft and had committed several torture murders—or so the police claimed.

"Heard of us, huh?" Larry asked. "Scared, huh? Don't worry, Mr. Barrman, we wouldn't harm a flea."

"We just wanta shoot the breeze a little bit," the white face said. "Your lady tell you we rode with her this morning?"

"She said you tailgated her."

The white face split in a jaundiced grin. "We figgered she'd tell you, Span, baby. We wanted you to start thinking about us, kind of subconsciously expecting us, being ready for us, ready to accept us, like sundown, you know, or night, 'cause we're a part of your life now, baby, gonna share a destiny, a sacred immortality, like it says in the stars. That's why we gonna get together now and get it going like it's written, so don't fight it. We gonna be so close together we gonna all be one."

"We like to get close to folks!" Larry squealed. His voice had a way of changing from bass to girlish in the middle of a sentence. "Don't we, Boots?"

Boots's thin lips curled over his teeth: "One foxy lady you got, Span. Hey, what you catch?"

"An eel."

"An eel? What you gonna do with it?"

"Smoke it."

"Smoke it!" Boots whooped. "Hey, Larry, he gonna smoke it! Hey, man, I got to see that! How you gonna keep it lit?"

Then the two Space Angels laughed in unison, a vaudeville laugh, "Waa Waa Waa! Waa wa wa wa!"

"See you at your car, Span," Larry said. "We don't want to come down there and mess up our good boots."

The two heads disappeared.

It was over a hundred yards to his car, Span calculated. He could beat them to it if he hurried. They had to travel over pathless hogback, slopes strewn with bare rock and thick brush. If he made a run for it he'd be out of sight under the bank, and the trail along the water was flat all the way to the old summer house. He could be ahead of them by enough margin to start his car and get away. If he didn't go now, this second, he might never get another chance. He looked up. There were no eyes looking down at him. He jammed the end of his pole into a small fault in the rock where he'd been putting it for years. He dumped the eel back in the river. It floated, belly up. He stepped quickly to the corrugated rock rib that blocked his path back to the car and served as a natural buttress to hold up the overhanging cliff. It was tricky to step around it without getting his feet wet, but Span knew how to hug the rock and place one foot on the other side and slide forward till he could put his weight on it and then lift his back foot and swing his body around. He'd only fallen into the river once in five years, and that was due to drunkenness. This time in his fear he did it not only perfectly but fast. Then, as he was about to make a dash for his car along the narrow rock pathway, he was hit in the chest by a rock as big as a golf ball. He staggered back against the buttress and looked up. A massive man with long matted hair and beard towered over him. The man was dressed in a black leather jacket, black leather pants, and black boots with the toes painted white to resemble cloven hooves.

"Where you think you're goin', Cross-Kisser?" he rumbled. He raised a rock the size of a cabbage in his right hand. "How'd you like to have this on your skull?"

Span grabbed the buttress and swung himself back to the other side. His heart was bouncing around in his chest like a bell tongue. He wondered if he were having a heart attack. Was the pain in his chest due to the blow from the rock or to a ruptured aorta?

"Stay where you are, Aries," the big man's voice came to him, "for five minutes, till we've had time to get to your car. Then come and join us. Don't try anything funny. There's thirteen of us."

Thirteen. A coven. Span wasn't sure what that meant, but it reputedly gave official weight to whatever evil witches planned.

There were only two other possible escape routes. He could swim for it and drown in the swollen river, or he could try to go upriver. On the north side of his fishing alcove there was a natural column very like the one on the south, except that this one was thicker and he would have to step into a foot of water to get around it. After that there was nothing but fallen overhang to deal with. In thin formations the red Stockton sandstone was fragile. He had expected the roof over his alcove to fall any day. The possibility lent an excitement to fishing that was not inherent in the act itself.

Span's tackle box was his favorite possession. It held not only his fishing knife, his flashlight, and all the tackle he would ever need, but a sandwich, cigarettes, and a fifth of vodka. Because it was heavy he had left it behind when he set out to race the Space Angels to his car. But now that he was going to try to travel north till he found a place where he could climb out of the riverbed, he took it with him. All his life he had had trouble making calculated decisions. Even on the most important crossroads of his life he had tried to reason calmly but had ended up making impulsive moves. Looking back, as he often did, he saw that he had been wrong more often than right, but this did not change him into a deliberate man. The time between leaping back into his alcove with the throbbing rock bruise on his sternum, and wading around the north column with his tackle box in hand, was approximately eight seconds.

Immediately his path was blocked by the fallen overhang. Between this leaning slab and the curved upright of the cliff there was a rough triangular tunnel that afforded crawlspace, at least for as far as Span could see. Around a curve ahead he could see a reflection of daylight. Without hesitation he put his tackle box down and started to crawl, pushing it ahead of him. There was just room for his body to wiggle through, stretched out full length. He made it to the curve in only a minute, huffing and puffing but feeling elated at being out of sight from the mouth of the tunnel. His chest still hurt from the blow of the rock, but he had never been so full of dynamic energy in his life. He felt that if the slab settled on him he could push it up again. Then he made a sudden, sickening discovery. He had arrived at a bottleneck that would not accept his shoulders. Nothing would give. The rock on all sides of him was solid. He could not crawl backward. He had a sharp stinging pain in his neck from holding his head in an unaccustomed position. He let his head down to rest his neck and consider his situation. If he did manage to back out by some set of undulations that he could not visualize at this moment, he would deliver himself to the Space Angels. If he stayed there for any length of time and the river continued to rise, he would drown. His choices seemed to be limited to how he preferred to die.

He became aware of sharp stings and aches along his body, including what felt like a crown of thorns poking into his forehead. He had snaked himself convulsively in one wild surge into the tunnel, ignoring the rock rubble and grit beneath his soft body. Now he felt the sharp points digging into him and the abrasive surface burning his skin. The torture of the Space Angels had existed only in his mind; to escape it he had created his own torture. He raised his head and looked at the bottleneck again. The narrowness only lasted a foot before opening out into a wider passage. The blockage was caused by a protuberance on the underside of the fallen slab. He managed to open the latches of his tackle box, but with both arms outstretched out ahead of him he barely had the strength to force up its lid far enough to slide his left hand in and rummage under the bottle of vodka and find his knife. He brought it out and waited for his breath and his strength to come back. Then he began to shave away the surface of the rotting sandstone in the cliff wall to his right rather than trying to attack the protuberance in the slab on his left, which was higher and more difficult to reach. The work went fast enough to encourage him, to give him strength. A dim hope at first, it now seemed possible that he would be able to chip and gouge and scrape his way around the bottleneck before he ran out of strength or starved to death. He scraped with his right hand till it got tired; then he shifted the knife to his left hand and, reaching over the back of his head, tried to gouge with it. On one such clumsy stab the knife astonished him by going in to the hilt. He pulled it out, took it back in his right hand, and stabbed again and again, frenziedly, like a maniac stabbing a corpse.

A chunk of rock wobbled beside his knife. He twisted the blade and the piece moved toward him. He pried and it came out, falling on his shoulder, heavy as a brick. Behind it came a chill subterranean odor, like air from an ancient tomb.

"Jesus." He groaned as he let himself sink down. The sound resonated. He had broken through a wall, and beyond it there was Something. For a few seconds his reason left him and the expectancy of a quick death at the fangs of some unimaginable beast whose hibernation he had disturbed caused him to lie there, resigned and spiritless. Then logic took over again and he forced up the lid of his tackle box and squeezed his left hand inside, pushing the vodka aside and this time bringing out his flashlight. The batteries were weak. But he could see hairline cracks, tiny veins in the deteriorating sandstone wall of the cliff. The hole was big enough to see through, but there was no room for him to raise his eyes to that level. He bumped his head trying. He twisted around and somehow managed to get his body on its left side so that he could hold the knife in both hands and work at enlarging the hole downward. The river's rough tongue had been lapping at this spot for centuries, and the lower part of the wall was the thinnest. Within minutes he had cut the bottom edge of the hole down to a level where he would be able to look into it by wedging his head into the triangular space above. As he was about to do this he heard:

"Hey, Mr. Barrman, shame on you!" It was the bearded Angel's voice from above. "You tryin' to embarrass me? The Angels left me here to keep track of you, and now you go and try this sneaky stuff. You think you are going to get away from us? You some kinda crazy? We got thirteen of the sharpest Angels in the world, man! Where are you? Answer me!"

Span remained silent. After a few seconds the voice came again: "Larry told you we wouldn't hurt you, didn't he? Now, come on out. We just want to talk to you. You are going to save all of us a lot of trouble if you cooperate. You hear?"

The source of the voice was moving and Span got a sense of its urgency. The man was worried about ridicule or punishment from his cohorts if he allowed their prey to escape. He tried another approach: "Listen, you God-loving cross-kissing son of a baptized bitch! Do you know who I am? I am One-of-Three! You don't understand that either, you Bible-thumper? One-of-Three who say Two-to-One or Three-to-None if you are to live or die! When you are before the High Priest, you filthy mongrel good-worshiper, you will need my One! And you will be before him before this moon is gone! Either you show your face this minute or you have lost my vote!"

One-of-Three's threat bore such conviction that Span was momentarily tempted to give himself up. But he kept still. One-of-Three uttered a few more threats: He swore that the Space Angels would wait for Span as long as necessary to capture his ass. And then there was silence.

Span raised his head as high as it could go and held his flashlight to the opening. The beam was so feeble that at first he saw nothing. Then, possibly more because of the resonance even his breathing had than from anything he could see, he became aware that he was looking into a chamber of indeterminate size. As his pupils dilated he saw that the ceiling was about three feet higher than his eye. He could not look down because his eye was at the lower edge of the hole he had cut, and could go no higher to look over it. He had no way of telling whether the floor of the room was an inch below his line of

sight, or a foot, or a mile. At the outer limits of his vision—
six feet away, he guessed—he finally made out a curving wall
with what seemed to be a small tunnel beginning about a foot
and a half from the ceiling. It was a perfect waiting room, he
decided, if the floor was not too far below. He wondered if One-
of-Three was standing just above him, waiting to hear a sound
confirming his presence. The consideration lasted only a moment. The prospect of having a little room to turn around in,
to have a drink in, to have a smoke in, to doze in while waiting
for the Space Angels to get tired of waiting for him, was an
inspiration. He began to chip and carve at the hole vigorously,
careless of being heard. The stone was porous, crumbly, easy
to cut, but there was a lot of it. The position from which he
had to work was awkward. His body was not used to this kind
of effort. His heart bumped ominously again, but he paid no
attention to it, except to think: If it goes, so what?

It took two hours to enlarge the hole so that he could get
first his arms and then his head and shoulders through. He
shone the light down, ready to recoil, half expecting to see a
nest of water moccasins or some unknown monster from the
netherworld. What he saw was the rounded curve of the floor
not four feet below his head, shaped like one end of a huge
gourd, with an inch or two of water in the bottom.
He pulled back quickly, got his tackle box, and shoved it
through the hole ahead of him. He lowered it as far as he could
down the near wall, then let it slide. He aimed the light at it
and saw that it had come to rest upright in the little puddle of
water. He then lowered himself headfirst, able to control his
speed by exerting pressure against the sides of the hole, until
his hands touched the tackle box and he was able to use its
resistance to help him slide comfortably to the bottom.
He opened the tackle box and found his matches and struck
one. What he saw was ordinary but magnificent. There was
nothing but red sandstone curving up and around him to form
a moist, womblike hollow. It was as though it had been sealed
since time began, a bubble in the caldron of creation, one of
God's little imperfections. And now he, Spanish Barrman, silly-

named nonentity, siding and insulation salesman, had been chosen in the Eternal Lottery to enter it first; to break, as it were, one of God's earth's maidenheads.

He calculated that if he'd been left alone to do his fishing he'd've had at least three vodkas and three cigarettes by now. All right, he'd catch up fast. He tilted the bottle and let a jigger or more of its sweet heat slip down his throat before he stopped. Then he lit a cigarette and leaned back and smoked hungrily. Was this the first time since earth's creation that tobacco smoke had perfumed these walls? Probably. To celebrate this miracle, he had another drink. It was three-thirty. He was tired and drunk and hungry. He felt illogically elated, like a man of accomplishment. The Space Angels were a bunch of impotent loudmouths. They would wait and wait and finally get tired of waiting and go looking for somebody else to torment. Oh, they would vandalize his car, probably, but then, what were vandals for? He laughed out loud. The laugh echoed hoarsely back from the little opening in the wall opposite his entrance hole. To sound like that it must go in a way, he thought. He resolved to look into it after he'd rested a bit. He ate his bologna sandwich and his little pack of Fritos and took another drink of vodka and smoked a cigarette. Then he slept in the arms of God.

When he woke up he was disoriented and stiff. He ached all over. It took him a few moments to remember where he was. He had no idea how long he had slept. He looked hard at the face of his watch, but could not distinguish the minute hand from the hour hand. He got his glasses out of their crushproof case and put them on. He saw that it was five minutes after seven. He assumed that meant evening of the same day, Sunday. He had slept three and a half hours. Giving the Angels patience they probably did not have, they could be still waiting. Well, he was in no hurry. He had his fortress. He could wait all night. If a face came through his entrance he would put his knife up its nose. He stood up uncertainly and stretched. His joints cracked. His hands just touched the ceiling. He got his flashlight and crawled, slipping and clawing, up the slope of the floor to the round opening opposite his entrance hole. His light was so dim that he could see only a couple of feet past the rim, but it was enough to tell him it was a tunnel and it probably went someplace. He fancied he heard a roaring sound at a great distance, but, listening closely, he decided it was probably the vodka and his own blood making the sound in his ears. He whispered, "Hey," as though to awaken gently someone he loved and feared, such as his drunken father when he was a boy, and a remnant of the sound came back to him expanded and elongated and octaves lower.

He slid back to the lower level of the floor, sat down with his tackle box between his legs, and lit a cigarette. He took another drink and was surprised at how little of the vodka was left. He looked in the box to see if any had seeped out while the bottle was lying on its side. None had. To pass the time, he inspected his little room. The walls were moist and cool and webbed with hairline cracks. On the ceiling were several clusters of little white nodules that looked like popcorn. Otherwise, except for the two holes, one leading out and the other inward, it was a plain, undecorated rock cell.

At nine o'clock, when he was sure it was dark, he began to struggle back through the entrance hole. It was far more difficult than coming in had been. Gravity had helped him then, and fear. Now he had to force his soft, sore body up through the hole. He could not get traction on the slanting floor, and there was nothing outside for him to get hold of to use his arm strength to move his bulk. For a few minutes he had to confront the possibility that he would not be able to get out. His vodka was gone. He was, he admitted, drunk, and therefore not at his physical or mental best. Then the specter of death gave him new strength and cunning. He leaned his tackle box lengthwise on the upward-slanting floor, stood on the end of it, and gave a mighty shove with his legs to get his arms through past the elbows. Then, hooking his elbows against the rock face on either side, he pried his head and shoulder through, twisted on his side with his head facing in the direction of the car, and pulled his legs out after him.

Before showing himself in the clearing where he had left his car, he peered out from the underbrush. There was no sign of the Space Angels. He ran to his car and jumped in and locked

the doors. The car had not been damaged: It started immediately. As he turned on his lights he saw a piece of paper on the
seat beside him. Instead of picking it up he drove away from
the spot as fast as he could. Not until he had parked under the
light in the parking lot outside the building did he pick up the
note and read it. It said: "Mr. B.: It is written in the stars."

3

He saw that her car was in a different spot: She'd been out again.

She was waiting at the front door with tears in her eyes. She had been at the window, watching for him. When she saw his wet, soiled clothes she gasped: "What happened?"

"I'll tell you about it." He stepped past her, trying not to touch her, not to let her know he wanted to touch her.

"Oh, Span, I've been so worried."

She was telling the truth, he knew. She almost always did. She detested lying. She only lied to avoid hurting him. He had once, three years ago, asked her about another man, expecting her to lie and reassure him. She had told the truth and he had been suicidal for three days. Since then each time he had felt the urge to confront her he had told himself no, suspicion's ache is better than confirmation's dagger. Live with it. These are the jokes, man. As long as there's any doubt, keep it, even if it's fractional and invented for your own comfort. She did not wánt to hurt him. She hated to hurt anybody or anything. But today there was no doubt in his mind, even though he wanted to find some; there was only lack of final confirmation. He smelled Jerry's musky perfume even stronger than when she had come home at noon. Had she got past the delicacy that was uniquely hers, of impeccable cleanliness even in her lust, of personal spotlessness? Did he detect an almost imperceptible coarsening? She was barefoot, her dainty feet peeking out from under the hem of her long, loosely tied robe. Her breath smelled of wine, just slightly sour. There was a limberness in her walk, a lassitude, a sense of deep satiation. But her tears were real, her concern honest. She loved him as well as she knew how to love. And he was not asking, and she was not confirming, so he was not crushed. He was dying a slow death. But who wasn't, in this world?

She took the vodka out of the freezer and poured him one, and gave herself some more champagne, going through the motions vaguely, automatically, her mind elsewhere. She made him a steak and a salad. Her cooking was not bad. It could be good, he thought, if she put her mind to it. But her mind had only been on one thing since the day he met her, to his certain knowledge, and since long before that, according to her own admission. She read French as well as English. She had gone to school in Paris at a time when she had not yet completely focused on sex. By the time the Italian government moved minor diplomat Santorini Pellegrini and his wife and pretty blond daughter to London, Yovi was thirteen and obsessed with her own body. In the ensuing thirteen years the obsession had not abated.

Span tried to tell her about his encounter with the Space Angels, but her reactions distracted him. She seemed utterly responsive and vulnerable. She went "Ooo!" and "Aah!" and licked her lips and looked frightened and shocked. Her robe fell open and he saw her small, firm breasts tilt and quiver as she lifted her glass time after time to her mouth. She had a way of sticking her tongue into the bubbles of a full glass, as though feeling them pop against her sensitive flesh were a special experience. As she did this now she hiccupped daintily. She smiled at him: Excuse me. It was as though, for a moment, she hadn't been listening to his tale of the day. He had not told about the little cave. Somehow he didn't want to yet. He told her only that he'd been forced to hide to save his skin.

Then she said: "You have to tell the police."

"What do I tell them?"

"Well, what you told me."

"But they didn't do anything. They were just there."

"They threatened you."

"But they didn't do anything. I did it all myself."

"What about the note?"

"'It's written in the stars.' Hardly a threat."

"Well, just the same I'm going to tell—" She stopped. She had been about to say "Jerry." She had wanted to tell her lover, the assistant district attorney, young man on the Way Up. He would protect her nice, potbellied, comfortable old husband from those Bad Guys. After all, wasn't he the prosecutor? Span was not surprised at her near slip. She felt no guilt and no real need to hide what she did except to protect the feelings of those she loved, those who often had strange hang-ups about perfectly normal and wonderful things. He felt a perverse gratitude to her for having made this adjustment for his sake. And he was proud that her hesitation was less than the time of a hiccup before she caught herself and ended her statement with "—Judge Youngford. He'll know what to do."

Walter Youngford was the judge who had handled the divorce case of *Spiegel* v. *Spiegel* when Abraham Spiegel had divorced Yovi. Although the judge had given the aggrieved husband everything except the rose-gold anklet, he had treated Yovi not as a scarlet woman but as a lady. In the past year, working as she did occasionally in the district attorney's office, she had got to know him and had begun to consider him a friend. He was an elderly gentleman who was looking forward to retirement so that he could spend his last years on his first love, archaeology.

"Well," Span said, eating a piece of the fat he had trimmed off his steak, "you let me know what His Honor says. Meantime, if I was going to do anything, I should've done it right there and then. I should've called their bluff. They're probably all talk."

"What if they're not?"

"Well..."

"I mean, it is spooky, Span, you'll have to agree, that they followed me and tormented me while I was in your car, and then they followed you and did all this. I mean, I know they didn't actually do anything, but they do have this sort of bloody reputation, and they must've done something to deserve it, don't you think? So you did the right thing, hiding and all. I mean, you're here. That proves it."

"Maybe. But you know who I thought about there for a while? My dad."

"I'm not surprised."

"I was thinking that he always wanted to do something he was proud of, some big thing, some life-or-death thing, on his own— you know—bet it all on one roll, one time, before he died. But he never did. And now it's too late. I was thinking of that. And I feel the same way he does, in a funny way. But I've never done it either. Maybe it's too late for me, too, but I hope not."

She looked at him with just a trace of a smile. "You've done something marvelous, darling, the biggest thing ever. You've found me."

She was flirting with him. At times like these he felt fury and resentment, and sometimes he could not help showing it. The bawd, after all the others, wanted him too. He had never tried to explain this reaction to her because he was sure she would never understand it. There was no ego mixed with her sexuality, no possession. He fought to keep his face neutral. She was hurt: She saw the fight going on. She stood up.

"I may pop over to Emily's for a nightcap."

He won his battle. He wanted her more than he hated her: "Please don't."

She was surprised. She recovered from her hurt as quickly as a child, the way she recovered from—exhaustion. She arched both brows: "Oh?"

He reached out suddenly and clasped, through her robe, a tuft of her pubic hair between his thumb and index finger. He was rough. He held on. She smiled—a slow moist distortion of lips. "Oh, Span...Chic."

Something had stopped him from telling her about his cave. Now he would have to wait for a more appropriate time. Maybe in the morning.

Later that night he dreamed about it. In the dream he went back to explore it, but the river had risen and flooded it. It was gone. He woke up in a sweat. He had the impression that he had cried out in his sleep. He could not be sure; Yovi had not stirred. He got out of bed, careful not to awaken her. She lay on top of the sheet, naked except for the anklet. It represented a priceless moment to her, something secret and wonderful that she could not share. All the distress around it, the ugliness of her leave-taking from the man who had put it there, had not altered the strange magic it held for her. There had been times when Span had wanted to slip his finger under the chain and rip it off, but its aura had stopped him. He would as soon have been able to poke out one of her blue-green eyes. He went silently out of the bedroom and closed the door.

There had been a word on his mind: *talus.* In his younger days, when he had been proud of being a teacher of English, he had collected words. One of these had been *talus,* but now he could not remember what it meant. It had something to do, he knew, with his adventures of the day. He looked it up in his old *Webster's International:* "*Geol.* Rock debris at the base of a cliff or slope...." He had been in two caves that day, a talus cave and—another kind.

His one-volume encyclopedia was twenty years old. It contained little about caves he didn't already know. The most famous ones were listed: Carlsbad Caverns, Mammoth Cave, Luray Cavern, Wyandotte Cave. Everything American was listed first. Then came Altamira, and Aurignac, and Kent's Cavern, and Fingal's Cave.

He let his mind crawl through the manhole-size opening in the east side of his little rock room. It went on and on, winding and scraping till it came out on the other end at a great domed railway terminal of a room, hung with dripping stalactites, and with wet stalagmites like whale penises thrusting up from the floor to meet them.

His head spun. He closed his eyes and tried to come back to now. His day of exertion and excitement and fear and discovery and vodka and—finally—Yovi had done him in. He staggered back to the bed, being careful again not to disturb her. He was exhausted. Even looking at her perfect golden body sweetly sleeping, covered with nothing but her own clean scent, did not make his flesh come back to life. Yet, he could not sleep. He lay beside a goddess who would turn to him if he touched her, but his mind was not there. His mind was having an orgy of eidetic images, monsters, natural wonders, a kaleidoscope gone mad. He got up, fearful somehow that the electric storm in his brain would awaken her. He sat in the kitchen, drinking coffee and letting his imagination go its own wild way, till he saw dawn spreading upward. Then he put a raincoat over his pajamas and went down and got in his car and drove along the river and turned off at the quarry and went down to the old ruined house and parked and sat there staring at the river as it ambled along. It told him nothing, except that it was not concerned with him.

W hile he was changing clothes to go to the shop, Yovi woke up. She did not know, or pretended not to know, that he had not slept and had gone out. She made coffee for him and fried two eggs. She saw that the coffee pot had been used and asked him if he'd made coffee in the night. He said yes. She looked hurt and asked him why, if he couldn't sleep, he hadn't awakened her. He answered with a helpless shrug. When he left the apartment, feeling dizzy and light-headed, she followed him to the door and kissed him with her wide, soft lips and asked if he was sure he was all right. He said he was. She told him she was going to work a half day at the D. A.'s office, addressing envelopes, and if she ran into Judge Youngford she would tell him about the Space Angels and ask him if Span shouldn't tell the police.

On his way to the shop he forgot for a moment where he was going and cut a corner so short that he ran over the curb and bent his hubcap.

When he walked into his office, which was only a space partitioned off in the converted barn that served as a shop, Dorothy told him he looked like death warmed over. Dorothy had survived three owners of the home improvement company that now bore this untalented newcomer's name. She knew where everything was in the casual filing system. She knew everything about roofing, siding, insulation, and storm windows, and she remembered every job the company had done for twenty-two years, and whether the customers had been satisfied or not, and whether the company had made a profit or not. She lived just across the street with her widowed mother in a house that needed all the improvements that Barrman Home Improvements had to offer, but which she could not afford, even at company discounts, on the salary the company could afford to pay. She had, in fact, been grudgingly generous enough to defer her salary for two or three weeks at a time on a number of occasions when the company coffers were bare. She had been there since the first owner opened the doors. She was a plank-owner and she knew it. The business could be sold and transferred in an orderly fashion without Span, or Bobby, or any of the others, but not without Dorothy. Without Dorothy it was only a big barn full of roofing and siding and workbenches and obsolete equipment.

She followed Span into his office. There was no door in the opaque glass partition, just a gap, so she had never acquired the habit of knocking. By the time he had sat down and looked up, she was standing there, powdering her puffy, discolored face.

At that moment Span realized that she was one of the reasons he hated his business. Prior to that moment he had not even been sure that he hated it, or her. He had always thought he resented her because of the little ridges of powder that gathered in the folds of her neck when she perspired, and her not-very-secret contempt for his inadequacies as a businessman, and her obvious awareness that she was irreplaceable. Now in one flash he saw that he had no control over whether she intruded on his mind or not. The lack of a door to his office that could be closed and locked was symbolic of his helplessness against her presence.

She snapped her fingers, the way a hypnotist brings a subject out of a trance. "Hey, hey, hey. Is this any way to start a Monday? Your eyes look like the windows in a vacant house. That's what you get, marrying a young woman, an old fuck like you. Try to keep up and you turn into a zombie. Believe me, I know. I made many a man holler uncle. Still could, if I ever found one worth the trouble." She swiveled her hips, which were narrower than her waist, and patted her neck with the powder puff emphatically, making powder fly up in a cloud. "Bobby called. The truck broke down on the way to the job. Nothing serious—fan belt. But hard to get a fan belt for that old model. I told you last year, get rid of that old heap. It makes the company look like it's on its last legs, which it is. Bobby will be two hours late getting to the Dwyer job. The carpenters are keeping the walls open, so they have to get the wool in there today, he said, before too much rain gets in. Mrs. Heller called and said the leak at the corner under the eaves is still there, and if it ruins her new drapes she is going to sue. Bobby was going to go by there today, but I doubt he'll make it now. You're going to have to go by there and do something about that, first thing, even if you have to stand there with a bucket till Bobby can fix it. Mrs. Heller sued the hospital when they delivered her daughter of a kid with a clubfoot. Believe me, she sues just to keep busy, so make her happy. And Mrs. Frank called about the insulation. That's the job we did in Ringoes two years ago, the one that said you saved her four hundred dollars in heating bills the first year. She said she heard that kind of insulation causes cancer and she wants it out. In her case I hope it does cause cancer, the old bitch. You look like you been dragged through a knothole. You didn't hear a word I said. I'm going to put some coffee in you and shove you out the door to Heller's house."

She went out, powdering her arms. In this humidity she would have those little furrows full of powder around her neck before noon. When she came back in with the cracked mug full of black coffee she reminded him that he had a lunch date with

Zeke Goodman at Colligan's at one o'clock: "His new meat lockers might get us out of the red for the quarter."

He left the shop in a steady light rain and drove along the river toward Mrs. Heller's house. The river was up, it seemed to him, since he had seen it early that morning, maybe as much as six inches. And the current had picked up speed. He saw a log in mid-river that looked as though it had traveled a long way. It must have been raining hard upstream for several days. He estimated the hole he'd made to enter his little cave was about two feet above yesterday's waterline. Another foot and a half and the water would start spilling over the lip. Another three and a half feet and it would start to flood the tunnel, his Tunnel to The One Extraordinary Moment in an Ordinary Life. He understood now why he had not been able to tell Yovi about his cave, why he would not be able to tell anybody till it had been explored. It was his. The way Yovi's anklet was hers, the cave was his.

He drove past the turnoff to the Heller place and went instead to the Hunterdon County Library. His head felt clearer but still light and unworldly. He got all the books he could find on the subject of caves and spelunking and piled them around him in the reading room and put on his glasses and lost himself in them. The first thing he found out depressed him: His cave was probably not very big. It was a freak. Most caves are either caused by weakly acidified water dissolving limestone, or they are fissure caves, caused by faults. The latter are irregular, the result of their violent birth, not round and cozy like his. And his cave was in sandstone, red Stockton sandstone.

His cave, it seemed, had no right even to be there. The books said that sandstone caves are formed at the bases of cliffs. Well, his was at the base of a cliff. But the books went on to say that they were formed by water running down the face of the cliff, causing the sand grains to be washed away. That didn't fit with his cave at all. His cave existed inside the face of the cliff. He personally had cut away the sandstone to make an entrance. What the books were telling him was that his cave was not a cave at all but a freak bubble, and the tunnel—which the books all called a passage—in the inner wall four feet or so off the floor probably did not go anywhere of any importance. It probably petered out after a few feet because there was no logical way it could have been carved out of the sandstone in the first place.

He tried to reason with himself that he should abandon the whole thing and go back to work, but another part of his mind told him that if the bubble existed against all logic, the passage could go to a bigger room against all logic. Did God abandon logic only in little things? And what was a little thing to Him? A great domed football field of a cave would not be a big thing to Him. And logic was no big thing to Him either—certainly not man-made logic.

He read until his head was spinning. He hadn't had his eyes checked in years and he was sure he needed new glasses. He decided not to take out any of the books because he didn't want to answer any questions, especially from Yovi, about why he had suddenly got interested in caves. She had her secrets, he would have his.

From the library he drove toward the Heller place in a steady downpour. The look of the river shocked him. It seemed to have surged upward, to be not flat but rounded, with the midstream higher than the sides, piled up, and angrily charging south. It looked mean, unreasonable, crazy. He wondered if he was personifying it, endowing it with his own paranoia. No, the river had nothing to do with him. The river did not care about his cave. The river was going to flood his cave, not because it was his, but because it was the river's job to flood whatever it could flood. It was part of the immutable idiocy of things, just as he was. "We're in a race," he said aloud to the river. "It's either my cave or yours."

For the second time he drove past the turnoff to the Heller place.

Yovi had gone out. For once he
was glad. He hurried to change to old shoes, blue jeans, and
worn-out dress shirt. His fishing khakis and deck shoes were
still damp from yesterday. He got his yellow slicker and rain
hat. He made two bologna sandwiches on white bread with
plenty of mayonnaise. As an afterthought he picked up an old
wool sweater, remembering that the books had said it was chilly
in caves. It was green, stained at the neck, raveled at the cuffs,
stretched out of shape at the waist—a long-ago gift from the
Cow. He was hungry. He took a drink of vodka from the freezer
and stuffed two slices of bologna in his mouth. Then he grabbed
two packs of cigarettes from the carton on the counter and ran
out the door. On the stairs he stopped to put on his yellow
slicker. He had started sneezing. He averaged three or four colds
a year and was not surprised to be catching this one.

On his way to Charlie's Rod and Gun he stopped at a liquor
store where he was not known and bought a fifth of Stolichnaya.

It was five dollars more than his usual Phillips, but he felt this was an important day that should be toasted in style.

Charlie's was not the ideal place to get what he needed, but it was the closest. He ordered things brusquely, impatiently, in a way Charlie had never known him to do. In the past he had always stopped to chat about shad runs and new bait theories and such. By the time Charlie got through hobbling about on his arthritic legs and putting the stuff on the counter, Span had bought three of the four light sources recommended by the books: a six-cell flashlight that could be broken in two and stowed in his tackle box, a two-cell waterproof light he could snap on his belt, and a half dozen candles, plus matches in a waterproof container. When he mentioned a carbide lamp, which the books had called an invaluable aid to cavers, Charlie looked at him as though he had suddenly started speaking Greek, and Span said, "Never mind. I guess you don't have a hard hat either."

Charlie dutifully got the other items Span ordered: a fifty-foot length of polypropylene rope, no thicker than a pencil but tested at four hundred pounds, and a four-pronged steel grapnel the size of his open hand, any prong of which would bear his one hundred eighty–odd pounds if he had to climb a ledge. The grapnel could be folded flat and stowed.

"Goin' mountain climbin', Span?"

"Huh? Oh, no. I, uh—got to tow a boat." He had a sudden image of himself lost in a maze of passages. He added: "Let me have some fishing line, too, Charlie. Forty-pound test. You have it in hundred-and-fifty-yard spools? Good. Give me about a dozen of those."

Charlie scowled at this, playing it back in his mind for a moment or two, then stepped up on his stool and reached a dusty box on the top shelf and brought it down and counted out the dozen spools slowly, as though giving Span a chance to say he'd made a mistake. All Span said was that he'd like the whole order in a plastic bag. Charlie found a green garbage bag and loaded the stuff in it.

"Span, what the hell do you think you are going to hook in the Delaware that's going to need forty-pound test?"

"Maybe nothing," Span said. He felt silly making such preparations for looking into a passage that could stop after five feet. He paid Charlie, took up the green garbage bag, and went out.

Span was parked in front of the church across the street from Charlie's. As he was about to get into his car he saw a tall young man with delicate features leaning against the iron fence of the churchyard. He was dressed in black leather pants and jacket and black boots with the toes painted white to make them look like cloven hooves. He was smiling at Span.

"Hey, Mr. Barrman," he drawled in a peculiar breathy contralto voice, "how you makin' out?"

He was bareheaded, and his blond hair was neatly cut. It was all in ringlets. Span got the impression it had been set. He imagined this young man spending hours curling his hair. "Fine, thanks," Span answered, as though he knew the young man but didn't have time to talk. He got into his car and drove away, not looking back. He cut his eyes to both sides of the street as he went along, but he did not see a motorcycle. He turned right at the first corner, and then, in a burst of panic, speeded up and turned left at the next corner. He drove several blocks at higher than normal speeds, changing directions at every corner, glancing behind him, listening for the roar of choppers. When he found himself in front of the A&P, he was inspired to turn in and park at the far end among the shoppers' cars. If they were following him they would have to pass there. They would not expect him to park at a grocery store. He listened. After a moment he heard the sound of many bikes. They came closer, then, without coming into sight, moved farther away, finally fading out of earshot. Span lit a cigarette. His hands shook violently. He took the Stolichnaya out of the paper bag, opened it, pushed his left arm against the door to steady it, held the lid in his left hand, poured a lidful below the level of the window, and tossed it into his mouth. He could not bring himself to tip up the bottle. It represented something to him, the beginning of the last phase of degradation, that he was not ready to face in himself. He was too well known in the area. Someone was sure to recognize him and say they had seen Span Barrman drinking alone out of a bottle in the parking lot at A&P during working hours. That could make business worse than it already was. He quickly drank five lidfuls.

Two things of seemingly equal importance struck him: Stolichnaya was sweet and smooth and did not sear his tonsils, and his fear was gone. He drank another lidful. Then he capped the bottle and kissed it in a fervor of gratitude for his new courage and put it back in its sack, speaking to it aloud: "Wi' usquebae, we'll face the Devil!"

As he turned off at the quarry he noted that the stonecutters had gone home. It was after four-thirty. *Quarry:* an open excavation for obtaining stone; also: the object of a hunt; a prey. The Space Angels had been watching him; they knew he went fishing every Sunday. He never went during the week. They would know that. And this was Monday. Defiantly he parked in his usual spot, in the very tracks he'd made yesterday by the rotting cottage shell.

Six inches of water covered the path that led to his cave. He sat on an outcropping and took off his shoes. They were old but there was no point in ruining them completely. He remembered the warnings about the low temperatures in caves, but in his present euphoric state he found future discomfort inconceivable. He put the shoes under the outcropping with the socks neatly tucked inside. They would be dry when he came back.

The rain still fell steadily and gently, a silver curtain that almost obscured the other side of the river. There was not a breath of breeze; the curtain hung straight down. It sparkled. It looked innocent, benign, and yet, it was the goad that made the river roil and race. He was glad for his yellow slicker and hat; though he had put them on too late to avoid a cold, they would save him possibly from worse.

He rolled up his trouser legs and started barefoot along the path. The water was so murky he could not see where he was stepping. He had to feel with his toes for the path before transferring his weight. All kinds of trash and filth were riding on the high water: paper cups, cigarette packs, a torn straw hat with HOTSTUFF printed on the crown. He had never noticed before that his feet were dough-colored and incredibly tender. They were surprised by every inch of the rough path.

His fishing alcove was underwater. His pole had been washed away but his chair was still there, with water halfway up to the seat. He kicked it aside. It fell into the water, rolled over, and sped away in the current.

Then he heard the bikes. At first he thought it was the vodka or perhaps the sound of the river compressed between the high banks, but when the roar came on and on, growing, a battle cry, he knew. He ran, guessing as best he could at the location of the solid surface hidden under the water, barely righting himself again and again in time to avoid falling into the sucking current. When he reached the talus he saw that he would never be able to negotiate the narrow crawlway encumbered with the yellow slicker. He tore it off and stuffed it out of sight into a fracture of the fallen overhang. He kept the rubberized hat; he knew he would have a fit of sneezing the minute the air hit his damp hair. He floated the garbage bag carefully in the six inches of water under the talus while he took out his ragged sweater. As he squirmed into it he realized how stupid he had been to leave his shoes behind. He could have put them in the garbage bag with the rest of the things. The awareness that he had once again had a logical thought too late to act upon it caused him to shrug. Years ago he had cursed himself for the same kind of thing, but time had made him accept himself as one step behind the game, or possibly not in the game at all. He was not even ashamed of himself for this. He carried this burden as a man does a shriveled hand. He knelt and pushed the garbage bag ahead of him and tried to crawl into the passage under the talus. He had remembered it all wrong: He had not been on his hands and knees the first time; he had gone most of the way on his belly, like a bloated snake. He would have to do it again in the six inches of filthy water. He had no sooner got a full length in when he heard Larry's voice almost directly overhead: "Goodness gracious, Mr. Barrman, you are a surprise. What did you leave down there that was so important you had to come back on a day like this? Come on out, now. We won't hurt you. And we certainly don't want you to drown."

Span did not move. He lay full length in the water with his head up like a water snake. He recognized One-of-Three's voice: "Hey, Mr. Barrman, we found your shoes. But don't worry, we won't wear 'em! Too shabby!" There was a burst of laughter, then another, but it was drawing away. He decided to move forward, whether it was a trick or not. This strange group of fierce yet effete bikers would not dirty themselves to follow him. They would wait till the water drove him out. Or they would leave, the way they did last time. He crawled forward, pushing the heavy bag ahead of him, keeping it upright. Eddies had brought trash close to the shore. There was a separate current going through the talus passage, carrying with it an amazing heterogeneity of debris. He felt something with weight bump the garbage bag; a moment later he found himself face-to-face with a drowned rat. It brushed his chin as it went by. He imagined that it was not dead, that it was clinging to a pulse of life, and that when he went through the hole into his cave he would find it hooked by its claws to his trouser leg, yellow teeth bared, ready to contest possession of the territory.

He would not be able to hold his head up much longer. His neck muscles were growing weak and throbbing with pain. In a few minutes they would give way and let his face down into the water. His heart quaked crazily. He wondered if what he was doing was a form of suicide. He came to the entrance to his cave. The water was within four inches of the lower edge. He calculated that since about this time yesterday the water had risen two feet, or an inch an hour. If the rate stayed the same he had four hours before the river would start trickling over the lip of the hole into his little room. It would take perhaps another hour to fill the room, and several more to start flowing into the passage, which was higher than the entrance hole. By then he would have seen all he needed to see. He wished he had brought along a flash camera. Suppose he found a stately pleasure dome at the end of the tunnel, in caverns measureless to man? Buck Rogers had come to pass, had he not? Why not Coleridge? Anything was possible. But now, no matter what he found, he'd never be able to prove it if the river came in. Like so much of his life, this, too, would be rewritten in retrospect, with regrets.

He stuck his long flashlight through the hole and followed with his head. The light was strong and for the first time he saw the little chamber clearly. It was plain, gracefully rounded, empty except for his tackle box, which lay at the bottom where he had left it. He pulled his head out and got the garbage bag and put it through, holding it and letting it down till he heard his vodka bottle clunk against his tackle box. Then he slithered in and piled up at the bottom with his gear. The isolation, the impregnability of his cozy fortress—temporary though it was— delighted and exhilarated him. He got out his vodka and his cigarettes and treated himself to a five-minute break. He was soaked to the skin, but it didn't bother him. He took stock. What was different from the last time he'd been here? Possibly nothing, but he'd been too confused, too astonished, to gather the experiences and be aware of them. Now, he noted, the responses of his senses were clear and separate. He vaguely remembered an echo. He coughed deliberately and listened. He had not dreamed it: The cough echoed in the room itself, then came back from afar, rumbling low in waves from inside the unexplored passage. Another thing: The air moved. He remembered the sensation of it tugging at him as he came through the hole. He had not accepted it as possible. But it was. He felt it now, changing direction, moving out instead of in. The cave was breathing. And its breath smelled—yes, he was sure of it now—of salt. But that was not possible. It was due to vodka, to his physical state, his light-headedness, his stuffy nose. He sneezed. His feet were cold. He regretted leaving his shoes and, most of all, the slicker. For a moment he felt faint, dizzy. When he stood up he staggered. The dizziness left him, but it had made him aware of threats other than the Angels and the river and the unknown—his own stupidity and weakness.

The Archangel Beezle, high priest of the Space Angels, stood at the top of the rise above the river. Dressed all in black, except for the white hoof markings on his boots, he was like a shadow on the dark sky. His sleeves fluttered in the breeze, and the little wisps of his long hair and drooping mustache lifted and waved. He was displeased, his displeasure mounting toward punitive rage. His agents, all gathered about him, had failed again to bring Barrman to him, and time was inimical to their ceremonies now.

"He has found a hole to hide in, like an animal," Beezle said. "After tonight he will be useless to us." The high priest had the diction, the intonations, of an educated man. He carried not only his personal dignity but the weight of his office with natural grace.

"If it pleases you, revered Archangel," Larry said, "One-in-Three and I have a plan. We can stand almost exactly over the spot where we know the offering to be hiding. We can arrange for the other parts of the ceremony—again, with your permission—to be held on this spot. We have access to a large amount of dynamite. We have sent for Fruity, who was to have joined us tonight for the great copulation rites, but who may now be of service to us earlier, since he is accomplished and experienced in the use of explosives."

"Let us discuss this plan," Beezle said.

6

She had decided that she didn't really like Milca, any more than she really liked Jerry. But you couldn't limit yourself in this world to only people you liked. You couldn't wait at the store to buy a wedge of Brie till you found a clerk you liked. And anyhow, she didn't actively dislike Milca and Jerry. They were just functionaries, useful elements. It was very nice to come to Milca's apartment and have her treat you like a treasure. The apartment was dark and too full of depressing furniture of several inharmonious periods, and long-furred cats, and hanging plants. Milca was forty. She had an overripe body with sagging melon breasts. She was possessive. She smoked grass and was always trying to get Yovi to smoke with her, though Yovi didn't even smoke tobacco, and couldn't inhale one puff without having a coughing spell. Worst of all, she had a boring mind that was always spewing out political clichés as though they were great new intellectual discoveries. But she kept vintage champagne in her fridge for Yovi, and petits fours, and she was clean. That was the main thing: Milca was always scrubbed. She smelled good. If a person was clean you could forgive them a lot of faults. And it was very nice to sip cold Moët et Chandon brut of a good year and not be alone and just lie there on Milca's enormous, incredibly soft bed and let her purr to you how beautiful you were, how perfect in every detail.

7

After only a few feet the passage narrowed. Span decided that before he went another inch forward he would see if he could turn around. It was almost but not quite impossible. He bumped his head, hard, and scraped his elbows and his knees. He got a cramp in his left foot, the one that always cramped when he was tense and it had no weight on it. When he was aimed forward again he looked carefully ahead with his waist lamp, which he wore on his right forearm, and saw that the passage seemed to widen. It went straight ahead and down at an angle of about thirty degrees for about ten feet, then turned off to the right. If it constricted even one inch more, he knew, he would have to turn around and go back. He doubted he would be able to crawl backward very far up a thirty-degree incline.

He had never been in a cave before, even on a guided tour. And this was a virgin, at least as far as he could tell. No cigarette butts, no plastic cups, no wadded Kleenex. The unknown around the turn in the passage frightened him. He whispered, "Are you there?" The sound rolled over itself and lost its shape, then was gone. Then it came back, fearfully altered, a deep-throated moan. Nothing alive had answered him. He inched forward, pushing his tackle box ahead of him. His trousers were being shredded, his knees scraped raw. His neck began to hurt again. His head could go no higher than his back, which was already touching the top of the passage. But the passage widened, and when he could see around the turn he felt the bare rock under him suddenly tilt more steeply down, heading straight into the bowels of the hill. He guessed the down-angle at twenty-five degrees. The floor was increasingly wet, but rough enough to give him plenty of purchase when the time came to ascend back to his little room. As he moved forward now the walls diverged steadily and the ceiling rose. If this continued he would indeed soon be able to stand upright, and he could claim the discovery of a true cave. The sound of his tackle box scraping on stone grew louder and reverberated. The air was chill. He sneezed. The sound was all around him. From the farthest distance it came back a growl.

The downward tilt of the floor was such now that he could not just push his tackle box ahead of him. He had to hold on to it for fear it would slide away on its own and disappear. He decided to check his ability to climb back the way he had come. It was more difficult than he had expected. The tackle box felt twice its previous weight, and friction made it stick to the floor. Each time his bare feet slipped he suffered agony. He was sure he was losing the skin from the bottoms of his feet. He looked, shining the light on them. There was blood.

He was breathing with difficulty. He sat down to rest. Air! Could he be running out of oxygen? He lit a cigarette. The match burned steadily: There was plenty of oxygen. He took a gulp of vodka. His breath was easier now. It was the short experimental climb that had made him breathless. The vodka caused him to feel unexpectedly silly. He flipped his cigarette butt down the passage. It bounced off the sides and the floor, sparking. Trash. The first human defilement of this immaculate Mesozoic salon. "Beware!" he shouted, and waited for the sound to come back in its many forms. "Beware! I am Man, the All-Fouler!"

Exhilarated, he resumed his descent, one part of him alert to the angle of the floor. How much steeper could it get before it became impossible for him to climb out again? Five degrees? Would he detect five degrees of change with just his eye and the difference of feel in his raw hands and knees? Was there a surer way? Of course. His vodka. He removed the bottle from the box again and set it in front of him between his legs, holding it carefully by the neck. The liquid made an angle with the printing on the label that he guessed in the dim light to be thirty-five degrees. He had forgotten his glasses—a subconscious compulsion, he knew, because they gave him a headache. With his fingernail he pressed a line down the center of the label at a right angle to the lines of printing. Then he set the bottle on its base again and stretched himself out as near to eye level with the surface of the liquid as he could get, and made a mark with his fingernail parallel to it, starting at the conjunction of the horizontal printing and the vertical mark. His first guess had been roughly correct: The angle was about ten degrees less than forty-five, which he found by making another line approximately splitting the right angle. He would check every few feet. If the angle reached forty degrees he would turn back.

His light dimmed. He moved forward with such caution that he became aware of the mechanics of his own breathing. When he checked the slope of the floor again it had increased two degrees, or possibly three. His measuring device would not be accurate to one degree. An inner voice told him to turn back, but he continued to descend. The vodka in his system argued with that in the bottle. He was accustomed to this dispute between logic and vodka. He recognized the symptoms. Sanity almost always won. In all things important, in matters grave, sanity, as he now thought he recalled, had always come to the wire a nose in front. Why, then, was sanity having such a battle this time, and one-hundred-proof bravado threatening to steal the race? Suddenly he knew: He was feverish. He was, in fact, the vodka bottle against his forehead told him by its remarkable contrast of temperatures, burning up. Well, he'd had a fever before. He was still in his right mind. He would continue to advance prudently, keeping close tabs on the angle of the floor. If he could stand raw knees and raw hands and raw elbows, what was a little fever? The waist light tied to his right forearm was definitely growing dimmer, but he still had his six-battery flashlight in his tackle box and plenty of candles and matches. A true explorer had no need to worry.

As though to confirm his belief that a benevolent Providence was now in charge of his life, the floor ceased getting steeper, then actually began to level off. Best of all, the ceiling started getting higher. Within fifty yards he was able to stand up and walk on a floor that was, by actual vodka-level measurement, only slanting at twenty degrees. At first he had to stoop, and twice he bumped his head surprisingly hard on the dripping ceiling, but soon he was able to stride down the pleasant slope fully erect with a great sense of joy and accomplishment. Surely at the end of this glorious road there was a miracle, a godhead, something so rare, so special, that the very seeing of it would be a great deed, and the very trip itself down this long chaste throat to see it a sacred act. He ran, splashing in the trickle of water coursing down the floor. He lost track of how far he had come, how long he had been running. The floor continued to level off, the passage to open out, the ceiling to rise, till suddenly he stopped, feeling lost. His weakening beam showed the walls to be twenty feet away on either side and the ceiling forty feet or more above him. And he heard a sound, a sound that had been trying for some time to get his attention, the sound of water falling. Had the river broken through into his little room? Was it coming down the passage for him now, divine retribution for his violation of the virgin cave? No. It was ahead of him, farther in, and it was the sound of water falling on water from a great height. Before he could start forward again he felt a disembodied lightness. He thought he had better lie down and rest before going on. Then he heard his tackle box hit the stone with a faraway heavy clunk, and he wondered why he had put it down so carelessly. He hoped he had not broken his vodka spirit-level. He felt a jarring painless blow on his right shoulder. There was a dark sweetness in his brain....

8

It was eleven-twenty-five when she arrived in front of her apartment building, exactly the time she would have got home if she had gone to the movies, as she planned to tell Span she had done. Jerry, the mean bastard, had twitted her about being square when she got up at precisely ten-thirty, took her special shampoo/conditioner and her hair dryer out of her purse, and showered and washed her hair and dried it and brushed it a hundred times till even Jerry had to admit it shone like a sheet of Florentine gold. To try to keep Span from knowing meant that she cared. To not try to keep him from knowing meant she didn't care. And she did care. Even if Span did know, she wanted him to know she didn't want him to know. God, she was drunker than she thought.

There was a police car, its top light flashing, in front of the building. It had nothing to do with her, obviously. She always drove more prudently after champagne than before it. She drove around back. There was another police car in the parking lot

with two officers standing beside it, talking. Maybe Mrs. Radi-
qualt was squinked again and throwing things. Span's car was
not in its spot. Good, she would not have to lie. She hated lying.
She got out of her sleek Veloce Spider not looking at the officers
and knowing they were looking at her, and walked with perfect
sobriety toward the stairs leading up to the apartment.

"Mrs. Barrman?"

"Yes?" God, wasn't she walking straight?

"You left your lights on."

"Oh. Thank you." Why did they call her Mrs. Barrman? How
did they know who she was? She walked carefully back to the
car. As she leaned in to cut the lights she felt the cool metal
of the door through her dress and had a moment's uncertainty
about straightening up and regaining her balance. Champagne
with Milca and then more—but cheaper—champagne with Jerry
had been almost too much! Oh, yes, and she had forgotten to
eat dinner. No help, that.

"We'd like to talk to you a minute if you don't mind, Mrs.
Barrman."

She felt suddenly very hungry, and she needed to go to the
bathroom. What were they doing there at this time of night?

They had walked over to her while she was turning off her
lights. "We were wondering," the older of the two said casually,
"if you could tell us where we might be able to contact Mr.
Barrman."

"Well, he should be here, any minute. What's this about, if
you don't mind?"

"We're not sure. But..."

She was surprised to hear herself giggle. "You want to talk
to someone and you don't know what about? Gentlemen, forgive
me. It's rather chilly out here, and I'm starving."

"Maybe we could talk to you while you eat. I'm Detective
Sergeant Healey," the older man said. "And this is Sergeant
Dierk."

Healey was sort of a family-man type, she decided, loyal to
Mom and the kids and the Church. His broad flat rump and his
ill-fitting uniform made her uncomfortable. Dierk was tall, wide-
shouldered, with a craggy face, a big, crooked nose, and a thin-

lipped mouth that looked both cruel and sensual. He made her uncomfortable, too, but she did not want to think about the reason. She told herself it was because she felt some deeply serious purpose in him. "Span hasn't done anything wrong, has he? No, he wouldn't've."

"No. Not that we know of," Healey said.

"Well, you can wait for him upstairs, I suppose."

She went to the bathroom and then changed to a floor-length zip-up housecoat. She had felt the dark eyes of the tall one on her as she walked up the stairs ahead of him and she did not want Span to come home and find her talking to two cops in nothing but a thin cotton dress that did not cover her knees. She had a sudden inspiration and she hurried into the living room, pulling the zipper all the way to the top under her chin. The two men were sitting on the sofa. They stopped talking when she came out of the bedroom. Both stood up politely. They had not accepted her invitation to pour themselves a drink.

"No, no, please sit down. I've just realized where he must be. There's a baseball game, isn't there? Sometimes when he starts watching a game— He's got a little black and white set at his shop—"

"We've been there, Mrs. Barrman," Healey said. "He's not there."

She felt a clutch of cold fear. "Something's wrong," she whispered. "What is it?"

"Don't you want to get something to eat before we talk?"

"Please—tell me." She sat across from them, grateful for her virtuous housecoat. When Span came he would see how decorous she was in front of strange men.

"We don't want to alarm you," Healey said. "We just need some information."

"What kind of information?" Then, to her astonishment, she spoke to Dierk: "Don't you talk at all?"

Dierk gave her a slit of a smile that had no humor in it. "Only when I have to," he said.

"I'm sorry, that was a silly question. I'm afraid I'm a bit light-headed. Petits fours don't make much of a dinner." She picked up an orange from the bowl on the coffee table, and the little fruit knife, and began to carefully score the peeling. "Please go ahead, Mr. Healey."

"His car has been found, badly vandalized."

"His car?"

"He didn't say anything about it being stolen, did he?"

"No, he—vandalized? Where?"

"At the river, near the quarry."

She put the orange down. "At the river?"

"Yes, ma'am. Tires slashed, upholstery set afire, windows broken—pretty messy. A lot of graffiti too. Probably happened around eight o'clock. About the same time or maybe a little bit before the explosion. The upholstery was still burning when—"

"Explosion?"

"Yes."

"What explosion?"

The two men glanced at each other. Healey said: "Do you mean to tell me, Mrs. Barrman, that you didn't hear—don't know about—the explosion?"

"I don't understand. Was Span in an explosion?"

"Would you mind telling me where you were this evening?"

"Was he? Has he been hurt?"

"We don't know. We don't have any evidence that—"

"Why are you doing this to me? I'm frightened now. Has something happened to Span?"

"Mrs. Barrman, we don't know. Where could you have been that you didn't know about the explosion?"

"I went to see *Downhill Racer.*"

"In Flemington. Well, I guess they didn't hear it there. There was a hell of an explosion at the river tonight, Mrs. Barrman, not too far from the quarry. Whole side of the hill came down."

"Well, what does that have to do with Span?"

"He fishes along there. His car was found—"

"But he wouldn't've been there today!" It all seemed unreal to her, as though she were having a dizzy spell and everything was too fuzzy to comprehend. She picked up the orange and began to peel it, her hands shaking violently. What were these two uniformed men doing sitting in her apartment on her lovely blondwood divan, which Span had had built to her own specifications so that she wouldn't have to look at the awful Macy's-Gimbelsy stuff they had started out with? Somehow she managed to tear loose a wedge of orange and bite into it.

"—and there was a note on the windshield."

"From whom? What did it say?"

"Mrs. Barrman," Healey said, and his voice took on a sudden stern, demanding quality, as though he expected her to not want to answer, "does your husband have any connection, friendly or otherwise, with a gang called Space Angels?"

"Space—" She gasped and swallowed a half-chewed bite of orange. "Oh, God, don't tell me they really did something to him! They threatened him, but he didn't take it very seriously....What did they say?"

Healey took a piece of paper out of his pocket and unfolded it. Yovi had gone ghostly white.

"They read this to me on the radio a little while ago. I copied it down word for word. I'm sorry, Mrs. Barrman. I hope it doesn't mean what it says. It says, 'To feed Space God he was sacrificed, not with blood as—'"

"Then they did it! They really did it!"

"We're not sure they mean Mr. Barrman. Let me finish. '—not with blood as wanted, but death is death. He was right sign, Aries native with Capricorn rising and a Taurus moon, born one-thirty-one A. M., April eighteenth, 1923.'"

"That's Span's birthday!" She started crying softly, closing her eyes and brushing away the tears quickly with her fingers. She held her hands together in front of her lips and prayed like a small child, in a small child's voice: *"Notre Père qui est au ciel, que votre nom soit sanctifié—"* Then she almost leapt to her feet and walked away from the two men and got a box of Kleenex from the kitchen and came back blowing her nose and drying her eyes. "I'm sorry." She took her seat again across from them. From the set of her face they knew she was ready to face the truth, whatever it might be, and help them if she could.

"I'm sure you understand we don't like having to do this. You say they threatened him?"

"Only Sunday. They followed him over where he was fishing and tormented him and left a note in his car. He—"

"Do you have the note?"

"No, but—"

"Do you know what it said?"

"It said something like 'It is written in the stars.' Something like that. God in heaven, why would—? But it's not sure, is it? If they were—around his car—I mean, they could've got his birth date off his driver's license, anything. I mean, it's not sure. It may be just a joke. People don't really—I mean, a sacrifice? To the— the Space God? No. It's got to be some sort of elaborate joke, psychological torture, some sort of symbolic ritual, play-acting, don't you think? You don't, do you? You think he's dead, don't you? Well, I don't! I don't believe it! I mean, why? Span, Span wouldn't hurt a soul. He couldn't've done anything to them, to anyone. He's the sweetest man I ever—so gentle, so vulnerable, so easy to—to hurt. I ought to know, I've hurt him, God knows. Please, tell me you think it's only a joke. Please."

"I think it's possible it's a joke," Healey said. "Definitely possible. But I have to be honest. I think it's more likely they've set off this big explosion for the purpose of burying Mr. Barrman alive—"

"No! I don't accept that! No!"

"At this point it's only a theory."

"But an explosion of what?"

"We don't know yet. Probably dynamite. Believe me, Mrs. Barrman, thousands of tons of earth—"

"But where would these crazy people get— I mean, wouldn't that take an awful lot of dynamite?"

"Yes. But—"

"And what do they say? The Space Angels. Have they been arrested?"

"These things take time. We weren't even sure it was the Space Angels we wanted. The M.O. was theirs, but till you confirmed that they'd threatened him . . . You see, they didn't sign the note." He turned to Dierk and said: "Better call in, tell 'em it's the Angels we want."

Dierk stood up, looked down appraisingly on Yovi for a moment, then went out.

"They're already looking for the Angels," Healey was saying. "We were already pretty sure."

Her face remained blank, incredulous.

"I said," Healey repeated, "that we were already pretty sure the Angels were the people we wanted. I'm very sorry, Mrs. Barrman. As soon as we know anything, we'll be back in touch with you. You'd better eat something now, don't you think? I won't take any more of your time. We'll hope for the best."

Yovi's bleak unseeing eyes flooded with tears. Healey had already risen and was starting to go when the phone rang. Immediately her wet face shone like a light. "That could only be Span," she said. "Who else would call this late?"

She took a deep breath before she picked up the phone. Healey waited, halfway to the door. "Hello," Yovi said, hopefully. Then her expectancy wilted. "Oh, Ida, I'm so sorry.... Yes, it's probably a blessing, I agree. He's better off. I know it was difficult, Ida. You're better off it's over.... I'm sorry, Span's not here. He's—he's— They're working late on a roofing job because they're expecting more rain.... I'll tell him as soon as he— Yes, no matter how late. I'm glad your sister's with you, Ida. If you need anything— All right, Ida." She hung up. After a few moments of shaking her head mutely, she managed to say: "Span's daddy died. Can you imagine? They both died on the same day." She tried to stuff both small fists into her mouth to stifle the little-girl's wail that came out of her. She cut her wet eyes wildly once at Healey and ran into the bedroom and fell across the bed. She was barely aware of the solid thump of Healey closing the front door. "Oh, Span, Span," she sobbed, "I hurt you. I hurt you. Oh, God, I'm so sorry."

9

Jerry Odessa slept in silk. The only child of Russian immigrants, he was endowed with the same fervent need to rise that had precipitated his tough, rectangular father out of his harness-making apprenticeship in the Black Sea town of Ochakov and into the bare-knuckle life of Brooklyn. Osip worked furs. His tiny, silent, durable wife, who never learned to read, also worked furs. They rose. Their boy fought in the streets but he went to college. He had the same flat-muscled square-cornered body his father had, but bigger: a six-foot stud-boar of a man, hard, black-haired, bristly. And like his parents he rose. After he'd passed his bar and was eking out a living defending shoplifters and whores in Flatbush, he went to night school and got rid of his Brooklyn-Russian accent. His English became standard, as good as any actor's. Only his voice remained rough, a grunting growl most women described as sexy. He pushed them over, if they needed pushing. He had no time to waste on niceties. Either they went or they didn't, and if they didn't, good-bye. He only had time to spend on Success. His quest for it was patient, meticulous, focused. He knew he was going to Be Somebody for one simple reason: Nothing was going to stop him.

His wake-up chimes sounded every morning at six, whether he had been in bed eight hours or one. This morning he allowed himself to lie in bed for five minutes, thinking of Yovi. She was, he decided, perfect for him, for his situation, in spite of her fanatical adherence to time schedules so she could keep up appearances with that middle-aged, overstuffed old man of hers. Last night she'd annoyed him a lot because he'd wanted her again so much he could taste her after watching her brush that crazy hair of hers, but she'd left him on the dot at eleven like a virgin going to Sunday school. Still, she was great. She had that dynamic mix of Yugoslav and Italian blood, with just enough Slav genes to respond to that vestige of him that once, he believed, roamed the tundra on a shaggy horse. And she was willing, easy. Except for that stupid time fetish of hers she was compliant. And she was, God knows, convenient. And she required no commitment. And best of all, when they disconnected she was a crushed petal, sticky and aromatic with love, and he was the Tsar of all the Russias. Oh, sure, she was a tramp, but a classy little tramp, with brains and taste and vulnerability and quiet tenderness and mystery—yes, mystery, that was it, sort of closed in, not quite there yet there in person, doing what she did magnificently but with a sort of aesthetic distance. And silently. What a blessing that was, a girl with all her qualities, yet not a stupid chatterbox. No question about it, for him at this time in this situation, she was perfect.

He got up and started his routine: stretching exercises, fifty push-ups, a cold shower, orange juice, black coffee. His phone rang in the middle of his push-ups. He let the machine take a message: Nothing could interrupt the push-ups or the cardio-vascular benefits would be lost. When his entire morning schedule was completed he sat nude on the side of the bed and played the message on his answering machine: Call Chief Poussi's office right away.

He called. The duty sergeant told him about the explosion

and the roundup of the Space Angels, but did not mention Span Barrman. He did not want to give the impression that anybody would think that the assistant D. A. would know who Barrman was. He did not want the assistant D. A. to guess that everybody around the station and around the courthouse knew that Barrman dying would make a big difference in Odessa's life, on account of Mrs. Barrman. Playing dumb was smart in a case like this.

Jerry lived a few miles north of Flemington. He was as surprised as Yovi had been to hear of the explosion.

"They called you last night several times," the duty sergeant said.

"I had my phone cut off," Jerry said.

"That's what they figgered," the duty sergeant said.

"I disconnected it. From the phone jack. I don't like to get calls at night." He wondered why he was overexplaining to this meathead.

"Yeah, that's what they figgered," the duty sergeant said.

"I'll be there in a little while," Jerry said, and hung up.

Chief Christian Poussi was six feet eight inches tall. He weighed 294 pounds and was not fat. There was no record of anyone ever having found anything funny about his name or his appearance. He moved slowly and surely in all things. He had left word that when they picked up the Angels or even one Angel they should give him a call at home, but not until they had got the Angels' lawyer, that frizzy-haired smart-ass Dolf Header, over there to make sure everything was on the up and up. The Chief enjoyed the idea of getting Header out of a warm sack at some crazy hour. Header considered it his political duty to defend all "underdogs," meaning all riffraff, as far as Poussi was concerned.

Around three A. M. two of the Chief's men, Bill and Darryl, had cruised over to the river in answer to a noise complaint and found a gang of Space Angels high on wine and hash and coke and grass and whatever else they could find, and having a boisterous orgy. Bill and Darryl estimated there were twenty of them, all naked, including two females. The two females and about half the men escaped, some by jumping in the river.

The Archangel Beezle had not tried to get away, however. He had stood his ground, fondling and displaying his enormous engorged penis and laughing derisively at Bill and Darryl. The two outraged and frustrated police officers, instead of arresting the nonresisters, ran around trying to grab and tackle the fleeing Angels and cursing and yelling threats. Beezle called them a long list of imaginative obscene inventions and begged them to please touch him just once. He would get the Civil Liberties people down there and see that Bill and Darryl got new jobs washing cars. Beezle was having so much fun that not only did Larry and One-of-Three join him in taunting the cops, but seven other Angels came back from escaping and offered themselves for capture so they could have fun too. They loudly compared the authority figures to exotic animal feces. The drugs and the wine and the laughter made them so weak they were helpless. They offered no resistance, but Darryl had to call for reinforcements because he and Bill had only two pairs of handcuffs. State troopers came and cuffed all ten and linked them together with their own bike chains.

When the Chief got to his little jail he found Dolf Header there, needing a shave, wearing bleached jeans and a T-shirt and tennis shoes, and already admitting defeat because he had tried to get the Angels to refuse to answer any questions at all till they got their heads on straight again, and they had refused. The Chief went down in the basement to see the ten Angels. They were held there with one man guarding them because the single cell would only hold three men. Beezle did not call the Chief any picturesque names. He was polite and identified himself as the Archangel Beezle, high priest of the Space Angels. The other Angels made no sounds at all except for an occasional drug-inspired giggle or sob, quickly stifled. The size of the Chief, his reputation, and his long hound's face, which had too many creases in it to be readable, did not inspire levity.

Beezle was muscular and pockmarked. His long hair and pendulous mustaches had touches of gray. He was a third-year college dropout and well spoken. He was proud of Space Angel accomplishments. He told the Chief that he and all the Spacers had been planning to sodomize Spanish Barrman and then kill

him and cremate him while he was full of their combined eja-
culate so as to send their reproductive atoms into the upper
atmosphere, where at this propitious conjunction of planets the
Space God could reach down and pick them like periwinkles.
They had been following Barrman for several days. One of the
Spacers had an aunt who worked part-time in the Hall of Records, and she had pulled his name and address for them, not
knowing why they wanted it, only knowing that for their ceremony they needed someone—anyone, male or female—who
had been born within fifty miles of Lambertville on April 18,
1923, as soon after midnight as possible. They had got the date
and the location from a Gypsy in Philadelphia. Their sole reason
for selecting Barrman had been that he fell neatly within these
limits and was available. Some of the Spacers, Beezle assured
the Chief, had been disappointed when the offering turned out
to be a male. Others had not, but none had refused to take part
in the projected sacrificial space-out. Barrman had been chicken,
though, Beezle said, and didn't want to be immortalized. He
had been hard to catch. The lunar phase was about to change
and that would have invalidated the ceremony. On the last good
day, which was yesterday, they had followed him, looking for a
chance to take him but thinking all was lost, when the Space
God had come to their aid and guided Barrman, against all his
habits and all logic, back to the river and into the same little
rubble-cave where he'd hidden from them the day before. As
time was running out for the benevolent conjunction they had
decided to take the big load of dynamite they'd spotted under
a shed at the quarry and blow him to Kingdom Come. With the
help of two Space Mamas all twenty-one of them had shot sperm
on the rocks where Barrman was holed up. Then they put the
dynamite in place and went back up to the top of the ridge to
watch Fruity, who had once worked with a famous safecracker
and claimed to know all about explosives, set it off. Fruity blew
himself into a million pieces, along with the offering, Barrman.
Fruity had miscalculated the force of the boom so badly that
part of the hill had gone into the river, almost taking the rest
of the Spacers with it. The Spacers weren't going to worry about
Fruity, though. Fruity had no family except the Angels, and he

had done his job well and had been atomized along with the astrologically compatible offering and the whole coven's space sperm. Who could ask for a better end than that?

The Chief taped Beezle's statement. While Beezle talked the Chief was thinking how lucky it was he had this modern equipment, so that Odessa and the others could play back what this batty bastard was saying and maybe translate it into American. Beezle spoke clearly and earnestly and seemed to think he was making sense, but the Chief was so befuddled by his vocabulary and the assignment of ordinary status to weird concepts that he could only think how much fun he would've had arranging accidents for these creeps in the old days before the psychiatrists and the do-gooders started interfering with law enforcement. Well, if anybody could put these perverts where they belonged for life, Jerry Odessa could. The Chief had not called Hi Rettly, the incumbent D. A., because Rettly was barely surviving constant alcohol abuse and, at fifty-eight, just waiting for retirement. He did not like to be disturbed for any reason. The Chief was glad Rettly would not be around to screw up the prosecution. Odessa was a tough, ambitious son of a bitch and would hit these assholes with the book.

When Jerry Odessa got to the little jail in his silver Cadillac, sporting an open-throat monogrammed shirt, Chief Poussi was waiting for him with the completed tape. He did not want to spoil the effect by mentioning to Jerry that Barrman was involved. He wanted to just sit there and listen with Jerry and watch the expression on his face when he found out his girl friend's old man was under about a thousand tons of rock. He wanted to see how cool Jerry Odessa really was. Would he have a reaction that would let the cat out of the bag? "This here is the tape of the statement of this character that calls himself the Archangel Beezle. He's kind of their high priest, I guess you'd call 'im," he told Jerry. "He talks about an old friend of yours in here. Remember old Fruity?"

"I heard Fruity was already back with the gang." Jerry had sent Fruity up for sodomy of a fifteen-year-old boy two years before. "What's he done this time?"

"You'll see," the Chief said. "Let's listen."

Jerry listened to the tape, taking notes. When Barrman's name was mentioned, he did not blink or react in any way. The Chief was impressed.

After hearing the tape, Jerry interviewed Beezle and the other Angels. Dolf Header, the dedicated antiestablishment lawyer, insisted on being present and told Beezle he should say nothing more until they had time for a private consultation. Beezle fired him on the spot. Header, patient beyond his years, told Beezle he would be available if he changed his mind, and left.

The Angels talked freely. They had, they believed, accomplished an historic triumph. Jerry fleshed out the information on the tape and reconstructed in his mind the sequence of events. He gave no indication that the death of Spanish Barrman meant anything more to him than to anyone else. He knew that the Angels would renounce their confessions and say they were coerced or intimidated, but Header had been present during the entire taping of Beezle's statement and his voice was on the tape, urging Beezle not to talk, along with Beezle's obscene rejection of his advice and insistence that he was making a voluntary statement for the "edification of posterity." So it was an open and shut case except for one small item: no corpus delicti.

One piece of information stood out in Jerry's mind: A Space Angel lookout who had been posted across the river on the Pennsylvania side had seen Barrman shuck a bright yellow slicker and hang it on an outcropping before crawling into the "rabbit hole" formed by the fallen overhang. In their haste to set the charge and get out of the way the Angels had left it there, and it had been buried along with its owner.

Jerry took Beezle with him to the site. Beezle, with his hands manacled behind him and a cop on either side, proudly walked through the physical layout of the scene before the blast. Jerry thanked him for his cooperation. He told the cops to take Beezle back to the Chief.

When he was alone he stood looking down over the long loose incline of dirt and stone that had once been a hillside and a riverbank. The Angels were right, he thought, in their assessment of their accomplishment: One steep rocky scrub-grown hillside and one water-carved red sandstone river cliff were permanently merged into perhaps a ten-thousand-ton mausoleum for two cadavers. There was not enough money in the county to finance the recovery of those bodies. Where the riverbank once curved in, it now curved out. How many freaked-out gangs of losers had ever changed the course of a river, even slightly?

He made his way down to the water's edge. The new surface was still settling and defining itself. Each step he took caused a minor dirt slide. He was ruining his lizard-skin loafers, but it did not seem important. Some element of this case, something of importance that he had not yet grasped, seemed to be signaling for his attention from a long way off. He sank to his ankles in a hollow that filled quickly with dirt and stone chips when he withdrew his foot. He was proud of his ability to treat fine things, including women, with disregard of their true worth when his goal was big enough. He was not sure what his goal was, but he was sure it was important. Yovi was a widow now; he was walking on her husband's tomb. Everything had changed. Everything had to be thought through again, and carefully.

He put a piece of gum in his mouth and rolled the wrapper in a tiny ball and tossed it in the river. He followed it with his eyes for a few feet. Then he saw something flash yellow under the edge of a huge slab tilted into the water. He had found it without realizing he was looking for it—Spanish Barrman's rain slicker. What he could see of it had been shredded by the blast and seared by heat. It was almost as good as a corpse.

She had awakened late and
started to cry again. She saw her red nose and swollen eyes and
for once in her life didn't care. The phone had rung twice
persistently and she had not answered it. She had eaten the rest
of the orange she had started the night before, then a small
apple, and had drunk a split of Piper-Heidsieck. She felt better
physically but something was torn inside her and she could not
stop crying. The phone rang again. After a ring and a half it
stopped. That was Jerry's signal. When it began to ring again
she picked it up, managing to say hello without sobbing.

Jerry's voice had a strange timbre. He sounded tense and
cold and he was very abrupt: "Yovi, I'm sorry about what has
happened. I really am. I know you liked him a lot, maybe even
loved him. I don't know. Anyhow he was your husband and this
must be a terrible shock. Listen, this is important. Don't talk
to anybody about it. They'll be wanting to talk to you—the
reporters, and the cops, even the neighbors. Don't say anything.

Nothing. Not a word. I'll explain why. I'm on my way over there."
He hung up as she was saying, "Wait. Wait. Jerry, please, I—"

What time was it? Noon. Jerry would be at his office, or—
anywhere. No way to keep him, one of her sources of guilt, the
main one, from coming. She had felt guilt, this kind of guilt,
only once that she could remember in her life. No, twice. The
first and most appalling time was in Paris at the age of twelve.
She had been taking private English lessons and had fallen in
love with her tutor, a twenty-two-year-old secretary from Kings-
ton upon Thames, who had migrated to Paris to work in pro-
duction teams of English-speaking movies. Her name was
Fredericka. She was tall, athletic, brunette, and a good teacher
in all things. She was also as vulnerable, as helpless in the
throes of infatuation, as the child Yovi. When it became known
that the reason Santorini Pellegrini had arranged tutoring for
his daughter was to prepare her for an unexpected move to
London, Yovi swore to Fredericka she would die before she
would leave her. Pellegrini was delighted with Yovi's progress
in English, complimented Fredericka lavishly, and even indi-
cated to her that she could, if she were properly discreet, enjoy
his private attentions. These she rejected gently but firmly,
saying she was flattered by his interest but unworthy of him
and fearful that she might find him irresistible and cause a
scandale. The result was what Fredericka wished: Signor Pellegrini was both put off and put on, and did not remove his
daughter from under her wing.

One day without warning Pellegrini announced to his family
that he had been transferred to the Italian Embassy in London
and they would be leaving immediately. Yovi went to say good-
bye to her friend. Fredericka was not expecting her and was not
at home. Yovi said good-bye to the two Australian lovebirds they
had bought together and which they had named Yovi and Fred.
She wrote a note to Fredericka and to her parents and shut all
the windows and turned on the gas and lay down on Fredericka's
bed and waited. Fredericka came home and found Yovi unconscious and the two lovebirds dead. She revived her friend and
destroyed the notes and the whole thing was passed off as an
accident, but Yovi cried for days because she had killed the

birds. Since that day she had never had a pet. When she thought of the birds to this day, fourteen years later, she felt a rush of shame to her cheeks and tears in her eyes.

The second time she had felt deep guilt was almost equally devastating to her, although being older she had come to accept her deficiencies more philosophically. When Spiegel had found her in bed with Span she had felt no guilt, only a sense of relief that she and Span no longer had to sneak about, and an inexplicable sense of vengeance on Spiegel for not having held her love. Yet, when she had told Span about having sex in the afternoon with a stranger at the Black Bass Inn, and had seen his face and the hurt that showed even in his walk, that sounded even in his breathing, she had felt the same flood of overwhelming guilt that she had felt at the death of the lovebirds.

And now she felt it again, only this time stronger than ever before, almost unbearably strong. It had to do with her carelessness on Sunday. Jerry always splashed himself with a musky cologne. She hated the odor of it except when she was excited. He liked to play with her hair. To make her instantaneously moist and receptive he had only to grasp a big handful of it and use it like a rope to pull her head back so he could kiss her throat. He always did this and he always left his cologne smell in her hair. On Sunday she had taken her usual shower before going home but had failed to wash her hair. Span had smelled the cologne. She had literally seen him smell it, and wince. She had felt the depression, the sadness, the loneliness, flow over and through him. She had not known how to stop it, how to change it, how to say she was sorry. And now he was gone, dead, forever destroyed, and the last thing in his heart was the sadness she had put there, the loneliness of being married to a woman with another man's scent in her hair. She could not stop herself from crying. She did not wash her face to try to bring down the puffiness of her eyes or the redness of her nose. She did not brush her hair. To hell with Jerry and everybody else, and everything. She put on the same chaste robe she had worn for the detectives. She found a pair of panties that she only wore when she had her period, and put them on. Jerry would not touch her hair today.

She heard his special tap and went to let him in. She had never seen the face he showed her now: eyes transformed to darting, glowing bits of onyx, red blotches on his high cheekbones, lips drawn dry and bloodless white. He moved quickly, jerkily, stepping inside with one long stride and about-facing in his tracks to firmly shut the door. He seemed about to give off sparks.

He spoke abruptly: "I told you on the phone how sorry I was, and I am. I know he was a nice guy, and I know you're all broken up. Okay, that's normal. But let me tell you this, Yovi: You're going to have the greatest solace a widow can have. You're going to be rich. All this is confidential. You're not to repeat a word of it. The quarry—"

"I don't want to be rich," Yovi said. "I don't want to talk about money. How can you be such a boor? Don't you understand what has happened? A nice man who didn't deserve to die has died horribly. And you stand there like a pig talking about money!"

"Shut up! Do you hear me? Shut up! I don't care what you think of me right now. You're going to listen, because it's important that you know what's going to happen before it's too late."

She turned away from him, sobbing, and collapsed on the blond-wood sofa. He followed her and continued talking with the kind of intensity for which he was noted in local courtrooms: "That quarry over there—Bozener's—it's not just a little locally owned business. The Bozener family sold it ten years ago, after Marshall Bozener died. Who did they sell it to? They sold it to Tri-State-Tronics. Tri-State-Tronics is a conglomerate involved in heavy construction, trucking, baby foods, pharmaceuticals, solar energy, and a half dozen other things. A billion-dollar conglomerate. And they have mishandled five hundred pounds of dynamite. Do you understand what I'm saying? They've disobeyed all the rules and regulations regarding the handling of explosives, and this has led directly to the death of an innocent man, your beloved husband. I am going to prove that your beloved husband died because Tri-State-Tronics—not just Bozener's Quarry—left powerful explosives lying around where criminal elements could have easy access to them. This callous corporate octopus with a computer for a brain has lost track of the importance of the individual, the worth and the rights of the human being, the little man. To save a few pennies they left a deadly cache of dynamite in the open under a shed, unlocked and unguarded, and as a result you lost the person dearest to you in this world. Tri-State-Tronics is going to have to compensate you for this criminal negligence. And I'm not speaking of a few dollars. I'm speaking of a million, minimum. That's all you need to know right now. That and the fact that you adored your husband and his loss will leave you with a vacancy in life that can never be filled."

"That part is true! It's true!" She would have screamed it at him except that her voice was drowned in tears.

"Save it for the jury, Yov. For the record I'm a family friend. We not only never made it together, we've never even thought of each other in those terms. Any stories about us are outrageous lies. Got that? And I haven't even been here this morning." He leaned down and patted her on the shoulder. "I know this is a tough time, kid. Hang in there. I'll be in touch."

He went out. She hardly noticed his going.

He became conscious of a light. He felt nothing and he saw nothing. The light was less seen than sensed. It was diffuse and he was not sure it was there. His awareness of anything at all was so dim that he could not at first challenge the phenomenon of light that had no form and revealed nothing. Then he knew out of dawning strength that the light was coming through his closed eyelids. To see the light properly would require that he open his eyes, a simple-seeming act that he could not accomplish. They were stuck shut. Where was he? Indeed, what was he? He thought about this for several moments, then stated to himself: I am a man.

This knowledge only led to further confusion. If he was a man, why did he not feel anything? Or hear anything? Wait. He did hear something. Water. Water falling from a height. It was not far away, but it was not, he judged, as close as the light. The light was close, and moving about. He tried to open his eyes again but his eyelids would not budge. Then maybe he wasn't a man. Maybe he was only a consciousness, a helpless disembodied awareness or nonawareness floating in dark space. He could not confirm the existence of arms or legs, or even a body. Yes, now that he tried he was aware of being cold. And then there was his mouth. His mouth was suddenly part of reality: pasty, sticky, evil-tasting. His throat was real too. It seemed to have been stuffed full of nails. He reconstructed himself in his imagination. If he had a right arm it would have to be in a certain place, growing out of his shoulder just to the right of his nail-clogged throat. By consciously willing it he moved his right hand. It was trapped under a weight. He felt it against his groin. Now he knew he was lying on his right arm and he could not move. Then his left arm must be free. He induced strength into his left shoulder by thinking hard of its location and willing it to move. His left arm came up slowly. The elbow did not want to bend, but he forced it. It was his elbow and he was going to be the boss. As his body stirred he felt scald burns. He thought: Christ, I'm lying in my own filth. When the tips of his fingers touched his face he reacted with shock. He had a stubble of beard such as he could only get by not shaving for maybe ten days. Is that where he was—in the North Woods with the Cow and Bicky and Sticky? That's who he was, now, he remembered. He was Spanish Barrman. But that trip to the North Woods, which was supposed to be for a month, had only lasted thirteen days because the Cow had driven him mad with repetitions of stupidities he had previously found bearable because he was away from her most days and several evenings a week. Then—

God in heaven, he was in a cave. Yes. He remembered it all, the Space Angels, Yovi, the Great Discovery, the exploratory zeal, and then—blackout. Wait. If he was in the cave, what about the light? Caves were dark. Oh, of course. Simple. It was his own waist light. It had been on when—and it was still— No. He'd been here awhile. He had a beard. The batteries would be dead by now. Then someone was with him. That was it. Someone who had a light was beside him. But why didn't they speak? Didn't they see him moving his arm? No. He was alone. He was—in the hospital! Yes! He'd hurt himself, he'd been found, and he was in the hospital, in some kind of traction. Where else could he be so chilled, so uncomfortable? Where else would he be allowed to lie in his own waste?

With his numb left hand he touched his left eyelid, felt the gummy, glued-together lashes. He scratched and pushed and tugged at the skin till the eye came open. At first he saw only a blur of formless light, and colors. No, it was not formless. It was a grotesque luminescence, and it moved about. This was probably consistent with a diagnosis of concussion. He must've received a terrible blow to the head, maybe even a fracture, and was just— No, it was not grotesque, it was symmetrical. And it was controlled, purposeful. It moved slowly closer, hanging in the air at an angle to make itself comfortably visible to Span's one open eye. It was multicolored, glowing, translucent. It had a long cylindrical body about—Span guessed, but with only one open eye he could not be sure—the size of a dachshund. It was the color of antique ivory, and curved, and it ended in a pair of short bowed legs to which were attached paddlelike appendages more resembling plastic swim fins than feet. For reasons that he was not capable of considering in his condition, Span had no fear of what he was seeing or thought he was seeing. While his first impression was that the legs were ugly, he saw now that the emerald greenness of them, the rare depth of color into which he seemed to see as into stained glass, made them beautiful. There were front legs, too—or arms—of the same color. They were almost as long as the body and legs combined, unaesthetically disproportionate yet oddly right for the whole. The wrists were thick—he thought of Popeye—and the huge hands had long, tapering fingers. He had only a brief glimpse of one hand as it flicked open in what he took to be a greeting, but he believed he saw three fingers and an opposing thumb, all connected over half their lengths by webbing. There were no shoulders on the sausage-shaped torso, but just below where the arms were attached, two tiny wings grew out of the back— or so he surmised, although all he saw were two gossamer blurs, as one would expect from the wings of a giant hummingbird. Span wanted to see the wings. To lift this thing, to make it float in air, if it was solid—and if it was real—the wings had to be as strong as steel and capable of beating with the speed of a tuning fork. The creature, or thing, as though hearing his thought, stopped its wings and held them open proudly for his appraisal, substituting for their power a rapid flapping of its long, protruding ears and its paddlelike feet, and maintaining its position in the air with ease. The wings were what Span expected, although more beautiful. They were thin, as though drawn on the air with cobwebs, and narrow and curved upward to needle tips, each resembling a silverpoint sketch of a scimitar. Most astonishing of all, they had not made—or at least Span had not heard—a whirring sound or any sound at all as they fanned the air. Nor did he, he realized, hear a whir from the ears and feet that substituted for the now still wings. This was undoubtedly due, Span reasoned, to the sound of the falling water.

Out of the rear end of the apparition (for such it was; now he was sure) grew a long prehensile tail. As it switched and undulated in what seemed to be a friendly manner, its glossy surface rippled with light and dark hues of hammered gold.

All this Span had taken in in a few moments of awestruck staring, not sure of being awake or of being sane if he was awake. Now he saw, or thought he saw, that the apparition was smiling at him. He had not dared before this moment to look it straight in the face, so unearthly was its shape, so blinding-bright its eye. But it was smiling. Its small pink fishlike mouth was turned cherubically up on both sides, and this gave him the courage to smile back. Immediately its smile broadened and it nodded its head and made squeaky gleeful noises. Its two tiny horns, shaped like its wings and gleaming with the delicate purple of pomegranate, tilted toward Span in greeting, and its long limber forked nose, as controlled apparently as an elephant's trunk, bobbed and waggled, shimmering satiny hues of canary down. The eyes were two extraordinarily brilliant aquamarine bulbs on movable vermilion stalks, twisting and flicking about like antennae, seemingly capable of seeing forward and backward and up and down and sideways all at once. The head itself was a light sky blue that seemed as clear as air. The entire apparition, or specter, or astral spirit, or poltergeist, or whatever it would eventually turn out to be (Barrman's brain was beginning to work again), could have been built of tinted plastic or blown glass or spun from sugar candy and lit from within. But the movements, the gnomish grin, the giggle—they could only have been made by God (God! If you want me to believe, now is the time to speak!), or by an aberrating brain. Why did it seem to find Span amusing? Its grin was as pink and harmless as that of an imbecilic old man, but it was annoying. It posed no threat, except in the acceptance of it as real. To accept it, even its seeming benevolence, would mean he was insane, and he did not want to be that. It drifted closer to Span's face, to his one open eye. Its feet and ears stopped flapping and hung motionless while the wings resumed the burden, whirring silently. Span had a moment of deep sad fear or hurt—he didn't quite know what it was he felt. Had he seen this thing before, someplace, a long time ago?

Again it seemed to hear his thoughts. It beamed down upon Span such love, such pure innocence and joy, that Span was terrified. Then it was true: He was crazy, incontrovertibly, certifiably mad, insane. Unless— Wait, this could only happen in one place: He was—he must be—dead.

The creature moved his head slightly—shyly, it seemed—but perceptibly from side to side. A horror even worse—illogically—than the thought of being dead swept over him. This thing was hearing his thoughts! The impression of previous contact, previous awareness, grew stronger in Span. As the past drifted toward him through the fog and became discernible, the thing nodded and smiled encouragement. Then it was there, and he knew—knew—that he was either insane or dead. He was seeing The Skook, and The Skook was not real. He, Span Barrman, had invented him—it—a creature full of maddening logic and complex guile, but with a sweet, guileless voice.

Bicky and Sticky lying in their bunk beds (Bicky the tomboy in the top one, Sticky the fatso in the bottom) had always missed the complex part, the part he, Daddy, liked best. Bicky only liked the part where The Skook sped with the speed of a laser beam, ears, wings, and flipper feet flapping, and speared the villain with his horns, then twisted around and sliced the dirty badso up like cole slaw with his scalpel-like wings. Bicky loved to know the rotten meanaroonie was dying, with blood splashing the ground like rain. She always asked, when he had finally expired amidst myriad screams, hisses, writhes, groans, and moans: "Daddy, was Armbruster McStink the dangerousest crinimal in the whole world and the whole outer space and the whole university?"

And Daddy always answered yes, and Sticky always grumbled that he ought to finish the story. The part Sticky liked best was when The Skook, having dispatched Armbruster McStink (or Poohead Hockeypuck, or Firesnorter McWhorter) and saved the lives of the two brave heroines, Kibby and Kitsy, who were pretty and sweet as could be, produced a fresh coconut cake and a fresh chocolate cake and a rainbow-colored lollipop the size of a big skillet with the lid on, which they shared in celebration of being saved. When Mom heard the sounds of smacking and squealing as Kibby and Kitsy and The Skook tore off big chunks of the cakes with their hands, she always came in frowning at them and tucked the covers around them and adjusted the windows so there would be fresh air but not enough breeze to rattle the blinds, and checked to see that the outside door was locked, and sideswiped each of her daughters' cheeks with a kiss, and glanced at Span in the final throes of tearing apart cakes and stuffing chunks in his mouth as though he were The Ultimate Idiot of the World, and went out.

Oh, God, that was on another planet, a life ago.

The Skook hovered in front of him, smiling. With that open toothless smile, Span thought, he was sure to drool. But he did not.

Now Span noticed something he should have noticed sooner, something odd enough to invite attention: The Skook, though glowing with an inner light strong enough to mix and metamorphose his beautiful colors as he moved, did not illuminate anything around him.

Only madness or an illogical assumption of awareness after death could account for The Skook's presence there. But then Span reminded himself that there was no logic to account for this cave, either, or his own presence in it. Was there another reality he was only now discovering?

"I know who you are." Span's voice sounded gurgly, disembodied. He had to force it out of his throat. "Therefore I must be mad. I know I'm not dead because I hear myself speaking. The Skook I invented could also speak."

"You remember." The voice was sweet and soft, like that of a child. It shocked Span, not because of its quality, but because he heard it. What was it doing there? The Skook came only in answer to the urgent needs of the pure of heart. Span was certainly not one of those. Was he then the enemy? Was The Skook there to do him in? Was The Skook the reason for his being there, the author of miscalculations, missteps, and misplaced self-confidence that had brought him there? No. The Skook killed directly when he killed, without subtlety or delay. The best guess was that he was a temporary aberration that would go away when Span got stronger.

The Skook smiled and withdrew a few feet and settled to a resting place on the same level with Span. His wings continued to move gently, slowly, the way a butterfly's open and close on a flower.

Summoning all his strength, Span tried to move his body. It budged. It felt cumbersome. A pain shot through him like fire, the pain of scalded skin. He was wet and filthy. Well, he'd been lying there long enough to produce a beard as heavy as a poodle's coat. He wondered what color it was. Was it old-penny copper like his hair used to be? Not likely. It was no doubt jaundiced gray, like his hair was now.

Numbly, creakily, agonizingly, he moved. He gathered his separate parts together, mobilized himself, and got to a sitting position. Nothing was broken, probably. The feeling began to flow back into his right arm. The Skook watched with an expression that conveyed polite concern. It was nice of him, Span thought, considering that he (Span thought of The Skook as a male, though he was probably polymorphous) could fly away from any place, even a solid steel box with no openings, at any time he wished, on wings of blithe disdain. And in a world of total darkness he was a light. Though he illuminated nothing he was a reference point. With the vagueness and vertigo in his head, Span was having trouble even remaining in a sitting position, and The Skook, while stationary, helped. His best balance guides, though, were his bruised raw buttocks, which told him quickly when the pressure changed on any part. Sitting was thus a sort of minor accomplishment, but it was only the beginning. Now he must rise to his feet and wash and eat and grow strong enough to walk out of this God-damned cave.

He rubbed his right arm and almost cut himself on the broken glass of his waist light, which had been tied to his arm when he fell. He had lain all this time on top of that rectangular metal lamp, with it crushed against his rib cage. No wonder he had a pain in his side when he coughed or took a deep breath.

Deep in caves, he had read, there was no night or day. The temperature was almost unvarying at the mean annual temperature of the outside air of the region. And humidity was close to a hundred percent. That's why he was still alive. Being without water for long enough to sprout this beard would have killed him anywhere else. He hawked and spat. Breathing through his mouth seemed to help clear his throat and lungs.

He groped for his tackle box. His hand fell on rocks, pebbles, little puddles of water. When he had covered the area he could reach from where he sat, he contrived to shift his body a couple of feet in the direction in which he calculated he must have been going when he fell. This was the logical place for his box to have fallen, was it not? No. He remembered having heard it land before he fell. Since he had already gone to the trouble of moving, he searched quickly where he was, then moved back along what he hoped was the path he'd already traveled, using his legs and arms for propulsion and sliding excruciatingly on his buttocks. Each time he started covering a new area inch by inch he had to fight back panic. His mind was full of snakes and rats and nameless fanged terrors. Seeing The Skook had made him believe it was perfectly possible for his hand—which he could not even see when he brought it to within an inch of his eye—to land on a creature unknown to man that, when awakened, would hold him in a hundred vise-like arms and eat him, small bite by small bite, starting with his nose. There was no precedent in his experience for being isolated in impenetrable blackness. He continued to move his fluttering hands around him to find what they could find. His alternative was to sit there and die.

He touched his tackle box about ten feet from where he had fallen. It was upside down but still shut. The latches had held. With fingers that seemed to belong to someone else in their numbness and weakness, he managed to open the latches and finally the lid. A stench hit his nose. The bologna and mayonnaise and white bread, all loaded with preservatives, had putrefied. The bologna gave off the vilest, most noxious vapors Span had ever smelled, far worse than the stench of simple carrion. He recoiled, retching bile. Averting his head, he felt for the sandwiches, closed his hand around his Stolichnaya bottle instead. It was unbroken, the cap secure. No leakage. He held it, wondering if a drink would make him feel better. It always had. With his other hand he searched for the sandwiches, found them, soggy feculences in waxed paper, and threw them away from him. Then he rummaged blindly again and found what he wanted—his two-piece six-battery flashlight. He put his vodka back in the box, fitted his flashlight together, and turned it on. It was bright. The first thing he saw was the floor around him, red sandstone flecked with quartz. It was flat or nearly flat, covered with rock debris ranging in size from grains of sand to great flat tables weighing several tons that had apparently fallen from the ceiling. There were sharp pebbles the size of peas that dug into his tender flesh, and shallow puddles of water. The floor was a shadowy wasteland. He aimed the light upward and saw nothing. When he looked down, befuddled, he saw The Skook, who seemed to be waiting, with an expression of benign commiseration, for Span to speak. Span resisted, lonely and frightened though he was, not wanting to hear The Skook's voice answer him. He preferred to think of himself as sane. He preferred to accept unsolved the mystery of the invisible ceiling. It was one of many. Then he saw that The Skook's face was oddly distorted, one eyestalk doubled back on itself, one glowing aquamarine bulb—the right one—extinguished by having been pressed into the sky-blue substance or nonsubstance of the face. The trick was accompanied by a wide, shiny, toothless grin. It was a fearfully ugly sight, grotesque yet suffused with what appeared to be genuine kindness. Several thoughts struck Span at once: First, The Skook was replacing speech with a charade containing a message; second, The Skook was refraining from speech because he knew Span wanted him to; third, whether The Skook was actually for him or against him, he was being most discreet and courteous; and fourth, the message he was trying to act out must have to do with Span's inability to see the ceiling of the cave in his flashlight beam.

These unspoken thoughts were answered by vigorous nods from The Skook, an even broader, shinier, uglier smile, and finally a series of hideous physiognomical acrobatics consisting of the right eyestalk popping straight out to its full length with the bright orb at the end of it glaring bluely at Span, then folding itself double again and blinding the eye against the face. This curious activity was repeated several times with great rapidity.

Suddenly Span exclaimed: "Oh, for God's sake! Of course! Thanks, Skook!" He had forgotten to open his good right eye. It was still stuck shut. As he rubbed and tugged and scratched to get it open, The Skook let his right eyestalk resume its normal, slightly curved attitude and acknowledged Span's thanks with a slight bow.

With both eyes open Span's vision, even without his forgotten glasses, cleared passably. He aimed the light straight up again and saw the bare red-brown arch of ceiling a hundred feet above him, sparkling and shining with the condensed mists that rose up and bathed it, and the minute quartz reflections scattered like glass beads everywhere the small weak circle of his light could reach. There was beauty there, he knew, and grandeur, if he could only see it as a whole.

Immediately his thoughts turned to exploration. He shined the light on the floor around him in a big sweep, and there it all was—the heart-stopping expanse of underground space that meant a great cave. In one direction—no doubt the one from which he had come—he saw a solid wall of red sandstone relieved only by cracks and ledges and the round black mouths of two passages. Almost a hundred and eighty degrees away from the wall his beam reached out and faintly found a wide diaphanous waterfall. It originated somewhere in high shadows and fell to disappear in mists. To either side of him the floor went on and on past the reach of his light. It was breathtaking and yet it was in some strange way disappointing. It was not a dream-cave, a cave like other great caves. It was—the fearsome immensity of it stifled his analytical acuity—what? Barren. Yes, it was barren. There were no stalactites, no stalagmites, no wonderland formations. He swept with his light again. It was not entirely barren. There were the blocks, fallen from the ceiling, there was the waterfall—fresh water, if he could reach it!—and there was something else, something not visual but that gave a sense of variety, of richness, of mystery, something of the senses—an odor, yes, the same odor he had detected and thought impossible on first breaking through the sandstone wall that had kept the river out of the cave, the odor of—how could it be?—salt water, seawater. No, it was a trick his olfactory nerves, swollen and disoriented, were playing on him. And there was something else: the millions of tiny sparkles in the stone, the flecks of quartz. Very pretty. A welcome decoration. So his cave was not like other caves, but it was a very nice cave all the same. It was like a huge abandoned dock house on the seashore, with sequined walls.

There was no sign of animal life. This was both a relief and a despair to him. He would not be attacked but he would not have anything to convert to food either. Never mind, he wouldn't be here that long. The time had come to walk out. If he had no food he would only get weaker. He struggled to his feet. They were numb, chilled to the bone, the soles bruised and swollen. He began to walk, lifting each foot a fraction of an inch and placing it forward six inches, like an old man learning to walk again after a stroke. He could feel the blood run hot down his shins from the reopened scabbed-over places on his knees. After three steps he saw the feathery gray curtain of oblivion coming down on his brain and he knew he was falling again.

Salacious stories about the second Mrs. Barrman, long circulated by those locals who professed to have—and in some cases had—firsthand knowledge of her departures from moral rectitude, suddenly proliferated wildly as the details of the crime were made public. Gossip gave way to suspicion and veiled public speculations. Had Yovi Barrman arranged her husband's murder? Had she been a secret part of the weird sexual ceremonies of the Space Angels? Why had she refused to give a statement to the police until several days after the murder? Was it not fortuitous that an assistant district attorney widely credited with being one of her intimate friends was preparing to prosecute the accused?

Many of these questions were answered to the satisfaction of all but the most cynical when the widow, in deep mourning including a black veil, was asked at a public inquiry into her husband's presumed death if she could identify a yellow rain slicker as his. Her answer was an uncontrollable torrent of sobs.

She buried her face in the shredded garment and collapsed. The inquiry was recessed and she was removed, unconscious, to the emergency room at Hunterdon Medical Center.

When she was able to resume on the following day she identified a pair of shoes and socks that the Space Angels had found stashed at the scene of the crime as having belonged to her husband. She wept during this ordeal but managed to answer the questions that were asked of her without delaying the proceedings.

Jerry Odessa, who had emphasized that the plans he was formulating for an assault on the treasury of Tri-State-Tronics depended on the visibility and sincerity of her grief, sought a moment in public when they were apart from the others ostensibly by chance, and told her that in her efforts to be convincing she was possibly overdoing the emotion. She was so shocked at this misreading of her feelings that she ran to the ladies' lounge. She sat on the plastic sofa and gave herself up to her anguish, her black veil thrown back over her hair. She would forgive Jerry his insensitivity because she had not been able to explain to him her true feelings for Span, nor her own gnawing guilt over having hurt him so deeply. She would also forgive Jerry because even if she had explained he probably was not capable of understanding, and she could not hold anyone responsible for being what they were. She was involuntarily what she was, the result of forces she did not understand, of genes she did not control, and she accepted this as she accepted it in others. She felt guilt only at having hurt others when she could have avoided it, as in the case of Span's having smelled Jerry's lotion in her hair on the last day of his life. And now he was gone forever, this sweet man, and she had helped make his last hours less than happy, and she would never get a chance to work for his forgiveness.

She felt an arm around her shoulders and peeked out past her soggy handkerchief to see a uniformed matron seated beside her. The matron's face was lean and wrinkled. She wore no makeup and her tanned skin contrasted with her light blue eyes. At first Yovi was startled, thinking it was a man's face, but then she saw the skirt, and the rest of the person, and felt the understanding human closeness of a woman against her body, the long bony arms and hard hands, skilled at soft touching. She let herself cry. The matron was strong. She held Yovi close. Yovi felt that the matron had all the time in the world, and would hold her and steady her as long as she needed to be held. This was the most calming thought of all. After a few minutes Yovi felt comforted enough, wept-out enough, to wipe her eyes and blow her nose and look straight into the sensitive leathery face of the matron. She smiled and the matron returned her smile, the papery skin around the eyes crinkling to become narrow slits that only a sliver of blue shone through.

The same light was there, coming through his eyelids, and this time he knew what it was. He did not want to open his eyes at first because he did not want to face The Skook, the invincible, the fearless, the intrepid challenge-loving Skook, in this condition of abject failure. When he did look, for want of any other choice, he saw the maddening beast in his usual serene self-satisfied mood, hanging effortlessly in the air a few feet away.

"If you're so God-damned great, you garish bastard, why don't you help me?" he shouted, or tried to shout. The sound came out more as a petulant gurgle. Even as he heard himself, he thought: Why does my fear always show up as belligerence?

The Skook, amiably calm, responded with what could be taken for regret: "You know very well I can't."

Span decided to be sensible and save his strength, dole it out carefully, not waste it in emotional storms. He whispered: "You helped Bicky and Sticky."

"Never."

"Yes. You did."

"Not once."

"Oh, I mean Kibby and Kitsy. You helped them."

"Happily."

"Out of tougher spots than this."

"Gladly."

"Then?"

"Sorry."

"But—please, Skook—why?"

"Must I say it?" The Skook smiled conspiratorially, as though whatever the reason, Span should see the wisdom of not putting it into words.

This subtlety was lost on Span, who thought The Skook's angelic voice and shiny pink smile more and more repellent. "Yes, say it. Dammit, you helped them. Why not me?"

"Don't you remember?"

Span struggled with and finally controlled his impulse to shout again. It would only be a waste of strength. He would conquer this beast by superior intelligence, force him to help or go for help. Was not man God's favored son? Did he not have dominion over every living thing? He spoke calmly and, he thought, with admirable reasonableness: "No, Skook, I don't remember. If you're not here to help me, why are you here?"

"You called me."

"No, I didn't."

"You very clearly did."

"I didn't even remember you. How could I have called you?"

"You had me locked in your past. When you got sick and didn't remember to forget me, I escaped."

"Well, go back. If you're not going to help me, go back."

"You don't really want that."

"The hell I don't!"

"After all, I'm all you have."

"Then help me out of here!"

"Goodness gracious, you are forgetful."

"You helped Bicky and Sticky, God dammit!"

"Kibby and Kitsy."

"I mean Kibby and Kitsy!" He heard himself sob. Was he going to give in now, a pitiful, unmanly petitioner, and grovel? No. No. He held in his sounds, commanded his breathing to be regular and deep, in spite of the pain of the waist-light bruise on his lower ribs and the—he remembered now—bruise on his sternum caused by the rock thrown by One-of-Three so long ago. Finally he was able to speak with almost casual matter-of-factness: "Skook, tell me why you helped Bicky and Sticky and not—"

"Kibby and Kitsy."

"Kibby and Kitsy, I mean. You helped them, but you can't help me."

"If you want to remember, you can."

"I want to remember!"

"You want to think you want to, but you don't really want to."

"Damn you, Skook! I can't remember!"

He remembered. Kibby and Kitsy were wonderful, angelic, sweet, obedient, pure, tender, thoughtful, responsive, concerned, gentle, honest—all the things, in short, that Daddy always wanted Bicky and Sticky to be, and which they were not. The goodness of Kibby and Kitsy permeated the air around them with the Perfume of Purity. The Perfume of Purity was a rare arrangement of atomic particles that bridged the Gulf from World to Otherworld and allowed The Skook to fly directly into their lives. Traveling in the only medium that would sustain him, The Skook came from Otherworld, able after crossing the Gulf to fly in worldly air and retain his skookly powers. Kibby and Kitsy never got into any trouble except in combating evil. The Forces of Evil sometimes overcame their goodness and imprisoned them in remote escape-proof cells where only death, slow and agonizing death, could find them. At such times these brave children called The Skook. They always apologized for troubling him, and always asked him how they could convert their enemies, the Evil Ones, without destroying them. This was the infinite range of Kibby and Kitsy's goodness, the source of the inexhaustible flow of the Perfume of Purity that allowed The Skook to voyage back and forth between the two worlds without plunging into the Gulf between, bereft of his skookly powers. The Skook had once saved Kibby and Kitsy from an airtight box made of foot-thick oaken timbers fastened together with railroad spikes. He had plunged his horns point-deep into the oak by ramming it at full speed, and then, by flattening down his long eyes and nose, and making his sausage-shaped body as rigid as a steel beam, and beating his wings and webbed hands and flipper feet till they hummed with the hum of a million hummingbirds, had turned himself into a giant drill and bored a hole right through the oaken wall. And once, when Kibby and Kitsy were thrown from an airplane by a wicked witch who wanted to rule the world, The Skook had hooked them both gently under the straps of their sunsuits, one on each horn, just in time to keep them from being smashed to bits on the jagged rocks of a mountain. He had then taken them with him as he streaked into the sky and caught the witch's private jet and landed on top of it and forced it to go in for a landing at the nearest airfield. The witch had been so frightened of The Skook's powers that she had radioed ahead personally and begged the forces of law and order to meet the plane and take her into custody to protect her, promising in return to give up witchcraft forever and get married and have children and be a good mother who never never fed her children soft canned spaghetti but always cooked it fresh *al dente*. The Skook had even followed up on this case and had been able to report to Kibby and Kitsy that the witch had kept her promise and was now Mrs. R. D. Lebenschreiber of Stockton, New Jersey, and had five lovely children, none of whom had ever needed spanking.

The exploits of The Skook had been as beautiful and numerous and uniquely structured as the flakes of a heavy snowfall.

"I remember, Skook," Span whispered. "I understand."

"Mr. Barrman," The Skook said with grave respect that worried Span even more than his usual flippant detachment, "don't you think you should turn off your flashlight?"

"Oh, yes, thank you!" The six-battery light was ominously dimmer. He must've been unconscious for an hour, maybe two or three. He switched it off and lay there in the blackness, able to see nothing except The Skook, whose light, incredibly, illuminated none of the objects around him. Span made a note to ask The Skook to explain—or help him remember the explanation of—this phenomenon. But there were more urgent considerations: "You were very kind to remind me, Skook. I shall need this light."

After what he took to be an hour's rest, he worked his way to an upright stance, turned on his light again, and began to shuffle determinedly in the direction of the passage through which he had come. There was another opening to his left, but he was sure it was not the right one. It seemed to go downward.

His light was failing fast. His legs were as unsure as hinged stilts. He got to the entrance to the passage, stopped, and turned to look back. The Skook had not moved. He seemed to be waiting for something. Let him wait, Span thought. This was a big place. Who had ever seen an underground waterfall? He would walk out of here and bring back a party of real speleologists and find out what was really here. No, he would get title to the land before he told anyone. Then he would develop the cave, Barrman's Cave, and let people enter for a fee and see the marvels he, Spanish Barrman, had discovered. And his father would know the triumph, finally, of something bigger than nine-to-five, the rent, the bills, the sitcoms, the ball game, the God-damned gummy white bread he ate because the label said ENRICHED. "Skook," he said, "you can stay as long as you like. I'm heading out."

The Skook did not answer. Span started up the wet path of the wide opening of the passage. It surprised him by being steep, right away. But then he'd been going downhill on the previous trip. His heart pounded erratically but he was not afraid. He knew the way. His dimming light showed him several steps ahead. He would have to crawl part of the way on bloody knees, but so what? And before they healed he would be back with the exploration party. As the leader of it. He was not going to step aside, play second fiddle, turn it over to somebody else, be modest, the way he'd always done in other things, all his life: "It was nothing, really. Just luck." "Go ahead, I'm in no hurry." "That's okay, pay me later." "I don't mind." "You're probably right."

No more of that kind of nonsense.

The path grew narrower, the climb steeper. He remembered it that way. But the air was stale, stuffy, dusty. He didn't remember that.

Then the passage stopped. The ceiling had come down, one solid piece, and pinched it off. He examined the cul-de-sac with terror-palsied hands. He was in the wrong passage. The one he should have taken was the one beside this one, the one that seemed to slant down but undoubtedly, after a few feet, turned up, and would lead him back to daylight.

He hurried back down the passage, inspired by the cloven hooves of death he heard behind him. There were probably many corridors leading off from the grand salon. That would be normal for such a large cave. He had chosen this one on the fatuous assumption that it was the only one other than the one that seemed to descend. He would look again when he got back to the big room, and find the right one this time.

The Skook showed no surprise at his return.

He was trapped. There was no doubt. The passage that began by descending had continued to descend for thirty feet and then narrowed to the diameter of a sink drain. He had been able to find no others.

The Skook had waited Sphinx-like till Span came literally crawling (he had fallen again but not lost consciousness) back to him, defeated.

"Skook," he said, his voice a shaky whisper, "I'm ashamed to admit it, but I'm scared. I'm finally down to that. I'm plain scared. I'm going to die, and I don't want to. I don't know how to. What does one do? Just sit here and wait? I mean, I'm weak, I'm starved, I'm sick, I'm scalded and smelly and scabby and skinned and bruised and scared, and I'm pretty damned close to just collapsing and ceasing to exist. How can I accept that? I'm only forty-eight. I'm young. I want to get another look at green grass. Another look? A look. I never really looked at green grass. I never really noticed it unless it had just been mowed and I smelled it. And now I'm going to die down here in this God-damned blackness without ever having seen green grass. I can promise you now that if I ever get topside again I'm going to look at it closely. Under a microscope! I'm going to roll in it. I'm going to eat it. I'm going to—" A sob escaped him. "I'm going to die down here. I'm done."

The Skook hung in black space in front of him, his face as full of unspoken thoughts as the *Mona Lisa*'s. This infuriated Span.

"God dammit, Skook! When someone is dying, is that all you can do—look smug?"

"What can be done with a quitter?"

"I'm not a quitter!"

The Skook's reply was a slight adjustment of angle toward Span to better reveal his look of distant serenity.

"I repeat," Span shouted, "I am not a quitter! I'm a realist acknowledging a certainty!"

"Of what?"

"Of death! My death!"

"Hardly a revelation, unless you know when."

"How could I?"

"Then it's really the same problem you had in the upper world. You know you're going to die, but you don't know when. Up there you tried to think of ways to live instead of ways to die."

"Such as what?" Span was petulant. "What ways? What ways?"

The Skook, superior and imperturbable, drifted away from him.

Span tried to yell at him but his throat only made low quavering sounds. "Name one God-damned way!" It was clear to him now. For his sins The Skook had come to make his last few breaths unbearable. He continued, saving his energy, knowing that The Skook heard his lowest whisper, even his unspoken thoughts: "You can't think of one way for me to live, can you, you little bastard? All you can do is issue taunts and accusations and act superior to me—me, your inventor, your creator! Well, you're not superior! And let me tell you something: There's water down there, and where there's water there may be fish, and if there are I'll catch one. I'll survive longer than you think, and you'd better hope that's quite awhile, you smug freak, because when I'm done you're done. Bicky and Sticky won't have any more use for you, that's for sure. And the Cow banished you years ago. All right, you won't be dead. You'll be lost somewhere in the cellars of their minds, decommissioned, which you eminently deserve, and not likely to be recommissioned. But in spite of the fact that I'll be saving you at the same time, Skook, I'm going to keep myself alive!" As he finished in a fierce hiss Span's face— a greasy nose, grimy forehead, and two red eyes burning through a matted beard—was vibrant with invincible spirit.

The Skook bounced up and down in the air, and spun around so that his colors blended and blurred. "Bravo! Bravo, Spanish Ulysses Barrman!"

"For God's sake! Don't say my middle name out loud! Those initials: S. U. B. Who wants to be called Sub all their lives? Substitute infielder, substitute teacher—twelve years at Lockatong Prep and never had a contract! A substitute, officially, the whole time I was there."

The Skook circled, pointing at his flashlight.

"I know, I'm wasting my batteries again. I haven't stopped being stupid. But I want to confirm my existence by looking at myself in the light for a change. Anyhow, as a sub English teacher, it made it easy to let me go, don't you see, after the so-called scandal, caught in bed with Yovi. No tenure. Story of my life, Skook: No tenure." With these words, the last of which he could barely say, S. U. Barrman fainted.

When he came to (he had no idea how much later, although his beard felt longer) he was almost too weak to move. But his mind was clear. At least it seemed clear to him.

"How long have I been out, Skook?"

"What is time in a cave?"

Span started to tell The Skook that he was about as likable as castor oil, but he refrained. Instead he groped for his flashlight. It had been in his right hand when he passed out. He was lying on his right side. Logic told him the flashlight was near his right hand, which was near his waist. It was there. He was getting good at dark logic. The batteries were dead. He had failed to turn it off.

All right, no crying over spilt milk. Fight back. Down to business. He opened his tackle box, which he had been wise enough to keep close at hand. The vodka was on top, cushioned by the folded plastic garbage bag. He took the bottle out, set it carefully between his legs, and felt under the garbage bag for the screw-top waterproof container of matches. His hand found a pack of cigarettes instead. He took them out, sniffed them. He had no desire to smoke one. He even felt slightly nauseated at the thought. He put them back. Then he brought forth a glass container, opened it, took out a book of matches, and closed the lid tight. As he moved his clothes stuck to his skin. When the cloth rubbed against itself it made a scratchy hissing sound. His head floated away and he willed it back in place. Unable to see anything but The Skook, he accepted The Skook as the only reality.

He had done things in the wrong sequence again. He should have prepared the vodka and the wick before getting the matches out of the jar. Never mind. It was done. What wick? The most nearly wicklike substance would have been his socks, but he had stashed them with his shoes before coming into the cave. You were right, Deena Jane, I am the Ultimate Idiot of the World. If you could only see me now, you would nod that nod of yours, smile that razor-thin smile, and say something brilliant and appropriate, such as "As ye sow, so shall ye reap," and walk away to the refrigerator and get a can of Bud, and light an unfiltered Camel, and turn on a rerun of Groucho. That's my memory of you, laughing and spilling Bud on your chin when the plucked duck falls. But you never got to call me Sub, because you never knew about Ulysses. I expunged it from my life as soon as I left Trenton. I even had new birth certificates made without the Ulysses in my name. Nobody knows, except Mom and Dad, and they're sworn to secrecy. Not even Yovi knows.

He snapped out of his trance and began the blind tactile labor of making a vodka lamp.

16

It worked but it didn't work. A piece of damp trouser cuff held upright by a fishhook in the bottle cap full of vodka finally caught fire and held a small blue flame. It had cost him a book of matches, plus one match from a second book, because by the time he had got ready to light the wick the phosphorus on the striking surface of the matchbook had already absorbed so much moisture that it was like mud, and when he drew the sulfur head of the match across it it skidded instead of striking. And now that he had done all this work in the dark and had a flame it was so small as to be almost useless. Holding it up between his thumb and index finger, he could see nothing but the hand that held it and part of his forearm, and his broken watch, stopped at six-thirteen. Still, dim as it was, it was better than darkness. He got a spool of forty-pound test nylon out of the tackle box and attached a leader and a shad hook to it with a clinch knot. He had no trouble finding—half by smell and half by the feeble light—the rotten bologna. If there were fish they would be blind. They would feed by sound or smell or motion detectors. If by smell, the bologna would be great bait. He put it on his hook. It smelled sweet now; it smelled of promise, of life.

His vodka lamp went out. When he had first lit it it had seemed like almost nothing. After ten minutes it had seemed like his link to life. As he watched the last wispy firefly tail of light disappear he started to whimper. The Skook, a sort of animated rainbow, was even more impressive when viewed through the prisms and blurs of tears, but his air of imperturbability infuriated Span.

"Skook, you're an idiot! Only an idiot or a hangman would enjoy seeing a grown man reduced to infantile blubbering, craven terror, helplessness, pridelessness, ignoble groveling with no one to grovel to, almost ready to call for his mama like a two-year-old in a nightmare! Yes! I almost did it! I almost let it out! If you hadn't been sitting there gloating, I'd've called my mama! And I don't give a damn! You're not a man, so you don't understand. Everybody dies, yes, but very few men die like this! Only men trapped in disabled submarines or deep mine shafts! And it's well known that many of them cried out and went crazy with the knowledge that they were spectators at their own funerals!" He gave way to whimpering again. He felt he had a perfect right to whimper and to lose his mind, yet he could not ignore the look of contempt on The Skook's face.

"Why do you sneer, damn you, Skook! Answer me, damn you! Answer me!"

The Skook seemed to shrug. "If you're sure you want me to."

"I said so, didn't I?"

"Then let me remind you that your case, and that of the submariners, are not comparable. Those unfortunate individuals have nothing but the certitude of a slow and agonizing death. You have air, water, and a newfound knowledge of yourself."

"Bullshit. The only new thing I know is that I'm doomed!"

"Do you mean you aren't newly aware that, in spite of endless brags to the contrary, you're afraid of death, can't face it bravely or even with dignity, and want desperately to live?"

"I admit it. That is newfound knowledge. And I'd just as soon not have it, considering how I got it."

"That's not all. You've also learned that in your panic, your seemingly bottomless cowardice, you assure your death, because you can't remember anything that's important. You're frozen."

"What do you mean? What can't I remember?"

"I'm not going to tell you. You're too chicken-livered to deserve it."

At this moment Span's hatred for The Skook was limitless. He wished only to express this rare—to him—hatred in a way that would have meaning to the seemingly impervious Skook. "Skook," he said, after a few moments of scheming, "the one thought that I will cling to and that will give me peace as I die is that with my death you will cease to exist. Bicky and Sticky will certainly never resurrect you. They and the Cow will die and you will be obliterated."

The Skook smiled sweetly. "Will I know it?"

"Not only that," Span continued, ignoring the question, "but you are not all-knowing. I am capable of acting. I'm not frozen. I'm a man and I intend to die like a man. You'll die, too, but you won't be mourned. Nobody knows about you, or gives a damn. But Yovi will mourn me. In spite of her aboriginal morals she loves me in her own way. I know that. And in her own way she'll mourn me. How is that? Not by abstinence, that's for damn sure!"

Span was astonished to hear his own laughter. It echoed and lost itself in the distant clatter of water.

The Skook's face took on an expression of one forced to hear an oft-told tale.

"You don't believe me, do you? I don't quite understand her, and it does sound farfetched, but I believe I know her better than anyone, and I can say without any doubt that what appears to be shallowness in her is only skin deep!" Again he laughed, or cackled, and the thought came in the middle of his laughter that he was hanging on to his mind by only a frayed thread. He continued compulsively: "Yovi was brought up a Catholic. When she was a little girl her parents moved to Paris from Italy. Up until she was twelve or so, I believe, she told me she was very religious. Went to mass and loved the Catholic ritual, still knows the Lord's Prayer only in French. Now, even though she never goes to mass, or confession—who'd have time to listen?—when something like this happens, she'll do like every other Catholic, astray or not astray. She'll go to church and pray for my immortal soul. She'll get comfort from a priest. In her mourning even the most attractive young padre might be off-limits to her, or he might not be. But no matter. She will have gone to him for comfort in her bereavement, and who are we to say what comfort is? And she'll wear black. And she'll go to the church at odd hours and light candles for my soul. Candles! Candles!"

Seeing Span speechless for a moment, The Skook was so pleased, he rose in the air, fanning his wings, his webbed feet, and his ears, and undulating his long tail. He rotated his protruding eyes in opposite directions, like a tassel dancer, and crowed.

"Skook!" Span growled. "Why didn't you remind me I had candles in my tackle box?"

With the first circle of yellow candlelight he had sought and found a candle holder. It was a flat chip of stone shaped like a spearhead. It not only kept the hot wax from dripping on his fingers but preserved it for some future use. He had not spoken to The Skook, or even looked at him, in an hour. He would live or die by his own efforts. He did not need a Skook to remind him of his faults.

Holding the spool of nylon line in his right hand and the candle in his left, he moved with small agonizing steps toward the edge of what he now sensed to be a deep chasm. He feared he would lose consciousness again at any moment, but the roar of the nearing waterfall excited him and gave him strength. Holding the candle high in front of him, he fancied he could see the sparkle of the cascading water. It was close enough now that the sound was deafening. It was falling several hundred feet, striking the surface below in a ceaseless cannonade, sending back a pulsing roar in gusts amplified in the vast chamber of the chasm. The sea smell was strong. Hypnotized and nearly shocked to insensibility by the buffeting waves of sound, he almost stepped over the edge into the void. It was suddenly there, under his forward foot—nothing but mist and the absence of rock. He swayed outward, felt faint, and was tempted momentarily to let it have him once and for all. It sucked at him, then gusted. The candle flickered, the flame bowing sideways in all directions. Far below Span thought he had seen specks of white phosphorescence during the one second he had swayed outward. He fell backward, dropping the spool so he could break his fall and touch the solid floor with his hand, with his whole body. He did not let the candle fall. His instincts were healthy. Even death is relative. He was already dead, but not dead. He still had his fevered corpse, feeding off its own fat, a few candles and matches, the hooks and lines, and his pulse. He lay on his side. He felt for and found the spool. The spoiled bologna was still on the hook. There would logically be fish down there, all right, blind fish, and they just might find this odoriferous junk food irresistible. He felt for his belly. It was no longer there. In its place were folds of loose skin. He was cannibalizing himself and there was not much left to eat.

Beside him, ghostly soft in the yellow light, was a flat rock the height and size of an orange crate. He slid on his side, not wanting to further damage his raw knees and buttocks, till he could reach out and brush away the pebbles and other debris at the base of it, then he pulled himself up and leaned against it achingly, facing the chasm. A foot beyond this was another, larger, rock, also flat, and a few inches taller than the one that served as his backrest. He put his candle holder on it. He was only three feet now from the edge of what he guessed to be a sheer cliff dropping straight down two or three hundred feet to water. He estimated the distance to the cataract opposite him to be two hundred feet. How long the chasm might be, or how deep the water at the bottom, he had no way of even trying to imagine. But the most fascinating mystery was—

He was startled when The Skook darted past him, circled, then came back and hovered in front of his face, squeaking, "Crisis! Crisis! Crisis!"

"Crisis? Of course crisis. Ongoing."

"You don't understand, Spanish Barrman. You are allowing yourself too much complacency."

"An achievement, under the circumstances."

"A defeat. You're like a weary trapper lost in snow. You'll go to sleep, never to wake up."

"Nonsense. I was lost in deep contemplation of an important question. Can you explain—?"

"When do you eat?"

"I'm not hungry right now. Listen, Skook, you're so bright, how do you explain the incongruity of—?"

"Anorexia. No desire to eat. You dream of life as you accept death."

"I feel great. Just answer me this riddle: Water from an underground river almost surely sharing sources with the Delaware, and therefore fresh, falls hundreds of feet into an underground pool, or lake, or whatever it turns out to be, that smells like the ocean. How? Why?"

"If you live, Sub, you may answer that someday yourself. Do you acknowledge that one must eat to live?"

"I do."

"Will you admit you haven't eaten in days? Maybe fifteen? Maybe more?"

"I don't know."

"Judging from your beard..."

Span felt his beard. At the same time he noticed that his buttocks had anesthetized themselves and no longer throbbed excruciatingly. His beard was long enough to be soft, and not scruffy but full. He wondered how it looked. He stroked it. "Yes, a beard like this takes awhile."

"Some time ago you said you were hungry."

"I was."

"Did you eat?"

"No."

"Then what happened to your appetite?"

"You'll have to admit that's quite a stumper, Skook: fresh water and seawater all in a cave."

"What about your appetite?"

"It went away."

"It won't come back unless you eat. And unless you eat we're done for."

"I'll eat in a little while."

"You'll eat what?"

"Eat what? Fish. I'll eat fish. I'll fish for fish; don't worry, Skook. But I'm so comfortable right now. My butt doesn't even hurt. And I'm about to figure out the riddle."

"Sub, listen to me. How many people ever escape from a place like this? You could be one of them, a unique accomplishment."

"I could be." Span yawned. "I could be." Even he recognized the timbre of the very old man's voice coming out of him. "And I will be, soon's I take a nap." He closed his eyes.

The Skook flew up and squawked. Span's eyes opened. The Skook darted at him, straight at his eyes, astounding him, then at the last split second veered away.

"What the hell was that all about?" Span tried to yell, his voice hollow, his larynx gone slack and uncontrolled.

The Skook buzzed him again, and again, barely missing him. Span dodged as though under attack by stinging horseflies. Then he realized that there was no air turbulence around his face as a result of the near misses, no sound of humming or buzzing from the blur of beating wings, ears, and feet. The Skook was—of course!—nonmatter, and couldn't touch him.

"Oh, yes, I can!" The Skook squeaked, hovering right before Span's eyes, answering his thoughts before they were spoken. "The closer you get to death, the closer I can get to you. I'll touch you, all right, if we go on like this, but it'll be too late for both of us. We'll both be in Otherworld."

"Why can we touch in Otherworld but not here?"

"I told you."

"I don't remember, Skook." He yawned and closed his eyes again.

"When you die you regain innocence, honesty, purity. You will be surrounded by the Perfume of Purity, the only medium in which I can fly. So I can touch you then, but it'll be too late. Your dead brain will be unable to animate me, and I'll be done for, same as you, old boy, unless by some miracle Deena Jane

— 116 —

or Bicky or Sticky energizes me again and calls me back. But of course nothing will ever be able to call you back."

Span did not answer. His head dropped to his chest. He swayed. The Skook darted at him and screeched. Span did not react. The Skook began to circle his head so fast it was a blur of colored light like a spinning halo. He screeched shrilly: "S. U. Barrman! Spanish Ulysses Barrman! On your feet! Up and at 'em, Sub!"

Span's head snapped up and his eyes popped open, wide, unfocused, seeking. The Skook stopped circling and treaded air in front of him, very close. Span was aghast. "Skook, you touched me."

"Only briefly, I'm happy to say."

"But—how?"

"For a moment you were—" He stopped himself and shrugged—or seemed to shrug in spite of having no shoulders.

"You mean I was actually—?"

"For a moment, yes. In my world. I lost control and ticked you with a wing."

"My God."

"Get up, Barrman. Get up on your hind legs and save yourself."

Span braced himself on the rock and struggled upright on recalcitrant legs. His feet were numb. His knees wobbled as though, if he were not strictly attentive, they might bend in any direction. Then, driven on by The Skook, who darted back and forth in the air, exhorting him in his high, childish, insistent, sometimes petulant, sometimes congratulatory, sometimes pleading, sometimes threatening voice, Span moved his arms, took deep breaths, shored up his courage, swore on his mother's head to never surrender, and started paying out the baited hand line toward the water. He sat on his rock with his candle at his side on the taller rock beside him, and let the line slip through his fingers. At about two hundred feet he felt it slacken. It had found the surface. He had hardly had a second to become aware of this when he felt a tug so strong the line sped through his fingers, burning them, causing him to drop the spool and hang onto the line with both hands, which were jerked out in the direction of the chasm. He could only say

"Skook!" before he fell forward off the rock to his raw knees. His line was bent over the edge of the precipice. He tried to lean out and free it before the rough rock cut it, but something was taking it out so fast, he realized he needed the help of the rock to slow it down. It was cutting the fingers of both his hands. Then the pull weakened slightly, and Span had a sense of impending victory. He managed to get seated again with his back to the rock, his knees up, and his feet braced on the rough floor. By leaning forward and extending his hands over the void and propping his elbows against his bleeding knees (which did not hurt), he managed to bring up a few feet of line, then a few feet more, which he wrapped around the apex of the triangle formed by his bent left leg. If whatever was on his line pulled too hard he had only to straighten his leg and the loops would pop free.

Suddenly the pull stopped and he fell back against the rock. His catch was off. He'd lost it, and he'd never be able to stay conscious long enough to bait another hook and try again. Wait. There was something—a weight—on his line still. He was lifting something, something that wasn't there when he put his line down. Whatever it was, it was immobile and not very heavy. Encouraged, almost daring to be jubilant, he began to bring the line up as fast as he could, wrapping it around his knee.

Then he heard something that he believed at first to be taking place inside his own skull—a sound, a sound like no other, a sound surely caused by blood vessels breaking in his own head. He had heard his dad describe the beginning of his stroke as the sound of a long unearthly scream. This, then, was a stroke. He waited to fall over, to be paralyzed. Then he heard the lingering echo of the sound come from far and near, overlapping itself. It was real, the sound, real and not happening in his own skull. The certainty froze him. The reality of it was more terrifying than a stroke, than death.

It came again, closer, more sustained, a mournful howl-roar. It was part thunder and part high-speed drill going into a steel plate.

Starry-eyed, his jaw slack, Span shook his head like a demented old man. He whispered hoarsely: "My God." Then, revived by fear, he went back to hauling in his line.

There was a fishhead on his hook. The body had been bitten or torn off just back of the gills, leaving a head as big from the side as Span's, but only half as wide. The eyes resembled demitasse saucers, proportionately huge, and porcelain, blind. From under the milk-white film that covered them they seemed to be trying to stare at Span, to question him.

Span stared unbelieving at the head. The hook was straightened out. The head was only hanging by the barb, stuck in cartilage. As he stared at it it fell away from the hook. He lifted it, his hands responding imperfectly. Blood and aqueous fluid ran between his unfeeling fingers and down his arms as he placed it on the flat rock behind him. Ten years ago, or six, before he met Yovi, he'd have wondered what to do with a fishhead. Deena Jane had always thrown them to the cat. But Yovi—how did she know so many things?—had taught him there were four fillets in the head as tender and savory as any part of the fish. With his knife he pried up the hard scales of a cheek and scooped out a morsel of pure flesh the size of an oyster. It was repellent to him rather than beautiful, as he knew it should be, but he put it dutifully in his mouth and chewed it. It was delicate and sweet. It only took him ten seconds to begin to relish it. He inserted the point of his blade under an armored covering at the back of the skull into a hollow beside a cartilaginous ridge and found another piece of flesh, oblong and larger than the cheek fillet, which he impatiently popped into his mouth while still chewing the first bite. He smiled at The Skook, who treaded air—more accurately Perfume of Purity—in front of him, waiting for his reaction.

"Sushi," Span said. "Without seaweed and ginger root and rice and white radish and sake, but perfect nonetheless." He turned the head over and began extracting the other two fillets. "Simplicity is the essence of greatness. Emerson said something like that. But then, so did almost every other wise man. Skook, you want to hear a joke? When I was on an aircraft carrier in the Pacific, they gave us a little survival manual. It told us that if we were adrift in the wide wide sea we could eat raw fish, actually eat raw fish, and survive. Sounded pretty farfetched to us dumb squeegee jockeys, reading in our bunks. Latest survival discoveries, huh? Okay, Admiral, we'll try it if we're desperate. They never mentioned that the Japs, our enemies, had made an art of raw fish dishes since before there was a U.S. Navy." He held a perfect lump of flesh on the point of his knife. It quivered and glistened in the candlelight. "Behold a moment of classic perfection, Skook. My first two bites were those of a starving man feeding. Now you shall see me dine." He bared his teeth and parted them just enough to allow the insertion of the chunk of fish between them. Then he bit down with just enough pressure to hold the flesh and remove it from the knife point. Then he took the whole piece into his mouth, closed his lips over it, and slowly masticated, the comic model of a Groton grad at tea with the First Lady.

The Skook was so pleased, he bounced up and down, slapping his webbed feet together. There was no sound.

"How is it, Skook, that I can hear you when you speak, but not when you clap your feet?"

"You can't hear me when I speak. You hear my thoughts, which send electric waves from Otherworld on the Perfume of Purity and are picked up as sound waves in the air. My slapping my feet together—unlike my thinking—produces no electric turbulence to be transmitted to your air."

"I don't believe you, Skook." Span spoke haughtily, still doing his impression of upper-class dining decorum. "If what you say is true, why do you move your lips when you speak?"

"Because that seems normal to you," The Skook said, moving his lips. "I don't wish to dislocate your reality any more than has already been done."

Span pondered this as he dug out the last of the four choice bits of fish, the one remaining in the niche on the right side at the back of the skull. "And now, Skook, being a caveman, I shall dispose of this final bite in accepted caveman style." He took the treat in his fingers, tossed it in his open maw, chomped on it rudely, and with many satisfied oohs and aahs and smacks and animal grunts dispatched it. Then he sucked on his teeth for a few moments, sighed as though preparing to undertake an unpleasant but necessary task, and belched with great emphasis. "Skook," he said, "I just flat don't believe you."

The Skook began to speak without moving his lips. His mouth remained tightly closed as he said: "You don't need to believe me, unless you want to retain what sanity you have."

Span was frightened speechless. This illogical act seemed somehow more impressive than all the other illogical experiences he had had. He felt helpless, betrayed.

With his mouth still closed The Skook asked: "Convinced?"

"Yes! Yes! For God's sake, Skook!"

The Skook moved his lips and spoke: "I think we ought to keep everything as nearly normal as we can, don't you?"

"Yes, yes," Span said. He felt sick. What was left of the food in his mouth tasted salty and soft. "I have to rest now." He lay over on his side, put his arm under his head, and sighed heavily, as though about to sleep. Then suddenly he raised up on his elbow, flashing damp blank eyes. "Skook, there's something down there."

"No kidding."

The Skook's tone made Span realize what a stupid statement he had made. It had been intended as a preamble to a question about a mystery or something that had to do with a mystery, but now he did not want to ask the question, even if he had been able to remember what it was. He put his head down on his arm and fell asleep.

He dreamed of bizarre and formless things, images seemingly without origin in human experience, surrealistic seascapes with mountainous waves and gigantic creatures just below the surface, imperfectly glimpsed. And with it all he dreamed the Answer. The Answer was overwhelming and exhilarating. He wanted to tell The Skook but he could not wake up. He struggled to come out of his dream, or he dreamed that he struggled, but even in the dream he failed, and finally it dissolved and he was in nothingness, oblivion. When he finally awakened the dream was far away and indistinct, a weblike tracing on his mind. The Answer was gone. Nothing of it remained. No, there was something close at hand, illogical, something that, placed in perspective, explained away the illogic, made it all make sense. He groped desperately for it but it remained elusive. He coughed lightly.

The Skook waited, smiling his sweet maddening smile, perched on the taller of the two flat rocks, the one on which Span had placed his lighted candle.

They were now in the dark. Span had left the candle burning and it had used itself up as he slept.

He coughed again, more deeply, then was suddenly racked with spasms. Because of the sweater he was no longer chilled, except for his feet. Odd that a long-ago gift from the Cow should now be so important in his life. Yet, neither his uncomfortable feet nor the blessed sweater nor his persistent fever seemed as important now as the answer to the question he could not even formulate. Whatever the question was, it was new, therefore it had to do with something reasonably new in his life, some recent addition. What were the recent additions? Dispossession? Deprivation? Disorientation? Terror? A new spatial concept? Self-awareness? Acceptance of fate? What? Those were concepts. Was the question about a concept? Or a thing? What were the new things in his life? Cave. Waterfall. Dirty pants. Chapped ass. Fishhead. The fishhead! It had something to do with the fishhead! He lit another candle and placed it on the rock by the mutilated head. What was it trying to say to him? He slipped his hand under it and lifted it. It dripped slime. Beneath the milky semiopaque rind that covered the round eye nothing looked out at him. Blind before but trying not to be, it was now blind beyond caring. It was a huge head. How big had the whole fish been? Sixty, maybe seventy pounds. A basslike fish. Then the answer came. "Skook ! This is a saltwater fish!"

The Skook, his homely features marked with skepticism, waited.

"Very few freshwater fish ever grow this big. The sturgeon—and this is no sturgeon. And it's not a muskie either. And I'm no ichthyologist, but anything big enough to bite this son of a bitch in two would be in the sea. Sea monsters existed—I said existed—in the sea. And that body of water down there is a sea, an underground saltwater sea fifty miles from the nearest ocean! Don't you smell it? No, you're in Otherworld. Well, I can smell it. Those are the facts. I caught a deep-sea fish. A monster bit it in two. And this nose on my face that has smelled the sea before smells it again. Go ahead, you smug little bastard, refute that reasoning. Go ahead. I'm waiting."

"Maybe there's just a salt deposit down there, Barrman. Maybe there's just a deep old-fashioned sump lake with an opening to the outside we don't know about, and an alligator ate your fish."

"Skook, this place has no bats, no kind of the usual cave-dwelling animals at all, no sign of anything up here where we are. I don't think this place has ever been opened to the outside world from above till I did it. And that thing down there that made that noise—that was no alligator. I heard a big bull alligator once in the Florida swamps. This thing made a sound no alligator ever made. It's two hundred feet down there, and whatever it is I hope to God there's no way for it to get up here. Wait a minute—two hundred feet. My guess—my memory—is that I followed that passage down at least two hundred feet to get to this level. That means the surface of the water is four hundred feet below the spot where I broke into the passage. And the top of the rise above the river there is another hundred feet up, and on the maps that rise is five hundred feet above sea level. Sea level! That surface down there is at sea level! And it's got to be salt water!" He was seized with a fervor. He must know for sure, and as soon as possible.

He attached a hook to the end of his line, folded his yellow slicker hat, and ran the hook through the brim on two sides to form a waterproof dipper of the crown. He lowered it carefully, hoping not to cause the Thing to make its sound again. Within minutes he had brought up a hatful of water. He tasted it. It was salty. He looked at it under the candlelight. It was cloudy. It appeared to contain tiny organisms. It was incontrovertibly seawater. His wonderment was sublime. He forgot everything, even his hunger. "A sea," he gloated, "a living underground sea!"

"Eat."

"What?"

"Eat," said The Skook, "and cover your feet."

"Skook, listen to me. I've discovered an inland underground sea. It's undoubtedly connected to the Atlantic by a subterranean salt river. As far as I know, such a discovery has not been made in the history of mankind. What could be more important than that?"

"Staying alive."

"You're right. I must be feverish. I can't seem to keep my mind on survival. Thanks, Skook."

The next baited hook he put down was lost. There was a powerful tug on the line, then nothing. When he drew it up he found it had been bitten through. The next hook was attached to a wire leader, but that, too, was severed. Span's competitive spirit was challenged. He tied both ends of four wire leaders together, separated two of them along the bight with frets made of three-hook assemblages, one wire going through the eye and another laid into the *V* where the three hooks met. Then he separated the other two wires in the same way. The result was a single leader made of four separate leaders, each a half inch from the other, an assembly next-to-impossible to bite in two, he thought. He attached his one bluefish lure to this with a clinch knot. Then he painstakingly laid out five lengths of forty-pound test line a hundred and fifty yards long, and tied them together at twenty-foot intervals, ending up with a single five-strand two-hundred-pound test line a hundred and fifty yards long. He secured one end of this by a bowline knot to the four-wire reinforced leader bearing the bluefish lure, and the other end to a second hundred-and-fifty-yard-long five-strand line with double bowlines. Just above these connecting loops he wrapped the second line once around the chair-high flat rock beside him, which he judged heavy enough to serve as a bollard. This would give him another hundred and fifty yards to pay out by letting it slip around the chair rock in case he needed to play the fish—or the unseen monster with the wire-cutting jaws.

He stood back from the edge of the precipice and tossed the bluefish lure—a plump, weighty, four-hooked object—as far out into the mists toward the cataract as he could, and let the quintuple-strand line slip over his fingers a loop at a time. He could not hear the lure hit the water two hundred feet below, but he felt the slackening in the pull and the slowed payout of the line. He envisioned the old lure with its rusty hooks waggling its way downward through black waters where no man-made thing had ever gone, past creatures no man had ever seen or even dreamed of, strange atom to strange atom, rust to phosphor, steel to living fossil, wonder touching wonder, all connected by nylon threads to the one man of all mankind who knew of the existence of these wonders, Spanish Ulysses Barrman.

All the loops were gone from his hand. The weight of the lure still pulled, at the end of four hundred and fifty feet of line. Subtracting two hundred feet for the distance to the surface, the lure was at a depth of two hundred and fifty feet. He loosened the loop around the chair rock and continued to give out line until more than half of the second line was gone, another two hundred and fifty feet, he guessed, five hundred in all, and still no bottom.

He began to bring the line in with little jerks to make the lure spurt forward and dodge and hesitate to imitate living food. Within seconds, while still at great depth, something hit the lure. Span felt a sudden hard tug that ripped the strands out of his hands. The loop tightened around the rock.

There were a few moments of violent agitation, during which Span got behind the rock and took up the rest of the line. It was slipping around the rock fast. Span's weight increased the drag and slowed it down. The agitation subsided and there remained a strong, steady pull. Span made another loop around his makeshift bollard and went forward and took up the line and hauled back on it, but he was not able to gain an inch. There was no fight, no movement at the other end, just a motionless strain like a dead weight. For a moment he thought he had hooked the bottom; then he gained a foot, lost it, gained it again, lost it. Maybe it was the bottom. Maybe he was only gaining the stretch of the line. Without warning there was a tremendous tug and he was almost pulled forward to the edge. He let go of the line and it snapped out straight and taut as a steel bar. Even with two loops around the rock it was slipping. He moved behind the rock and took up the loose line and let it continue to pay out slowly until, after five minutes, it went slack. He was trembling with the exertion and excitement. He sat on the rock to calm himself. During this time the line did not stir and he decided that whatever it was he had hooked had managed to free itself. He began to retrieve the line. When he had about twenty feet of it looped in orderly fashion in his hand he felt another vicious strike and then steady resistance. He managed to gain with each pull on the line, but it was like lifting a small barrel of water on a well rope, a steady stubborn weight. His heart clattered. He grew faint. He stopped pulling and looped the line around the rock so that he could rest. He was hungry again. He thought of his vodka. At least there were calories in it. The thought of it did not sicken him as it had before he ate the raw fish. He got it out of his tackle box and took a swallow of it. It was warm and sweet. He took some more. Immediately he knew he'd done the right thing. The warmth rushed through him. He was like a dry arroyo filling during a cloudburst. He coughed but the cough seemed trivial. He was thinking of the Thing. What if the Thing took his catch, as it had last time? He was tired. He'd have to take the chance. His fish would have to wait. Maybe it would grow weaker as he grew stronger. He took another gulp of vodka, capped the bottle, and put it away. He picked up his bloody knife from the rock and cut two squares of plastic from the green garbage bag and wrapped his feet and tied the plastic at his ankles with fishing line. His feet began to hurt, but he knew it was because they were warming and losing their numbness. He felt stronger, more optimistic. He went back to his fish.

The last two hundred feet were the hardest. As soon as it broke the surface it began to flop wildly. The line swung in a wide arc. Fearing the heavy grinding against the cliff edge would sever the line, Span kept it coming in as fast as his strength would let him. The effort seemed interminable. He finally decided he would never last through the struggle with the weight of the fish and the added thrust of rock against the line, and he would have to forget the possibility of fainting and falling: He had to pull straight up, hand over hand. He moved with great fear and caution on his buttocks to the edge and let his feet hang over the side. Then he leaned forward to get the line in his hands clear of the edge. Whatever swung at the end of his line, occasionally thrashing but for the most part hanging like a ball of lead, must weigh, he guessed, at least seventy pounds. Was it another of the basslike fish, this time whole? The extra weight he felt during its less and less frequent convulsions would no doubt be the maximum. This gave him the courage to loop the line around his body as he got it, to leave both hands free for bringing up more. As the arc of the pendulumlike swings grew shorter he knew his prize was coming closer. He leaned over the side to try to see it but saw nothing. The candle on the rock behind him left everything below him in its original stygian darkness. He began sobbing out the last measures of his strength. His tears and his weakness and the roiling mists were as blinding as the lack of light. At the beginning of the struggle he had prayed that the Thing would not take his fish again, and not make its awful sound, but now as his prospect of having nothing grew with the outraged bumping of his heart he would happily have settled for a nice big fishhead. He was now more caught than catcher. His backbone felt as though it were being pulled apart. He wondered if he'd be able to straighten it, or rise, or bring his catch over the edge onto the floor. Or would he at the last moment fail, and fall into the chasm with his conqueror? The arc of the pendulum grew small. He peered down and saw a form. He leaned back and pulled with all that remained of his strength. He lifted his legs up out of the way. He could barely command them. Ignoring the agony of his raw knees, he crawled away from the edge, dragging the last fathom of his fishing rig, half five-strand nylon and half four-ply steel leader, up to the level of the cave floor. Then he walked a turn around the rock with his line, then another, and another. He was not going to give back one blood-bought inch. Then he removed all the line from around his body and put it down beside the rock in neat coils and took several steadying breaths. When he felt able he took up the candle and stepped carefully, his left leg brushing the taut line all the way, to the edge to see what he had caught.

Two round milk-blue saucers—sightless eyes—glowed in the candle light. The face was that of an armor-plated bulldog. The wide mouth was open, showing irregular, stumpy teeth. The four steel leaders disappeared down the throat. The fish had gulped the lure and now hung by its pierced inner parts, bearing its ordeal stoically except for involuntary spasms in the area of its gills. It appeared to be resigned, defeated, yet proudly withholding surrender. Span had never seen anything like it, yet there was something familiar about the fierce countenance. He bent lower and held his candle to the side to get a look at the body. It was long, possibly five feet—and covered with armorlike rough scales. Just abaft the rear shoulderlike head plate, large fins grew out of the ends of short arms—the strong deformed forearms of a dwarf. Span bent lower, held the candle close. The fish could not see him, so Span was not afraid. But it must have heard his breath, or smelled him, or sensed his body heat, for in a fraction of a second the powerful tail slapped against the side of the cliff, flinging the body outward and up, the left forearm fin rotated up and forward over the edge toward Span, slapping the cave floor with a thunderous *thwak* and launching the fish in a leap toward Span's face. The great jaws disjointed themselves, stretched astonishingly wide, and hissed with a powerful intake of air that almost sucked Span forward into them. Then they snapped shut with the sound of a cleaver hitting a beef joint. Span fell backward and dropped his candle. The last thing he saw before the light sputtered out and the black of the cave closed over him was the maddened fish waddling toward him on its stumpy fins, snapping and gulping air. Span scrambled and flopped and squirmed away until he was by his estimate fifty feet from where he had last seen the fish. He listened, imagining that somehow it had followed him beyond the limits of its line and was about to take his leg. But reason, what little he had left, told him it was hooked and secured to the rock. Span could hear it gasping and burping the air it had swallowed.

The Skook's particolored glow was visible, but shed no light on things around him, so Span was not sure he hadn't moved. "Skook, are you still seated on the rock where the candle was before I took it?"

"I am."

"Do you know what I think that thing is? It's one of those

whattayacall'ems—coelacanths. Remember when they caught that one back in the thirties? The papers were full of pictures. Living fossil, they said. I was just a kid in school. We studied all about it in our *Weekly Reader,* or something. My God, I caught a coelacanth!"

He overcame his fear and, guided by the sounds of the dying fish, made his way to his tackle box and got out another candle and lit it. Then he went as close as he dared to the coelacanth, which was mortally hurt, vomiting its own blood. It was at once a fearful and pitiful sight, feebly fanning, expiring. Its color was changing from mottled brown to oily dark blue, and the once luminescent blind eyes were blank.

Because he had handled the divorce case of *Spiegel* v. *Spiegel* and had caused much comment with his decision to let Yovi Pellegrini Spiegel retain the claspless rose-gold anklet as part of her person, Judge Walter Youngford disqualified himself as trial judge in the case of the sacrificial murder of Yovi Pellegrini Spiegel Barrman's second husband, Span.

It was for this reason that the county coroner, Roderigo Bruque, heedful of the many accusatory whisperings about the widow Barrman, went to visit the good judge in his tall house on the hill overlooking the Catholic cemetery. He wanted to discuss her for his own peace of mind before issuing the death certificate on Spanish Barrman. Assistant District Attorney Jerry Odessa had presented eyewitnesses to the presence of the presumed decedent in the area now covered with many tons of rock as a result of the explosion. Odessa had also presented him with the signed confessions of the leaders of the Space Angels. Mrs. Barrman had dramatically identified the yellow slicker found at the scene as that of her husband. Still, Bruque, a careful man, as befitted his position, was concerned about the possibility that Mrs. Barrman might be engaged in some sort of complex scheme to defraud the insurance companies. Could his friend Wally shed any light on her character?

Youngford was only too happy to help his old pal Rod. Yes, he had got to know Mrs. Barrman since her divorce and re-marriage because she sometimes worked as a part-time secretary for the district attorney's office and their paths crossed. She still wore the anklet he had ruled a part of her person, and had told him only recently that she would never take it off. It held some mystic meaning for her; the judge respected her for the intensity of her feeling for it. As far as he could tell she was— except for her extramarital adventures—an honest person who, in some inexplicable way, loved and even respected Span Barr-man. He was sure that she would be incapable of hurting him or anyone else deliberately. She was simply not that kind of person. He would bet his life that Mrs. Barrman was as dev-astated by the tragedy as she had seemed to be.

This matter taken care of, the judge invited the coroner for a drink and the two men walked down the hill to The Swan.

The death certificate was issued without delay, and the in-surance company that held two policies on Spanish Barrman's life paid them. One was in the amount of $40,000 to beneficiary Deena Jane Edwards Barrman, former wife of the deceased, and the other was for $30,000 to Yowa Pellegrini Spiegel Barrman, the widow.

Yovi communicated with Jerry by calling him from a phone booth. He had told her her phone might be tapped. He urged her to take a trip, go to England perhaps and join her parents for a while, during the deepest pain of her mourning. When she demurred he told her his real reason was that he was sure since she wasn't getting any from him she would go out and get some from someone else, and if anybody caught on to how fast she could drop her black mourning panties it would com-pletely screw up the secret investigation of Tri-State-Tronics he was conducting on his own time and without the knowledge of the D. A.'s office. The important thing was that nobody but nobody see her being a merry widow. In England nobody would notice. Yovi told him he was the most detestable person she had ever met. She hung up on him. The second she walked in her door she went to the refrigerator and got Span's half bottle of Phillips vodka that was still in the freezer and drank a slug of it and went to bed and cried herself to sleep.

The Space Angels withdrew their confessions, just as they were expected to do when they came down from their chemical highs and got legal representation. This and other events leading to the trial got extensive coverage in the press. The name and likeness of Assistant District Attorney Jerry Odessa were prominent in the stories. As prosecutor he would be one of the stars of the sordid drama. His immigrant background, dynamic personality, and virile good looks made him a sought-after interview. He was the American Success Story. The trial was going to expose a populous netherworld of witchcraft, bizarre sex, and sacrificial murder. It was going to be more famous than the Manson trial, and more significant. Jerry Odessa was going to be at the apex of it. There was little doubt that he was going to be the next D. A. and, after that, governor or senator. In his interviews he was terse, dedicated, and dignified, as befits a crown prince. A columnist said that he had the charisma of a Kennedy and the girls to prove it. And wasn't this in the tradition of red-blooded leaders? He modestly admitted that his research had begun to place the Space Angels in a hitherto unimagined historical perspective. They were interconnected with other depraved tribal organizations, covens of modern witches, metropolitan street gangs, and so on, all virulent social growths that fed on public apathy and threatened to undermine the foundations of democracy.

A few thoughtful citizens noticed that Odessa was endangering the case before it went to trial by revealing too much in public statements. It would be difficult to find a juror in the area who had not been influenced by the pretrial coverage. Judge Youngford, at his usual seat on the church bench at the rear of the old bar at The Swan, wondered aloud why a man of Odessa's experience and obvious intelligence would let himself fall into this trap.

The flesh of the coelacanth is soft and oily. It has the consistency of putty or dough. When Span first ate the cheek fillets from the severed head he was in such a state of physical and mental deterioration that none of these characteristics registered on him except in retrospect. But now that he owned an entire five-foot fish that probably weighed eighty-five pounds, and realized that he was sentenced to eating it uncooked at every meal, he became aware of every aspect of the mixed blessing. His first bite of dorsal flesh from the new fish was depressing. If he had not known it to be fresh he would have thought it unfit to eat. In his mouth it felt and tasted like things he had been conditioned to spit out. When he chewed it and swallowed it he had to resist the efforts of his stomach to reject it. When he had forced as much of it down as his throat would accept, he cut armholes and a neckhole in the green garbage bag, put it on like a shirt, and lay down to sleep. He was racked with coughing and almost lost his meal. The vodka and food and his new plastic jacket warmed and thawed him. Where he had been numb he was now sensitized again to his damp, filthy clothes, his scald wounds, his cough, his open sores. He was perversely grateful for this. It meant he was alert, aware, and dealing in reality. He smiled at The Skook, who smiled back.

"Skook, how long would you say we'd been here?"

"Does it matter?"

Christ, Span thought, here we go again. He turned his back. He would somehow shut the ugly apparition—who seemed to consider it his function to make Span feel like a simpleton—out of his consciousness, out of his life. He had an idea for keeping track of time, but The Skook was certain to knock it down. Therefore he would keep his own counsel.

He tugged at the growth of hair on his cheeks. It was like a water spaniel's coat. How long had it taken? Three weeks? He'd been unconscious part of the time, but from now on he'd keep track. Three hungers and one sleep would be a day, just as they were in the upper world.

But would that help him? Would it depress him to know how long he'd been there? Would it begin to mock hope? Would he not finally think: God, I've been here three months, I've found no way out, I'm dead to the upper world, I'm doomed? What good would knowing time be? Where was he going? Who was he meeting? Wouldn't knowing time, collecting the weight of it, only drive him sooner to madness, utter madness, rather than the partial madness he doubtless suffered already, and wouldn't utter madness make him fall or jump over the side to drown or be eaten by the Thing—or shredded and eaten by many smaller Things? And would that be madness—or logic? Would that not be the simple honest practical thing to do, and the least painful—far less painful than a hideous lingering disintegration in a black hole? Wouldn't it be an act of sanity rather than insanity to accept the inevitability of death and go to meet it? On the other hand, didn't that question obtain in the upper world too? The difference was that in the upper world the travelers to inevitable dissolution found ways to pave the path to the end with moments of forgetfulness—drunkenness, love, sex, gluttony, laughter, work, drugs, sports, gambling, music, even movies. Some, it was claimed, even managed more good moments than bad before they went down the throat of the Thing. That was the ideal in the upper world, the thing most striven for.

Well, this, the lower world, was his world. This was where he had to strive.

He tried to forget time. He ceased trying to measure it. Time was only now. There were two parts of time: life and death. Life was one grain of sand, one heartbeat. Death was infinity. He understood vodka now as never before. Vodka was for stopping Time. Without vodka he had only work for stopping Time. Stopping Time meant forgetting it. When you thought of Time you could not escape it.

He began to work compulsively. He did not sleep till he shook with fatigue, till he knew that he could sleep, even with his deep cough and his scalds and sores, the minute he lay down. As his strength returned so did his ingenuity. He found that he could squeeze oil out of a handful of coelacanth flesh. To have a place to put the oil, he emptied his tackle box. With a thread rubbed with fat and dipped in sand he sawed his empty vodka bottle in half, to make a vessel of the bottom half. Once he got used to not caring how long it took, it was an easy job.

His plan was to collect enough oil to fill his tackle box and make a fire big enough for drying his clothes. Then he would bring up salt water and wash himself. He would wash his sores with healing seawater, and rinse his clothes and dry them, and put them back on and luxuriate in them, sitting before the oil-fire. He would even rub fish fat like unguent on his flaming raw skin.

When he wanted coelacanths for oil he fished at five hundred feet. When he kept his hooks at thirty feet or less he got the saltwater fish all anglers bring home, except that his were blind. The best for eating raw were the bass.

His cough grew worse. Sometimes a hard spasm brought up flecks of blood and left his ribs aching.

This did not deter him from his first goal of getting enough oil to have a big fire for drying clothes. Washing himself was his obsessive dream, but this would be useless, futile, if he had no clean clothes. He found a third flat block of sandstone the size of a footstool about fifteen feet from the two blocks that were the center of his little camp. In the top of this smaller block there was a natural hollow in which water had collected. It was not potable. He removed the dead batteries from his flashlight and used the case to scrape away stone and enlarge and deepen the hollow. Then he poured the oil from his tackle box into it and held a match to it. Nothing happened. The oil was actually, of course, liquid fat, laboriously wrung and pressed by hand out of chunks and strips of flesh. There were pieces of solid fat in the small pool too. It was all cool, turbid, nonvolatile. Span held the match close to the surface till it burned down to his fingers, but the oil did not take the flame. He tried submerging the candle till the wick was level with the surface of the pool, but still he got no fire. He poured what was left of his vodka onto the surface and lit it. The vodka fire heated the surface enough to make it burn, and slowly, slowly, the pool pushed up a small finger of fire that grew in breadth. When the whole surface, about nine inches in diameter, was finally ablaze, Span put two hatfuls of seawater in the tackle box with a small sea bass and set it over the fire. When it began to simmer he became excited. He was going to have a cooked meal. Fresh fish, delicate and aromatic, boiled in naturally salted and seasoned water. He found a small slab to use as a platter, washed it in a hatful of seawater, and waited, trying to figure out what to use as pot holders before the fish got overcooked. Everything he had taken from the tackle box was on the big rock by the candle. He went back to it quickly, lit the candle, and selected the grapnel and the pack of cigarettes as his two pot holders. The cigarettes were useless now. He had involuntarily quit smoking while unconscious and had no desire to start again. He hooked the grapnel under the handle at one end and the fragile cigarette pack under the other and lifted the makeshift pot off the fire. He dumped the bass onto his stone platter, letting the cooking water spill. With his knife he dug into the side of the steaming fish and brought up a chunk of meat. It tasted of burned enamel and rancid coelacanth oil, but it was still better than unseasoned raw fish. Soon the enamel would be burned off and the rancid oil boiled away. He was going to eat well beyond his original expectations.

He could not stop himself from idly counting hungers, although time now seemed to him not time at all but a curious liquid that flowed around him and did not seem to require consideration in terms of quantity. Still, after much successful fishing and eating and oil-collecting, during which he dreamily noted fifteen hungers, he felt ready for—and, more importantly, that he had earned—his bath. He had enlarged two natural depressions in the floor of the cave, one to serve as his major oil reservoir, and had put in it an estimated three gallons of oil, all hand-wrung from the flesh of the plentiful but difficult-to-haul-in coelacanths. In the other he poured four hatfuls of seawater. Before he used this for washing he brought up seven hatfuls more and filled his tackle box. Then he strung a nylon line that slanted down from a high jut in the back wall to his chair rock, passing at a height of six feet over the floor-level pool of oil.

He had, wisely—and for him uncharacteristically, he reflected—kept oil burning in his small cooking pool in anticipation of lighting this new large surface. Now he dipped up some of the flaming oil in his flashlight case, singeing his hand, and poured it carefully onto the larger pool. As it had before, the flame climbed to a small peak and then, as its base grew to the full two-foot diameter of the pool, bounded three feet high.

It was like a sudden sunrise. Span stepped away from it and looked about in wonder. It was the first time light had opened the great salon to his eyes. It was a ghostly, frightening sight, a brown rock wasteland shimmering with flecks of quartz. He looked up and saw for the first time the dripping cathedral-like dome a hundred feet above, carved by some unimaginable force in wild imperfect layered arches, a misshapen thing built by a mad giant, an architect without compass, working in an eons-long frenzy of drunken creativity to build a vast many-leveled ceiling lined with millions of tiny reflecting chips of glass, a sight unique forever in the yellow dancing flame of Barrman's fire. He cried. It was at last the wonderland he had dreamed. Without stalactites, stalagmites, or any of the picture-postcard formations he bore in his mind, it surpassed anything he had been prepared by life to see.

Pulling his eyes away, he looked across the cavern and saw the huge glowing curtain of falling water. His cave was not pretty, the way small shapes and colors are pretty. It was beautiful, as only things with size and grandeur can be.

When finally he was able to stop his awed turning and staring to return to his personal needs, he took off his damp, filthy, stinking jeans, rinsed them thoroughly in the pool of salt water, and tied them on the line near but out of reach of the flame. The water dripped into the fire. It sputtered and smoked, but it kept on burning, a sight as beautiful to him, Span thought, as the island of San Salvador to Columbus.

He looked at his naked midsection in the light. It was a frightening sight. He was like a leper. His penis and testicles were covered with raw, festering patches of flesh. His inner thighs and buttocks had open sores, pustules, boils. And yet, even the first few minutes of exposure to the damp sweet air of the cave had made the discomfort less severe.

With the lower half of his vodka bottle he dipped the dirty water out of his bathing pool, which was no more than a shallow sitz bath. Then he filled it from his tackle box and lowered his buttocks into it. He had a few moments of agony, which he expected, as the water both chilled him and burned his wounds like fire. Then, miraculously, the water felt warmer, and his raw skin began to welcome the salt and the minerals in the water. He leaned back, soaking, and closed his eyes in a kind of incongruous bliss. He had not, it suddenly came to him, thought of or seen The Skook since his last hunger, and a hunger was coming on him again. He looked toward the first two blocks of sandstone he had found. The Skook sat motionless on the smaller one. He seemed dimmer in color, and diminished in size. How odd that the little creature should wax and wane in importance in his life like a moon. Span decided not to speak to him, not to rouse him. The Skook, though unreal, somehow was a conduit for the most painful realities. Span leaned back again, luxuriating in his bath, and looked up at the ceiling, with its million specks of quartz aglitter. It was like a small sky full of stars.

Standing in his dry jeans in
front of the fire with only his garbage-bag gown to warm him
while he waited for his shirt and sweater to dry, he dreamed of
fresh water. Cooked fish with its altered fluids did not satisfy
his thirst the way raw fish did, and he knew that he would have
to continue to eat raw fish at least part of the time not only to
replace drinking water but to conserve oil. He had become a
hunter-gatherer, gone back to the primitive state of man, spending all his time on food and warmth, basic survival activities.
He could see the waterfall—fresh water—on the other side of
the abyss. Getting it would become his next major project.

Bathing had chilled him. He coughed, almost losing consciousness as the pain hit his injured ribs. And yet, his cough—
possibly even a fever—seemed less important now. Everything
was moving upward on the scale of hope. Health would come
naturally with victory over starvation and despair.

When he had dried his shirt and sweater he put them on, lit

a candle, and extinguished his big fire. He dipped up half a cup of oil with the upper half of the vodka bottle and, using the neck for a handle, lit the contents and congratulated himself on having made a fine flambeau. Immediately the heat shattered the glass, almost splashing him with burning oil. Using only the light from the candle, he began the long process of scooping out a hole in a brick-size piece of sandstone to make a portable lamp. He used the point of his knife at first, but seeing how it wore he switched to his watch case, which he had managed to bend by hand, then pound with a rock till it was folded double. It made a fine drill, though slow. He had only to twist it with pressure in the small hole begun by the knife point, and to let time envelop him like warm amniotic fluid instead of sweeping him into swift currents. When the hole was deep enough to hold a half cup of oil, he rubbed the outer sharp edges against the floor till he had an oblong oval that fit comfortably in his hand. Then he filled it with oil, lit it, and set off exploring. He felt strong, excited, anticipatory, optimistic in spite of his cough. With measured steps—in deference to the remembered treachery of his legs, strong one moment, jelly the next—he walked toward the waterfall till he was within ten feet of the edge of the precipice, then turned right, and, holding his little torch high, moved slowly into new territory. He had never known himself to be afraid—more afraid than others—of heights; yet, now he felt fear of approaching the drop-off where, conquering or ignoring his fear out of necessity, he had spent so many hours bringing up fish. Wondering about this, he concluded that he had proven that the edge where he had worked was solid, not rotten, as so much of the sandstone was, and deep within him was the dread of testing another section of the cliff with his weight. Furthermore, when he had approached the edge near the two rocks, he had always been seated. Now he was upright, wearing slick, uncertain plastic footgear, and he could not rule out another attack of vertigo.

Step by step he revealed more of the barren massive sameness of the cave, the shallow indentations full of brown, undrinkable water, debris ranging in size from pillboxes to boxcars fallen from the ceiling, the waterfall, a wide, thick sheet that seemed to be forcing its way between two immense rock plates deep in the unreachable gloom. Span was amazed at the vast unchangingness. He had expected—not expected; dreamed or hoped for—more wonders. There were no small wonders, only big ones. There was the wonder of the place, the wonder of his being in it, the wonder of the wild Thing or Things below in the salt sea, and the salt sea itself: Yes, that was the biggest wonder of them all, a marvel—an inland underground sea. There had to be a connection to the ocean there, a subterranean salt river to the Atlantic fifty miles away. Yes, that was a wonder.

He came to a place where the wall came close to the edge. He sat down, lifting his garbage-bag gown so as not to wear it through, and worked his way sliding on his slowly healing bare buttocks to the edge. If the wall came so close, he surmised, the edge could bear another—what? He felt his bony thighs, the loose skin of his belly—150 pounds, maybe 140, down from 180. And if it couldn't, well, it would save him a lot of misery. Or so he told himself. Still, as he drew near the edge, his heart remembered the chunks of rock the ceiling had let fall without the extra push of his hundred and whatever pounds. He thought of his own flesh being shredded and minced in a frenzy of competing teeth in the black chasm, but he forced himself forward. It was time to conduct his experiment. He had come as far to the right of the waterfall as he could come, although not as far as he would have liked, being stopped by the wall that approached the edge. His aim had been to get as far from the fall as possible in the hope of being beyond the mists and being able to see the surface. He had thought of his experiment as he dried his shirt over the fire. He had cut a strip from the tail, dipped it in oil, and put it in his pocket, wrapped in a square of garbage bag left over from cutting armholes. Now he took it out and draped it over his leg. When he got to the edge and dangled his feet over into the blackness—an act of faith in itself, not knowing what was there—he held his little stone lamp up and leaned forward and tried to peer around the obstructing wall. After only a few feet of six-inch ledge it widened out again and continued beyond the reach of his light—how far was something he would try to learn at another time. His pressing project of the moment was to see the surface of his cave sea. He held the oil-soaked piece of shirttail over the flame of his lamp till it caught fire. He dropped it on the rock beside him till it burned brightly, then he flicked it out into the void and leaned forward to watch it flutter downward. It fell with surprising slowness, both its own heat and the updraft from the water pounding the surface, making it drift like a wounded bird instead of falling straight down. And suddenly the surface came into view. It was flat, with no swells or waves, textured with the ripples sent out by the battering of the waterfall. It seemed a complacent, predictable surface except for a few small crosshatching swirls made by hunting or hunted creatures. The flame tumbled lower; a shadowy shape materialized under the surface, and then rose upward, causing a massive dislocation of water, like a breaching whale. The shape was deformed by the waters pouring off its back, but before Span's flare landed and snuffed itself out he saw a long arched neck, a giant serpent's head, and powerful shoulders flinging foam and spray. The jaws cracked wide as the cloth hit the water. In pitchy blackness the monster screamed, his sound filling the cavern, a single long weird ululation that almost split Span's eardrums. Stunned, near to swooning, Span jerked his legs up and fell away from the edge, spilling the oil out of his stone lamp. It flared and spread over a one-foot circle, and Span barely moved away from it in time to avoid being burned.

"Skook! Skook!"

A rainbowlike streak of light arced across the space between them, and there was The Skook, hanging in black space before his eyes.

"Skook! I saw it! I saw the Thing! A living prehistoric sea monster, the kind they reconstruct for museums! And I saw it in its secret inland cave sea, and even heard it scream! Good God, Skook, if I could show this to the upper world, they'd have to revise all their geological thinking, all their theories about the heaving and settling of tectonic plates, about evolution and extinction, and all because of me— Sneer, dammit, Skook, but you can't belittle this! You can't deny me this one moment of triumph! Admit it!"

"Sub, you've got to quit wasting oil and matches."

"Damn you, Skook! Do you know what I consider the main attraction of the upper world? You weren't with me there." He crawled back to his two base rocks in the darkness, keeping the sound of the falls to his right and feeling no panic, because he no longer feared placing his hand down on some inconceivable man-ripping creature. He dipped up more oil and managed to light his stone lamp again. Finally he said: "You're right, Skook. From now on I'm going to keep a small fire burning. That's what really counts. Whether this other stuff happened or didn't happen means nothing to the history of the world or to the history of Spanish Barrman. I was inconsequential when I came down here, and I'll be inconsequential to the end. Nothing I do here will keep me from being of no consequence. I'll die here, and it'll be as though I never existed, and what I did here will never have happened. The thin wall I broke through to find this place is now a God-knows-how-thick pile of rock. This cave will be safe from man's intrusion for another jillion years."

He felt a cough coming on, but by tightening the muscles of his chest he managed to suppress it. "I don't know why I called you again just now, Skook. I was getting along fine without you."

"You needed me because you wanted to confide in me that you were inconsequential, hoping that I'd say you weren't. But I didn't, because you are. You're inconsequential because nothing you do is consequential unless another human being tells you it is. If you were strong enough to value your accomplishments without needing outside confirmation you would place yourself as part of The Great I Am. It is because you can't that you are inconsequential."

Span was seized with a paroxysm of coughing. He spit up blood and almost lost consciousness. A sharper pain than usual told him he had reinjured his ribs on the right side. The thought came into his mind again—and lingered, not flitting through as it had done a few times before—that one moment of sweet death in the jaws of the Thing would be the best way out.

J erry Odessa's sudden fame
caused great excitement in the garden apartment of Ossie and
Mavda Odessa in South Brooklyn. Ossie and Mavda had become
local celebrities since their son's involvement in the Sacrificial
Murder Case. Never had they been so grateful for the decision
to change their name, which they had made thirty-six years ago
on their arrival in the United States. Their identification papers
said Osip Tchartorizhsky and Mavda Tchartorizhsky and son
Pyotr. No one at Immigration could pronounce the family name
or spell it. America was in the depths of the Great Depression,
and Europe and Russia were in violent social upheaval. Sergei
Kirov, Stalin's close collaborator, had just been assassinated in
Leningrad. The world was on the verge of a nervous breakdown.
The Immigration officer dealing with the entrance of the Tchartorizhskys wanted to delay processing them until a Russian-
speaking officer could interrogate them. The murder of Kirov
had occurred only a few days before this hard-muscled man with

the blue-black hog-bristle hair and his tiny wife with the almost inaudible barn-swallow voice, and the intense, restless, inquisitive four-year-old brat had debarked from Odessa with very new-looking papers. Why would a man bring his family to America at a time when bread lines stretched around the block and millions of native-born workers were jobless, homeless, hopeless? Maybe this man from Odessa was part of the Kirov murder plot.

So Osip and Mavda sat on the concrete floor at Immigration, leaning against the scarred wall, waiting and not knowing what they were waiting for, or why. Little Pyotr, as usual, inspected every inch of the drafty, ugly room, climbed onto everything, and stared at everyone. Osip, to retain his sense of well-being, fingered the buttons on his home-sewn coat. Each button was a small gold coin, which Mavda with her nimble fingers and her curved fur-sewing needle had covered with glove leather. They did not appear to be any better than the buttons on any other unpretentious coat, but Osip got great pleasure out of fondling them. When the Russian-speaking official finally arrived, little Pyotr had grown tired and hungry and was lying on the concrete floor among the cigarette butts, crying. The official's heart melted. He took them out and bought them all hot dogs and Coca-Colas, although his own salary was barely enough to keep his own family fed and housed, and he had waked up only the night before in a cold sweat after a nightmare in which he had been dismissed from his job. He advised Osip that if he were going to become an American he should change his name to something pronounceable. Just as he was saying this, the mean-spirited officer who had suspected Osip of being involved in the murder of Stalin's cohort, and had caused the Tchartorizhskys to have a miserable afternoon, stopped at the sidewalk vendor's cart to get a cream soda. With the responsibility now off his own back he was very genial:

"Hey, there, Odessa," he said. "Already found out about franks, huh? You're a real American."

This was the third time Osip had been called by the name of his port of debarkation. A man of action, of decision, of foresight, Osip changed the family name to Odessa on the spot. Mavda fought him on this, but after a week he prevailed. She refused to change her given name, although he longed for her to call herself May like a good saluter of the Stars and Stripes. He changed his own first name to Ossie, and Pyotr was renamed Jerry, after Jerry Blum, the Immigration officer who had bought them franks and Cokes that first day. Five years later Jerry Blum's wife received as a gift a mink coat, hand-stitched at home after hours by Mavda with odd-size skins she and Ossie had bought at a discount at the loft where they spent twelve hours a day, six days a week, cutting and sewing furs. It was not in the characters of the Tchartorizhsky-Odessas to forget that memorable first day. Thirty-six years later Jerry Odessa, assistant district attorney and heir apparent to some as yet unchosen high American office, still got his greatest gastronomical thrill by stopping at a cart on a street corner and eating a frank piled high with piccalilli and washing it down with a Coke.

Ossie and Mavda (he now a wizened face capped with wispy strands of white hair perched on a short round body, and she more birdlike than ever behind her improbable glasses, which were so thick and heavy, she constantly fingered them to take their weight off her sharp little nose) sat at the kitchen table with their neighbor Mrs. Catarina Barca, who had brought over a flan she had just made to have with tea. Ossie had been told by the doctor not to take sugar in anything, therefore he refused to eat the flan.

"Mavi," he whispered (something in the last couple of years having diminished his once strong voice), "would you please put one piece that chelly in mine tea?"

"Grape chelly iss sugar, Osip." When she was stern with him she would not call him by the name he had taken to help him be an American. Her voice was permanently hoarse now, much lower than his.

"Iss also fruit."

As he stirred the jelly in his tea the news came on the radio that Jerry Odessa had resigned as assistant district attorney and prosecutor in the Sacrificial Murder Case and would go back into private practice. When the reality of this announcement sank in, Ossie Odessa began to cry as only old men and little children can. Mavda, tougher by far than her husband, lit a dark cigarette and stared at the table as she puffed. Catarina, not knowing what to say in such an incomprehensible tragedy, excused herself and went out quietly, leaving her beautiful delicate flan untouched on the table.

After Mavda and Ossie had sat in funereal silence long enough for her to smoke two brown cigarettes, she rose and, taking her ashtray and blue pack of Gauloises with her, slid her worn felt slippers along the floor in her peculiar skating motion into the tiny living room where the black telephone sat in a wall niche beside the fishtank. She dialed her son in New Jersey, in spite of the fact that it was only four-fifteen in the afternoon and the cheaper long-distance rates had not gone into effect. He was not in his office. She left a message for him to please call his mother. She dialed his home number and got his answering machine. It frightened her but she managed to leave a halting message for him.

When he called back at seven-thirty, a half hour before their unvarying bedtime, she upbraided him for treating his parents like strangers, letting them find out about him only through the papers and the radio. "Why should you do such a thing, get all the way to such a big case, could make you famous, you could write a book, then you turn your back? Why?"

"Listen, Mama, I know it sounds crazy to you and Papa, but what I'm doing— Let me put it to you like this: You and Papa will never have to worry again."

"We worry about our boy. Otherwise we already don't worry."

"Mama, I mean—and listen, this is strictly confidential, do you understand?"

"I understand confidential. That's all I understand."

"As long as you understand that, Mama. Listen, I'm going to be rich."

"You going to be rich?"

"Yes, Mama."

"Honest?"

"Yes, Mama. Honest."

"No, I mean, not crooked."

"That's right, Mama. Legit."

"Legit?"

"Legitimate."

"So what is it?"

"I can't tell you yet."

"It's legit but you shouldn't say it?"

"Not yet."

"So, you going to got money."

"Plenty, Mama. You and Papa will never have to worry."

"You going to be somebody?"

"Sure, Mama. I'm going to be a millionaire."

"That only is to got something. You going to be something?"

"Like I said, Mama—"

"No. Your father and me, we want our boy should be something, not only got something."

"Mama, you'll just have to trust me."

"My son, when I could trust a person, I don't need he should tell me. Come see your papa and mama sometime when you got a minute. We never knew a rich man." For the only time in her life, Mavda hung up on her son.

$\mathbf{N}$one of the partners in the conservative law firm of Byrne Berg and Borden of Flemington, New Jersey, liked or trusted Jerry Odessa; and yet, when he came to them with the proposition that he use a spare office in their building as his temporary headquarters, they listened politely in spite of themselves. "We're not discussing a partnership here," Jerry said. "I mean, nobody, not even a biggy like Jerry Odessa, is going to screw up the alliteration on your front door, right?" He waited for their smiles, which came. "I'll be here two months, maximum. I pay handsomely. I leave the secretaries alone. My name—" he waited again as one of the partners chuckled more knowingly than the other two would have liked—"my name doesn't go on the door nor my number in the book. Frankly, most of the time I'm not even here. What I need, and without indicating in any way that I am part of the firm, is a quiet, dignified office for discussing business with a couple of clients. By no act or word or association will I tarnish the ivy-covered respectability of Byrne Berg and Borden."

The partners each had the same thought separately: We shouldn't do this. Each admitted this to the other over lunch after they had done it. They analyzed their having been steam-rollered: Each, in accepting Jerry's presence in their midst, was expressing subconscious need for some relief from the interminable predictability of their lives and the unchanging hushed gentility in which they had trapped themselves. They decided they were glad they had done it, even though they were sorry.

The first client to visit Jerry in his temporary office was Yovi. He had given her instructions and she had obeyed. She was all in black. Her hair was coiled on top of her head in braids. The secretaries were stunned by her regal appearance, her dignity, the evident depth of her mourning. There was no trace of the notorious blonde with the long flying hair who had been seen dashing about the area in an aquamarine sports car. Here for all to see was a widow in whose heart her departed mate had left an ever-aching void.

When they were alone and his oaken door was shut, Jerry said: "My God, Yov, if you'd been an actress and concentrated on fucking producers you'd've been a star."

"Jerry, I've told you, I detest vulgar language."

"I just got carried away, baby. You're sensational."

"I dressed like you said because you told me it was important. My sadness, whether you believe it or not, is real."

"Okay, Yov, if you say so. Let's get to important matters. I want to remind you of the rules. Nobody's going to hear us in here with these deep rugs and these tapestries and these hard-wood doors. So whatever you want to say, say it. But anywhere else, we're lawyer and client, period."

"You've said that several times."

"A reminder. I just want to be sure you don't forget in front of these people and show affection for me."

"I don't feel any affection for you."

"Good. You will. By the way, let's get the business aspect of this thing out of the way first. I hope when this is over you and I will get together permanently; therefore—"

"I don't think so. You're a cruel, insensitive person. And you've been very mean about Span."

"I know you, Yov. All that stuff will pass. What counts with you is I get you off. And you get me off. We're good together. If we were together all the time I'd be enough for you. You've never had that. That's why you have those alley-cat habits of yours. If you were with me you'd stay home and cook, baby, and you'd like it, because you'd know you were going to be taken care of the way you like it. But just in case you're right, and we don't get together, I want you to sign this. It's a contract saying I get half of whatever I collect from Tri-State-Tronics on your behalf."

The contract was two pages long. To prove that she was not what he thought, Yovi read it. She did not really care what it said, but she was in no mood to be pushed around by Jerry. She objected to the part that said his expenses came off the top and then they split fifty-fifty, and she told him so. He was surprised that she had understood his legalese and had been able to reduce it to the vernacular so easily. She insisted the full amount be split fifty-fifty, and that his expenses come out of his half. Behind her softness he detected armor plate. He accepted and had the page retyped. She checked all four copies before signing them and folding one and putting it in her purse.

"Good fences make good neighbors," Jerry said. "Now, Yov, have you ever heard of Trevor Sandaski?"

"No."

"He is the chairman of the board of Tri-State-Tronics. Tri-State-Tronics, as I told you, is the conglomerate which owns one hundred percent of the stock of Bozener's Quarry. I went to see Mr. Sandaski to tell him that someone—not I, because I was, at the time, of course, the prosecuting attorney in the case—someone was almost certainly going to look into the prospect of bringing suit against Tri-State-Tronics for negligence in the death of your husband. He was very upset, and asked me if there was any way he could avoid a suit. It would be embarrassing to Tri-State-Tronics, which was in, among other things, the baby-food business. I told him that the widow had already mentioned to me that she was going to sue, and the only way to stop it in my opinion was to offer a generous settlement to her, sub rosa, and quash the whole thing before it got started. He suggested five hundred thousand dollars, with no urging at all. It was so easy I couldn't believe it. And there was something—"

"Jerry, I want to accept it. I don't want to go through a lawsuit."

"Wait a minute. Hold it. The guy was in such a sweat I couldn't believe it. I decided to let him simmer awhile. I went back to the office and got to looking through all the records on the Space Angels. At this point I still hadn't made up my mind to resign. I thought we might get a small settlement and split it and I'd have to keep on working. That was my downside scenario. So I went ahead, preparing to prosecute those creeps, to really do a number on them and put them away for life, the whole gang. If I managed that the benefits would be enormous—if I managed it. I'd be well known, maybe do a book, maybe get into politics, maybe even get elected—if I did all the other stuff. So I was digging. I had all the transcripts of all the court proceedings involving Space Angels for about the last ten years, and I was holed up going over them line by line, looking for— whatever. All of a sudden, guess what? I saw the name Sandaski. An Angel named Ruben Sandaski, twenty-four years old, indicted with three other Angels in Atlantic City for homosexual rape of a liquor store clerk, robbery of the store, and arson. Defended by a very expensive Atlantic City lawyer. Never brought to trial. Who was Ruben Sandaski? The son of Trevor Sandaski, that's who. The son of R. Trevor Sandaski, R. for Rosswell, chairman of the board of Tri-State-Tronics. Nice, huh? I went through the records, shuffling them like cards, looking for the name Sandaski. I found it. Six times. I called Papa Sandaski, asked him to have lunch. Over drinks I told him. He cried. He cried, I'm telling you, into a Booth's House of Lords martini, very cold and very dry, straight up with an olive. Yes, his boy Ruben had always been a problem. Five kids, two boys, three girls, all fine except the youngest, Ruben. One of the girls a doctor, one a teacher, one married to an artist—a really fine painter, poor but honest. The other boy a college grad, a lawyer, very successful, headed—hear this—headed into politics. And Ruben determined to make everybody in the family feel like they did

something wrong. We had another martini. He'd done everything a father could do, and more, to straighten the boy out.
Had created jobs for him, had kept him out of jail, had even
sent him to a shrink. Finally he'd got him a job at Bozener's
Quarry. Ruben only showed up when he needed something, so
the quarry was a good place for him to work by the hour. If he
needed money he'd show, if not he wouldn't. What embarrassment, what harm, could even this habitual ne'er-do-well cause
the family if he were relegated to cutting stone and perhaps
driving an old truck on county roads a hundred miles from the
family home? To get Ruben into this work, the no-longer-doting
Papa Sandaski caused the boy to be hired without the usual
security checks. This was necessary because he could not have
been hired to work around dynamite if his felony convictions—
three of them—were a matter of record at Tri-State-Tronics.
Ruben's promise that he had seen the light, and Papa Sandaski's
assurances to the personnel director that he, the chairman of
the board, would remember his cooperation, resulted in a freaky
Space Angel becoming a sometime worker at Bozener's Quarry.
Papa Sandaski and I had our third martinis. I believe I was
enjoying mine more than he was enjoying his. We were at
Lorenzo's. Remember we met there once when we were still
being careful?"

"Yes." She had been staring stonily at him. Now she looked
down at her hands in her lap.

"Papa Sandaski confided all in his pal Jerry, the well-known,
soon-to-be-famous prosecuting attorney. Of course his moti-
vation was to get me on his side and somehow keep his boy out
of jail, somehow keep his boy's name out of the papers, somehow
keep the widow Barrman from suing and creating an embarrassment for TST. Well, I figured that there was still something
missing. He was too much of an old warrior, he had too many
scars, he was too tough, too much of a survivor, to let a no-
good kid—a kid who had been a problem from the beginning
and to whom he had adjusted—reduce him to tears in front of
a stranger. There was more. There had to be. So I told him I'd
do what I could, couldn't guarantee anything, and I'd get back
to him. His rotten Ruben was not one of the Angels arrested,

so maybe I could keep him out of the trial, I said, though the whole gang would be on trial and his name would almost have to come up. Chairman Sandaski said he wanted it clearly understood that he was not offering me a bribe—he'd never do anything to circumvent the law—but if his boy's name did not come up in the trial, if the name of Sandaski never came up, he would look upon me as a friend, and no friend of his had ever found the friendship unrewarding. Are you ready for this, Yov? I dug into Chairman Sandaski's life a little bit. He gets $700,000 a year in salary and perks, and there is a move afoot to oust him. He is vulnerable. If this thing goes public it would be the straw that breaks his back, and he knows it. So it's not young Ruben he's trying to protect, or Tri-State-Tronics. It's his own ass. It's those seven hundred big ones per annum. The thought of losing those is what makes chairmen of boards water martinis with tears. I went back to him and told him I could maybe keep him out of a lawsuit and his boy out of the papers and out of jail, but it would require a lot of untraceable cash. 'Oh, yes,' he says, 'I couldn't pay by check. That'd be a dead giveaway, very incriminating. How much are you thinking of?' I told him I was thinking of two million. He almost fainted. Two million? Impossible, he says. Maybe he could raise six hundred thou, maybe even seven. But two million? Forget it. Okay, I said. I don't blame you. It's a lot of money. We'll just let things take their normal course. Who knows, you might even win your case. 'But we can't have a case!' he says. 'For God's sake, give me some time! I'll tell you what I can come up with!' 'Well,' I said, 'think of it this way: You're trying to get me to risk everything, to compromise my job, my career, my reputation. What's that worth? I've got to be offered some motivation. And what about Mrs. Barrman? She's so broken up, she refuses to even discuss anything other than a trial to punish TST. She believes—she's a very idealistic person—she believes this sort of gross corporate negligence is a blight on the earth, has gone unpunished long enough, and it is every moral citizen's obligation to see that it is punished. How much are her principles worth? I don't know. Maybe they can't be bought. I'll have to handle it very carefully, very tactfully. I can only go to her and ask if she'll accept *X* dollars under the table to save a very nice man, a man who is the victim of his own love for his boy. I don't know if she will or not.' He promised to get back to me to let me know the absolute maximum cash he could raise and how long it would take. This is a pretty nearly sound-proof room, Yovi. Admit that you think I'm not only a great lay but a great businessman."

"You're a blackmailer, and I won't have any part of it."

"For Christ's sake, Yov! This is an accommodation! I have—we—you and I—have something Sandaski wants and he's willing and able to pay for it. He's willing to pay more than we'd've got through a suit against TST, and quicker, without all that long legal hassle. Look, I'm an honest guy, as people go. I took every reference to Ruben Sandaski out of the pretrial material I turned over to the D. A. before I quit, on faith, and I told Papa Sandaski so. He was fervent when he told me he was going to move heaven and earth to get what it took to solace the widow and pay me for my efforts. Isn't that nice?"

"*Nice* is a word that has nothing to do with you."

"This is business. And you'll learn to respect it, or at least accept it, when you see the results."

"My God, Jerry, you're a barbarian."

"That's why you find me exciting."

"At least that Sandaski person had a sentimental reason for breaking the law. But you—"

"Pity the gullible father. Should he be rich, and should the wrong leaf blow from the wrong tree and flutter down on his head at the wrong time, a jurisprudent legerdemainist such as Jerry Odessa can turn it into a broadsword."

S pan sat on a narrow ledge over
the water, twenty feet below the level of the cave floor, and
drank fresh water. It was cold and sweet, and he found himself
remembering his first taste of it at least a hundred and fifty
hungers ago. Then he had found it better than even Stolichnaya.
Now it was only water, and he drank it carelessly, the way people
in the upper world do, thinking of other things, and even spilling
some.

Holding tight to the end of his water-fetching line, he struggled back up to the level of his little encampment with its one
ever-burning stationary lamp. He carefully hooked the big loop
in the end of the line over the bollard-rock. This was a critical
act and his heart always beat faster till he had got the line safely
secured. More than almost anything he feared a momentary
inattention or weakness that would cause him to drop the end
of the line and let it slide off into the cavern. He knew he would
never have the strength or the patience to rig another. The loss

of his water-fetching line would be his signal to carry out his oft-fantasized dive through black air to the red gullet of either the Thing or the other creature he had heard—a creature that roared instead of screamed. One of his rationalizations for delaying his plunge was that this new creature had to be seen. The hot thunder of its roar gave promise of another visual wonder for Span to carry into afterlife. In his proximity to death Span had reversed many of his previous contentions. Whereas once he had sneered at the belief in another existence after the present one, he now thought it silly not to believe. Belief was a comfort. If one gets comfort in the tortured skin he wears in this world from such a belief, the belief is justified, even if it turns out to be false. And if it is false, who will know?

Having made fast the water-fetching line, he lay back in that half swoon–half slumber he had got accustomed to of late, and let his mind wander back over his great triumph in bringing water from the falls.

After much thought he had tied a long, irregular chunk of rock (his grapnel having long since been turned into fishhooks) to the end of a length of forty-pound test line, stationed himself at the edge directly across from the cascade, and begun to try to cast into it. His theory—his prayer—was that there had to be irregularities in the wall behind the falling water, and if he was patient and continued to cast into it his rock would eventually catch in a crevice and anchor itself. His patience and his strength were sorely tried. When he was able to swing the rock around his head with sufficient speed and let the line go at exactly the right time so that it reached the falls, it invariably fell through; and often when it swung down against the cliff under his feet, the rock shattered. Then he had to find another rock of the proper shape and start again. Oddly, he felt no urgency. He could live as long as he was going to live by chewing the flesh of raw fish. Trying to get fresh water was only a game, to see if God rewarded this sort of mad patience.

And God did. One day or night, after Span had been casting intermittently for at least eight hungers, the rock caught and held. Span's gratitude was tempered with irony: His last challenge other than escape or a brave death had been answered.

In his explorations he had discovered, not only the accessible ledge twenty feet below the main floor, but a shelf twelve feet above the floor on the wall thirty feet back from the edge of the cliff. He could climb to this shelf by using stacked rocks. He prepared his water trolley by weaving loops of nylon line through the brim of his yellow rain hat and inserting his cross-cavern line through the loops, so that the hat looked like a tiny punt swung from a boat fall. Then, carrying the hat and the free end of the line, he climbed—breathless as much from excitement as exertion—to the high shelf and watched the yellow hat slide down to the falls. It was not heavy and it went slowly. He urged it on by shaking the line. It moved with magnificent predestined inevitability, as though Span had taken the entire rig out of a da Vinci notebook. When it came under the falls the sudden weight almost ripped the line out of his hands. He feared the stone anchor would pull free. The hat bounced crazily, like a lemon-colored cat caught in a machine-gun barrage, but everything held, including—just barely—Span's grip on the line. He hurried down from the shelf and forgot his many pains as he scurried across the floor recklessly down the incline to the ledge below and pulled the line taut. The water hat ran down to him. He grabbed it and spilled half of it in his sudden compulsion to gulp it. What poured over his chin and neck and chest was as good as what he drank.

That had been at least a hundred and fifty hungers ago. At the time he had not expected to live long enough for bringing water from the falls to become a commonplace. Yet, here he was, setting records, in all likelihood, for surviving in caves. Or was he setting records? If he was, he would gladly trade the honor to one of those college kids who think records are worth setting, like the ones who had told him one time they were going to push a roller bed bearing pots of growing garlic from Hoboken to Santa Barbara, to get their names in the record book. What had happened to those kids, anyhow?

Thinking back, writing in the dust with his finger, he calculated that, based on remembered hungers and remembered sleeps, he had been in the cave through ninety-five days, or sleeps, not counting his incalculable period of unconsciousness in the beginning. The hungers he remembered were three hundred and twenty-four. This worked out to thirty-nine more than three hungers per day for ninety-five days. He had often been hungry more than three times a day, therefore he preferred to believe in his count of sleeps. In his previous world he had averaged about eight hours sleep a night by the clock, but how does one know without a clock if one has had a true sleep or only a siesta? Still, the fact that the hungers at three per day tallied so closely with the sleeps at one per day...

He lost track of his calculations. In any case, he told himself, time as he figured it here was the true time because it was the only time being figured. His life was not on Greenwich time. His life was on Barrman's Cave time.

He felt The Skook watching him, just as he always did when he thought a lot about time. The Skook was eerily silent these days, reflecting possibly Span's conviction that death was on its way. While there had been secret hope, however faint, there had been little bounces in his spirits, but now everything was sunk as deep as the unfound bottom of the cave sea. He was sick, weak, lethargic of mind and body and spirit. He was no longer racked with heavy sieges of coughing. These had long since given way to frequent but weaker spells that always brought up blood. He knew it was hopeless now—more certainly because he had accepted it. He was ready to welcome it, if it could only be quick. He searched for the courage to act out his plunge to feed the monsters. He would not, would not, would not, die groveling in this dust on this cold floor with nothing but a bloodless Skook to watch him go. He kept his back turned to The Skook because he did not want to see the all-knowing supercilious smile he knew was on The Skook's face, the smile that was always there to taunt him when The Skook heard his self-pitying thoughts. He wanted only to slip away in peace. There was finally nothing, nothing, left in him. Let the great bird of night sink his talons in and soar away.

"Skook," he croaked hollowly, "save yourself. Leave this place. Go visit Kibby and Kitsy. Let them—"

"Bicky and Sticky, you mean."

"Damn! Yes, Bicky and Sticky. Why do I always get those four mixed up? Beatrice and Stella, Bicky and Sticky, in their little homes with their little lives—their unremarkable little lives, which would seem so remarkable to me right now! Go to them and somehow announce yourself, so that they can keep you going. Because I can't. I'm finished."

"You forgot, Sub, they'd have to call me."

"Maybe they will. Maybe someday they'll get their minds off themselves and onto their kids, the way I did for a while. Though, looking back, Skook, I'm ashamed I spent so much of my time ignoring them."

"They probably appreciated that very much."

"They loved me then, Skook, I think. Maybe even now they love me a little. I mean, maybe they try to love my memory a little, like I try to love theirs. I don't really know them anymore, but time changes—damn time! There it is again!—it changes everything, even selfish, rotten, shallow, insensitive brats like Bicky and Sticky—true inheritors of all the spiritual values of the Cow. And yet, someday, they may tell bedtime stories to their kids. I can just hear Sticky's fat little voice: 'When I was a little girl, my daddy used to tell me stories about the Gook or the Kook or the—ah, The Skook! He used to tell us Skook stories. Would you like to hear a Skook story?' 'Oh, Mommy, yes! Tell us a Skook story, Mommy, like Grampa used to tell you!' I'm a grampa, Skook. Four times. And two of them I've never even seen. Bicky's boy Sanford. He's three, I think. They call him Sandy. And Sticky's daughter—whatsername. Regina. Can you believe it? Just like fat, self-satisfied Sticky to call her daughter by a grand name. Damn, I'd like to see those kids, just once."

Span began to cry, not noisily or even very damply, but profoundly, softly, mysteriously relieved by the cool, nurselike rustle of death beside him. It was as if he were sleeping in a clean hospital bed, dreaming of iced tea with his eyes closed and smelling the perfumed whisper of the starched white uniform of his nurse, the big-breasted comforting one with the squeaky rubber-soled shoes, the one who lifted his head every night when he'd had his pill, lifted him gently with her surprisingly strong hands, pulled his pillow away, let him down again, the back of his head to the sheet, a reassuringly dizzying experience, as she fluffed his big pillow and shook it vigorously, her great mammaries bouncing and perfuming the air like a bellows and making his pillow twice as big as it had been, and firmer, and dry and fresh. Then she lifted his head again with that woman's hand that has lifted worlds, and slid the pillow under and let him down again as on a cloud, the whole act expressing love that asks for nothing in return. He sighed a deep, painless sigh. He heard it come through his slack mouth. If it was his death rattle he was glad. He felt nothing, nothing but floating bliss, a morphine drift of sleep.

"Hey, Sub, is this it, then?"

He heard The Skook, the unwelcome obtrusive voice edged with derision and disbelief, and refused to acknowledge it, the way as a boy he had refused to acknowledge his mother when she came in his room to tell him it was time to get up and get ready for school. If he did it well, feigned deep sleep, she would often take pity on her little boy—her child who wasn't ready for this heartless world any more than she, Ida Lee Spanish Barrman, was—and tiptoe out and let him have another ten minutes of dreams.

"Come on, Sub, up and at 'em. I'm not ready to be frozen. Who knows if I'll ever get thawed?"

"Frozen? Thawed? What?"

"Get with it, Barrman!" The Skook screeched the words.

"Leave me alone, Skook. It's over. I'm going."

The Skook flew very close to Span's ear and shouted in a squeaky, dwarfish voice:

> This is the way the world ends,
> Not with a bang but a whimper.

Span opened his eyes. They were blank like a dead coelacanth's eyes. Then they focused weakly on The Skook. "Neither," he whispered. "No bang. No whimper. Nothing."

"What if Bicky and Sticky never thaw me?"

"Thaw?"

"It's as though I were one of those people who have themselves frozen. When you go I'll be in suspended animation, frozen till one of three people thaws me."

"Let me go."

"You could go out in an unforgettable way."

"Any way I go will be forgettable. There won't be anybody to remember."

"Let me ask you something," The Skook said, and his voice was insistent. "What if—just by some miracle—I escaped via Deena Jane or Bicky or Sticky, by their calling me, and suppose one of them, or one of their kids, turned out to be as good as Kibby or Kitsy, and I could swim right into their world on the Perfume of Purity and tell them what had happened here. Wouldn't it then be worth it to you to have gone out with a bang in a unique once-in-the-history-of-mankind way?"

"If my grandkids, or my great-grandkids, could know?"

"By some long-shot happenstance."

"Would I know they know?"

"We have no way of knowing."

"Skook, I'm finished. You're making me hang on with all this speculative sentimentality. You're like a stubborn doc who won't disconnect a terminal patient's life-support system, even when the patient begs."

"Are you begging?"

"No."

"Because that would be a whimper."

"Damn it, Skook. Let me go."

"Sub, think about this for a moment. You take a flare to the edge. You hold it out over the chasm. When the Thing—or that other monster, the one that roars—when they detect the light and start to howl and roar, you go over, you and your flare, a yellow streak falling through the void, a shooting star, straight into the fang-lined maw of a prehistoric monster, the first human being in the history of the modern world to commit suicide by feeding himself to a living cave-sea fossil."

"God almighty, Skook!" Span's voice was stronger. "I've

thought about it, but I haven't had the guts. That would be ending with a bang all right, though I might whimper just a little when he crunches me."

"That would be allowable, I should think."

"What scares me is, what if I fell between 'em? What if smaller things got there first and piecemealed me, like piranhas? Or what if they all missed me and I drowned? I can't stand the idea of drowning. That's the one way I've always been petrified of. Anything but that. Anyhow, even if I had the guts to do it, I haven't got the strength. I doubt if I could get up again."

"Just think what you've accomplished down here, Sub. You've not only stuck it out this long but you've caught fish for food and oil. You've kept a light burning. You've brought fresh water from across the gorge. You've washed in it, cooked in it, bathed in it. You've learned to live with hopelessness. You've lived with pain and no aspirin, no doctor, no number to call for help. You've accepted your own unworthiness, your unimportance. You've accepted death. With so much accomplished, why not go for a capper, a topper, a pièce de résistance?"

"I'm tired."

"Sub, Spanish Ulysses Barrman, ponder this: Ulysses, true Greek moniker Odysseus, king of Ithaca, famed as a strategist. Bone-weary after the long siege of Troy, it took him ten years to get home to Ithaca. On the way he encountered great dangers, including the Cyclops who imprisoned him in a cave. But he escaped. Nor did six-headed Scylla get him, nor Charybdis, nor any of the other hazards on his way. His wife, Penelope, had many suitors in his absence, but when he finally came home to Ithaca he killed them all and once again was king. Why don't you be one of those few, one of that infinitesimal number of human beings saddled with a great name who has the courage, the strength, the will, to try to rise to that name?"

"I just wish—I just wish—" Another sigh, this one enough like a death rattle to be mistaken for one by the night nurse in the terminal ward, escaped from Span.

"Wish what? Wish what, Sub? Tell me. What do you wish?"

"I just—" The whisper was too slight to stir the flame in the oil hollow six inches away. "I wish I could've seen—the other one—the one that—roared."

"That's it!" The Skook exclaimed with such energy, such glee, such vehemence, that Span's eyelids fluttered, then half revealed the dim eyes that strove to focus on The Skook. "That path, your water path," The Skook squeaked, fluttering and darting as though to stimulate the nearly sightless eyes reaching out to him. "Remember when you first found it? You went down it about twenty feet below this floor, came to the little flat place where you could stand, and decided that was low enough to make the water hat come to you down the line. So you didn't go any farther down. You chickened."

"Too narrow."

"There was a narrow spot there, yes, but not too narrow. And the monsters were raising hell. It was worse than an elephant stampede in a Tarzan movie. You were terrified you'd fall and the whatevers down there would get you."

"I wanted to."

"Wanted to fall, sure. That's what scared you. Beyond that narrow spot the path widened out again and went down as far as you could see with your little flare."

"Yes!" Span burst out with a vehement croak. "Yes!" His dull eyes stared; light flowed back into them. Then, with long groans and a mighty physical effort, the near-corpse struggled up on one elbow and gasped: "That would be a final act, a great act, a truly great, unique act!"

This was a moment of rejoicing for The Skook. He fluttered and soared.

Span slid his body a few feet and put his back against the chair rock. Then he managed to smile at The Skook. "You know something, Skook? You're like one of those electric machines they carry in ambulances to jolt the old ticker back into action. I was finished, but somehow you got me cranked up again, at least for a minute."

"You're wasting precious time, Sub."

"Now you're the one hooked on time. Give me a little while to savor this, Skook. I'll write it in the dust. No, that'll wash away when the cave is flooded. Or will it be? Won't this place take all the Delaware has to offer and not even notice? This whole formation is likely to sink again someday, after a millennium, the way it rose. To be safe, I'll scratch it on the wall. I'll take my time. I'll live long enough. How? I'll will it, by God."

"Attaway, Sub."

"I'll scratch: *Barrman was here*—like Kilroy. No: *S. U. Barrman was here. Committed suicide by offering self to living prehistoric monster, Nov. '71.* Somebody, someday, may find it, Skook!"

His enthusiasm left him weak. He chewed some squid and fell asleep. When he awoke, feeling rested and more realistic, he took his old Bulova watch case, bent double and almost ground away by his having used it to hollow out stone lamps, and scored the sandstone wall: *S.U.B. '71.* Anything more would have been too much. Let them guess. Let him, dying, be preserved in undying mystery. If in some age to come his inscription were found, some archaeologist would amuse himself for years piecing together the evidence that the *'71* was for 1971, and that a person named Spanish Ulysses Barrman had disappeared in that area that summer. He would learn this only if there were still newspaper morgues, or libraries with microfilmed papers. And if there weren't, well, so what?

If he did not go soon he would have to fish again. He had chewed his last bit of squid and all he had left was a chunk of bass two sleeps old. He ate it, fearing it would make him ill, but reminding himself that he would not be alive long enough to get sick, unless he got sick quickly. This was possible, judging by the roundfish—his name for it— at the far end of his floor to the right. He had caught it only one sleep before the bass and it was already glowing with the phosphorescence of rot. It was a fish he had never seen in the upper world—short, thick, ugly, its flesh bitter. He could not eat them so he kept them for bait. He had noted they worked better after they were tainted. He kept them in this particular spot because the action of the waterfall between his camp and the rotting fish caused an updraft that carried the odor away to some distant part of the cave. He had used this area for his personal needs, too, and cleaned it daily with hatfuls of water.

With the roundfish and his own wastes he realized he had started a whole new cycle of evolution. Living organisms that had not touched this stone floor in the past—tiny living passengers in man—and others, different, surely, common to fish—were now at work here. Would they find each other and establish a chain of life? What would a man breaking through into Barrman's Cave ten thousand years hence find living on this floor?

"You're stalling, Sub."

"Let me finish my Last Supper, Skook. You know what I resent? I resent that God, or Whoever or Whatever is in charge down here—is anyone, or anything?—is letting me have this taste of Barrman's Cave, which is about to cost me my life, and not letting me know the rest. If I pay so much, why can't I have the whole thing?"

The Skook had moved closer to him, and was hovering a few feet in front of his face. "Are you asking me?"

"No, Skook, I'm not asking you. I'm asking God, if He's there."

The Skook giggled and chirped and did several tight loops, then hovered even closer to Span's face, smirking. "I suppose you're going to say now that if He doesn't answer He doesn't exist."

"No."

"Then how long are you willing to wait for an answer?"

Can condemned men laugh, actually feel the bubbles of joy rise in them and burst from helpless mouths in gusts of mirth? Yes. Span answered: "Indefinitely." Then he and The Skook laughed so hard that Span's hurt rib cage brought him up short. He ended in an excruciating fit of coughing.

The Skook watched as he spit up blood and struggled for air. "It's time to do the deed, Sub, while you still have the strength. I remind you you've taken an oath on Yovi's head—"

"No."

"—yes—that you would not end with a whimper."

"Not Yovi's head."

"Remember, you do not need to speak it aloud for me to know."

"That was a secret oath!"

"You know you have no secrets from me."

Span felt suddenly sick, whether from the tainted fish or from fear he could not tell. It was time to go.

26

He wanted the exhilaration he had felt when he had made the decision. It had seemed a gesture of such magnitude as to merit immortality, and the prospect of immortality, even unrecorded, should have inspired joy, a zealot's bliss, at least. But nothing of the sort rose in him. He trudged—staggered, rather—feeling queasier by the second, to the top of his water path and started down on rubber legs.

Immediately after the flare was lifted over the chasm the voice of the roarer was heard: a rumbling growl at first, then rising in anger or anticipation to a roar. Span was glad it was not the Thing, the howling, screaming thing he had first heard and then seen briefly as his flaming strip of shirttail fluttered down. He wanted to see this growler, this roaring thing, before he died. He was collecting these great moments for the edification of his immortal soul. Another thunderous roar came from farther away, then another from far down the cavern, farther than he'd suspected it reached, resounding and echoing. The roaring things must have driven the howling things away, Span thought, or perhaps the things had only migrated to other hunting grounds, given way to new tenants. For whatever reason, Span told himself he was glad to die in the jaws of the roaring thing rather than the ugly lizard mouth of the howler.

He stopped, half from habit, he thought, and half in terror, on the lower level he had used for getting fresh water. He whimpered once, or seemed to whimper, a sound escaping him that could have been called a whimper by an impartial judge; but he denied it to himself, and then aloud to the unseen Skook. It was a groan of pain, he said.

He held the torch close to the end of the platform where its narrowing in the past had discouraged his further progress downward. Now he was determined to go farther either by moving past the narrow spot or by falling. If he fell he would avoid the nausea he felt coming on, but he did not want to fall by accident. He wanted to go as near the water as possible and try to see the roarer before it got him. He wanted to look his death in the face. At least in his mind he wanted to. He wanted, in his mind, to go to the wall without a blindfold, toss away a cigarette with a gesture of contempt and face the end with a sneer the way the Cuban police chief had done when Castro sent him to *el paredón*. That was his mind's wish. His body's wish was to go back up the path and drink fresh water to quell his nausea. His body did not want to try to negotiate the scant shelf past the bellied-out wall that would give a mountain goat pause. His body wanted to live. It wanted to whimper.

"Go not as a quarry slave, scourged to his dungeon, but sustained and soothed..."

Span felt The Skook's eyes on him. He moved to the edge of the shelf.

"...by an unfaltering trust, as one who wraps the drapery of his couch about him..."

As far as he could see by his smoky flame it went downward, eighteen inches to two feet wide, no more, steep and wet, with the wall leaning out over it.

"...and lies down to pleasant dreams...." Am I remembering

that right? Could Bryant have said that, at seventeen? You'd have to be seventeen to believe that.

If the path got narrower he would not be able to go on, but still he would go. There was no coming back. He put his right foot on it, reaching out, facing the void, pressing his body against the wall, keeping his center of gravity as far inboard as possible. He slid his left foot over to join his right. His arms were spread wide as though to hug the rock behind him. His leading arm, his right, held the torch, and the other palm was open against the clammy wall. The sandstone there was covered with a slick hard glaze, the result of incalculable ages of mists from the falls, each droplet leaving its infinitesimal burden of mineral as it trickled down to the salt sea. The mists rising from the impact of the falling water were trapped in the gorge, roiling against its walls and condensing and running back, never to escape. These mists now shrouded Span, wetting his face, coursing down his cheeks like tears, calling forth true tears, and further blinding him. He slid his right foot forward again and then his left to join it. There was a sudden storm of hideous sounds from what seemed to be a menagerie of monsters below him. The nearness of the roars and howls—the howling things were back—shook the air around him, strained the thin fabric of his courage. On the verge of blacking out he continued still to move downward, the conviction growing that to see the roaring thing, to confront his death, would be a kind of ultimate bliss. And yet, the ear-splitting roars, the howls, and the deafening crash of the falls buffeted his resolve, even his physical orientation. The wet mists swirled around him. He smelled the salt, tasted it, mixed with his tears. His torch fluttered and hissed. By commanding his body to obey he moved, half step by half step, down the ledge, which he perceived to be steepening and narrowing still. To preserve his courage he stopped looking down, feeling his way with his feet. When the path should finally give way he would fall, but he would not have to suffer it till it happened. One of the roaring things was now just below him, how close he could not tell, but closer than he could have imagined it being an hour before. It roared incessantly and seemed to be leaping and falling back. It had apparently established this spot as its territory and smelled the advent of dinner, and there was nothing down there with him to challenge him. There was another sound, too, a chilling solid click that could only be two rows of teeth the size of ax heads slamming together. They were for Span. They would not be long about their work. But Span would see them. He would have this one moment of recognizing himself as a unique accomplisher, a doer of unduplicatable deeds. He would look upon it, whatever it was, and in some future existence he would have a memory of it, and this memory would place him among the special ones.

He judged he was within fifty feet of the water, or less. He heard the roaring thing that near, breaching and falling back with a cannon-shot splash and a pistol-shot clack of jaw teeth missing prey, missing smelled red meat, intoxicating blood, slamming together like boulders in a riverbed under a broken dam, then opening immediately to let out a thirsty roar that sent up billows of heat that Span could feel and smell—a mammal scent, not reptile.

Span knew the path did not go all the way to the water. If it had there would have been, at some point in the secret closet of time, a living thing that would have made its way up the path to make a life for itself somehow, to be there to greet Spanish Barrman, great explorer, when he entered the cave. This fish or insect or mammal or reptile would have evolved, mutated, adapted, and changed the high cave floor into something with a life cycle instead of the great damp stone desert it was.

Something else: The wall beside him was different from that higher up—grainier, rougher, unglazed. Span felt sand and rock chips on the path. His footing was surer. This was a new path, the last hundred feet he had come, only a thousand or so years old, perhaps. The condensed mists had been running down the path and had finally cut off another slab, which had toppled into the gorge, leaving this new ledge. In another few thousand years—or in a moment—another slab would fall, and the path would be down to the water, and something would find it and climb up it to his camp and start a new family of specialists who live in caves.

His right foot touched nothingness. He had gone as far as he could go on foot. The rest of the way would be through air. Through the whole toilsome descent, full of fear and doubt, he had not thought of The Skook. Now there was The Skook in front of him, framed in the sparkling mist.

"Well, Skook," Span said, "this, as they say, is it. I want to thank you for your company. You've been amusing, and—"

The living things in the lower mists set up such a bedlam of sound when Span spoke that he could not hear his own words. One sound stood out—that of the roaring thing that had established itself exactly below him and maintained that position for at least the last hundred feet of his progress along the path. Span raised his voice:

"You've been amusing, and—"

"You don't have to shout, Sub. I hear you perfectly well."

"Oh, yes, I forgot."

The sounds below were the sounds of a zoo at feeding time. Span's shouting had stirred the monsters to a frenzy. He continued speaking now in a normal tone that he knew the Skook could hear even if he himself could not:

"You've amused me, you've kept me company, you've even, I believe I can say with truth, helped me prolong my life, though I'm not sure that has been a worthwhile service. Still, I thank you for it, Skook. The thing you have not been—and you're fully aware of it, I'm sure—is a comfort. But I suppose I couldn't expect that, could I? At any rate, thanks, Skook, and I hope Bicky or Sticky—see, I got them right, that time—or even Deena Jane—I really shouldn't call her the Cow; she's a human being, doing the best she can like the rest of us, eh?—anyhow, Skook, I hope one of them resurrects you."

"Thank you, Sub." The Skook, for once, did not have anything flippant to say, and did not smirk. In fact Span was gratified by the gravity of his mien. He was even encouraged to do something that had been on his mind, though repressed, during the entire time of his descent to the level where he now found himself:

Give thanks to God. Yes. He had finally decided for once and all, having toyed with the idea several times but not made it final in his mind, that it was foolish to deny the existence of God. He reasoned that man was a fool to set himself to judge such things. If God does not exist, Span's thinking went, He does not need to be denied. And if He does exist He can't be denied. So why get into a no-win situation? Wasn't He a matter of definition, anyhow? If man created God in his own image, so what? Did not Spanish Barrman create The Skook?

The Skook smiled at this thought—not a frivolous, triumphant smile, but more of a gentle pious smile of thanks.

"God," Span said aloud as the mists boiled hellishly around him and the hidden monsters that were about to be fed human flesh deafened him with their impatient cries, "God, I thank you for the experience of this cave, for the uniqueness of it and of my life, and for not having led me into a cave full of hanging bats with needle teeth, a filthy cave with bats hanging together like a thick fur coat on the ceiling, raining down fleas and dung on the floor and on me, a cave full of rats and snakes and the remains of dead things, and most of all I thank you for not having let me find here beer cans and plastic cups and old paper napkins with mustard smudges on 'em. I thank you for the clean bare cave and for the time to sort out my life and my love for Yovi, and to understand, too late though it is, that she is one of your most triumphant works, and I'm one of your least successful, least deserving, least perceptive, least accomplished. But the least shall be—what? The most? I know the last shall be first, God, so there must be something for a guy like me, a guy that was just there, just around, not helping much and maybe not hurting much, either, but just there, like trees are there, and grass, and caves. Anyhow, God, now I know I'm special, and I can die. I don't understand why you picked me to do this, or what it all means, but you did, so, well, thanks, God."

He stood there crying, holding his pathetic sputtering torch, unable to move, to act. Finally he spoke again, so low he could not hear his own words, although he guessed if The Skook could hear him, so could God: "One last request, God. I'm going to look down, hold my light low, try to get a look at the loudest one, then jump. Don't let me chicken out, please."

He pulled in one last wet breath, held his torch as far out as he could, and peered down.

For what seemed a long time there was nothing. He questioned his sanity, his relationship to time and place. His flare did not illuminate the water or pierce the mists except to form a golden glowing circle like a globe around him. Still, his senses told him the surface was less than fifty feet away. The sound of the water of the falls landing in the gorge reverberated from both walls, crashed back upon itself in waves hard enough to make heads ache and bones vibrate; yet, above it rose the cacophony of animal sounds. Time seemed suspended, reality non-existent, for this unmeasurable period of his looking down. Then, slowly, or he thought slowly, for it all was clear, burned on his mind in every detail, an apparition formed in the gold and silver mists, a ghost yet not a ghost, a memory of circuses and zoos and *National Geographics*, the albino head of a bear too big to be a bear, rising whalelike with the ponderous irresistible thrust of tons, matted moon-hued fur flinging spray, two laid-back ears as far apart as casket handles, unseeing eyes seeing back to seal hunts in the Ice Age, shoulders emerging out of the gloom behind the head, hairy-mammoth mounds of exploding flesh, rising, rising, out of the sea, out of the past, propelled by some magic force up toward Span, on and on, up and up. Then the jaws opened and there were the railroad-spike fangs bared to rip him and the two long rows of sledgehammer molars to crush him, and the deep red final gullet. The gusting roar battered Span with its wind. The heat of its breath struck him.

Span's nerve broke. He straightened up with an involuntary flinging of both hands over his head to flatten himself against the wall, to be as small as possible. At the same time the bear—if something in the form of a bear that was as big as an elephant could still be called a bear—brought up his paws at the end of long humanoid arms and slammed them together like a thunderclap, expecting to find a meal between them. The paws, as big as footstools and bearing claws long and curved like wild-boar tusks, passed within inches of Span's nose, drenching him with salt spray. They went by so fast—though they seemed slow at the time—that there was a partial blurring of detail, but Span would later say that he believed he had seen that the space between the great toes was webbed, thus accounting for the loud report as the paws came together.

All of this happened in an instant. As Span threw his arms in the air in panic—though he did not whimper—he slammed his torch against the wall beside him, breaking it and splashing blazing oil along the wall. This gave the scene a flash of light as if to fix it forever in the memories of the participants.

A split second after the hairy paws slammed together there was another sound, a sound like that of a match put to an accumulation of propane under a cooking pot, though thousands of times stronger—BOOF!—and from shoulder level to his right no more than an arm's length away a horizontal column of blue flame thicker than a one-man submarine shot to his right halfway across the cavern, instantaneously boiling the mist in its path and turning it to steam and singeing Span's hair and beard. By this flash, which would have incinerated Span if it had not been angled away from him, he saw the giant bear glide from sight into the nether mists. Had one paw taken with it a chunk of the ledge beneath his feet? He had felt it go. Or had it fallen the way other pieces of rock had been dislodged as the wall behind him shook with the blast? Now the blackness was complete except for the nonilluminating Skook, who hovered nearby with a bland expression on his face. Span, in shock and ready to tumble off his perch, did not look at him. When he started to come back to himself and realized he was trapped on the narrow ledge in pitch blackness, he regretted briefly that his legs had not let him go to the cave-sea bear, and that he had not been standing directly in the path of what undoubtedly had been a coal-gas explosion. It was going to be harder now. He had done something else extraordinary and he was still alive. He had seen a two-story-tall cave-sea bear, descended from bears trapped by some freak glacial action and forced to adapt. Span had read about the discovery of giant bear skeletons, bears the size of hippos that had once roamed the earth. And here were these cave-sea bears that, confined to water and not limited in their growth by their ability to carry their own weight, had grown in their buoyancy like whales into enormous furry predators, ready to turn a grown man into two bite-size morsels.

"Skook, I didn't jump."

"No."

"Help me do it."

"You don't need to do anything. Just stand there till you topple in."

"I'm afraid that's what I'm going to do."

The stone was chill against his back, but comforting. It told him he was alive, not falling. The blackness all around him was like death, nothingness. It was his shroud. He strove to remember his camp, the color of the stone, his oil flame. Not red sandstone. It was the color of strong iced tea with ice in it, flashing out at him. That would be the moisture in it, the irregularities of the wet surface, the sequins of quartz. It had not been ugly, not at all. He longed to see it again. There was still a light up there, burning in his scooped-out oil bowl in the rock.

"Skook, I have an idea, but I'm too far gone to try it."

"How do you know?"

"I can't move."

"Why don't you die trying? Beats the hell out of toppling."

"You're right." Span began to inch sideways back the way he'd come. He pressed the rock with his spine. It stuck out now. He imagined he looked like a cadaver. He thought of himself as an ant crawling with a simple goal—to go inch by inch through darkness into light. Another roar of a cave-sea bear rolled down the canyon, a plaint of disappointment. It was followed by a howl from a monster reptile throat. These did not shake Span's purpose in the pale flicker of his mind: See the light. Inch by inch he felt his way toward the top of his path till his left hand reaching upward told him, by the absence of wall to touch, that he was almost there. He continued with barely controlled urgency—not fall, not fall now—till he could with dread that it be not there after all turn his head and look above the ledge, and see the beacon to the wandering son.

27

In his previous life Span had heard it said many times that there is strength in hope, and along with all the other clichés that ceaselessly assaulted him he had brushed it off like snow on his shoulder. Now, however, this sociologist's truism became to Span a great discovery, a philosophical Rosetta stone, a Koh-i-noor of the psyche. There is strength in hope. In hope there is strength. Yes, the unforgettable truth. Must pass this on to the world. Must escape and shout from mountaintops this key to all human triumph.

His strength of spirit soaring and his physical strength flowing back after a short rest seated on his chair rock, he became aware of something seemingly foreign in the cluster of hair and beard that framed his face. He absently reached up to remove the stray hair that blurred in front of his eye. He felt for it, got it between his fingers. It was coarse and straight and not attached. He held it out where he could see it. It was as long as a hair from a horse's mane, heavy but flexible, and yellow-white.

"Good God, Skook! Do you know what this is? It came from the cave-sea bear! It's priceless! I've got to get out of here, and take this with me!" It was at least an hour before he could stop fondling it, and sniffing its strangely familiar wet-dog smell, and communing with it, feeling its amuletic powers. Finally he tied it for safekeeping to the handle of his tackle box.

He began to fish deep for oil fish and shallow for food fish. His strength grew. He continued to have fits of coughing, but these were of shorter duration and brought up less blood. His ribs hurt less. On instinct he had begun to chew the bones of fish to combat his occasional diarrhea and it had worked. He felt real hunger again, a zest for food rather than the mere need of it. He caught a four-foot shark. When it finally stopped thrashing and snapping he cut out its liver and chewed it. It made him ill but after he had thrown up he ate more of it, and kept it down. After a sleep, his seventh since his face to face encounter with the cave-sea bear, he felt stronger than he had felt since he had awakened in the cave 160 sleeps ago. During this time he did not discuss his plan with The Skook. He knew The Skook knew and approved. He knew this from the indifference with which the creature hung about in the air, watching as though barely able to stifle a yawn, showing no disapproval or disdain. This constituted high praise from The Skook.

Span had caught roundfish, which were the proper size for his plan, and put them to rot in the updraft area to the east— or what he had designated as the east—of his camp, based on his memory of the side curve of the passage by which he had first entered the cave, and its angle to the riverbank. Two of these fish now glowed strongly, creating a small dome of blue-white light.

He collected oil with vigor. Ironically the treasured coelacanths that had been caught off Africa and trumpeted by scientists throughout the world as living fossils were as commonplace in Span's private sea as groupers off Nassau or porgies off Riverhead. He wrung oil out of their flesh till his tackle box was full.

The passage, which had been full of gas till his torch ignited it, would be full of gas again. If he was to explore it he had to do it soon or the coal gas would overcome him. He would light his way with roundfish so as not to set it off again.

He put the rotting roundfish in the remaining half of his vodka bottle. The stench was sickening. If the coal gas—he had to assume it was coal gas—did not overcome him, maybe the rotten fish would. The prospect did not frighten him. It seemed trivial. He was like a prisoner condemned to die at dawn who escapes from his cell and now must go over the wall. Is he going to be afraid of the height of it?

He made his way back to his water path. His lamp was like a giant firefly, or the luminous dial of a big clock. It was more comfort than light to Span as he felt his way foot by foot downward toward the bottom end of the path where he had met the cave-sea bear. The way down seemed familiar to him, though he had only traveled it once, and this time he was not serenaded by bloodthirsty howls and roars as he approached the water. His phosphorescent lamp could not penetrate the blindness of the cave beasts.

His feet remembered—and his back too—the place where the path abruptly narrowed and then merged with the wall. As he reached it his heart stopped again for a moment and his body froze as he saw again that terrible yard-wide furry face and its blank mother-of-pearl eyes rise out of the mists to him, splitting crosswise into a maw framed with fangs and bone-cracker molars. The brief image made Span cringe. Then it was gone. There had been no roar, no spray-flinging paws, no hot breath. It had all happened in his memory. Or his imagination. Had it happened at all? Yes. The hair proved that.

The hair. Had he actually found it? Or had he dreamed that too? No, he had found it. He had tied it to the handle of his tackle box.

He reached up and out with his right hand and found the aperture through which the shaft of blue flame had issued. It was exactly shoulder-high. His fingers explored the near rim. There were enough surface irregularities for him to be able to get a grip. He planted his right foot and swung around, feeling for a foothold with his left. He found one, a niche big enough for his bare toes, about halfway up to the floor of the passage.

Resting there, he placed his glass of roundfish as far back in the passage as he could reach and then, finding a grip for his left hand, swung himself up into the mouth of the passage on his belly. He kicked and squirmed forward, then stood up almost to his full height before he bumped his head.

Holding his fish lamp in front of him as far as possible to favor his nose, and walking slightly stooped over, he penetrated the passage, mounting steadily upward and curving, according to his judgment, to the southeast. A trickle of water an inch deep moved past his sore feet, refreshing them even as bits of debris from the explosion of seven sleeps ago tore at them. There were splinters as long as the cave-sea bear's fangs, and blocks ranging from the size of bricks to one as big as the crate Span's new blond-wood console-model television set—a gift from Yovi—had come in. This one almost sealed off the passage, but Span managed to squeeze past it. He tasted the water from the inch-deep stream. It was fresh seepage water, coming through tiny fissures in the sandstone formation and finding its way down to the sunless sea. That was the way of poets (Span remembered having told his eighth-grade class—to glassy stares), divining the existence of things before science could prove they were there.

The passage tilted sharply upward. He had to climb, slipping and falling to his tender knees—which, along with his much-abused feet, were now numb to all but the most grievous physical insults. If the grade got much steeper he would be stymied. He estimated that now he must be under the hills overlooking the river to have been able to go up so steeply for so long without reaching the end of the passage or breaking into the open.

He began to feel light-headed, vertiginous. That would be the coal gas. But where was the coal? He held his fish lamp close to the wall and put his eyes within inches of the surface. He saw that the monotonous red of the sandstone was relieved by a dark streak of something, a vein. He touched it with his fingernail. It was moist, pulpy. Lignite. Not coal but lignite. Farther along, the sandstone began to give way to some other rock, darker and harder, also shot through with damp lignite bars. He sniffed their musty odor. Some great upheaval in times past had caused this odd juxtaposition. Span recalled an obscure fact: There was a geologic fault under Stockton, New Jersey. It was not hard to reconstruct the explosion now. The lignite had thrown off its gas for centuries, filling the highest chamber first and finally the entire passage all the way to the opening over the water. It would have gone on forever had not man added fire. And now the passage had started filling with vapors again.

The angle of the floor was so steep that Span had trouble climbing and carrying his glass of luminescent carrion. He came to a piece of fallen ceiling, an irregular cube of what appeared to be granite, dislodged by the explosion and effectively blocking the passage to anything larger than a groundhog. This seemingly unconquerable obstacle dashed Span's optimism. He inspected both sides and the top of the blockage as though disbelieving the obvious facts. Then he sank, or rather wilted, to a sitting position and heaved such an outsized dolorous sigh that he brought on a coughing spell.

The obstruction shone, in the greenish glow of Span's lamp, with all the dour majesty of an open tomb. It was gray-black, adamantine. Specks of quartz glittered in its side.

Span stifled his coughing and spit up his usual teaspoonful of blood. His gloom was profound, his defeat or capitulation complete. His head fell to his chest. Then, in spite of himself he heard the persistent nagging voice of The Skook:

"Does an oath on the living head of the only sacred love you've ever known mean nothing?"

Span closed his eyes. Salt droplets crept from under his eyelids. Yes, sacred love. Too bad he had only understood here, in extremis, that it was love, deeper love than he had thought he would ever be capable of experiencing, deeper than he had known existed. Why did he, Spanish Ulysses Barrman, ordinary man forced to extraordinary deeds, always come late to any important realization? In the upper world, with its constant scramble to pay phony ego debts, Yovi had been only an errant wife, a self-indulgent amoral hedonist who put horns on her hardworking husband's head. Here, far from the incessant pounding of that world, she had begun to take the shape—or regain the shape—of what he had seen when first he looked upon her, when she "belonged"—what an excruciatingly canonical concept!—to someone else: an angel of blondness and softness and grace, something beyond human perfection, with an inner glow of honesty (*honesty:* truthfulness, fairness, the absence of deceit and dissembling) that put her apart from anyone he had ever met. Had she not told Abe Spiegel when she married him that she was incapable—and did not aspire to being capable—of being true to one person in the sense of dedicating her body to the service of that person? And had not Spiegel, in his blind love-lust, chosen not to believe her? Had she not told Span the same thing, with the same result? Had she not explained to him carefully, her blue-green eyes wide and full of the tears of sincerity, that *love, honor,* and *obey* meant very special things to her and that he should understand them before he linked his life with hers? *Love* meant wanting to be near, feeling good with, wanting to stay with forever, die with, early or late. Love was when you would step in the path of a bullet and die to save your lover. *To honor* meant to not diminish by bad thoughts—spoken or unspoken, to him or to others (it all flooded back now into his lonely brain)—the person loved. To honor was to not deceive. It meant being to the other person what you claimed to be, no more and no less, and not dissimulating ever, except when the other person wanted you to.

Oh, God, had he not driven her to dissimulation by his reaction to her first honest affirmation that she had been with another man? She had known after that what he wanted, according to the ground rules of their lives: to not be told. And it was true, because he had not believed her when she had said what she was and what she would do, his ego and his sutured accumulation of public stances not letting him believe, and his need to possess, to possess exclusively another human being for his own use, and the historical precedents for his belief in this right, not letting his ears hear or his mind accept the truth she had told him in the beginning. So she, Yovi, his all-blond all-sweet angel, had given him truth and he had given back lies. She had honored him in sharing her ultimate self and he had dishonored her.

And obey? Yes, she had said, she would say "obey," but only

if he understood that *obey* in her definition meant "obey within the parameters of our love as defined by mutual understanding." No person who truly loves another would ask for obedience the other would not want to give, unless mastery and slavery were parts of their love. She had said all this. To her it was her soul. To him it had been words.

If only he could have the time with her, the few moments he would need to tell her that he understood it all now and loved her the more for it, he would be able to accept death. But he was not going to have those moments, and he was going to have to accept death anyhow.

But without a whimper. He would not place this last insult on the uniquely wonderful head of his Yovi.

"Listen, Skook, I'm not going to sit here and wait for this immovable block of granite to be my tombstone. I'm going back to the open end of this passage and try to jump again."

"Gravity," The Skook intoned.

"Gravity?"

"If it'll work when you jump, why won't it work when you don't?"

"Gravity? Good God, Skook! Yes! It's on a steep grade! Maybe if I pulled on it! Skook, you're a genius!"

"I did nothing, Sub. You thought of it."

"Yes, I did, didn't I? Oh, Skook, I feel something in me, something gathering. Where does it come from?" He struggled to his knees, groaning. He held his lamp (it seemed an ordinary lamp to him now, wonders being relative) close to the block of granite that had closed his passage. There were irregularities in the side, finger grips. He placed his lamp behind him at a safe distance and groped for a hold on the stone. He stationed himself so as to bring his own weight and strength to bear, and then he put himself together: muscles, brain, will. He drew them all up into one explosive knot. The moment came when everything in him was all compacted and ready for the fuse of his spirit. He told himself "Go!" and every fiber of him burst into flame. His heart thrummed. His brain flared. His backbone became a white-hot steel rod, his whole body one great consuming agony.

For a moment, almost the last moment of his strength, nothing happened. Then the stone moved, slowly, almost imperceptibly at first, then faster, sliding of its own great weight down the wet slope, swinging sideways a foot, and another foot, then stopping with one ponderous sparkling corner pointing down the passage.

As it moved Span fell on his back. He had had his feet against the wall and his hands locked like meat hooks into the stone, and had uncoiled somehow with not only all the strength he had but all he would have after his next rest. He had asked for and got an advance on his strength and had spent it and now there was nothing, not the force to bat an eye or move a finger, hardly even enough to pull air into his chest. He felt the seepage water crawl past his backbone and his almost-fleshless buttocks. The stream had grown shallower and narrower, a mere tricklet. Even in his depleted state, flaccid, with nothing but a faint heartbeat and a fainter mind, he understood what that meant: He was near the surface.

Strength, as it had done so often, began to grow in him again.

"Skook, I opened the door. I feel Christ-like, ordained, infallible." He took up his precious stinking fish lamp and moved past the block, which had turned just enough to accommodate his emaciated frame, and no more. The passage above the block widened, and the ceiling rose. Span found himself after only a few yards in a chamber of sorts, a round terminus like the bubble at the end of a giant thermometer, full of debris shaken loose by the gas explosion. The floor was thirty-odd feet in diameter, and on it were two blocks of the same dense gray-black rock as the one in the passage, only larger. These were surrounded by smaller pieces of various shapes, like a furniture depot for a tribe of troglodytes. Span began to feel dizzy, queasy. He was about to throw up. The lignite gas had refilled this room. He knew he had to leave here or he would fall unconscious, but he refused to leave without having seen the ceiling. It was only twelve or thirteen feet above him. He scrambled to the top of the biggest block and held his fish lamp over his head, straining to stave off his vertigo and nausea. Then he saw it. He had just time, just breath enough to cry out: "A root! A root! Skook, a root!" Then he began to vomit and fell to his knees. Somehow he managed to place his precious vodka-glass lamp on the flat surface of the rock. It was the last thing for some time that he was able to do with full awareness of what he was doing. It was by instinct that he slid off the slab onto the rock-littered floor and crawled blindly back down the passage through the narrow gate he had made by moving the slab, and several yards beyond into a lower part of the passage before he collapsed. The trickle of water was dammed by his body. Then it flowed past him and mixed with the blood of his knees. He was not unconscious. He saw himself wet and sick like a drunk in a gutter, momentarily helpless. He could think of nothing but the root the root the root. It was a hairy taproot. It had split the granite like a carbon-steel wedge, driven by forces heavier than sledgehammers yet as sensitive as ants' antennae for finding the tiniest fissure. It had entered the fissure and conquered it with the same patience the sea had shown in making this cave. Barrman's Cave. Barrman's Caverns. Barrman's Underground Sea. Barrman's giant cave-sea bear, *Ursus barrmanus*. "Spanish Ulysses Barrman, 1923–" (It says in the *Encyclopaedia Britannica*) "American explorer, discoverer of—" The root the root the root. At the other end of that root was a tree, tossing its head, fluttering its skirts, celebrating its life in the Upper World. No, the explorer Barrman was not going to die in his cave. He was within a root's length of the open air and he was going to breathe that air again. The gas? That was not to be breathed again. It was to be used.

28

He unraveled almost his entire sweater, and made one long thread of it by tying more square knots with his numb fingers than he had tied in all the previous forty-eight years of his life. Then he soaked the thread in coelacanth oil for one day (one sleep, three meals, and the feeling it was near time for another sleep). Instead of sleeping he began to wrap the nylon line with the oil-soaked wool, and continued feverishly, fighting off drowsiness, till he had made a fuse long enough to reach from the Root Room to well below the Jesus Stone (as he now called it), well below where he estimated the gas would have filled the passage by the time he was able to lay his fuse.

The rock where he had put his fish lamp when he was first taken sick in the Root Room (and from which he had rescued it later, throwing up every step of the way) had been part of the ceiling of the Root Room, which had come down in the first explosion. The next explosion—or the one after that—would bring down the whole roof, taproot, tree and all. Or so Span's feverish brain projected.

A fit of coughing left him gasping. His fuse was completed. He coiled it in a tight loop and put it in the pool of oil to soak while he stretched out to take a nap.

He rested but could not sleep. His brain was too full of the moment. He was getting out. There was no longer any doubt about it. Yes, there was a small doubt, but he would not think about the one doubt, the one fear. He would control his mind and wait for rest to give him the last surge of strength he would need in the cave.

The cave. A cave of mysteries, none of which he had solved. He took a deep breath of the fresh wet air. He had a theory about that, at least, and when he was in the upper world again he would tell it to the scientists. They would be astonished to find not only that the condition existed but that Span Barrman, layman, had figured out why. Somewhere a hundred miles or so away, where the Atlantic tides rise and fall on the eastern shores, there must be a cavern, a hole, that is uncovered by the tides once or twice a day, and fills with air, and then is suddenly sealed again when the tide comes in. The air becomes a great bubble forced into the underground sea, pushed along by other bubbles till it reaches Barrman's Cave. And when the pressure of the air in the cave gets high, bubbles—other ones—are forced back out along the same deep hidden salt river to the shore, to emerge as one monstrous eructation after another somewhere off Red Bank or Point Pleasant or Seaside Heights or even Barnegat Light. Fishermen must have seen them, these mysterious globes of air that break the surface, rolling boats alarmingly at times, causing folksy explanations: "Neptune just farted," the captain might say, and he and the crew might talk about it in the bar that night, and even ask an oceanographer one of them happens to know. The scientist would shrug and offer some thought such as: Some old sunken hull was maybe turned over by the current, releasing a bubble trapped in it for God-knows-how-long. Something easy and sensible, like that. Secretly he thinks the seamen exaggerate the size of the bubble they saw, anyhow. Is there an oceanographer in the world who would say, even while deep in his cups, Well, fellas, maybe there's a big old hole down there that leads to a cave somewhere? No.

Span could not sleep. His wildest surmises, desperately drawn out, could not shut out his one remaining fear: On his final trip to the passage, to light his fuse, he would have to carry fire. Fire would be light, and this light might penetrate, however dimly, the thick blindness of the cave-sea bear. He had barely survived the last leap of the bear. Would he be so lucky the next time? When he had descended the path that led to the gas-filled passage he had been on his way to death. He had been on Death Row so long that the idea of dying was part of him. Then he had found the new passage and he was no longer condemned. He was now a prisoner the commutation of whose death sentence was being considered by a sympathetic governor. What if now, at this last moment, carrying the sacred flame to the fuse to freedom, he ended in the jaws of the cave-sea bear? It would be like the lost map to the gold mine, or the winning lottery ticket that blew out the window. Span had always scoffed at the thought that death to a millionaire could be a more anguishing thought than death to a bum, but now he knew it was true. He was a millionaire now, or almost one, in reach of the grand prize, but instead of being able to rest, to collect himself for the last walk, he lay there frozen in fear, feeling himself drift toward catatonic panic. He was tempted to summon The Skook, but memories of The Skook's coldness and derision stopped him. Was it not the pattern of the pre-cave Barrman to always do that which in the end would prove to have been ill-conceived? Was the now-Barrman unchanged from the then-Barrman? No. The now-Barrman was another man, not remotely resembling the ordinary Barrman who once roamed the earth in search of surcease from his own inadequacies. The now-Barrman would not drown his fear in vodka, even if vodka were available. He would fight his fear and beat it and walk out and see his Yovi.

If only he could have discussed his fear now with Yovi, it would have gone away. Yovi knew how to listen, understand, feel. He could have lain beside her and told her, without qualification or embellishment or—he only realized at this moment—embarrassment, that he was afraid, uncontrollably afraid, that the cave-sea bear would get him on his last trip down the water path. He did not know if his heart would survive the sight of the bear again. The howls of the Things (he would tell her) and the roars of the cave-sea bears congeal my blood, even from a distance. How can I face those swiping paws so close again, those paws as big as footstools, Yovi, I swear. Yovi, listen, I know you'll find this hard to believe, but—Do you remember the bull fights in Mexico City? Remember those black bulls, their horns? Well, I swear the cave-sea bear's claws are the size and shape of those horns, even colored like them. Can you understand why I'm so scared of seeing those claws so close again, so close that—Look, Yovi, look here—here's a hair that flew at me with the spray as those paws slapped together where they thought I was, like a fly. A hair as long as a hair from a horse's mane. Can you imagine a paw with hair like that?

Do it to me, Span (she would say). That's what she had said after—in fact during—the bullfights, and they had missed the last two bulls. Do it to me slowly, Span (she would say if she were there). We'll take all day. It'll be so nice. And afterward we'll go together, and I'll carry a tiny torch, no bigger than a match, and cup it in my hand, and that nasty old bear won't even know we're there.

"That's it! That's it!" Span shouted. "A small, hooded flame!" The Skook did not answer. Span was grateful.

Inspired again, he took up his fish lamp and his coil of oil-soaked fuse and made his way down the water path to the passage to the Root Room. Once in it he climbed quickly to the Jesus Stone, held his breath, and darted on his unsure sticklike legs upward into the Root Room, where he hooked the knotted end of the fuse under a rock and made his escape like a drowning man coming to the surface back past the Jesus Stone, carefully uncoiling the fuse as he went. He brought it out well below the gas level, as best he could imagine, and then took several deep breaths and went back and made sure the wool-wrapped line was propped up on small rocks along the side so as not to be near the trickle of water in the lowest part of the floor. It all went just as he had imagined it, without a hitch.

Back in his camp, he poured out the contents of his carrion lamp—it was liquefying—and rinsed his shortened vodka bottle with fresh water and set it upside down to drain. Anticipating human contact, he was suddenly vain, even anxious, about his appearance and his odor. He brought several hatfuls of water from the falls ("Barrman's Cascade Water, from the underground falls in Barrman's Cave, guaranteed pure, bottled at the source, 89¢ a gallon. S. U. Barrman and Co., Inc.") and bathed himself from head to foot, even washing his hair and beard and drying himself—or rather, brushing away most of the clinging water—with what was left of his wool sweater. Unable to dry his hair, he wore his water hat—formerly his rain hat—to warm his head. In spite of this he began to sneeze and cough again. He saw that his body, which he had avoided inspecting for many sleeps, was white as paste and splotched with sores and scalds and raw spots and scabs. His knees, mercifully numb most of the time, were half scab and half raw flesh. On the exposed flesh where the scab had been lost he saw pockets of pus. Before his new optimism all these things had seemed as nothing compared to the end he was expecting. Does a man on his way to the gallows worry about his laryngitis? But now all values were changed. Not only his physical health but every minor detail of his physical appearance seemed important. The sight of him as he was now was sure to disgust poor Yovi. Even though she loved him—of this he was now certain—she would not be able to look upon this rotting living corpse without repugnance. No one would.

He was feverish. He felt it. He should not have bathed. Never mind. Nothing that he had now would be difficult for the doctors in the upper world to handle. Good food, love, warmth, and maybe a little penicillin would bring him around.

He hurried the making of his new lamp. He found a rock splinter, flat at the base, that fit into the bottom of his sawed-off vodka bottle and tapered quickly up to a pencil-like stem. He wrapped this in two layers of oil-soaked wool thread. This would support the fire for lighting the fuse, without being bright enough, he trusted, to alarm the blind beasts of the cave sea. To make sure, he wrapped a piece of green plastic around the glass and tied it with fishing line.

He had been wearing the cutoff sleeves of his sweater on his feet when he slept, and sometimes, when the agony was too great, when he walked about, but in precarious situations, such as his descent along the water path to the Road to Glory (sentimental names for everything were popping into his head now), he always went barefoot, even though the extra traction meant extra pain. He briefly considered wearing the sleeves on his last trip, however, secured around his ankles as always by nylon line, because he did not want to appear in public limping on ugly ulcerated feet, but the possibility of slipping put this last vanity out of his mind. He washed his pants and his frayed shirt and dried them over the Olympic Flame and dressed himself for his ascension. The clothing had a smoky perfume but it was clean. With it and his unsoaped but rigorously rinsed beard and hair, finger-combed, Span believed that he did not look like a person who had been carried beyond the known limits of mortal strength to survive unimaginable tests. Only his wraithlike torso, transporting itself on heron legs, revealed the deprivation he had suffered. Yet, without a mirror, and without any image of himself other than that which his hands and poor vision had constructed and accepted and dwelt with for many sleeps, he could not see that he was only a shaggy head wobbling uncertainly atop a skeleton loosely wrapped in battered skin. He thought of himself as quite presentable except for his admittedly disgusting feet. New thought: Walk barefoot, but carry the sweater sleeves to wear outside. He stuffed them and their strings in his belt.

He took one last look around his camp. He would not miss it. He would leave his oil pool burning. It would be nice to think, in the upper world, that here below in a place no one but he had ever seen there was a cheery man-made fire ablaze. Perhaps it would still be burning when he came back with an expedition of incredulous scientists. He seated his rain hat-cum–water hat tight on his head, fought back a cough, and lit the stone-and-wool wick in his lamp. It burned with a weak, sputtering flame that threatened to expire at any moment. He hurried without further delay to the water path and down. His lamp threw off too little light to see by, but he felt his way, his feet remembering the surface. In the distance—a distance so great, it canceled all his previous imaginings about the length of the cavern—a cave-sea bear roared. It was not, Span knew, in response to his presence, and it was not answered nearby. The blind brute was just reminding his world that he was there.

He felt his way to the edge of the dropping-off place, keeping his back tight against the wall, not trusting his balance. He did his now-perfected maneuver of holding his lamp in his left hand, grasping the lower lip of the Road to Glory in his right, pivoting on his right foot, and swinging his left up to the niche that allowed him to transfer his weight to his left foot and lean his upper torso into the passage. There was a moment of terror as the strength went out of his fingers just before his left foot landed in the niche, but his momentum carried his left arm with his little lamp and then his chest and shoulders over the lip into the passage and he was secure. The terror, so quickly there and gone, made his faith absolute that whatever this next phase of his design might entail, he was destined to complete it.

He took a few deep breaths, then wiggled his way into the passage. He rose on palsied legs and ambled upward toward the end of his fuse, cursing himself—but not as roundly as once had been his custom, having got used to his own peccadilloes—for not having made a fuse long enough to reach all the way to the mouth of the passage, so that he could have ignited it from the end of the ledge and waited there in safety till after the explosion instead of having to scramble out ahead of the blast and then having to climb in again with his failing fingers. But it was done. He found the end of the fuse at the spot where the passage tilted drastically upward. He put the fire to it and watched for a moment as it burned and traveled. It went faster than he had guessed it would, leaping along like a forest fire in a high wind. He had the sickening feeling that he was not going to get out in time. He put his lamp down carefully in a deep fissure in the wall and ran on his wobbly bone-stilts toward the mouth of the passage. He knew from the sound of the falls when he had got close. Reaching the lip, he let himself down and swung sideways to the firm footing on the end of the ledge. He had hardly touched it when the whoosh of a blast shook the air around him and then the sound came down from the Root Room, a hollow boom with the rumble of falling rock and a general quaking of his footpath and the wall that pushed against his spine—pushed out, it seemed to him, harder than he pushed in—an obvious neurotic judgment, as he was still upright and not falling. His race to the mouth and the narrow margin by which he had escaped being a pea in the peashooter had left him—in spite of his conviction that the Almighty intended him to succeed—on the verge of fainting. For the second time he was on the ledge in the impenetrable blackness, and this added to his weakness. His own movements seemed disembodied. When he raised his hand to touch his face, the two seemed not to meet at the proper time. Then, without warning, a thunderous roar began just below him and came up toward him, closer this time, he felt, than in his first experience. He flattened himself against—almost into—the wall, and held his breath. There was the flung spray again on his face and the smack of the paws meeting with nothing in them. He felt the blast of air on his face. Had the sound of the explosion brought the beast there to defend his territory, or was it after all the odor of red meat in the air that had made it jump again? Span did not waste further moments on conjecture. He set a new record doing his swing up into the passage, instinct making him act without considering the idea of failing. On the way to flopping on his chest and kicking his way forward he knew again the exhilaration of invulnerability. He was chosen.

He tied his sweater sleeves on his feet, then rose and floundered blindly forward. He heard the cave-sea bear again, this time not leaping but roaring with disappointment and wild challenge. Somewhere the Thing answered. Let them fight over me, Span thought, I'm not staying around to referee. He lurched ahead and ran into a solid wall. He staggered backward, then advanced again discreetly, feeling for the obstruction. He groped his way to the side and found that he could barely squeeze past it. The second explosion had dislodged pieces of ceiling loosened by the first. He heard a crash behind him, then another more sustained rumble, and guessed that his way back to his camp was now cut off. If the way ahead should also be sealed, he would be the rat he had discovered once in an empty garbage can, endlessly jumping and falling back. Span had put him out of his misery, but he himself, here, if he was trapped in the passage, would not even be able to feed himself to the cave-sea bear. This thought was brief. His sense of celestial intervention lifted him to renewed optimism and he plowed on recklessly through the debris. He came to the preselected fissure where he had wedged his lamp, and saw that his string of miracles had continued: The glass had shattered but the oil-soaked wool on the thin spear of rock still burned. He took it up, holding it by the bare base, and scrambled upward with growing ecstasy, praying aloud. He came to the Jesus Rock. The explosion had moved it sideways and down so that it was easier to pass than before. Scrambling the last few feet, slipping and stumbling over new rubble, he found himself suddenly, incredibly, in the Root Room.

A feeling of ultimate horror spread from his throat down to his stomach. The roof had not come down. He held his flame as high as he could reach and saw nothing, not even the root, above him. There was one small blotch of light at the very top of the dome that reflected back to him his weakening flame. It was probably a slice of quartz, uncovered as stone beneath it dropped away. And where was his root his precious magic root his freedom root? He took another step; his way was blocked. The Root Room was full of heavy rubble. He climbed a foot, another foot. His light was dying. He held it high again. The quartz reflected as much light back to him as it had before. Then he saw that it was not quartz. It was a star.

He remembered climbing up over the taproot's leafless tree and finding himself on a high barren elevation in frosted night air. The star was gone. The sky was overcast and the brief appearance of the star fit perfectly the long chain of wonders through which he was living. He stumbled and crawled through the frozen night, or dawn, down the steep hillside to Route 29, the River Road. As there was no traffic he guessed the time at three or four in the morning. He walked in the middle of the road, using the yellow line to give him reality. Headlights. He moved to the side, floundering like a drunk, sobbing, waving both arms. Police car. Flashlight. Bright beam in his face. Unseen faces behind it. Voices.

"Jesus Christ! Look at that!"

"Hey, fella, where you headed?"

Span mumbled and sobbed.

"Wanta pick 'im up?"

"Shit no. Don't you smell 'im?"

"Jesus!"

"Crawl back in your hole, fella!"

Laughter.

"And have another drink!"

They drove away, whooping. Span staggered on. He saw himself as they had: a filthy drunk, Little Bigfoot in a green garbage-bag jacket and yellow rain hat, hair and beard like a pack rat's nest, feet wrapped in sodden sweater sleeves tied with nylon line—an apparition, even without the stench, to make any human being retreat. Well, he thought, they should've smelled me before I washed.

After a blank spot in his memory he discovered himself crawling on hands and knees up familiar stairs. He arrived in front of his own door, or—he sought to prepare himself—what was the door to the place where he had once lived. Where was the key? Where was anything? He had left the contents of his pockets in the cave.

The first to hear the stuttering sound of the doorbell was Jerry. It was just after four o'clock, and he was half awake. There were so many things to do, so many details to remember, that he had only half slept, if at all, and had been lying between sleep and waking for an hour. He looked at the clock when the first brief ding of the doorbell sounded and decided it had been a mistake, a neighbor coming home drunk and punching the wrong bell or staggering against it. Then it came again, this time insistently and long before a brief disconnection followed by another deliberate ring. Yovi slept, wrapped only in her perfumed skin. She did not stir as he got up and padded barefoot to the front door, tugging at his red silk pajama bottoms. The bell was ringing continuously, apparently stuck. Jerry looked through the peephole and saw nothing. The ringing stopped. Jerry checked the door lock and went back to the bedroom. As he got there the ringing started again, unsteadily, as though the ringer were trying to send

Morse code. Jerry turned on the light and awakened Yovi.
"Hear that?"

For several months, since Yovi had accepted Span's death
and passively allowed Jerry to replace him nightly in her bed,
she had been awakening to repugnance and self-loathing. Her
life had become a series of events allowed to happen. Jerry came
each night and left before dawn, playing out a charade that
fooled none of the neighbors. He was there tonight not because
she had asked him but because she did not have the will to stop
him. His ferocious spearing left her punished and forlorn. Her
afternoons were spent vengefully and unselectively deceiving
him. Some nights she was tempted to taunt him: Maybe he
would kill her. She knew why they were together: He was what
she deserved.

"Yovi, listen. That's the doorbell."

At first she was disoriented and disbelieving, then she was
alarmed. She sat up suddenly. The pink sheet caught for a
moment on her breasts, then slid down.

"Who could it be?"

"You'll have to go. I'm not supposed to be here."

She got up, clinging to some of her sleep, and started for
the front door with her unique erotic walk that contained all
the grace and undulating sensuality ever invested in woman-
kind, without a hint of coarseness or vulgarity or self-con-
sciousness. Jerry, hypnotized by this living sculpture, called her
back for her robe. As he wrapped it around her he cupped his
hands over the two sweet cones till he felt the nipples touch
his palms. Her silk rustled against his. Her ropy hair picked up
the green from the robe and turned canary yellow. He watched
it split at her shoulders, half falling over her breasts, the rest
down her back, saw her bare feet spring in the rug as she walked
away, her rose-gold chain glisten on her fine left ankle. She did
not tie her robe shut but held it together with one small fist.
He decided he was glad some idiot had forced him to wake her
up. She made being awake worthwhile.

Yovi looked through the peephole and saw nothing.

"Who is it, please?" Her voice emerged out of dreams, muffled.
If there was any answer from the other side of the door she

could not hear it. The ringing had stopped. She heard a faint sound as of something sliding along the wall, then another sound that could have been a groan, or a sigh, or the wind. She sensed Jerry behind her. She turned and looked at him. He stood in the bedroom door, puzzled, protective, only moderately concerned. She took a step back toward him and whispered: "There's something there. Shall I open?"

"No."

Then she heard a distinct moan. She caught her breath. She unlocked the door, and, in spite of Jerry's quick "No" behind her, opened it a crack, and peered out. She shut it reflexively and flashed a stricken glance at Jerry, then unhooked the chain latch with such breathless urgency that Jerry moved quickly toward her and hissed, "What the fuck are you doing?" She stared down at the pile of hair and rags at her feet. Jerry came up behind her and saw and smelled the object.

"Holy shit." He grabbed the door and tried to shut it, but Yovi, surprisingly quick and strong, put her body in the way and held it open without ever lifting her eyes. It was the yellow rain hat that held her, and something about the dirt-encrusted scabby hand that lay inert atop what now took shape as a human form.

Jerry tried to pull her away. "Shut the door, for Christ's sake. What a stink."

Then, in front of his disbelieving eyes, Yovi's robe fell open as she forgot to hold it, and she sank to her knees and covered the wretch with her naked body, softly keening.

Jerry, for all his overt physical and intellectual maleness, had many vulnerabilities. The faint odor of urine and excrement that rose from the heap of human garbage made him gag. He had to back away and hold his nose. But the incredible sight of Yovi's naked body straining to be close to such filth attacked his greatest vulnerability—his ego. He had long tried to conceal from himself that he did not believe as strongly in his own high destiny as others did. He had an aura of inevitable glory. He had learned to project it outward but not inward to himself. He was never more aware of the falsity of his image than at this moment when, pinching his nostrils closed against the stench and blinking his eyes to deny the sight, he was unable to close his ears to the childlike sound of Yovi wailing, "Span, Span, Span..."

As one is said to review his life while falling to his death, Jerry saw, in a second, what his new future would be if this pile of rags and bones were indeed Span Barrman: The one-and-a-half-million-dollar secret out-of-court cash settlement due to be paid to Yovi next week for the wrongful death of her husband would no longer be due; the insurance moneys already paid to Yovi, some of which had been spent, would be sought in lawsuits; Jerry's rich fiancée would be neither rich nor his fiancée; Jerry's proof that Barrman was dead would be nullified, along with his credibility; the public career he had abandoned in favor of his now-threatened financial independence would be next to impossible to revive; the condition of Barrman, who had obviously survived some harrowing experience, would inspire pity and admiration for him and detestation for the man who had caused him to be declared dead and then taken over his wife; the original suspicion that Jerry, known to many to be sleeping with Yovi, had had something to do with the disappearance of Yovi's husband would be refueled; it would be remembered that he had resigned as prosecutor of Barrman's "murderers," and appointed himself the widow's lawyer, and prepared a suit against Tri-State-Tronics—only to abandon it inexplicably a short time later. There would be a lot of explaining to do—more than could be done. The sum of all these thoughts was that if the status quo remained—the status quo being that what was left of the living Spanish Barrman was once more in the loving arms of his wife—Jerry Odessa was ruined.

Instantaneously rejecting ruin at any cost, he yanked Yovi up and into the apartment, then grabbed—though on the verge of retching—Span under his armpits and dragged him—almost too light to be an adult male—through the door and slammed it. Yovi had already picked up the phone, but Jerry knocked it out of her hand.

"I'm calling a doctor!"

"No. He's dead." He grabbed her arms just above the elbows and clamped down hard enough to leave five oval bruises above each elbow. The pressure and his dark look silenced her. His eyes glittered like chips of black lacquer. "He is dead. He didn't come back. He isn't here. We haven't seen—this."

Her eyes grew bigger than they had ever been. Through the light tan of her cheeks (on bright winter days, and with her skin heavily creamed, she often had sped about in her topless blue Spider, her blond hair streaming) the original fine-veined alabaster white appeared. She had almost never known horror, had seldom even imagined it. The moment of picturing Span buried alive had been the only time—no, the second time—in her life when horror had actually touched her. She was inclined to walk in flowered lanes in her mind. She could not fathom the seeking out of sordidness, danger, inharmony, ugliness. Was not every person, every sentient thing, put on earth to be happy if possible, to seek beauty and love? Should those who found it give it up because all could not have it? She had momentarily wondered from time to time when confronted with the hopelessness of others if she should not feel some guilt, possibly even be driven to some act to try to close the gap between her good fortune and the tragic lives of others, but unpleasant thoughts seemed not to be suitable to her mind, and giving up a moment of following her body's wishes was an unpleasant thought. She was a sunflower; she turned to catch the light. She told herself when she felt the world's opprobrium that she could not physically sin because her soul did not understand the concept of sensual sin, did not understand the giving of pain instead of pleasure or the taking of life instead of the sharing of it. And yet, here was her lover, not her love, speaking of—yes, unquestionably, unmistakably—murder. Murder. And not conceivable murder, not murder that murderers do for passion or money, but inconceivable murder, the taking of her adored Span's life, a life once taken, now miraculously restored. And yet, this lover of hers was bruising her flesh to impress upon her the importance of this inconceivable thing, this madness. No. It was conceivable that Jerry would want to do such a thing; she understood that now. But it was not conceivable that she would let him do it. She would die first. In her own pain—she thought in his grip her bones would snap—she shook her head from side to side, no, no, no, what you are saying can never be. No.

"Yovi, come to your senses. Nobody knows he's here. If anybody'd seen him they wouldn't've recognized him. I didn't. He's dead and he's got to stay dead."

"He's not dead!"

"He's going to disappear again."

"Then you'll have to kill me too."

"Then I will."

She stared at him in a long white silence. He took this to mean that she accepted the fact that he was going to kill Span and, if necessary, her, and that she did not wish to be killed.

"Now, listen carefully. We don't have much time. If nothing else the stink will drift down the hall and wake people up. It's almost four o'clock. We're going to wrap him in an old quilt or something and put him in the trunk of my car."

"No."

"You don't have to do anything but keep your mouth shut. I'll do the work. Just give me a quilt or a blanket—whatever you have."

Span made a sound and opened his eyes. Yovi dropped to her knees beside him. "Span. Span. This is Yovi."

As she spoke his eyes closed again and Jerry grabbed her and jerked her to her feet.

He hissed: "Are you crazy, touching that thing? Look at 'im, for Christ's sake. You don't know where he's been or what he's got. He could have anything. Leprosy. You name it."

Span was trying to speak. Yovi struggled with Jerry to get near him. "Span," she cried, "what are you saying?"

"Never mind what he's saying! Get me a blanket!"

"It sounds like *school*! Why would he say *school*? Or maybe *It's cool*. Maybe that's it."

Jerry spun her around with such force, she felt a whiplash effect in her neck. "Get the God-damned blanket. I'm losing patience with you." He shoved her toward the bedroom. She balked, set her feet, and turned back, just as Span said distinctly:

"Skook."

"Skook? Skook?" Yovi repeated the word, wonderingly, trying to come back to him. Jerry shoved her away, toward the bedroom, but she resisted. "Jerry, he's trying to tell us something!"

"He's dead, God dammit!"

"No!" She tried to fight her way past him, crying, pleading. She fell to her knees and clung to Jerry's legs. "For God's sake, Jerry! I'll give you anything! All the money! Anything!"

"You'll give me everything? You dumb bitch, everything is nothing if we don't do what we have to do, and do it now. There won't be any everything. For either of us. Not if he's alive! Can't you understand that? You're trying to blow the whole deal, and the son of a bitch is going to die anyhow! Look at 'im. Even if we called a doctor—"

"We've got to! We've got to try! We can't let him—"

"He's a corpse already! Is ten minutes of his life in this shape worth a million and a half bucks? Use your head, Yovi. We call a doctor and by the time he gets here we've got a corpse on our hands and no million and a half."

"Skook!" Span cried out with what seemed a last surge of strength.

"Span! What is it? What do you mean? What are you saying, darling?" Yovi struggled to get past Jerry, but he flung her away with a savage twist of his body, then lunged after her.

"He's finished! He's off his nut! Skook! What is that? It's nothing! His mind is gone, his body's gone. Let 'im go, for God's sake, Yovi, before you fuck up everything, all our plans."

"All right. No doctor. I'll save him in secret. I'll hide him. Nobody will ever know he's alive. I'll put him anywhere you say, change his name—"

"Where? How? It's impossible."

"I don't know. Anywhere. Somehow."

Her intensity held him. Was there a safer way? Murder will out. Two murders almost certainly. "How would I know you wouldn't blow the whistle on me as soon as you got clear?"

"What about me? Would I be clear? If I saved his life in secret and took the money as though he were dead, would I ever be clear? And if we don't call a doctor, or if you don't at least let me help him, will either of us ever be clear? We're criminals!"

"Criminals! A criminal is somebody who gets caught! And there's no way we can get caught if we do it now! He's already dead! You can't kill a dead man! What we are, if we accept his being here, being alive—what we are is idiots. We're kicking our own asses. We're flushing a fortune down the toilet." For the first time in fifteen years, since his speech course, he heard Brooklyn in his speech. It broke through in his pronunciation of *toilet,* just a hint of an *r* sound in the first syllable.

"Skook!" Span expelled the word, a death-rattle sound.

Yovi darted past Jerry and fell on her knees beside the still heap of rags. "Span! Don't die! Please! I love you! Stay with me! Oh, Span!"

Jerry bounded into the bedroom, where his jacket hung in an open closet, snatched a baby Beretta from an inside waist pocket, and was standing over Yovi with the pistol a foot from her head almost before she was aware that he had moved. When she looked up she was staring straight into the blue-black bore. She flinched, but held her ground.

Jerry said: "This thing makes a sound like if you broke a lead pencil. Nobody'd hear it if I pulled the trigger. Twice."

"Then what would you do?"

"Never mind. Just do as I say."

"Jerry, think a minute. Two bodies. Bullets from your gun in their heads. Your car downstairs. Signs of you all over the apartment. Even if you managed to get us out of here—our bodies—somebody would know. These flimsy walls—somebody knows already that something's going on in here. Heavy foot-steps. Doors. Urgent talking. And all at—let's see—four A.M. Can't be done, Jerry. You'd be nabbed straight off. And even if you weren't you'd have nothing. You need me to collect the money. So you'd have nothing, and you'd be on the run, wouldn't you? Now that I think about it, shooting Span and me would be stupid, and you're not stupid, are you, Jerry? Actually you're very bright in what I realize now is a sick way. Why don't you call the doctor now? You could be a hero instead of a rat."

Long before Yovi finished her desperate rationale, which did not reveal her desperation, Jerry had accepted her premise and was working on his next move. He was grateful to her for having gone on at such length; it had given him time to think. To signify acceptance, he slipped the pistol in his pocket and smiled at her—a superior smile that dimpled both cheeks and did not part his lips.

"Yovi, are you afraid of jail?"

"Jail?"

"If you don't do as I say, and help—help us both—get out of this, I'll see to it that you spend the rest of your life—or the rest of the good part—tucked away in a nice drafty little prison cell somewhere, with nothing but concrete and steel—and an occasional old bull dike—to keep you warm. I'll swear we planned Span's death. I'll swear we paid one of the Space Angels to organize the whole thing—burying Span alive, I mean—so we could be rid of him, collect the money, and live happily ever after."

"But that would convict you too."

"If I'm to have nothing, not even your blond pussy, you don't know how convincing I can be. I could make a deal. I know how. I'll prosecute your gorgeous ass off from the defendant's chair."

"I believe you would. My God, prison. Please, Jerry, I'd rather die than kill, and I'd rather die than go to prison. I'll do anything you say—short of letting poor Span die or hurting him more than he's already been hurt."

A car door slammed in the parking lot. An engine started. Jerry listened, revising his time frame. Somewhere in the building a toilet flushed. He heard hushed voices in the hall. Ordinary people starting their days. Who were these idiots, anyhow, getting up at this time of morning?

Span groaned. Jerry stared at him with revulsion. It was too late to try to dispose of him now. If awareness of him could be restricted to this room, then somehow a way could be found.

Yovi broke into his thoughts: "Jerry, please, let me help him. I won't call a doctor, I swear. But he needs nursing. It might even be safer, Jerry. I mean, he's out of his mind. What if he has the strength to suddenly start to scream?"

"That's why it'd be smart to put him out of his misery with this." He took the Beretta out of his pocket.

"I told you, you'll have to use it on me too. You're too smart to do that."

"You're right. I am. All right, Yovi, have at it. But you'd better keep him quiet and not let anybody outside this room know he's here."

"I swear."

"Then go ahead. I've got to get out of here before I throw up."

He went swiftly into the bedroom. As Yovi got brandy from the little dry bar she heard coat hangers clattering and presumed Jerry was dressing. She poured brandy into a spoon and parted Span's lips and tried to put some into his mouth. Only a thimbleful went in. The rest ran into the matted thicket of his beard. She had never seen him with more than a day or two's growth of facial hair. The rust-flecked gray of it and the fleshless white skin above it pulling the lips away from the teeth in a death mask made him appear a stranger. Only her heart knew he was Span. "Oh, God," she whispered, surprised at her words, "let him live." She forced more brandy between his lips.

He grimaced. He coughed. He smacked his lips. His eyelids fluttered briefly. She felt his forehead and found it flaming hot. She ran into the kitchen and poured milk into a saucepan and warmed it and put a teaspoon of honey in it and poured it into a cup and hurried back into the living room. The eyes in the shapeless pile of rags were open wide, clear sky blue, watching her.

She sat on the floor and cradled his head in her arm. "Oh, darling, darling Span, you're home. Don't try to talk. Just drink this. Here, darling." She held the cup to his lips and he drank, spilling and slobbering but getting some of it down.

Jerry came out of the bedroom transformed into a cool, controlled attorney, combed and scented, buttoned and zipped into a hand-sewn charcoal-gray suit. He watched the two on the floor for several moments, his face set in a mask of deep cruelty and distrust. Finally he said: "Yovi, don't forget."

"I won't forget."

Span did not take his eyes off the face of the madonna who held him to her breast.

Jerry went to the front door, listened for a few moments for sounds in the hall, opened the door a crack, looked out, then stepped out of the apartment and shut the door silently. Yovi did not hear his footsteps in the hall.

She fed him lightly and bathed him and put him into sweet-smelling cotton pajamas. She burned his sour rags in the fireplace. He slept. When he awoke hours later she sat beside him on the bed and they smiled at each other. These were moments of mysterious serenity requiring no words. She doctored his sores and scalds with unguents. She cut his hair, trimmed his beard as short as she could with scissors, then shaved him and splashed some of his old shaving lotion, sandalwood—which she had never removed from the medicine chest in the bathroom—on his bleached skull-bare face. If he had seen or heard Jerry that morning he did not choose to speak of it or, apparently, of anything. He seemed content to look at her and smile drowsily. Earlier, before he slept, he had told her only monosyllabically in response to questions that he had been in a cave. Now, after a half day of silence, he asked:

"When are we?"

"When are we what, darling?"

"I mean—what month is it?" His voice was surprisingly strong. "What date?"

"December eighteenth."

"December! My God!" He explained in short, breathless sentences how he had tried to keep track of time in the cave. He had underestimated by five full weeks. He had actually been underground for six months.

Jerry called and Yovi gave him a list of shopping. That evening he brought vitamins and honey and red wine, which Yovi believed to be good for the intestines and the blood of invalids. Span heard Jerry conversing for some time in the living room with Yovi, but he could not hear what was being said. When Jerry left, Yovi did not bother explaining to Span what was going on, presuming that he had made the correct assumption that her relationship to Jerry during his death no longer obtained now that he was alive again. Both understood the euphoric silence. Yovi was bursting with questions, but the time had not come to use his strength in answers.

That night she awakened beside him to find him looking at her. He wanted to talk. She started to turn on the light but he asked her not to. There was moonlight in slices coming through the venetian blinds, and he said he could see her perfectly, all her Cleopatran aura. The big lights, he said, hurt his eyes. He began to ramble, growing more and more excited by the realization that he was there, alive, and that his Yovi was hearing his tale and not scoffing. He told her everything in chronological order, more or less, or as nearly as he could remember, and without embellishment, leaving out only The Skook. She listened without any exaggerated or dramatic reactions, either to the sunless sea or the coelacanth or even the giant cave-sea bear. He did not ask if she believed him. He knew her. If she did or did not she respected the fact that it was in his mind and real to him, and that was enough.

When finally he needed to rest she got up without comment and went to the refrigerator and got a split of Piper-Heidsieck and came back sucking on it, her slender nakedness looking phantasmagorical in the striated moonlight. She lifted his head and gave him a sip of the cold froth. She leaned against the headboard and cradled him against her breasts. If she had had milk she would have suckled him, so helpless was he, so child-like.

He began to cry and she asked him why and he told her he had left his one proof of the existence of the cave-sea bear in the cave—a yellow-white paw hair as long as a horse's mane. He had planned to stop the scoffers with this strand, and by God, he still would. He'd go back and get it as soon as he was strong again. He'd take his dad, too, even if he had to carry him in his arms. What a day that would be! They'd see the cave together; Barrman's Cave, the falls, *Ursus barrmanus.* He'd have no need of the paw hair. He'd bring in searchlights and shine them down on the sea. The unlit sea would be lit. The wonders would be seen.

Yovi knew the bliss had to be broken. She could postpone for a while longer telling him that he was going to have to remain officially dead and would not be able to tell the world about Barrman's Cave, but she could not put off the truth about his dad.

"Span, darling, I'm sorry, but your dad—while you were gone—"

He had been going weakly from tears to laughter and exultation, and now he went to tears again, reading her eyes. "Poor bastard," he whispered. "Poor unsung bastard. If only he could've waited, even for a little while."

Yovi began to feel a sense of spiritual levitation. Her man, her real love, not a mere lust-thruster but a true love, was in her arms crying, communing, trusting her to know his deepest hurt. She believed their union was at that moment complete. When she had thought him lost she had realized that he was irreplaceable in her heart. She had known then that she would never stop mourning him, and that Jerry or any other man would never be able to numb her to her loss. This had been her revelation when Span was dead. Now, miracle of miracles, he was returned, and she had not only the awareness of her love but the object of it too. She petted him, kissed him, held him. She felt him shudder and go slack. He was sleeping. She kept him in her arms, not wanting to disturb him, until he awoke an hour later. Then they began to talk again.

She went back to the time in the living room almost twenty-four hours ago when he had first tried to speak. She told him he had said something she had not been able to make out. It sounded like *Skook*.

"Did I say that?"

"That's what it sounded like. You said it several times."

"Good God."

"Span, darling, what does it mean?"

"It means—I thought I'd dreamed all that, but—now I don't think I did. No, I didn't."

"Darling, you're not making sense. What does it mean?"

"It means I may be off my rocker. I definitely was, down there, and I may still be."

He told her about The Skook: its origins, its colors, its odd shape, its goadings at desperate times, their serious talks. She listened without comment, but Span sensed that she became uneasy as, in the telling, The Skook took on reality for him again. "I know I hallucinated the little bastard. I know that. What bothers me—and I guess it bothers you a little too—"

"No, no."

"—is that right now, as I tell about him—it—he's real. It's real. I mean, I remember it as well as I remember the bear or the coelacanth. If I hallucinated The Skook, which I obviously did, who's to say I didn't hallucinate the rest of it, the cave, the cave sea, my *Ursus barrmanus* two stories tall? He could stand on his hind legs and look in our window, for God's sake, Yovi—this second-story window—if he squatted down a little."

"You didn't hallucinate this one-hundred-pound body, this scabby sack of bones that once was my fat-bellied friend, did you? You didn't hallucinate being trapped under a landslide caused by a dynamite blast. That's documented."

"Then I didn't hallucinate the cave."

"No."

"Nor escaping from it."

"You're here."

"I sure as hell am."

"You lived through those months."

"So I didn't imagine chewing raw fish, and squeezing coelie fat for oil, and being scared almost to death by giant bear paws clapping together in front of my face. I didn't imagine those things. They're real."

"Then The Skook is real too."

"No. That couldn't have happened. I shouldn't've told you that. Until I can go back there with witnesses, The Skook puts everything in doubt."

"Not to me, Span. I believe in things like that."

"But you can't believe in The Skook, for the simple reason that I made him up, I invented him as the hero of stories to tell my kids. Don't you understand? He isn't real."

"How do you know?"

"Oh, for God's sake, Yovi."

"You say you invented him. Where did he come from?"

"Out of my imagination."

"How did he get into your imagination?"

"Listen, Yovi, will it make you happy to believe in him? Be my guest. But don't tell anybody I do. It's important to me to sound sane."

"All right. But I envy you knowing him. He sounds adorable."

"He's not that charming, believe me. If I was going to hallucinate something, I don't see why it couldn't have been you."

"You mean you didn't?"

"I did, but it wasn't—somehow—the same. By the way, I didn't hallucinate Jerry here, did I?"

"No."

"Does my coming back cut him out of the picture?"

"Out of the picture? It's more complex than that. Out of my bed—our bed—yes. Forever. But—"

"I know you and he were sacking out before I went away—"

"I thought you might, because I'm no good at sneaking. I do it badly and I hate it. I'd've told you, but I was sure you didn't want to know."

"I didn't. But I do. I accepted it then, and if I have to I'll accept it—"

She startled him with the vehemence with which she cried out: "No!"

"I mean, if that's the way you need it to be."

"I don't! I don't! Oh, Span! I need only you!" She pressed her face against his emaciated chest and began to sob, caressing him, clutching his loose skin as though trying to crawl inside him. It was a new experience for Span. He could not remember any woman—certainly not Yovi—bathing his chest in tears. He liked it. He liked the intensity with which she had said "I need only you!" This is the thing that made it impossible for him to stop his own tears. Had they ever wept together? He thought not. How long had it been since they had talked intimately about something within them? Had they ever? They had communicated through sex from the beginning, Yovi's universal language, her mother tongue, in which she had wished to address the world, one communicant—on occasion two—at a time. He had finally accepted this, though the acceptance had not diminished his resentment.

Then, in the cave, he had begun to see her as a mythic angel, devoid of sin, a pagan innocent. How could he have resented her being what she was? The purity of her response to her physical impulses had been there before he met her, and after. Her hungers, devoid of any concept of morality and thus incapable of being immoral, had not been kept secret. As a concession to those who saw her actions in a different light—including Span, at the time—she had been as discreet as possible, never flaunting herself or making a public display of her sexuality. In the cave he had realized that in another time, another setting—ancient Tahiti, for instance—she would have taken multiple partners in public orgies. This was fitting for a thing of wild beauty that should not be caged, not trammeled. He had sworn in that lightless world that if he should survive he would accept her as a golden-plumed bird to be glimpsed by any lucky eye as a flash of unexpected color in jungle clearings, and consider himself privileged to share the roost to which she returned at night. But just now, when he had started to tell her this, she had burst out "No!" She had even said that she needed only him. Could this be—impossible as it seemed, based on the past—true? Or was it the beginning of the disintegration of her honesty?

She stopped crying, grew calm, but continued to kiss his crepey skin. He caressed her hair. Could it have been Yovi who in days of legend dropped her cordlike tresses down from the tower window for her lover to use as a rope to climb up to her?

"Yov—you didn't let me finish. I was trying to tell you I understand and love you as you are."

She was motionless for a few moments, then she spoke flatly, dully, without looking up at him. "No. You mustn't." Then she sat up, looking away from him, and dried her face on the sheet. Not meeting his eyes, she got out of bed and walked impatiently around the room, stopping only to snatch up the split of champagne and empty it before taking it away from her lips. Then she paced again, reaching up with both hands and flinging her hair out behind her in a marigold spray, her breasts dancing primly ahead of her. Her anklet, which Span had once resented as secret-bearer of another love but now honored as a symbol of her inexplicable personal code, glowed palely in the dim light.

She came back to the bed and knelt beside it and kissed his face as one kisses an invalid. "I'm going to make you well, Span. I'm going to make you strong again, so you can make love to me. No one but you is going to have me—any part of me— again, ever."

In his fragile state, still uncertain as to reality, so recently lost in the realm of the cave-sea bear and The Skook, Span was not able to deal rationally with this reversal of all his fortunes, all his assumptions. He remained mute, stunned.

Yovi said: "Sleep, darling. When you're stronger we'll talk."

He understood from her manner that they would have plenty of time. He fell into a deep sleep.

Yovi was too full of joy for sleeping. Span had been purified: Being near him was a purifying experience. She felt like a little girl, immaculate, suffused with love.

It was difficult for Yovi to understand what had happened to her. She only knew that whereas she had in the past followed her hungers where they led and kept them separate from love, now they merged. She had only one love and he was to be henceforth the recipient of all her favors. She wanted not to belong to Span but to be a part of him, both the finite corporeal him and the infinite him. She had only had sex-in-love for one brief period (not counting her girlhood infatuation with Fredericka) in her life, with Abe Spiegel, and had experienced not only sexual release but a sense of soaring, of transcendence. This experience, unique to both, had been memorialized in the rose-gold anklet that Spiegel had locked on with his Weller needle-tipped electric soldering gun "so neither one of us'll ever be able to forget. It's something worth trying to keep, or to get back if we lose it."

They soon did lose it, and were not able to get it back. First the love, the main ingredient of the soaring, went; then the lust. Detestation moved in. Still, Yovi cherished the memory of those moments and the anklet symbol. Its barely felt caress was a reminder that magic, if it struck one time, could strike again.

She felt it coming on her now. The air was right, the ingredients were there, and she was older and more aware that love, like gold, can only resist time and tarnish if it is unalloyed. She had debased it by the addition of inferior elements. She must repurify it. This awareness had not come to her till she had counted Span dead. Then she had realized that he had been the one with whom she might have risen to those celestial heights whose memory walked with her always. It had not happened with Span because they had started with lust, carefree sex, not love. Then they had believed they felt love and had married, but he had already begun to resent her careless public passing around of what he thought of as his. He had wanted to possess her and she had refused to be possessed. He had grown hostile to her, and to him hostility and sex were not coexpressive. He was a gentle lover, except when it seemed right not to be. But out of hostility he could not draw passion. So the lust was gone or nearly gone from their relationship before he had gone into the cave, and the love, the sublimity, was not yet recognized. She could, in fact, define the exact moment when the revelation had arrived: She was with Jerry. He was doing the same thing he always did, pounding heroically, forcing them both toward that impersonal sky dive through the animal kingdom they knew together, and she was thinking of Span. Yes, she thought, I loved Span. Why didn't I know it in time? Why didn't I let him know somehow? She had then, for one of the rare times in her life, felt guilt.

And now he was returned and lying beside her. She raised her left leg, so smooth, so slender, so practiced in swinging wide to give access to her center, and bent her knee so that her ankle came near her hand. She inserted the tip of her little finger (there was no room for anything larger) between the amulet chain and her ankle and pulled it tight, almost breaking the skin, trying to summon somehow the spirit for which it stood, the genie in it. With this effort she brought to mind the several times brutish lovers (Jerry, twice) had tried to break it, to tear it off, vexed at her refusal to divulge its meaning, sensing it was a symbol of something beyond their powers to reach. But it had held. Gold is strong in soldered links, hairy-bellied Abe had told her, and that was why this chain would properly honor their achievement.

She slid it up to the bottom of her calf, then down as far as it would go to the tarsal protrusion of her size six foot, then round and round, grinding the memory in. Yes, it could happen again, and would. She knew what to do.

At noon that day, while Span slept and she watched over him, she got a call from Jerry. He told her to give Span a sleeping pill and come to his apartment. He wanted her. She told him that she had decided to make love only to her husband and never sleep with anybody else again, ever. Jerry yelled at her and made fun of her and threatened her and told her this was some God-damned female sentimental crap that would only last till the next time he grabbed her ass. She told him that was something he was never going to do again, and hung up. Span had been awakened by the phone. He listened to her side of the conversation and understood. Yovi saw by his smile that he was proud of what she had said. So was she. She leaned down and gave him a light kiss. She pulled her green silk robe around her and went to open the blinds so that he could see the day. What he saw first were her perfect buttocks, and he guessed that she had pulled the robe tight to give him this view. He felt a stirring in his groin. Then the blinds opened and he saw the wet, gusty sky.

"I'm sorry," she said. "It's not a very nice day."

"It's beautiful."

"Yes, I suppose it is. I forgot." She came back and pulled a chair beside the bed and sat looking at him and holding his hand. She was both troubled and flirtatious, trying to decide whether to continue petting him, soothing him, bathing his wounds, being as comforting physically and emotionally as his condition would allow, or to make him face the one devastating fact she had kept from him.

Span made it impossible for her to delay the truth: "Maybe you could call Mom and tell her I'm here."

"I can't," Yovi said. "It kills me to have to tell you this, Span, but I may as well be blunt and get it over with." She told him about the 1.5-million-dollar secret settlement she was about to receive from Tri-State-Tronics for his wrongful death. It was sort of a blackmail, she said, that Jerry had arranged, and she had to split the money with Jerry. Her impulse was to call the whole thing off, but unfortunately Jerry did not agree. He wanted the money, and her too. He was not going to get her, but he would kill them both for the money. If she did not maintain the deal the way it was, Jerry had sworn to have her sent to jail for insurance fraud. And he could, she thought, although she had done nothing wrong except sleep with Jerry. She would tell Span the whole complicated story later, if he would only understand now that he had to remain officially dead.

With what strength he had acquired in the short time he had been in her care, Span rebelled. He not only did not understand, he was not planning to try to understand. The whole point in being alive was that he would be able to live as he had never lived before, with the woman he loved, with his great discovery and the fame it would bring him. It was out of the question that he should remain dead.

It took Yovi the entire afternoon to convince him otherwise. She made the three important points over and over again: First, Span's insurance policies had been paid, to her and to Deena Jane. Jerry had sworn to testify that she had arranged for Span to be buried alive so that she could collect the money and be free to live with him, which she had been doing and which he could prove. Second, she had been forced to cooperate with Jerry to keep him from killing Span when he arrived. You can't kill a dead man, Jerry had said. And if Span came back to life Jerry would kill him or have him killed for revenge. Third, if he remained dead they had each other. They could go somewhere with new identities and be free. By the end of the afternoon it was this third point, plus Span's exhaustion, that made him acquiesce.

It was a great moment for Yovi. Now she could concentrate on his health and strength and serenity of mind, and their discovered love, and her yearned-for return visits—each time from now on with Span—to the enchanted celestial island she could not forget. She became a dedicated nurse-nutritionist. She went to Farley's Book Shop and brought home cookbooks and pored over them for things to tempt Span's laggard appetite. She made him eggs fried with garlic slices in sweet butter, and brought them to him in bed on a tray covered with a crisp white linen napkin. There was also a pot of hot, strong coffee, and whole-wheat toast and blackberry jam. For one lunch she cooked spaghetti perfectly *al dente* for the first time in her life (having never really tried before) and topped it with pesto that she had laboriously made herself, chopping the green basil with fresh garlic and mixing it with virgin olive oil. Each night she brought a new dish of red meat or fowl (he resisted fish)—steak and onions, broiled lamb chops, *poule au pot*—always preceded by at least one Wyborowa—not Stolichnaya—vodka straight from the freezer. And she stuffed him with vitamins.

His morale roller-coastered. Nothing she could do, no amount of perfection, could keep him from falling into profound depressions. For hours his cheeks would be wet with tears, till finally her optimism and contagious joy brought him out of it. He confessed that he occasionally felt suicidal, as though, having escaped death against astronomical odds, he had no right to be alive, and this was why fate had decreed that he remain officially dead and not be able to tell the world about his six months in the cave, thus obliterating them, nullifying them and the changes they had wrought in him along with them. It took a daily miracle in the person of Yovi to keep him sane.

Her personal miracle was that she, too, had been transformed. The frivolous blonde with the aquamarine Alfa Romeo Spider who formerly left Swanson frozen dinners in the refrigerator for her husband and disappeared for long afternoons and evenings now spent her days and nights preparing gastronomical delectations for him.

In the first week he gained five pounds. Between emotional troughs he declared he was strong enough to meet with Jerry and settle the details of the plan.

The meeting was arranged for Christmas Eve. Yovi dressed in her most conservative wool suit as a message to Jerry and a celebration of her dizzying new status as a wife glorying not only in her physical fidelity but in her psychic chastity as well. She let Jerry in without a greeting, as though he were an undertaker. He did not speak to Span but stared at him coldly. Span spoke with Yovi and Yovi with Jerry, and the decisions were made.

Chairman Sandaski of Tri-State-Tronics was to personally deliver the 1.5 million dollars (Jerry still doubted that this was all the cash that Sandaski could raise but had decided to accept it in the interest of expediency) in person to Yovi's apartment on December twenty-ninth. They would split the amount down the middle. (Jerry again insisted his expenses be deducted from the full amount, but Yovi said that she had signed an agreement with him stating that his expenses came from his half, and if he did not honor that agreement they would be back to Square One in everything. Both Span and Jerry were impressed with her strength. Jerry backed down. Span was not reassured by this.) Jerry, as Yovi's lawyer, would announce that she was going away to try to start a new life. The existence of Spanish Ulysses Barrman would remain a secret. Yovi and Span would take new names. Jerry, through his connections, would furnish them with passports for their new identities. Yovi would turn what assets she could into cash. The three would then fly separately to Corpus Christi, Texas, by commercial airliner, Yovi retaining her true identity till she arrived in Corpus, to avoid creating suspicion in case she was recognized. During the trial of the Space Angels, Yovi had become something of a media star. When Beezle and his two top warlocks were given short prison sentences, and the rest of the Angels put on probation, TV cameras had caught her telling members of the gang outside the courtroom "Kill me too. Nothing important will happen to you." Her beautiful grieving face was shown on every home screen and in every newspaper for several days. It was highly likely that wherever she went in the near future someone would point her out as the lady whose husband had been buried alive by a motorcycle gang. Span, sure not to be recognized, would be ticketed in his new name. Yovi would carry approximately eight hundred thousand dollars cash, which represented her and Span's total assets.

Jerry would borrow a yacht on the Gulf Coast from one of his trusted connections, then the three "friends" would leave on a cruise of the Gulf. It would all be very informal—just three people on a pleasure craft putting to sea for a short cruise. They would leave at night, and in all probability no one would notice them. Every effort would be made to keep anyone from knowing that Yovi and Span—in their new identities—were on board. Captain Jerry would head for the port of Vera Cruz, Mexico, where he would take the couple ashore outside normal channels and authenticate their documents. After that they were to lose themselves with their small fortune in cash, never to be heard from again. Yowa Pellegrini Spiegel Barrman would no longer exist. She would join Spanish Ulysses Barrman among those mysterious persons who have disappeared from the face of the earth without leaving a trace. And somewhere off the tourist trail in rural Mexico a retired American couple would be peacefully living out their lives in comfort. This would leave Jerry free to return to Hunterdon County and take up the practice of law with a nice nest egg of his own. He might even decide to go into politics someday after all.

When everything was settled, Jerry threw one more murderous glance at Span, then strode in silence to the door. As he started to open it he changed his mind and said: "People around here are not stupid, and they're not deaf and blind. They're bound to know somebody's here. They know I was hanging out here and they must've noticed by now that I'm not. We'd better agree on a story."

"I forgot to mention," Yovi said, "I've already put out a story. My brother is visiting from England and he's ill with the grippe."

"What's his name?"

"Arturo."

"That should do it."

Then Span spoke up, and his voice was surprisingly strong: "We'll let you know in a couple of days what our new names will be."

Jerry faced Span again and looked him up and down, from the fleece-lined beaded moccasins Yovi had put on his feet that morning, to his new navy-blue flannel robe and the white cashmere scarf she insisted he keep wound round his throat in his weakened condition to thwart insidious drafts, to the gaunt face that was getting its color back and the sunken eyes that were starting to shine again. "I can't do anything about passports till I know who they're for, can I? And one other thing, schmuck: Don't get any ideas about blowing this deal. If you want to live, stay dead."

He went out and pulled the door vigorously shut behind him.

Yovi went quickly to the door and slammed the bolt in place with a loud click that she hoped Jerry would hear. Then she went to Span, who had spent the entire unpleasant three hours seated upright in a straight chair, trying to look stronger than he felt. She sat on his lap and kissed him. "Merry Christmas, darling. The worst is over. We're going to be free, and together, and happy. Does that sound like something you could accept?"

"It sounds like something I've always wanted without ever having been able to define it."

"Oh, Span, I love you so much! I'm going to make you so happy! Would you marry me again?"

"Anytime."

"Because we'll soon be somebody else, and if we're somebody else, we won't be Mr. and Mrs. Barrman, will we? So we'll have to get married again. We'll have Jerry get us new birth certificates too. Everything. Then, in Mexico, we'll have some nice old pueblo priest marry us in a little stone church in front of one of those awful bleeding Christs—"

"A Catholic wedding?"

"What difference does it make?"

"That's true."

"And it'll be unforgettably picturesque. He'll be potbellied, and wearing a cassock of hand-woven cloth, very coarse, and huaraches, and he'll do the whole thing in singsongy Spanish—"

"Which I won't understand."

"But I will. And I'll see to it that it contains the pledge *pegándose únicamente y siempre a él*—'cleaving only and ever unto him'—and then we'll toast each other in Mexican wine, or whatever—"

"Tequila, maybe."

"Yes, tequila. That would be appropriate. Oh, Span, it'll be wonderful. And do you know what my first project will be? With your cooperation, of course."

"What?"

"Babies. I want to have babies. I want to be a mama. I want my breasts to swell up and drip milk. I might even get slightly plump, and carry a *niñito* on my hip, and put it to my nipple whenever it gets hungry. Would you like that?"

"I'd like that very much."

She jumped off his lap. "Come over here, where you can be more comfortable." She led him to an overstuffed chair. He melted into it happily, a well-cared-for semi-invalid aglow with being loved. Then she ran into the bedroom and he heard her rummaging around, and pretty soon she returned carrying a Christmas tree made of blown glass. It was about eighteen inches tall, dark green except for the ornaments. There were silver bells smaller than thimbles, shiny cherry-size balls of red, blue, yellow, amethyst, white and grass green, miniature white doves, candy canes that looked like red-and-white-striped cup hooks stolen from a cupboard, all made of glass like the blown-glass tree. She held it for Span to see; when he responded with an intake of breath and widened eyes she told him, "Wait, wait, this is only the beginning." She set it carefully on the table, laughing her special musical laugh, as fragile as the tree. She plugged in the electric cord that trailed from its base, and the tree and all its baubles glowed. Then she shut off the other lights in the room. As the tree heated up, a liquid in the hollow trunk and limbs began to flow, and the effect was that of a luminous plant moving to gentle breezes.

Span appeared to have felt a phantom's touch on the back of his neck. He started.

Yovi watched his reaction. "You know why I bought it, don't you?"

"It reminds me of The Skook."

"I saw it yesterday at an antique shop outside New Hope. They only brought it out for the Christmas season. When else would anyone pay the outrageous price? But I knew I had to have it for you. Span, we must never forget The Skook. I think he saved your life in the cave. Whether you believe in him or not, I always shall, and I'll always be grateful to him."

Span covered his eyes. "Turn it off, please."

Instead of obeying, she turned the other lights on and went to him and pulled his hands away from his eyes. "You must think of The Skook and remember you're here and not there. You must think only good thoughts when you think of The Skook."

She led him into the bedroom. He walked like an old man. She took his robe and hung it and seated him on the bed and knelt before him and removed his moccasins. Then she pulled the half-dozen bandages off his open sores and walked hand in hand with him to the shower. She bathed with him, washing his sores with pHisoHex and his hair with baby shampoo. Then she patted him dry with a soft towel and used the blow-dryer on his hair and oiled his chapped skin and put salve and clean bandages on the open lesions. She remained naked throughout, her wet hair sticking to her back, her anklet sending up little glints of pinkish light as her bare feet stuttered about him. Neither spoke. He suffered her to do as she wished. His eyes followed every motion of her body and limbs, drinking in her flawlessness, her grace, letting his mind savor like great music the promise of exclusivity she had given him.

The effort of standing to be treated left his legs trembling. Seeing this she hurried, completed her work, and helped him back to bed. They stretched out side by side and listened to the clatter of the harsh night. Then he sighed and dozed. She sought out undamaged parts of his skin to kiss—his chest around his nipples, the loose folds of his belly just above his pubic hair, his lips. He moaned happily. She moved down to the flesh of his thighs, which had been scalded by his long months in the cave, and began to kiss him there and to fondle him. When she felt him begin to swell she took him in her mouth. He grew to only a semblance of the thick, blunt staff she remembered but she became impatient, much to her own dismay, and maneuvered him onto his back and got astride him and managed to put him, only half engorged, into her. Then she leaned forward, keeping her hot flesh wrapped tightly around him, throbbing and pulsing, and glued her mouth to his.

Span responded only weakly. By his standards he was a failure. Yet, Yovi felt first a surge of joy that almost stopped her heart, and then a vertiginous sense of coalescing with him, brain and bone, and finally, like magma pushing up from secret depths, an almost unbearable heat. Then she was shaken by the most violent and enduring orgasm of her life. It did not subside until, at last reduced to weak, uncontrollable spasms, her eyes rolled up and she fell into a swoon.

The next morning, after long, sound sleeps, they awoke almost simultaneously, still in each other's arms. Span reported that she had whimpered in her dreams. He noted that, all things considered, he was the one who should have cried.

She told him no, not so. Whatever he had contributed to the event had been perfect for it. Still not recovered from the experience, she tried to describe it to him, could not, and finished by saying that her greatest ambition was to have the same thing happen again.

He said he would dedicate himself to helping create conditions conducive to its repetition, but he hoped his own inadequacy was not one of the essential ingredients.

Yovi bade him stay in bed. She got up and hurried out of the room. He dozed. After a while she came back and roused him and helped him on with his robe and moccasins. They walked together into the living room–dining room where the glass Christmas tree glowed.

"Look!" She cried. "Jolly old St. Nick was here!"

On the table beside the tree he found a leather-bound notebook with a lock, and a thick-barreled Mont Blanc fountain pen with a bottle of blue-black ink.

"This is for you to fill with your memories of Barrman's Cave," she told him. "Just put down notes, everything you remember, in no particular order, whenever it comes to you, every impression, every detail. You'll forget if you don't. You'll start doubting yourself. You'll start thinking it was only a dream. Put it all down, darling—the cave-sea bear, those coelacanths, the taste of their oily flesh—everything. And The Skook! Oh, The Skook is the most important. Here, look, I got you something else."

She handed him a wrapped gift. He tried to open it without tearing the pretty silver paper, but she grew impatient and grabbed it from him and ripped it open. It was a box of watercolors.

"You must sit down and paint The Skook," she said, "in all the colors you remember."

"I can't paint."

"Do it over and over till you get it the way you remember him. Please, Span, let me share The Skook with you just a little. I wish I'd been your little girl and you'd told me Skook stories."

"Maybe that's what I'm doing now."

"No. He exists. And I want him to exist for me too."

"I miss him, Yovi."

"That's normal."

"The other night— A year ago I couldn't have told you this— or anybody—and now I can. I know you won't use it against me. The other night I couldn't sleep and I got up and sneaked into the kitchen and sat there thinking about him, and I called him. I asked him to come to me, just for a second, to show himself so I'd know I wasn't crazy. But he didn't."

"Maybe—because you don't really need him."

"Maybe. Hey, I don't want to be depressing. It's Christmas. Look, you got me all this stuff. And I didn't get you anything."

"Yes, you did. Look. These cookbooks. And this—" She opened a big cardboard box under the table. "A food processor. It cuts, slices, chops, grinds—"

"But we won't be here very long!"

"While we are, darling, you're going to eat like a sultan! And look what else you got me—a case of Piper splits. Oh, darling, you were so good to me this Christmas."

"We can't afford all this."

"Of course we can. Your death benefit."

"Oh, right. I forgot. Jesus." He crossed to the big chair with its overstuffed arms that were getting greasy near the ends where people's hands rested on the flowered pattern. He flopped down in it and closed his eyes and shook his head in despair. Yovi followed him and sat on his lap.

"And Span, darling, last night you gave me the greatest gift of all; priceless it was—yet, it didn't cost a ha'penny. I'm still weak from it. I was on a peak above the clouds, the snow was crème Chantilly, not cold, and you were God and I saw directly into your soul." She licked his ear, forced his head to turn up so she could kiss his mouth. But he did not respond. She saw that he was trying to hide tears. "Oh, Span, Span, darling, what is it? Tell me please."

"It's my folks," he said, "and I don't want to talk about it because it's corny." He flicked some of the moisture away from his eyes with a finger, and she handed him a Kleenex. He blew his nose angrily. "It's all so stupid. My dad, an ordinary man who lived an unrelievedly ordinary life, just missed the one thing he wanted most to have before he died: to be part of something—just one thing—extraordinary. And my mom. All she ever wanted was her family, and she hasn't got even that. She's all alone, and I can't help her." He started to cry. "I told you it was corny. I hate it."

"I like its corniness better than my story," Yovi said. "My mama hasn't answered a letter from me since I 'dishonored the family' by cheating on Abe with you and getting caught. My papa didn't ever get appointed ambassador, and he's retired, and owns a seafood restaurant in Trieste. He's not in touch with the family disgrace either."

"That's terrible," Span sobbed. He could not stop crying. Yovi cried with him. He was resentful, disgusted at the spectacle.

"What the hell's the matter with us?"

"I don't know."

He emitted a wet snarl. "God dammit! We've never done this before."

Then Yovi said: "No, and we've never been so in love before."

This silenced them. They blew their noses and dabbed their faces with Kleenex and stared at each other through red, puffy eyes. Suddenly the maudlin depths to which they had fallen struck them as funny. They began to laugh and hug each other and mutter about how silly, how corny, how disgusting, they both had been, and what a way to spend Christmas. They said "Merry Christmas" to each other, then repeated the wish, incongruously, over and over again, in different ridiculous voices, high and low, loud and soft. She squirmed on his lap and pulled open his robe and began to lick his nipples. He felt himself stiffen powerfully. It happened suddenly: Her own robe came undone and she was astraddle him, covering his face with random kisses, her knees crushed between his thighs and the arms of the big chair, riding him slowly at first, seeking, then suddenly furiously, eyes shut tight, mouth wide in a silent scream; head twisting in seeming agony, moist hair flying, her whole body quaking continuously as though a high-voltage electric current were coursing through her.

Later, when he had got through his own almost unbearably long and intense unraveling, and some strength had come back into them both, she sat up and leaned close to his ear and whispered huskily: "Were you struck by lightning, as I was?"

"Yes."

"Atomized?"

"I don't know what happened. It was indescribable."

"Indescribable. Yes, that describes it. And it went on and on. I thought—I did literally think—I was going to die if it didn't stop. Span, I think I've been metamorphosed."

They passed the rest of the morning in their warm bed, content to hold each other and rest. Then they began to try to analyze their strange emotional adventures of the past twenty-four hours. They spoke of his long absence, hope after hopelessness, the excitement of his return, the season; they finally agreed: The only thing that could have caused the incredible intensity of their experiences was love, true love. Love was not just mutual joy, or happiness, or togetherness, or admiration, or sharing, or any of the other soapy conditions claimed for it. No. Love, true love, was synergistic, far stronger than the sum of its parts. Love was a multiplier. A small love was a small multiplier—a six, perhaps. A big love, which theirs had become, was a big multiplier—maybe a hundred. What the multiplier did was raise the intensity of every emotion, good or bad, shared by the two lovers. Hence the sobbing. Hence the devastating climaxes.

They declared confession time. By knowing each other better, or by admitting what the other had probably already guessed, they would be closer, they believed.

Span went first: "Well, I guess my most important confession is something you already know. The first time I saw you I couldn't think of anything but getting your clothes off. Love? Forget it. I'd thought I was in love with Deena Jane once upon a time, and that went sour. So love—forget it. That was my attitude. I just wanted your cute blond ass like all the other guys. And when I finally got it, wow, I wanted it again and again—"

"And got it."

"Yeah, and it was great, but nothing like this morning."

"I think we hit about a nine multiplier in those days."

"And that was great, considering we didn't know what could be reached. Anyhow, I would never—this is still confession time—I would never have dreamed of marrying you, if we hadn't got caught, if the crisis hadn't come. I mean, we were both married, for Christ's sake, and just fooling around. I think we just told ourselves we were in love after that, to make ourselves feel less guilty, or whatever, to make ourselves believe we wouldn't create such a big mess if it weren't love."

"I confess the same thing. You're right."

"And then the way our marriage limped along tends to prove that was the case. I got less and less pleasure out of your body because I knew you were passing it around, and I resented it, and it kind of froze me up. I didn't understand till I was in the cave that I shouldn't resent you being what you are. That's where I realized I really did love you, and even if you hadn't volunteered your oath of exclusivity, I'd love you still."

"Differently, Span. A whole part of what we have would've been left undiscovered."

"The multiplier would've been smaller, no question. But since our multiplier was already the biggest I've ever had—a nine, as you estimated, or maybe even as high as fifteen at times, which is more than most people ever get anyhow, or know about—I wouldn't have missed what we didn't find. Can you imagine having the multiplier we have now, somewhere between fifty and a hundred—who can measure?—and then losing it?"

Yovi said: "I'd kill myself." She got up and walked, fully recovered and making sure he saw her new vitality, toward the kitchen. "Want anything?"

"A vod, maybe, in O.J."

"Coming up."

When she came back, hurrying because of the sudden chill on her bare skin, she carried a bottle of her champagne and a glass of orange juice spiked with vodka. Propped up and tucked in, she sipped for a few moments to organize her confessions. "I'll keep mine general," she said. "No sweaty detail." She told him about spying on her father in bed with his mistresses when she was fourteen, and envying them and wishing she were one of his mistresses too. She'd had innumerable encounters since then, most of them onetimers or affairs of short duration, but had only realized recently that they had been little more than butterscotch sundaes. Only Abe Spiegel had given her love, before Span. She had really loved Abe for a while, in spite of his freckled bald head and his hairy potbelly and his uncouth habits. When you're in love you don't see those things. They had achieved a multiplier of about twenty-five, she'd guess, a miracle for the time, but only a molehill compared to this Christmas morning.

She threw back the covers and twisted sideways in bed and brought her left foot up close to Span's face. "You've always wondered about this anklet, haven't you, darling? Now you know. Abe put it on and soldered the last link shut so we'd never forget those 'biggies,' as he called them. Without even knowing that, you resented it, didn't you?"

"I did. I mean, it did sort of represent a part of you I couldn't have. But now you can take the damned thing off."

"But why?"

"It's been superseded by a one-hundred multiplier."

"But it's a monument to a discovery, darling. If I hadn't climbed those heights with Abe, I wouldn't have known they existed, and I wouldn't have known what I yearned to have with you—and got, in spades."

Span held her fine-boned ankle in his hand and toyed with the chain. He pulled her foot to him and kissed her toes. "In that case, Yoyo, I'll accept its presence without rancor if you'll let me hang a wafer-thin platinum tag on it, microengraved: *Span/Yovi 12/25/71 100 Mult.*"

"Darling, a wafer-thin tag would slice your back like a knife."

"Or maybe my shoulder." He kissed her toes again.

She pulled her foot away and put it under the covers. "Very likely. Suppose we put a couple of new links in?"

"With engraving? Who could do it that small?"

"Abe could, but I don't think we should ask him."

"No."

"Though he'd do it. He does have a yummy appreciation of jokes, Abie does—'specially raunchy ones."

Span, feeling safe and superior, asked, "But would he give us a discount?"

"Never."

"Then we'll get it done in Mexico."

This was the first time since yesterday's meeting with Jerry that either of them had mentioned what was on both their minds—the new adventure that awaited them. They had concealed the foreboding they both felt, the doomlike conviction that they both had and neither wanted to admit—that at some time during the coming trip Jerry was going to try to kill them.

Yovi had told herself over and over again: Jerry will have his share of the money. Why should he take the risk? And the answer had always come back to her in a tiny persistent voice: Jerry wants it all. He is capable of anything. At sea, far from anywhere, Jerry will say to himself, "Dead men tell no tales," and then he will do it.

Span knew too. Being already dead, he could be disposed of without consequence. Yovi, 110 pounds of vulnerability, could easily disappear at sea. If Jerry managed to keep their presence on board a secret as he planned, no one would even know that anyone had disappeared at sea. Span had decided that he would not alarm Yovi with his thoughts. He feared she might do something rash and cause them both to be killed now, or him to be killed and her sent to jail. If he made his presence known to the world he might save his own skin, but Jerry would surely manage to get Beezle or one of the Angels to swear that Yovi had hired them to do in her husband. Span decided to wait and watch.

Yovi, with similar thoughts, did not reveal them to Span. "My next confession," she was saying brightly, "is not only a confession but a revelation, something revealed to me only since you came back to me." She told him that she saw her old self now so clearly, it was as though for years she had been watching another person physically identical to her repeat a certain sexual pattern like a robot, again and again. "You might say I was a controlled obsessive-compulsive personality, if there is such a thing. Everything, including my orgasms, existed within safe limits. I never let go, never came undone, except briefly with Abe those few times. And even those, I realize now, were modified by an impenetrable wall of caution that surrounded everything I did. I thought I was free, but I was no freer than a grazing cow who never challenges the barbed wire around her world. Oh, technically I did become a good lover, don't you think, darling? But—"

"With all that practice, why not?"

"But that's over. My confession is that for the twenty-six years of my life I've been emotionally stultified, a twelve-cylinder power plant limping along on four and not even knowing it. You have awakened me, my prince. I hope my new power doesn't shake us apart."

"Our only hope is to stay fine-tuned."

"I'm willing. Oh, God, Span, this is a greater discovery—for us: I'm sure it's not new, except to us; I mean, Antony and Cleopatra, Abélard et Héloïse—God, there must've been millions of couples who hit the high multiplier before we did! But to us it's a greater discovery than Barrman's Cave! For us it's our own Elysium, our personal Olympus. We'll flower into gods together. We'll let our psyches bloom. This morning the walls came down and I saw all the way to infinity. I got—finally and forever—out of the embassy."

On the evening of December twenty-ninth, at exactly eight-thirty as promised, Sandaski and Jerry arrived together at the apartment. Sandaski, wet-lipped, frightened, breathing in short, rapid gasps, kept his overcoat buttoned and tried to seem convivial. He spoke only to acknowledge introductions, and smiled continually. Fumes of gin rose from him in such strength that Yovi fancied she could see them. Jerry carried the money. He was icy calm and businesslike. He put all the money on the table and counted it in its little bank wrappers rapidly and without once bobbling the amount or fumbling a stack. Then he put his share back in his scuffed leather weekender, closed it carefully, said, "I believe that does it. See you in Corpus," motioned to Sandaski, and led him out.

Yovi and Span locked the door, hugged each other, and then carefully fitted the money into a Vuitton bag that Yovi had had since she was a girl in London. They were ready to go.

33

J erry was due at the end of the private pier of the Sea Shell Motel at two A.M. They still had an hour to wait, but Span and Yovi sat in creaky straight chairs in their darkened room, searching seaward for any sign of a motor yacht. The broken venetian blinds on the inland windows were closed as well as they could be to thwart the busy red eyes of Mr. Dukes ("Just call me Jake, folks"), the proprietor. He had come twice to their door since they arrived, smelling of gin and panting like a hound, asking if they needed towels or Cokes or hamburgers or Southern Comfort or "anything at all." Each time he had tried to peer past Span to get a look at the mysterious blonde he had seen getting out of a taxi in front of the office, wearing a hat and veil. She had waited outside with the luggage, her back to the office, till her man had registered. They had then refused his help with the bags and had struggled with them, she with her face averted, past the office window, down the rickety wooden walk, and into the shorefront cabin they had reserved for one night only.

Now, an hour after midnight and with all lights off, Yovi still wore her veil, not only because it made a fine mosquito net, but because she thought there was a real possibility that Mr. Dukes, though his apartment-office lights had gone out half an hour before, might still be on the prowl, peering at that very moment through the many-apertured blinds.

Span tilted up a bottle of Stolichnaya, then set it carelessly down on the cracked linoleum. He slapped at something as it flew close to his face, and there was a sound like that of a peanut shell landing on the floor.

"Another one," he mumbled.

"If Jerry is late I shall be very cross with him," Yovi said.

"I thought I'd never be in a place again bad enough to make me look forward to seeing Jerry," Span said. "Flying cockroaches."

Yovi picked up the vodka. "I used to believe only uncivilized people could drink strong spirits out of the bottle. Now I realize there are places on earth—Cabin Four of the Sea Shell Motel, for instance—where a lady of civilized sensibilities can neither touch the glassware with her lips nor remain sober." She lifted her veil, drank daintily, then pulled the net down over her face again. "Am I wrong, Span, darling, or is that pier swaying as though it were afloat?"

"I'm afraid you're not wrong."

"Will it be safe to walk on, do you think—much less tie a yacht to?"

"The yacht won't be there long."

"Corpus Christi," Yovi said. "The body of Christ. What a name for such an ungodly place. You think Jerry's going to kill us, don't you?"

"He'll try."

"I'm sure you're wrong, but to honor your opinion, suppose I woke up dear Mr. Dukes—if indeed he needs waking and isn't peering at us through one of the many holes in the walls and windows of this awful place—and suppose I said to him, 'Hi, there. I'm the mysterious beauty in Cabin Four you've been trying to ogle all evening. Well, have a look.' Then he'd say,

'Hey, you're the lady on the telly, that they done her hubby in with the dynamite.' And I'd say, 'That's me, mate. My friend and I are about to go on a little cruise, and we think the captain's off his chump and is planning to give us the old deep six.'"

"Then he'd call the law," Span said.

"Exactly," Yovi said. "And we'd all, including Jerry, be detained and eventually charged with insurance fraud and sundry other things, and go to jail."

"Till Jerry knocked us—or had us knocked—off. We've been over all that."

"Suppose, then, darling, we didn't tell anybody, but told Jerry we did."

"In that case, if Jerry's planning what I think he's planning, he'd go right ahead and do it when he planned to do it, since he's not planning to come back here anyhow. No, the only thing that'd maybe work is to not meet Jerry. To split."

"Let's go. We have each other, and a *baise-en-ville* full of money."

"Futility. Jerry's outsmarted us. Why do you suppose he insisted on delivering our new passports on the yacht? Without them we're stuck in this country. If we didn't meet him he'd call the cops, describe us, tell the story—his version—and same result, jail."

"And separated. Oh, God, not again. Let's take our chances with Jer. I know the boy. He's mean, grasping, petty, selfish—but he wouldn't kill. Not us. He'll have three-quarters of a million tax free. He's not stupid enough—that's one thing he's not, and I'm sure of it—he's not stupid enough to jeopardize that by committing murder."

"He would, Yov. He will. But I agree, we've got to take our chances with him, play out the hand. It's not all on his side. I have an idea too."

"Tell me."

"I can't. Not yet. I'm ashamed of it."

"Why?"

"Look. Running lights. He's here."

"God—it's big."

The red and green sidelights, wide apart, ran straight toward them. The rest of the craft was dark, a shadow slightly darker than the sky.

"Let's go," Span said. He took up the Vuitton overnighter, complaining of its weight with an exaggerated groan. "Is this thing full of bricks?" He picked up the larger of the two remaining bags, of maroon imitation leather, misshapen and homely compared to Yovi's chic *baise-en-ville,* and started out. Yovi followed with the smaller bag along the dark unstable pier. Ahead of her, Span tripped and almost fell. He stopped and waited for her, then whispered: "Loose plank here. Watch your step. Might even be some missing."

"If you disappear, darling, I'll know not to step there."

The red sidelight disappeared as the tall yacht swung broadside onto the end of the pier. The only visible light was the green one. As Span and Yovi had waited in darkness, so Jerry had come in darkness, visible only as a long—Span guessed sixty feet—handsome silhouette with two diesel engines purring like great cats.

The pier shuddered as the motor cruiser, both engines backing, slid into a controlled collision with the truck tires hanging from the barnacled pilings.

Span stood still and Yovi clung to him with her free arm as the boards under their feet lurched and groaned under the strain.

They saw Jerry faintly illuminated by the glow of the instruments in the pilothouse, a yachtsman's cap cocked jauntily on his head. He called down to them with just enough volume to be heard no farther than the starboard beam as they arrived: "Sorry I can't come and give you a hand, folks." He sounded affable, relaxed, un-Jerry-like. "Hop aboard. That all your gear?"

"This is it," Span said. He heaved both his bags over the gunwale onto the deck, then took the one from Yovi and deposited it there, too, then stepped on board across the one-foot chasm, planted his feet, and gave Yovi a hand.

The moment her foot hit the deck Jerry said: "Welcome aboard." At the same time the twin diesels began to hum and the yacht started backing clear. The speed and precision with which Jerry acted to shove off belied his imitation Galveston drawl: "Come on up to the pilothouse, y'all."

They saw him spinning the wheel and manipulating levers. The huge craft suddenly shivered and heeled to starboard as Jerry shifted to forward speed and swung the bow to port and accelerated toward the Gulf of Mexico.

Yovi took off her hat and veil and shook her hair free. She groped for Span's hand and gave him a half-reassuring, half-fearful smile. Then she preceded him up the ladder to the pilot-house.

Span groped for his nautical vocabulary, twenty-seven years in drydock. The deck moving under his feet brought back the same foreboding he had felt on his first seagoing voyage on a destroyer at eighteen. Then the steel deck had vibrated as though trying to move out from under him, and he had stood like a fool in the sulfurous fumes from the stacks, listening to the black waters pound the fragile shell he rode on, an alien in a hostile world, being hauled away to seek death—his or the enemy's—to the west. He had felt that same helplessness in the cave, but it had gone away as he grew used to the idea of dying. Now he had got used to the idea of living again, and each step up the ladder to the pilothouse—his face only inches from Yovi's trim rump, which had come to symbolize all life, beauty, and pleasure to him—brought him closer to the man who planned to kill them both. Yovi knew too; he was sure of it. She was sensitive, intuitive. She knew but she denied it. He made a note to ask her why, to force her to accept reality. Only then would he be able to sell her his plan.

"I had a hell of a time in Galveston," Jerry was saying. "For a while I thought I was going to be late getting here. Too much to learn." He swept his arm grandiosely over the semicircular bank of equipment stretching the width of the pilothouse in front of him. "Look at this. Sonar. Radar. Loran. You name it. Autopilot. Soon as I get out of traffic—see those blips on the screen?—into open sea, I'll put this thing on autopilot and I'll be a better host." As he talked he flipped switches; lights came on—a bright range light above them, a bow light, a stern light, then a greenish dim light in the pilothouse.

"I see you came in under darken ship," Span said.

"Yeah, natives down here see a palace like this, they want to climb all over it. Span, you're getting fat."

Span, still almost skeletal and not feeling jocular, did not respond.

After an awkward silence Yovi said: "Jerry, I don't understand how, with so many old piers along this shore, and no lights on our motel or the pier, you came straight to it in the dark."

"Look astern," Jerry said. "See the radio tower with the red light on top? When that tower is lined up with the vertical line in the 4 in that OPEN 24 HOURS neon sign flashing below it, you're on course for the good old Sea Shell Motel. I came down here and scouted this place. That's why I chose it."

"We knew you didn't choose it for its luxury," Yovi said. "It has flying cockroaches as big as hummingbirds."

"Good training for Mexico," Jerry laughed. "From what I hear, you've got tarantulas and scorpions for everyday houseguests down there. That bother you?"

"Not in the slightest," Yovi answered quickly. "Does it, darling?"

"No," Span said. The flat tonelessness of his answer caused Yovi to glance at him. A leaden gloom descended on them for a few moments, then Jerry tried compulsively to revive the banter.

"Tricky in here this time of year, I'm told." He slowed the yacht and went into a long, slow course change to starboard. "The insurance people checked me out on this channel—on the charts. Got to keep that little red rascal there well to port, then the next one too. See that one to starboard, the red one? Got to stay in the turn till that one's to port too. Span, maybe this is a good time for you and Yovi to put your bags below. I'm letting you guys have the master stateroom. After all, you need the double bed, I don't. Go straight aft through the salon—by the way, there are four bottles of Dom Pérignon on ice in the galley. Bring one up when you've stowed your gear and we'll toast being millionaires. Take the ladder down from abaft the salon and then turn aft and you'll run into your stateroom. Notice the teak decks, please, and the air conditioning—and take a peek at those beautiful twin diesels—painted blue. How about that? I can't be all bad, can I, if I've got a friend who'll trust me with this beauty?"

The salon had bookcases, a stereo tape deck, a wet bar, chintz curtains that made Yovi's flesh crawl, a mounted wildebeest head wearing a yachting cap with gold braid, and a thick bearskin rug the color of antique ivory. Yovi hurried through, the decor having instantly depressed her. Span, wrestling with the larger suitcase and the joint-cracking Vuitton weekender full of money, stepped on the skin, looked down, caught his breath, and stepped back off it. He set the bags down and stood trembling at the edge of a nightmare. Feeling weak and exhausted, he needed several seconds of deep breathing before he could resolutely take up his burdens again and march across the skin, planting each foot firmly. When he caught up with Yovi, who waited at the bottom of the ladder, he told her he'd put the bags down to rest his arms.

"You're still not strong, darling," she said. "I should've carried those things."

Their stateroom had a double bed. This was a pleasant enough luxury to Yovi, who had never been to sea on anything, and who had always heard her girl friends describe yachts as cramped, uncomfortable, and unprivate, but she was overjoyed at the other facilities. "A real W.C., darling! All to ourselves! And a shower!"

Span shut the door to the stateroom, checked the flimsy lock, and kissed her. "It's not a W.C., or a loo, or any of that sort of thing. It's a head."

"Call it what you like, it's heaven to me. I had visions of buckets, and shared ones at that. And imagine, the nasty bastard even put Dom P. on the ice for us."

They heard the water sluicing past beneath their feet. They bathed, got into pajamas and robes, and went to the superb galley, where they found the cold champagne as advertised, but to Yovi's disappointment only the "wrong" glasses, the wide, shallow kind that, she complained, "they serve champagne cocktails in, to fat ladies with lacquered hair in bars."

She briefly considered rummaging in her suitcase for her

elegant fluted Baccarat, one of the few personal possessions she had found it impossible to leave in the apartment in Lambertville, but decided against it as too pretentious. "Besides, Jerry would probably think *it* was the wrong glass."

Span carried an unopened bottle and three of the wide glasses and they climbed back to the pilothouse, not having spoken of the odd cold dread that continued to grow in both of them.

"We'll be outta here pretty soon," Jerry said in greeting. He was still negotiating the channel. They saw land now on either side of them.

Yovi held the glasses, Span poured, and Jerry toasted them: "Here's to the new-rich—us. Only problem we have now is that old sailor's saw: 'Red sky at night, sailors' delight.' We sure as hell got no red sky last night. Not a glimmer. The whole western horizon looked real shitty."

"Still does," Span said, trying not to ruin the champagne moment with glumness.

"The way I'd describe it," Yovi said, "since my vocabulary is not limited to fecal images, is: 'It looks like a glass pot full of boiling asphalt.'"

"I'd say that's a bit farfetched," Jerry said, trying to do Yovi's British-flavored accent, "but we're pretty sure to get some weather before this is over, at any rate, and so what? *Cranky*—that's her name—*Cranky* is a blue-water baby. She can go anywhere. She was parked in Saint-Tropez last year, right next to Onassis."

Jerry's chattiness and good cheer, almost reassuring at first, began to seem more and more compulsive and somehow sinister. He kept up a monologue on inconsequential matters, sprinkled through with tense metallic laughter, till they had cleared Aransas Pass and felt the long powerful swells of the Gulf.

Jerry set course 135 on the autopilot and asked Span if he knew how to read a radar screen.

"I was in the Navy," Span said, as though that answered the question.

"You can't see much in this low ceiling with the naked eye," Jerry said needlessly, "but it's good at this speed to keep as sharp a lookout as possible dead ahead, both for surface craft and for floating logs and any kind of debris that could knock a hole in *Cranky* at twenty knots." He told Span he could override the autopilot just by spinning the wheel; then he took a big draft of his champagne. "Say, I never bought this expensive stuff before. You can taste the difference."

"Yummy bubbly," Yovi said. She finished her glass and held it out to Span for a refill. "Makes my splits of Piper taste like sauterne and soda."

Jerry allowed Span to replenish his glass, too. "Nice to think we'll be able to afford this stuff from now on, huh? Look, you guys are ready for bed, so why don't you go below and sack out. You must be bushed. I'm going to stay up here till daylight, then maybe you can take over for a while, Span."

Span was staring at the gyro compass. "One-three-five? Why southeast?"

"We want to clear the continental shelf and get away from the fishing fleets as soon as we can. By the way, I had a little trouble with the passports. Hope you don't mind being British."

34

Yovi carried a new bottle of Dom Pérignon into the master stateroom, got her Baccarat glass out of its box in her suitcase, and began to sip in proper elegance. Span did not, he said, care for more. Two glasses had done him in, and he was exhausted. They spoke only in necessary commonplaces, not wishing to dwell on their apprehensions.

Span tilted the only chair in the room against the door, its straight oaken back hooked under the knob. Then he crawled into bed without a word, lay on his back, and in a few minutes began to snore loosely.

Yovi sat up in bed with her individual reading light on, sipping steadily and listening to the throb of the blue diesels and the occasional long shuddering thump as the stern in which they were quartered smacked the bottom of one of the troughs, which seemed to be deepening as they moved south. The sudden decelerations at the bottom of the swells made the glass dip at the end of her arm. She decided that her fascination with this phenomenon proved that she was somewhat drunk, and that this was a natural result of her drinking. She considered the chair against the door. It proved, she concluded, that Span thought that Jerry might burst in on them and kill them in their sleep. She did not believe this. It would be too messy, too self-incriminating, too direct, too un-Jerry. Thus reassured, she set her empty glass carefully in its protective box and slid down in the bed with her tangled hair on the pillow. She was not naked, as was her bedtime custom, but chastely buttoned into white pajamas. She pressed herself as close as possible to Span's thin body, and slept.

When she awoke only three hours later she knew the weather had turned angry. She had trouble keeping her balance as she dressed quickly in white jeans and pale green cotton shirt. She turned on only the small directional reading light on her side of the bed so as not to disturb Span. Then she took away the chair against the door and went up on deck, clinging to stable things all the way and standing momentarily in air several times as the yacht dropped from beneath her feet.

It was as though dawn had not come. The sky was a funereal gray-black in all directions. There was no sign that the sun was hiding behind any of it. When she reached the level of the pilothouse she saw Jerry's back, and then the sea rose up ahead of them like a mountain born of subterranean forces. It loomed alarmingly over them for several moments, then quickly fell away. She took a steadying breath, then called out: "Good morning."

Jerry, except for a gunmetal blue stubble that she had always found perversely attractive, looked like a man who had had a full night's sleep. They exchanged pleasantries and she asked him if he'd like breakfast. He told her he'd been dreaming of eggs over light and black coffee for two hours.

In the galley she found more supplies and better equipment than she'd had in her own kitchen—propane stove, an electric coffee pot, a four-slice toaster, a shelf of exotic jams and jellies, fresh fruit, and a refrigerator stuffed not only with milk and eggs but bacon, fish fillets, lamb chops, sweet butter, hot mustard—everything, in short, that a good cook might need for making gourmet meals at sea. Unfortunately, she thought, I am not yet a good cook, so I shall not be able to utilize all this potential. But someday...if...

She made breakfast for Jerry and herself and went on deck, feeling triumphant at having managed without spilling anything or falling down. She was inordinately hungry. She ate two slices of toast, fig preserves, a scrambled egg, and finally—unable to resist the perfect cheese she had found on a marble wheel under a cover battened down with elastic straps and hooks—a third slice of toast piled high with runny Brie. It was a challenging balancing act.

"I've cut speed on account of this sea," Jerry said. "Instead of nine o'clock tomorrow night we'll be off Vera Cruz more like midnight, or later. And we've gone to 180, due south. Partly because that's the way we want to go—though I'd rather be five more degrees to the west—and partly because of our angle to the seas. On the wrong heading we could pitchpole."

"Pitchpole?"

"Ass over teakettle—kaput."

"Pitchpole. Where did you get all this nautical talk?"

"Well, honey, I'm a sailor. My first foray into the social big time was crewing on yachts—and you can elide that if you want to: was screwing on yachts—out of Manhasset and Nantucket. That's when I discovered not everybody had a Brooklyn-Russian accent."

"And unlike ordinary men, you adopted one you liked better."

"I'm glad you haven't forgotten I'm not ordinary. Span still sacked out?"

"He's still recuperating. But I can handle this while you sleep, can't I?"

"He'll never be any good again, Yov."

"Jerry, please—"

"You need a stud like me."

"Don't."

"Miss Insatiable with a worn-out old man. It'll never last."

"Jerry, you've been very pleasant since we came aboard. Don't ruin it."

"I'm only thinking of you, kid. There's still time."

"I love him, Jerry."

"Love, bullshit."

"It means different things to different people."

"You've got a mama complex, Yov. You love 'im because he needs you."

"I'm not going to try to make you understand. I don't think you ever could."

"It's your choice. Okay, look, sweetie. All you have to do is keep a sharp eye out ahead about forty-five degrees on either side for surface craft or junk in the water." He instructed her in overriding the autopilot, and in turning the wheel to go to port or starboard, and in sounding the general alarm, which would bring him racing to the pilothouse. "Okay. Got that?"

"I think so. Yes."

"Ever steer a boat?"

"No."

"Well, the autopilot'll take care of everything unless you have to override it. If you do, sound the general alarm and I'll be here in ten seconds or less—maybe bare-ass, but here. No—" He took her arm and led her to the portside wing of the pilothouse, outside the enclosed part, and pointed to a black instrument mounted on gimbals on the rail. "See this? This is a pelorus. Ever fire a gun?"

"No."

"No, you're not the type, are you?" The yacht was suddenly twisted sideways several degrees. The bow heaved up. "Hang on!" Jerry barked. He put his arm around her protectively and both grabbed the railing. The bow nosed down into the trough and buried itself, throwing out a curtain of spray high enough to drench them; then it bucked free and leapt straight up.

"This could get to be interesting tonight," Jerry said. He continued to hold her tightly in the crook of his arm.

She loosened his hold on her and stepped away. "If it gets any more interesting than this I'm going to be terrified." She saw that her pale green shirt was drenched and sticking to her, and her breasts showed through as though she wore nothing. "How does this thing—this pelorus—work?"

"Okay, look along this gun-barrel–type thing here."

She saw that as he talked he was staring at her breasts. She bent to the pelorus, pretending not to notice his eyes.

"Here's the front sight, and here's the rear one," Jerry continued. "Now, if you spot any kind of a surface craft, get its bearing by sighting along this, right? Here, take a bearing on something. The bow."

She took a pelorus sight of the stem. He checked it.

"Perfect. Now, if you take a sight on another vessel, leave the pelorus set on that bearing and look again every couple of minutes. If the bearing doesn't change, and the vessel keeps getting closer, press this button, pick up this phone, and I'll answer from my bunk. That's important. If the bearing doesn't change and somebody's within, say, five miles, call me. You know what that means, don't you, if the bearing doesn't change?"

"It means we'll run into each other."

"Bravo." He saluted her, looking at her breasts instead of her eyes. "You have the helm, ma'am. Hang on tight when we hit a bump." He started to go, then turned back to her, stared openly at her breasts, and said: "One of life's little tragedies— a world-class piece of ass retires to a nunnery."

"Pleasant dreams, Jerry."

He started to retort, but instead turned his back and disappeared aft. She wondered what Span's reaction would have been if he'd come upon them at the pelorus, she in her see-through shirt and with Jerry's arm around her. I'm guilty of careless enticement, she thought. From now on I'm going to dress more in character with the new me.

Jerry discovered Span in the galley, with a half-eaten apple and a cup of black coffee and fully dressed, including a nylon foul-weather jacket. Their eyes only met for a flicker as they exchanged nods. Then Jerry, who had not slowed his steps, went down the after ladder. Span heard the metal door of his stateroom open and shut, and the lock engage.

The first thing he saw when he went topside was Yovi taking a pelorus bearing of a supertanker headed north on their port side, halfway to the horizon. A quarter of a mile long, low in the water, it looked more like an island than a ship. The radio near the autopilot was sputtering on low volume.

Yovi sensed his presence and looked up. "Span, you're supposed to be resting." She saw him glance at her revealing wet shirt, then look away without reacting.

"Guess what? Our friend locked his door. He's afraid of us too."

"Span, I don't want you to get chilled—"

"Oh, found this nice jacket in our locker. I should've brought the other one, for you."

"I'll get it when I go down to change. What woke you up, darling?"

"A nightmare. I was in my cave, and my campsite, the whole floor under me, broke off and slid down into the water. I was just about to be devoured by a cave-sea bear when consciousness rescued me. Then I got to thinking about this rough weather, and I saw that you were gone, and I had this vision of you up here in a wet shirt and Jerry staring at your succulent knockers."

"I'm sorry." She looked down at her protruding nipples, the areolae lustrous, like veiled brown eyes. "I feel like such an idiot. He did stare at me, and it's my fault. I dressed in a hurry and I just didn't expect this to happen."

"Tried to get you to switch to his side, didn't he?"

"Please don't be angry."

"Yov, I know you wouldn't leave me for a lousy five multiplier. May I have a taste?"

She unbuttoned her shirt and held it open. The yacht rolled, taking a twenty-degree list, then pitched violently; yet, neither Span nor Yovi, though they had to make sudden grabs for the rail and hang on, lost the focus of their intentions. Span ceremoniously kissed the tender buds, then took each erect breast deep into his mouth for a moment of gentle suction. It was not foreplay, only a special good morning kiss, a *carezza*. Still it left Yovi panting. They clung to the railing and to each other as the yacht whipsawed through a trench.

"My God, Span—let's go below."

"Suppose we hit something?"

"'Sweet death to die,' as they say."

"Some sailor you'd make."

"I'd only make a sailor if he were you."

He pulled back from her and after a moment the smile went out of his eyes. "Yov, we have to talk."

Her shirt was still open; she stood precariously on tiptoe and arched her back and poked the two points up at him. "Please, darling—again."

"We have to talk seriously." He began to button her shirt. "We don't have much time. Jerry's going to do it. Any time we're both together it could happen. He may be getting ready for it right this second, though I doubt it. He was up all night and he'll want to rest first."

"You're wrong, Span."

"I'm right."

"I'm not going to believe it because I'm not going to let that kind of evil into my mind."

"Death is a reality, Yov. Killing is, too. Murderers are."

"I refuse to let such awfulness stay in my thoughts."

"Yovi, listen. I have all kinds of proof. Nobody—not a friend, not a broker—would lend or rent this little floating palace to a guy like Jerry for a trip like this *without a crew,* without an experienced crew. This thing would bring—what, half a million?—on the market. What's the insurance worth? What are the insurance company's expectations, the fine print? It sure as hell doesn't say let anybody who wants to take it anywhere they want to in any kind of weather, qualified or not, and without a crew. No. Look at this." He held out a shiny gold-colored matchbook with a black Gothic *S* stamped on the cover. He turned it over to show her the *TST* on the back in the same style. "I found this in the back corner of a drawer. I was looking for something, because I could see that Jerry had removed every sign of the owner's identity from this damned boat. Even the books on the shelves in the salon all came from the same used-book shop. Why? And there's a blank space in the salon where a small frame was removed from the wall. How much would you bet that that frame didn't contain a photo of T.S.—Trevor Sandaski, with a bunch of Tri-State-Tronics people?"

The supertanker was sliding past them like a gigantic sea slug four miles off their port beam. From its bridge a signalman began sending a flashing light signal.

"Can you read them?" Yovi asked.

"I've forgotten my Morse code."

"They're probably saying the same thing they've been saying on radio," Yovi said. *"Fuerza diez al sud."*

"What does that mean?"

"Force ten south of here."

"Christ, force ten. That's either gale force, or storm, or hurricane—something like that. Did you answer?"

She guided his eyes to the radiotelephone. It took him several moments of puzzled squinting to realize that the mike was unplugged, missing.

"Terrific. We can't transmit. Listen, Yov, you're a gentle person, and you're honest. But let's not let your gentleness and your intellectual allergy to evil overwhelm your honesty. I'm gonna give you irrefutable evidence that Jerry doesn't plan for us to survive this trip. That's when I expect your honesty to conquer your idealism. First—and these things are just in the order they come to me, not in order of importance; they're cumulative—first, he said he'd kill us both if we didn't do what he said, if we didn't follow some scheme that would satisfy him. Why did this particular scheme satisfy him? Isn't it risky? How did he know one of us wouldn't suddenly freak out and blow this whole thing? Answer: He didn't. But this was less risky—and less messy—than killing us at the apartment. Second, he agreed to split the money fifty-fifty and make all arrangements with Sandaski. But he lied about the deal. This yacht was part of the deal, part of the blackmail. Of course he had to hide that from us. How do we know what else he got that he had no intention of splitting?"

"There are other people with those initials. And he didn't hide the name of the boat from us."

"Of course not. *Cranky.* What does that mean to us? Nothing. And he has no intention of our ever being in a position to check and see who the owner is. Let me continue. Why did we have to meet him in Corpus Christi? Why couldn't we have boarded this thing in Galveston?"

"He was afraid I'd be recognized."

"Right. And connected to him and to this boat. You two

together—very noticeable, very newsworthy. On the other hand, if you're recognized in Corpus Christi, how serious can it be as long as it has nothing to do with him? We didn't use our new passport names at the Sea Shell because he insisted we not use them till Mexico, so no connection between the people at the Sea Shell and the people in Mexico could ever be made. Does that prove he expects us to get to Mexico? No. It proves that as far as the world knows, nobody got on this boat besides Jerry. *Nobody.* A boat nosed up to the pier at two o'clock in the morning and maybe it was noticed and maybe it wasn't. Boats do that all the time. And the next morning two people named Mike and Mary Jones are discovered to have left early from their cabin. So what? They only rented it for one night and they paid cash in advance. Lovers. They do that all the time, lovers. We did it many times. No connection between them and the boat that may or not've been seen stopping for thirty seconds at the end of the pier. See what I mean? Yov, we're not here! There's nobody on this boat but Jerry! And when Jerry goes back to Galveston alone, nobody will have disappeared, nobody will be missing."

"He couldn't be sure nobody was seen boarding. He couldn't be absolutely sure, and he wouldn't leave anything to chance. As long as there was a possibility that someone saw this boat, and saw two people get on it—"

"What boat? What people? A dark boat stops for half a minute, picks up a man long dead and a blonde in a veil. You don't think for one minute, do you, that Jerry told Sandaski or whom- ever in Galveston that he was coming to Corpus? He could've told them he was picking up crew at Freeport, or even at— Hell, he didn't even have to tell 'em he was going west. He could've said he was headed east, picking up crew at Sabine. We don't exist, Yov, and when we disappear—it'll be at night— nobody'll be missing. I don't think he'll shoot us on board. Too many clues, unremovable blood stains or unnoticed ones—you know, 'Out, damned spot!' and all that. No. He's waiting for the time and place. You know what's the most telling clue of all? A slip of the tongue. He said, 'We'll toast being millionaires.' We're not millionaires, and neither is he. You'd have to combine our money and his under one owner to create a millionaire. And why did he lock his door? Does he think we're going to disturb his privacy? No. He's afraid we're going to do unto him before he does unto us. He doesn't know we won't go back on our word and tell our tale and destroy him someday. We know that but he doesn't. It's sort of rare, wouldn't you say, for two people like us to be involved in one little deal—two people who separately or together would honor their word? He's not used to people like that. I doubt if he even conceives of people like that, even believes they exist. So does he believe our deal with him is real? No. And he won't feel safe till *we* don't exist. I already don't exist, so that part's easy. And you don't exist either—*in this place.* And you have a new name and a new passport. So he's running no risk, to his way of thinking, because no one will be missing. Not only that, but if three quarters of a million tax-free is good, twice as much is twice as good, and he'll be able to really toast being a millionaire, though he'll be the only one raising a glass. Now, are you ready to let your honesty break your rose-colored glasses?"

"You're very convincing, I admit, darling. Now, I know you have an escape plan. Tell me."

"We have to strike first."

She questioned the implication with her eyes, and when he nodded, she paled.

"I have a hunting knife in the lining of the big suitcase. Did you notice there are only round-ended table knives in the galley? I suggest that tonight I take him off guard with my knife—I won't hurt him unless I have to—tie him up, then run due west till we're within striking distance of the coast with the dinghy, then set the course of this thing due east on the autopilot, send out Mayday signals with a false location a couple of hundred miles ahead of the actual loran position—"

"Why false?"

"To give us time to make it ashore. We'll leave his money with him. We'll only take what's ours. We'll keep sending Maydays till we get answers, till we know there's awareness, then take off in the dinghy. That's our only chance, Yov."

She pondered this, breathing heavily. Her eyes welled with tears. Finally she said: "No."

"Yov, for Christ's sake!"

"He could have a collision. He'd be tied, helpless. He'd drown. We'd be murderers. What if he weren't found? What if he continued on till he ran out of fuel, then drifted till he starved to death? No."

"Would you rather die?"

"Than kill someone? Yes."

"Well, I wouldn't. Yov, death's not just a word, it's a permanent condition, where Dom Pérignon and one-hundred multipliers don't exist. I hope you change your mind, honey, because I can't pull this off—maybe not even with you, but certainly not without you. So if you don't reconsider—and soon—well, it's lambs to the slaughter."

35

The gale winds of which the supertanker had warned struck them. *Cranky* bobbed about like a cork, twisting twenty degrees off course in both directions. The swells peaked and grew beards. Span and Yovi clung to each other in the pilothouse.

At noon Yovi went below for food, lurching from one stationary object to another, clinging to each till she felt she could gain another foot or two. Finally she cut short her lunch and went straight to the master stateroom and changed into dry, heavier, curve-camouflaging clothes, including an orange nylon Windbreaker. Then she went topside to take over for Span so that he could eat.

The day wore on and they heard nothing from Jerry. Then as it grew dark they found out why: He was sick. He called up on the voice tube and they could hear the nausea, the misery, in his voice:

"I'm sorry, kids, you'll have to hang in there awhile longer without me."

He refused food and all offers of help. Yovi's commiseration sounded so genuine it irritated Span.

"He probably won't die," he said. "More's the pity. But it's a reprieve, anyhow. 'Tis an ill wind turns none to good."

They spent the night huddled together behind the water-blinded windshield. They could see absolutely nothing ahead of them—not even the bow of the boat. Several blips came on the radar screen but passed at a distance and disappeared. *Cranky* danced so wildly that they expected momentarily she would dive into a giant wave and never surface.

At an hour when they should have seen signs of dawn but saw nothing, Yovi went below and knocked on Jerry's door.

"Jerry, do you feel like eating anything?"

"Maybe." It was not spoken but groaned.

She staggered into the galley and made him strong tea (a feat of prestidigitation) and one slice of toast with butter and marmalade. He accepted the food through a minimal opening, then shut and locked his door immediately.

Yovi went to the master stateroom, locked her own door, stripped naked, and crawled under the covers. It had seemed prudent to be dressed for an emergency, but now she accepted the fact that the boat might founder at any moment, and nakedness was as good a state to drown in as any. She slept only fitfully, wondering why she had allowed Span, in his weakened condition, to convince her to be the first to go below and eat and rest. After an hour of clinging to the side of the bed and feeling herself alternately rise in air and press with three times her weight against the mattress, she got up and dressed again in the nonrevealing clothes, including the Windbreaker, and went back up to the pilothouse. This was a bruising journey, as she often miscalculated the boat's next zig or leap, and ended being a missile flying up against a bulkhead.

Toward night the wind began to abate. Jerry came on deck looking pale and embarrassed. He reminded them this was rendezvous night, and urged them to go below and get as much rest as they could before time to disembark.

In their stateroom Span and Yovi agreed that the time had come for Jerry to do whatever he would undoubtedly have done earlier if he had not been taken ill. They had been on a due-south heading since clearing the continental shelf out of Corpus Christi. This, even at reduced speed, was designed—on paper, at least—to put them fifty or so miles east of Vera Cruz in the pre-dawn hours of this night. Jerry, Span believed, had certainly not intended to hold such a course for such a long time, and had only done so to keep his passengers—unexpectedly still alive—from becoming suspicious. Span did not know how to work the loran but guessed that the storm, roaring in from the southeast, had blown them well off course and they were closer to land than Jerry would like. Zero hour was now. No bribed officials were coming out from Vera Cruz in this or any other kind of weather to put them ashore in Mexico with all their papers in order at this time of truth.

Jerry, affable as a tour guide, called them on the voice tube: "Hey, kids, come on up when you're ready. Bring your bags to the salon. I'm in contact with the launch. It'll be here in half an hour. Lucky for us the weather's coming around pretty good. We'd've never got you into a boat in the seas we had yesterday. Try to get up here in time for us to toast long life and happiness before they get here."

"Good deal." Span's voice was as easygoing as Jerry's. "See you shortly."

Without further discussion they put their agreed-upon plan in operation. Yovi took a stack of hundred-dollar bills out of her *baise-en-ville,* gauging by hand what she thought she could accommodate, went into the head and shut the door, rolled them into a tight cylinder, and put them into herself like a tampon. Span also grabbed a handful of bills and put as many as he could into various pockets without making obvious bulges. The idea was to play along as though they had no suspicions whatever till Jerry tipped his hand, and for Yovi to then appeal to him emotionally on the basis of their long relationship to let them live. He could have all the money. All they wanted was their lives. If he'd let them go ashore with their passports they'd swear never to bother him again, never to let anyone know that Span and Yovi Barrman existed. It was Yovi's idea that this entreaty would work on Jerry only if she abased herself, begged, sniveled, made him feel all-powerful, deific, unconquerable, and if she did it with Span present, standing by, acquiescent, passive, silent. She knew Jerry well, and he would not let them live out of pity or kindness, only out of some mad contempt for them, the way a matador turns his back on a noncombative bull. "It's an acting job," Yovi said, "for the highest pay any star could ever demand."

"Let's hope we don't close out of town."

"We may never open. Unless groveling turns out to be absolutely de rigueur, darling, I shan't do it."

As a last precaution, in case Yovi's act was a flop, Span felt in the lining of the large suitcase for his hunting knife. It was gone.

Each had secretly clung to an iota of hope that their fears were fantasies. This gone, they kissed each other fervently before leaving the safety of the stateroom.

"This isn't good-bye, darling." Yovi whispered. "The Skook will save us, because we've both been purified. I love you."

"I love you, too, Yov, and I'd rather die with you than survive you."

She was incongruously calm. He hoped she couldn't read his thought: Has she gone mad, to be able to joke about The Skook at a time like this?

They put on the orange nylon foul-weather jackets. Then, like summer lovers getting off the ferry in Nantucket, they wrestled their luggage up to the salon, groaning comically and—somehow transmuting their inner horror by a strange psychological chemistry—giving good imitations of carefree, anticipatory vacationers, with laughter, quips, and snatches of tuneless song.

The storm had almost blown itself out, but the waves were still high, with steep forward sides, and the night was still black with a low, glowering sky. Jerry was quartering to the waves. He had taken way off the vessel, and it seemed to be holding itself proudly stable in the turbulence. He stood sideways at the wheel, steering with one hand, the other in the pocket of his Windbreaker. He hailed Span and Yovi with horrible metallic good cheer.

"Hey, kids, everything's working for us. Weather's starting to behave, and look alongside to starboard—we've even got company."

At first Span and Yovi saw nothing. Then they made out two large vertical fins slicing along about thirty feet out on the starboard beam, visible mainly because of the trail of phosphorescence they were leaving.

"Nice to have an escort, huh?" Jerry said.

"Maybe they're just lonely," Yovi said. Span was proud that she could make a joke with such a truly light voice.

Jerry laughed, a short burst of mirthlessness. "Oh, right. Sharks get lonely a lot. Very sentimental people, sharks." Unhurriedly, and with seemingly no special attention, he took his right hand from the pocket of his Windbreaker. It held a .45 automatic, black and plump. He aimed it casually at them. "I don't want to use this. I like you guys, both of you, believe it or not. I mean, not *like,* really, but admire. You showed me something, Span, hanging on there in that God-damned cave for—what, six?—six months, and then digging out. Shit, man, you make a hibernating bear look like a piker. You're a real spunky guy, and you know what? I think Yovi really does honest-to-God love you, whatever that means. How long it'll last, who knows? But for now at least you have each other. Okay by me. I had the use of 'er for a while, no strings, so maybe this is best, huh? Onward and upward. But the money's a different matter. I'm sorry, kids, I really want it all, not just half. So look. You put the dinghy in the water, Span, on the leeward side—that's to starboard, in this case; oh, I forgot, old Navy man, sorry—and put your stuff in it, except for the expensive weekend bag, the one with the money—Oh, I checked. You'll be okay. You have your passports, and the dinghy has a cute little outboard motor. You'll be on the beach in no time, broke, but—like I say—you have each other. Whattaya say, Span, you know how to launch a dinghy, don't you, old swab-jockey like you? Better get started."

"That'll be just fine with us, Jerry," Span said. He measured each word out in a flat monotone. He went aft then without hesitation, leaving Yovi in the pilothouse with Jerry.

"What about the sharks?" she asked.

"What about 'em? They don't really feed on inflated rubber dinghies, no matter how lonely they get." He moved two levers and she heard the twin diesels hum together as the yacht picked up speed. "Got to keep enough way on to steer this mother, otherwise she may twist around on us and broach." He flipped several switches, and lights above and all about them perforated the night. "Got to give Span something to see by."

The lights spilled over to the surrounding water. Yovi saw that a third dorsal had joined the first two. She crossed to the starboard rail and leaned out to watch Span, trying to look as nonthreatening as possible.

Jerry held the heavy pistol at his side, not pointing it.

Span could not remember his small-boat seamanship. He was not sure now he'd ever really known it. He removed the little outboard with its push-button electric starter and lowered the orange dinghy by its bow painter. When the stern hit the water it floated out, bumping a curious shark. The shark, which looked to be about seven feet long to Span—smaller than the others—circled swiftly and inspected the new object, his snout and cold eyes awash momentarily. He found it not worth his interest. Span slacked off on the stern line, and the dinghy floated parallel to the yacht. He looped the bight of the bow painter through an open chock, and carried the loose end with him as he lowered the outboard gently by a hand line. Then he went down the Jacob's ladder with the end of the dinghy's bow line and passed it through the ring where the other end was tied, and stopped it with a simple half hitch. Then he secured the motor in place in the stern and pushed the starter button. It started. He left it idling as he climbed back up on deck and went forward for the bags.

"Hand me the one with the money," Jerry said.

Span brought it forward. Jerry waved the pistol toward him. "That's far enough. Put it down."

Span put it down.

"Shove it toward me with your foot."

Span shoved.

"Far enough," Jerry said. He waved the pistol.

Span backed away.

"Yovi, get on your hands and knees."

Yovi obeyed.

"Now crawl to the bag and open it."

When she had done so he knelt in place with the pistol to her head, let go of the wheel, stuck his free hand into the bag and hurriedly, without looking, confirmed its contents. The wheel spun violently and the bow swung to starboard. He straightened up and grabbed the wheel and fought with it to get back on his heading. "God-damned son of a bitch! Don't want to fuck up this late in the deal, do we? Okay, kids, bon voyage."

Yovi smiled and said: "Bye, Jerry." He did not respond, but when he looked at her she saw the same glittery pitch-black gemstone eyes she'd seen the night he wanted to murder Span in the apartment.

Span was waiting for her in the dinghy when she arrived at the starboard beam. Barely loud enough for him to hear, she said: "I didn't even have to grovel."

"Not yet. Hand me the bags, quick."

One at a time she let them down to him and he placed them as nearly amidships as he could, side by side. As she started down the ladder she asked: "Do we have food and water?"

Span snapped at her in a tone she'd never heard: "Shut up and get your ass in the boat, God dammit!"

Imbued with his urgency, she scrambled down the floppy Jacob's ladder—a thing she had never done before—into his steadying arms.

"Sit in the bow, facing me! Right here! Quick!" He shoved her forward and she landed heavily on the bow thwart. He leaned over her and untied his half hitch and put the loose end of the bow line in her hands. "Hang on to this and throw it off when I tell you." Then he half crawled, half lunged aft and sat on the stern thwart and flipped the stern line as far away from the boat as possible to clear the propellers, then gunned the motor. "Release the line!" he shouted. "Throw it clear!"

The moment she obeyed he backed down with a jolting spurt of power and the line whipped through the chock and splashed in the water.

"Haul it in!" he yelled, continuing to back, "or it'll foul the screw!"

She fought the wet line desperately. His voice told her that split seconds counted, although she didn't know why. As the line landed in a tangle at her feet she felt the boat lurch forward. She grabbed the thwart beneath her with both hands. They skidded into a sharp turn to starboard, almost colliding with an inquisitive great hammerhead shark, its flat yard-wide head planing as it got a look at this strange moving object. Yovi shrieked as the dorsal passed close aboard, then rose above them on a swell, looking as tall as the keel of a swamped racing sloop.

"Hang on and stay low!" Span yelled.

The dinghy, nothing more than an inflated oval tube with a flat bottom, skittered over the surface like a rubber ball. Span drove it astern of the yacht into a trough, and then along the bottom of it as far as he could out of sight of *Cranky*, before the water thrust them up again.

Jerry came out of a tight 180-degree turn and steered in the general direction of the dinghy, though he obviously had lost sight of it, as he was sweeping the surface with a powerful searchlight. It went past them, then snapped back on them and held them in its garish brightness. It was then that Span, facing forward, saw that a garden of dorsals of all sizes had suddenly sprouted around them. The crests of the swells were no longer breaking. Span sought another trough. Yovi understood now that he was engaged in some act of desperation to which she was not privy. He was acting on assumptions she had not made or did not understand, assumptions the sharks apparently shared with him. The sharks were closer now, more numerous, and more competitive for favored positions. There was something in the agitated motion of the dinghy, the alarmed buzz of its little motor, the timbre of Span's voice and the volume of it, the sudden tight turn of the larger boat, the long shaft of light stabbing out at them—something in these and other things, other unknown-to-man things—that drew these predators, excited them, brought them to the edge of mania. The great hammerhead bumped the tube near Yovi's hand, then slid one end of its grotesque head up over the side as she jerked away, almost falling out the other side. The single eye on the end of the long flat shape met hers for a moment, malevolent and merciless, then slid out of sight, leaving scratches down the side of the rubberized cloth.

Span saw her cringing from the sight, then covering her eyes against the blinding searchlight. Then as the dinghy was lifted breathtakingly up he heard something whine off into the night from beside him in the water, and a cracking sound like a breaking dry twig from behind him, and he knew Jerry was firing up at them from a trough and a bullet had ricocheted off the side of the steep swell.

"Get down, Yov! God dammit, get down!"

Unable to see Span because of the white glare, she obeyed him instantly, sliding as far down as she could, her feet bumping the two suitcases, her head on the forward thwart.

Another bullet hit the water beside them with a popping splash, and then another.

Span threw the dinghy into a tight skidding turn and in a matter of seconds they were diving down the slope past *Cranky*, going in the opposite direction. They had momentarily escaped the searchlight. As they passed close under the port beam of *Cranky*, Span saw Jerry wrestling with the controls and the pistol and the searchlight, and heard him cursing.

Yovi screamed: "Jerry, no! You don't have to kill us, Jerry! We're not going to do anything against you, Jerry!"

Jerry's answer was to swing the now-cumbersome *Cranky* into a dangerous tight circle to try to keep from losing his prey in the darkness.

As they passed through the yacht's churning wake they heard Jerry fire again, but no sound of the bullet. Then *Cranky* was astern of them again, and Yovi could see her long tongue of light licking over the swell-crests as Span sought the hollows, sought to dive as *Cranky* rose, and then to rise as *Cranky* fell. And Span was astonished—astonished at the white face of Yovi, her angelic eyes, her sudden look of saintly rapture.

"Skook!" she cried, and it was not a scream but more of a song. "Skook! We need you! Help us! Save us, Skook!" Her eyes widened, a look of spiritual ecstasy transfixed her.

God, Span thought, she's lost her mind, like I did in the cave.

Then the searchlight found them, and Yovi, incandescing in it, stood straight for several seconds in the dancing, skating boat, incredibly not losing her balance, and cried out again in a high soprano liturgical chant: "Yes, Skook! Yes, Skook! Yes! I see you! Yes!"

Christ, Span thought, don't let her freak out and jump overboard, please. He tried to guess from the searchlight's erratic strokes what *Cranky* was doing.

"It's The Skook!" Yovi cried. "Span! Look!"

He almost caught her madness, almost turned, but at that moment a vertical fin two feet tall appeared beside him within arm's reach, then sank out of sight. The black water and the black sky did not allow him to see shadows under the surface, so for a moment he thought it had gone, but as the brute dived the scythelike caudal broke the surface, switching, and barely missed clubbing him before it, too, slipped through to the other side of the opaque surface. Christ, if Jerry can manage to hit our little balloon these bastards'll finish the job, Span thought. Won't take long, won't take any longer or hurt any worse than the cave-sea bear, but I'd better have gone to him and got it over with, so we wouldn't even be here. Christ, I got out of the cave, saved my own ass, and now I'm causing Yovi to lose hers, though God knows in the shape she's in she won't feel a thing.

Her face, as he looked at her now, was celestially lighted. The searchlight had lost them again and yet, he saw her, supernaturally white, her wide eyes the color of drops of seawater falling through blue air.

He had not heard shots in several seconds. Now the light trembled on them momentarily and he heard two in quick succession as Yovi's soft enchanted voice spoke to both him and The Skook, although her eyes never wavered from whatever wondrous thing she saw or thought she saw astern of them:

"Oh, Span, he's just as you said. Oh, yes, Skook, yes! Oh,

Span, he knocked the pistol up in the air just as Jerry fired! Oh, God, he's aiming at us again!"

Then she stood up again, shot straight up in such a way, so rigid, that she seemed sure to fall. Her eyes popped, her mouth opened to a long vertical oval. She sucked in a gulp of air like a person about to blow out birthday candles, then held it, shocked into immobility.

"Sit down, God dammit, Yov! Sit down!"

But she neither sat nor fell. Some unknown inner gyroscope held her upright in the leaping boat, her eyes fixed on something behind Span, out of his sight. Then she exhaled with a horrified gust and her eyes gushed tears. "No. No."

She whispered the words, but Span heard them. Then he heard Jerry scream, and in spite of himself he twisted around to see the yacht almost upon them, but listed forty-five degrees to port, and Jerry falling over the pilothouse rail into the water, the water lit by all the topside lights of *Cranky,* now tilted so close to the surface, and at least twenty vertical fins streaking toward him as he splashed.

There was only time for Jerry to scream "Help! Oh, God! Help me!" before Span lost sight of him.

"Go back! Go back!" Yovi screamed. Her voice was human again, not angelic. "Span, go back! We've got to help him!"

"Sit down! I can't turn unless you sit!"

She seemed surprised to find herself upright. She dropped to the thwart and took a firm grip. "Please hurry!" Then she gagged at what she saw, and made a retching sound.

Span spun the dinghy around and found himself steering directly toward the feeding frenzy like a man unwilling to see what he was seeing: a great red foam rising on the black sea. The yacht had righted itself and was running away unguided. The crazed sharks ripped at everything in reach of their teeth, including each other. The death orgy built to fury. Span righted his mind in time to swerve away and open the throttle and bounce them wildly away at top speed. Their tiny bubble reared and plunged and skidded and soared. Span and Yovi clung to it with all their strength. After five minutes that seemed an hour he cut the engine and tilted the propeller out of the water;

they began to drift. He spoke low: "I don't want to give 'em any clues—any noise, smell of oil, anything. Let's just sit here and be quiet and maybe they'll forget about us and go away. In the state they're in, if there's a tiger or a great white among 'em, they'll eat our boat."

He saw that she wasn't listening. Her face still shone with the light of her vision.

The wind slowed; the swells grew
longer and began to flatten out. The drifting dinghy, alone in
the night, was lifted and held and turned around and then sent
swooping down the gentling forward slopes stern first, or sideways, or sometimes spinning according to the whim of *Neptunus
Rex*. Yovi and Span sat in silence, waiting for the return of the
tall fins, but they did not come.

They had no idea whether they were drifting seaward or
shoreward; there were no markers in the sky. After an hour of
drifting they were suddenly battered by torrential rains that
threatened to fill the dinghy. Span took off his deck shoes,
handed one to Yovi, and they bailed. Neither spoke, it being
understood that any sound at all might be the one that brought
bloodthirsty visitors. They were even careful not to scrape the
bottom of the dinghy with the shoes, and to empty the water
soundlessly over the side. In flashes of lightning they looked
about them and saw nothing but long hills of water speckled
by rain.

Then the cloudburst stopped and the solid overcast thinned. The cumulonimbus parted and stars winked through—one at first, then three, then whole formations. Span searched his memory for their meanings. Yovi recognized the formations but knew absolutely nothing about their navigational significance, explaining that it had never mattered to her before which way she was going. Finally Span found a constellation that meant something to him:

"The Big Dipper," he whispered. "Look. And there's Polaris."

It was time to make their move. He started the motor, set it on slow speed, and swung the boat around to put the North Star on his right. They glided uphill and down, almost without sound for several minutes as Span scanned the water on both sides, looking for fins.

Yovi surprised him with a tranquil smile. "We're going to be all right."

The craziness is still on her, Span thought.

Then they topped a swell and they saw about three miles ahead the lights of a big ship, not only the glitter of the masthead lights but both the green and red sidelights. It was bearing directly down on them. Span swung north and gunned his motor and they began again to skitter and skate over the changing slopes. When he was sure he was well clear of what he recognized now as a cargo vessel, he slowed again and headed west.

"Our unfriendly neighbors are probably following that one, waiting for garbage," Span said, trying to ease Yovi back into his world. "Let's hope they're well fed and deafened by those big engines. Kind of ironical, huh? Here we are in this flimsy thing headed for God-knows-where, not knowing if a great white is going to cruise up and bite us in two, or if we have enough gas to reach shore, and yet, we can't afford to be rescued. Here we are in *Cranky*'s lifeboat, and *Cranky*'s off somewhere, cruising along with a million and half bucks on board, and no skipper, nobody, a ghost ship full of money. How do we explain, and who'd believe us? The man who borrowed the yacht is missing, and here we are, alive. And some of the money—we don't know how much—is with us."

Yovi giggled. "I'd forgotten. No wonder I have that full feeling.

I never thought money could make me uncomfortable, but this has."

Thank God, Span thought, she's back. "Well, fetch it out, honey. Let's see how rich we'll be if we ever hit the beach."

Again she giggled. "Well, don't drive so bumpily, please." She slid forward off the thwart, turned her back to him, got on her knees, and modestly extracted the roll of bills. At the same time he took his from various pockets. They were pleased to find they had seventy-one hundred-dollar bills.

"We'd better figure out a story," Span said, "in case we're rescued against our will." He steered west at moderate speed. Behind them the eastern sky was starting to lighten. "We're going to be accused of murdering Jerry. We may as well face it."

"No one is going to believe The Skook saved us from him," Yovi said.

"Yovi, listen—"

"Not even you." Her tone was softly regretful, and her look both shamed him and forgave him. "Don't you want to know what happened?"

When I was the one who needed to talk about The Skook, Span thought, she listened, and she didn't ridicule me. "Yes, Yov, I do. Tell me what happened."

"Well, I called The Skook. I don't know if I actually called out loud, or—"

"You did."

"Well, he came. At first I saw this light, this crazy sort of fluttering iridescence in the air, the air over the bridge, and then it just swooped, sort of Roman-candle-ish—quite beautiful, actually—just swooped in a curve right onto Jerry, or into him— it was rather blinding for a moment—but it hit his arms, and the pistol, from underneath, and knocked his hands upward, and the pistol went off again—I saw the flash—but of course it was firing into the air. And then Jerry staggered back and yelled something—I don't know what—and then The Skook— and it was The Skook, Span, exactly as you described him— with those sharp wings and big duck feet and big ears, all flapping at once, and those bright eyes on long stalks, and all those marvelous colors—It was The Skook! He hovered for a moment and I saw him clearly. Then Jerry came to the rail again and tried to aim his pistol with both hands, and The Skook darted in like a streak of light and hit the yacht up front there—you know, on the bow—and made it bounce high and roll, and then roll the other way, and Jerry staggered. Then The Skook swooped in and shoved, and everything was whirring soundlessly just the way you said—feet, ears, wings—even the long tail was waggling like a snake! And he shoved, and the yacht rolled, and rolled, till it looked as though it was going to roll right over, and Jerry screamed—at least you heard him scream."

"I heard the scream."

"It was horrible. He screamed and lost his balance and fell overboard, and—" She shuddered.

"I saw the rest," Span said. He decided there was no point in trying to talk sense to her about The Skook till time had done its work the way it had done for him.

In less than an hour Span sighted land. At first it appeared to be a lowland with jungle coming down to the very edge of the water, but as they drew closer and the sky paled they saw the looming dark hills, and then, to their consternation, a half dozen primitive huts ranged along the shore. They heard a dog bark briefly, and a cock crow, but saw no human beings.

Span turned south and aimed for a landfall in the middle of the longest stretch of jungle between two huts. He cut the motor and paddled. As soon as the water got shallow enough he jumped out and hauled the boat up onto the narrow strip of sand. Yovi stepped out and the two of them dragged the dinghy into the jungle far enough to make its immediate discovery unlikely. They lifted their two pieces of luggage and the plastic box of emergency rations out and immediately plunged into the wall of ferns and trees and vines in a kind of mindless urgency to separate themselves from the evidence of any association with *Cranky.* They walked all morning with the energy of fear, breaking through the tangles by shoving their suitcases ahead of them. They seldom saw even glimpses of the sky. It was brightening—they knew from the greenish light that filtered through the leafy vaulted ceiling, and the occasional column of misted sunlight that found its way down to the wet rug of rotting vegetation that squished under their feet. Monkeys screeched at them, and birds with short wide wings and, Yovi said, "more and prettier colors than The Skook" swooped and darted among the seemingly impenetrable curtains of leaves and lianas, magically colliding with nothing, and screaming, whistling, and squawking their alarms. Span became suddenly breathless. They stopped. He trembled. There was no place even to sit. They stood in a two-inch-deep puddle of brown water. He would be okay in a minute, he said. They looked about them as he took deep breaths of the saturated air. Directly in front of them, two strides away, something caused Span to study a pattern of beautiful glistening horizontal curves. Slowly his eyes distinguished a brown tan-blotched snake, about ten feet long and as big around as Yovi's leg, draped on a low limb, absolutely motionless. Yovi, her arm around him both in affection and support, felt him start. She followed his eyes, saw the boa, signaled Span with a squeeze. They took a step back, then moved off to their right with renewed spirit.

"See," Span panted, "I told you I'd be all right in a minute."

At noon they sat on their suitcases in a clearing the size of a large closet, and ate some of their emergency rations—hard biscuits, peanut butter, chocolate.

"Either we're close to the home of a little old lady who keeps cats," Span said, "or there's a jaguar around here. All cats smell like cats, and I smell a cat."

"So do I," Yovi said, but she did not seem perturbed.

They decided to leave their bags so as to make better time. Span found the bare hipbone of a large animal, and decided to carry it as a weapon. He had been looking for a stick, but the only ones available were rotten. They had nothing with which to cut a green one. The hipbone was eighteen inches long, and heavy. It would be useless against a jaguar, but it was a psychological comfort, and it was helpful in knocking the vines aside to clear a path.

They continued to smell the cat, but saw nothing. Toward evening they came to a large clearing where two elderly Indian women were digging medicinal roots. Yovi spoke to them in Spanish. They understood, they said, *"un poco, no mucho."* Yovi showed them her British passport with her new name.

"Pasaporte. Inglesa." She made them understand that she and Span were tourists, had left their bus to take a short walk, had got lost, and had spent the whole day wandering in the jungle.

The women wanted to know if they had seen any snakes.

Not only had they almost walked right into the jaws of a boa lying on a limb, Yovi told them, they had been followed by what must have been a jaguar.

The two old women, when they finally understood what Yovi was telling them, laughed till they had tears in their eyes, slapping their legs with both hands, and showing two mouths almost devoid of teeth except for a few yellow stumps. They finally told Yovi the reason for their mirth: While she and her man had been worrying about a harmless boa and a rarely harmful jaguar, they had been at risk every moment of stepping within reach of the fangs of *el Capitán Matapronto*—Captain Killquick, the fer-de-lance, deadliest snake in the Mexican jungle.

"They are saying, dear," Yovi explained, "that it's a miracle we're still alive."

Epilogue

In 1979, Judge Walter Young-
ford of Lambertville, New Jersey, retired from the bench. This
occasion was toasted for several days and nights at The Swan,
much to the alarm of Irma Youngford, who feared for her husband's liver. At these celebrations Wally, as he was called by
most of the regulars, announced that he had only dedicated
himself for forty years to the law in order to finance his real
career, which was about to begin: archaeology. For two decades
Wally had spent his Sundays digging along the banks of the
Delaware (Span, on his way to his fishing spot, had often waved
to him—a tall, pink-faced man with wispy white hair, carrying
a small pick and spade and wearing a floppy wide-brimmed hat),
collecting arrowheads and other Indian artifacts. As he grew
older and spent more of his after-court hours in the convivial
climate of The Swan, Wally's tendency to corpulence became
more pronounced. By the time he retired, with his reputation
for integrity and evenhanded justice secure (typically, he had

disqualified himself as judge in the Space Angel trial because he had presided at Yovi and Abe's divorce settlement; and the victim's company, Barrman Home Improvements, had once roofed his home in a satisfactory manner at a fair price), he had become, in appearance, a tall, beardless, pink-jowled, round-bellied Santa Claus. He had spent several vacations studying pre-Columbian sites in Mexico, had memorized the First Commandment ("Eat nothing raw, drink only beer or rum—without ice cubes"), and considered that he and Irma were ready for their first real dig.

To commemorate Wally's many years at the same table, in the left corner farthest from the front door where he could look up and see *The Harvard Crimson* framed on the wall above the end of the bar, Jim and his partners had mounted a small brass plaque on the paneled wall above the church bench where Wally sat:

> RESERVED FOR
> JUDGE WALTER
> YOUNGFORD

Dedicating the plaque and toasting Wally in Mexican rum on the July night before Wally and Irma were scheduled to catch their flight to Mexico, Jim said: "If Robert Benchley can have his name on a table at 21, Wally sure as hell deserves his at The Swan."

Everybody cheered. That night Irma suffered a coronary occlusion and was rushed to Hunterdon Medical Center. Two days later, instead of installing his beloved Irma in the Hotel Colonial in Vera Cruz, Wally buried her in the two-grave plot they had reserved for themselves in the tiny cemetery at Buckingham Friends School. Unable to have babies of her own, Irma had said she wanted to spend her eternity near the laughter of children.

Left alone in the old house with only his Lenape arrowheads and a few pre-Columbian figures for company, the judge fell into a deep depression. He began going early to The Swan and staying late. He sat on the church pew in the corner in front of his plaque and had his glass filled with rum and soda as soon as it was empty. Some nights he switched to Scotch, others to bourbon. These were the significant variations in his routine. On rare late evenings one of the regulars—Roger the oil man, or Martin the doctor, or Frank the investor—having seen his foot falter, would offer to walk him home. He gained weight. Already fleshy, he seemed to swell from the neck to the beltline like a woman in her ninth month. His blue eyes, which once danced and darted, all but disappeared behind folds of skin, and his complexion changed from pink to red on the cheeks and nose and to gray on the jowls. Visitors seldom saw the plaque proclaiming his table because he was usually sitting in front of it.

Then, suddenly, after almost a year, the judge underwent a dramatic change. No one was sure what had caused it. Some say it was the proximity of the anniversary of Irma's death that made him aware of how his life was slipping away. Others theorized the reason was the embarrassing night he fell down in the men's room and had to be carried home and put to bed. He did not return to The Swan for two days after this incident. When he did stroll in, looking rested, he greeted his friends and the young bartender with banter, seated himself in front of the plaque, ordered a Barrilito and soda, drank it slowly, and left. His visits for the next week were equally short. He refused dinner invitations. He appeared to be losing weight. Then, three weeks after the humiliating accident in the men's room, he announced that he had arranged to go on a dig in Olmec country in the state of Tabasco, Mexico, and that he was leaving at five o'clock the following morning. All the denizens of The Swan were heartened by Wally's apparent recovery from his deep mourning. Appropriate toasts were offered and answered. In contrast to his actions on many previous occasions, the honoree prudently limited himself to small sips of his rum and soda, and left early with a sure and springy step.

Thus it was that, in the natural course of events, Judge Walter Randolph Youngford, retired, found himself in the Parque la Venta in Villahermosa, Tabasco, Mexico, on an oven-hot July afternoon in 1980. His tender pink face was shaded by a wide-brimmed Panama hat. His seersucker suit—the jacket flung over his shoulder in abandonment of his longtime personal dress code—felt like mohair to the judge, stinging his legs. Rivulets of sweat ran from the underside of his belly down the inner side of his thighs. And yet, it all seemed worth the effort. He was staring, entranced, at a colossal basalt head, six and a half feet tall, weighing, he had read, twenty tons, carved by the mysterious Olmecs circa 1000 B.C. Where had they come from and where had they gone? Why were the features of the colossal heads Negroid? Had a race of giant Negroes appeared out of the mists one day and been declared gods? If so, why had they been recorded in heads only, heads carved in great blocks of basalt that had to have been transported—how?—over hundreds of miles of roadless and bridgeless swampland. Why no torsos? And why were the heads buried? Had the giants these heads depicted—all with similar Negroid lips protruding beyond the flat noses—once walked among the Olmecs? If so, why had they not left their stamp on the Olmec features, on succeeding peoples?

As he marveled at these mysteries the judge felt someone staring at him. He turned to see a small boy, no more than seven, golden-skinned, with long blond hair secured by a figured headband, and dressed in the hand-woven bright colors of the Totonacs. The boy waited for the judge's attention; then, in unaccented English and with a sweet shy smile, he said:

"A message for you, sir." He darted forward and thrust a folded sheet of paper in the judge's hand. Then he ran, his bare feet flying over the rough pathway, and disappeared among the orange-flowered banana trees and the other jungle flora of the outdoor museum. The judge stared after the boy, astonished. With a sort of dread he unfolded the message. It was written in delicate feminine penmanship, neat and simple. It read: "Dear Judge Youngford. If your heart is strong, perhaps you would like to see two long-lost acquaintances whom you no doubt believe to be dead. As a clue: Do you recall a golden anklet which you ruled to be the property of the person on whose ankle the only open link had been soldered shut? We'll call you tonight

at your hotel. Please keep this matter in absolute confidence."
The note was signed "Reborn."

The judge, already feeling light-headed because of the heat
and somewhat enchanted from his communion with the misty
abysm of time, heard himself muttering: "Good God. Mrs. Spiegel. No, Barrman." Had it been fourteen years since the Spiegel
divorce? And more than eight since Barrman died and she disappeared with that lawyer, that whatsisname—Odessa?

So they hadn't died after all. Amazing. They had actually
concocted some intricate plot for reasons known only to themselves, and had disappeared, to live in a faraway place. A com-
mon-enough fantasy, seldom acted out.

Yes, the judge said to himself, I'd love to see them. Jerry
Odessa never was one of my favorite people—in fact, I always
thought of him as a giant rat—but it will be interesting to hear
their story and it'll make good talk at The Swan when I get
back.

At seven o'clock that evening, as the judge was relaxing in
the garish fake luxury of the Hotel Villahermosa Viva, sipping
his third Barrilito with soda—and no ice—the phone rang. He
snatched at it before it completed its first ring. He had been
waiting for this call since six, feeling very alone and very old,
hoping the author of the note would not change her mind. The
voice of the caller was Yovi's. She offered no explanation and
no details in the short, polite conversation: "We're very excited
at the possibility of seeing you, Your Honor," she lilted, "but
we're a bit frightened too. It's only because you're who you are
that we trust you. Could you meet us tomorrow at a little place
that we know on the road to Teapa?"

He arrived at the appointed hour next evening. It was growing
dark. His driver did not know the place and almost drove past
it, as it was fifty meters back from the narrow road in a small
clearing, and identified only by a wooden sign with the word
fonda crudely painted on it, nailed to a tree. It was a low pal-
metto building with a thatched roof and dim lighting. There
were no cars parked in front of it. It appeared to be a natives-
only place, gringos not invited. The judge saw no one, but smoke
rose through a hole in the roof, and he smelled meat roasting.

A dog came out and growled at him. He felt a chill of anxiety as he paid his driver and sent him away. The driver, a surly, flat-faced fellow whom the judge imagined to be a cutthroat in his spare time, accepted the generous pay without comment, smirked at the judge as though he were the craziest of the many *idiotas* it was his fate to have to tolerate in this world, and drove away, turning in a tight circle and skidding to be sure the rich *norteamericano* knew how he felt.

The judge walked into the empty restaurant and sat on one of the high wooden stools at the bar. For a moment or two, as no one appeared, he thought he had made a serious error. Then he heard children laughing. The sound came from the rear of the *fonda,* outside. Then he stood up as a full-figured woman materialized out of the shadows. She was dressed simply in a white cotton sack dress and huaraches. The dress was sleeveless, scooped low in front, and short, stopping just above her knees. As she advanced, smiling, he saw that it was Yowa Spiegel Barrman, metamorphosed. Her long blond hair was sun-streaked straw and copper, and cut straight across just below her shoulders by a pair of careless and crude—yet somehow apt—scissors. Her face was rounder but beautiful now instead of merely pretty. Her skin was tawny and seemed to glow. She wore no makeup; there was darting light in her blue-green eyes. The greatest change the judge saw was in her walk. At the time of her divorce from Spiegel her walk had been constructed (the judge remembered vividly) of several slender sections that did not all move in unison, balanced on feet that seemed to skim the ground uncertainly for short distances, like baby birds learning to fly. Her walk now, fourteen years later, was surer, springier, more compact, and somehow lighter, in spite of her added weight. A woman of heart-stopping allure—at least to the judge's eye— had replaced the easy slip of a girl. The dignity, the sense of self he had noted even back then, was still intact, though part of a composite now in which it was a perfect fit.

She offered her hand. He took it; it was not as soft as he remembered it.

"Judge Youngford."

"Mrs. Barrman."

"Thank you so much for coming."

"I wouldn't've missed it. I'm delighted to see you—not only alive, but beautiful."

"Thank you. I'm sorry to have been so melodramatic. I think you'll understand when you see the surprise I have for you."

"I believe I'm prepared for it."

"I hope so." She hesitated, smiling impishly into his eyes, then turned to the rear and made a gesture.

Span stepped out of the shadows. He wore loose cotton *pantalones* tied with a string, a pullover shirt, and native sandals. He did not come forward immediately, but waited for a reaction from Youngford, who remained thoroughly baffled. Now fifty-seven, slender, deeply tanned, his hair long and white and held in place by a beaded headband, Span had undergone such a physical and spiritual transformation that even if the judge had not thought him long dead he would not have been able to recognize him. Furthermore he had been expecting to see another man, and it was not possible to fit what he saw here into the skin of Jerry Odessa.

The judge passed his hands over his eyes as though to clear his vision and shook his head. "I'm sorry. I—"

Span walked up to him and held out a calloused brown hand. The judge, still lost, took it.

Yovi said: "I told you to be prepared for a shock, Judge, and I hope you are. This is my husband, Span Barrman."

Yovi's warnings had failed to prepare the judge for this moment. He was seeing a ghost, and he was shaken. "But—but—"

"I know," Span laughed. "I'm dead. It's a long story. Would you like a drink?"

The telling took Span six rounds of rum, a dinner of *cabrito asado,* and half a bottle of Mexican brandy, which, but for the rum that went before it and paved its way, would have tasted like liquid fire. By the time he arrived at his escape, he and the judge were both drunk. The judge was also spellbound. Yovi, who had drunk only white wine before and during dinner and a sip of the harsh brandy after, waited until Span had finished, then challenged him: "Didn't you leave out something important?"

"No."

"Perhaps the most important thing."

"I don't want to tell about that. I don't want the judge to think I lost my mind down there."

"Then I'll tell him," Yovi said.

"Would you folks do me a signal service," the judge said, slurring his sibilants, "and call me Wally?"

"Oh, of course. Thank you," Yovi said.

"Sure, Wally," Span said.

Then Yovi, over Span's drunken protests, told Wally the history of The Skook. Wally was in his cups deep enough that her story seemed perfectly logical to him. If there could be a blind cave-sea bear two stories tall, why couldn't there be a Skook?

During this long, animated discussion three Indian oil-field workers entered the *fonda*. Their khakis were black with crude and their faces and hands smudged. They had not bothered to wash after leaving their work. This was not the first place they had stopped for a drink that evening. Though the *fonda* was nearly empty they chose the table nearest the three *norteamericanos*. They ordered mescal and began to talk in an Indian dialect while staring insolently at Yovi. The barman became uneasy. Span and Wally, who had their backs to them, paid no attention to them. Yovi did her best to ignore them. As they got drunker they talked louder. One of them began to wave to Yovi and to make obscene gestures. Finally Yovi, who was just beginning to tell Wally the answer to the biggest riddle of all—how she and Span happened to be together in this place—stopped herself and said softly: "Excuse me." She rose. Span and Wally assumed she was going to the ladies' room, and were shocked when she stopped at the table of the three *obreros* and began to speak to them firmly in their language. They became very polite, almost cowed, immediately, and hung on her every word.

"What's she telling them?" Wally asked.

"Damned if I know," Span said. He tried to take a drink and shake his head at the same time. He spilled brandy on his shirt.

Yovi returned to her seat, still calm. "I'm sorry," she said.
"What happened?" Span asked.

Yovi held her answer as the three *obreros* rose abruptly, left
money for their drinks, bowed with great respect toward the
judge, and shuffled out sideways like crabs, still bowing.

"They were speaking a dialect, Nahuatl," Yovi said. "Naturally
they—"

"Isn't she fantastic!" Span burst out. Drunkenness had made
him boyish. "She's a tabula rasa. Picks up languages like a dog
picks up ticks. Nahuatl! She learned it just by being around it,
by osmosis! And Totonac too! She already knew Spanish, and
French, and Italian, and German, and—" He reached for her
and she placed her hand in his, smiling shyly. Wally thought
they looked like young lovers. "Christ, sweetheart," Span finished, "I'm proud of you."

"Thank you," she whispered. She seemed to blush in the dim
light as their eyes held for several moments as though they
were alone. Then she looked at Wally and said: "Excuse us."
Then she said softly to Span, squeezing his hand: "I'm proud
of you too." Then she broke her eye contact with him and
continued in a matter-of-fact voice: "Those chaps were discussing waiting around here until we left, and then beating us
and robbing us and raping me. They were pretty upset when
they found out I understood them."

"I can imagine," Wally said.

"Honey, you're great!" Span burst out again with his drunken
enthusiasm.

"So I just told them politely that having listened to them for
an hour, I knew where they were from, what their first names
were, and where they worked. I told them the tall, distinguished
gentleman was a *jefe* in the American Drilling Company, and
if they left quietly I would do my best to see that they were not
fired."

"You see? You see?" Span beamed. "And they left! She's a
genius!"

"It's a good thing too," Wally said. "I'll bet there are no
telephones or police within miles."

Span reached under his baggy shirt, brought out a .38 automatic, flashed it briefly, then put it away. "No, Your Honor (Span had not been one of the regulars at The Swan. Calling the judge Wally was going to require practice), I mean Wally, you don't understand. Yovi was trying to keep them from getting hurt."

"We don't actually depend on the *federales* out here," Yovi said.

"If we have a problem," Span confided, leaning close to Wally as though this part of the conversation, unlike the rest, were a big secret, "we handle it ourselves."

Wally peered hard at Yovi, squinting. Then he looked at Span, then at her again. He swayed in his chair. "Maybe we could have some coffee," he muttered. Then: "Excuse me." He rose unsteadily and went looking for the men's room.

Later, fortified with bitter black coffee, he listened as carefully as he could as Yovi finished with the story of how The Skook had saved them from Jerry's bullets and caused Jerry to fall among the sharks.

"God in heaven," Wally said, genuinely moved. "I thought I was too old to get goose bumps, but I got 'em."

"Span doesn't believe me. He says it was St. Elmo's fire."

Span put his hand out and stroked her hair in a way that said he couldn't believe her but he loved her.

"Span is afraid to give life to something metaphysical," Yovi continued. "It makes him doubt his sanity. But if a man is the only person in a cave, and sees something, what are the criteria of sanity? Against what is sanity to be measured? There is no other perception to be used as a benchmark. In just such a situation he saw The Skook, but now he's afraid of his own perceptions. I'm not. I know he saw The Skook, because I saw him too."

They sat in awkward silence. Span smiled and waggled his head drunkenly from side to side in negation. Yovi stubbornly nodded yes.

The judge finally said: "If I were on the bench I wouldn't accept her testimony. I'd accept yours, Span. But I'm retired. I'm old, retired, unwived, and drunk. I believe you, Yovi." He had tears in his eyes. Yovi moved her chair close to his and hugged him.

Span applauded vigorously and cheered. "I'm glad! Wally, I'm glad you believe her! You're great, Wally!"

The proprietor took the clapping as a signal. He appeared, fawning, hoping to be able to give them a final bill. Span scowled at him and he withdrew to a discreet distance.

"We got ashore with only $7,100," Yovi continued, "and a thousand of that went into bribes, and for a year we had no income, so you can see it hasn't been easy. But Span has been selling articles on his archaeological explorations, and has been rewarded by museums for a few pieces he's found—which would've made us rather rich if we'd channeled them out to foreign collectors—"

"I refuse to be a looter," Span said.

The proprietor coughed, and this time the reminder took effect. He had been engaged in advance by Span to drive the judge back to Villahermosa. They followed him out the side door to a Chevrolet with crumpled fenders, slick tires, a broken windshield, and—Wally would soon discover—no shock absorbers and no muffler. But it started. The engine ran on all six. Yovi embraced Wally. "Must you join that silly old expedition tomorrow? We'd love to have you come up to our house for lunch and see our children and Span's studio and just catch up on things. Please."

Wally hardly looked out the window as Span drove them in his Jeep eastward into the coastal mountains. The July weather in the region was notorious for its unpredictability. Only one thing was certain: It would be extreme. It had been suffocatingly hot when they left Wally's hotel; then, a half hour into their drive, they had run into a wall of rain; it continued now with monsoon-force winds. The four-wheel-drive Jeep crawled in fifty-foot visibility on narrowing upward-slanting roads. Wally was glad. He was sworn to reveal nothing of the whereabouts of his friends' home, and the less he knew, the easier his secret would be to keep. He was proud that after the peculiar history of their early relationship—judge and judged—they had taken him so to their hearts. He felt privileged. This adventure was bigger than any expedition into already-picked-over Olmec leavings could ever be.

Cramping the Jeep around sharp turns in the one-way rock road, which had to be climbed in low gear, Span brought them in sight of the house. It was perched on what seemed the very top of a promontory. On one side—Wally's side—of the road was a sheer drop that disappeared in mists.

The windows in the basalt-block walls glowed with light and distorted images. Span had parked as close to the front door as possible. An Indian woman with a wide guileless smile hurried out of the house with hooded ponchos for the men. Wally stepped out of the Jeep and she threw the garment over him. She herself was in a rough cotton dress, which was immediately soaked, as was her bare head.

"This is Huauchi," Yovi called from the open door, and Huauchi nodded vigorously in greeting, throwing sprays of water off her head like a shaking dog. Then the children came charging and tumbling out, past Yovi, almost bowling her over. Naked except for shorts, barefoot, they flew into the rain with screeches of ecstasy and threw themselves on their father. Span, struggling to get under his poncho without getting wet, almost fell under their attack. The least assaultive, Wally saw, was the seven-year-old blond boy who had brought him the note in the Parque la Venta.

Yovi, to honor her guest, wore a hand-woven Mayan dress of many bright colors. She had pinned a cluster of several small wild orchids in her hair, purple on gold. Her small sun-browned feet were bare, the nails painted to match the brightest red in her dress. Wally felt a sad flush of memory when he saw something the dim light of the *fonda* had not revealed to him the night before: the rose-gold chain, now bearing a conspicuous platinum link, in place on her left ankle.

She saw his eye drawn to it. "Yes, still there," she laughed. Then, to Span: "Darling, I've got things on the fire. Would you give the judge a drink?"

Span led Wally to the living-room area to the right of the

entrance. Wally's eyes had already strayed there, and he was half prepared for the shock a full view would give him. It held more Mesoamerican archaeological treasures than most museums. Dominating it on what appeared to be a mahogany pedestal carved from one log was a thirteen-inch-tall Olmec man-jaguar bust of blue-green jade, a piece similar to but larger than the famous Kunz ax that the judge had often admired at the American Museum of Natural History. In one corner stood a six-foot-tall stela of a nude male with erect penis and royal headdress. In another corner, on a second, smaller pedestal—this one made of a round base, a round top, and a simple column of common basalt—was a magnificent jade dwarf. The judge could not suppress an exclamation of pure awe: "Good God." The walls in that third of the great room were lined with shelves, all full of artifacts—a clay vessel with the bas-relief figure of a woman curled around it, a Totonac "laughing boy," braziers with the faces of old men, braziers with man-jaguar faces, wooden masks, figurines of jade, jadeite, serpentine—a fortune in unique and irreplaceable pieces.

Span's workroom behind the house was a jumble of archaeological jigsaw puzzles: arms, legs, heads, headless torsos and potsherds, all lying about, waiting to be fitted together. The tables were full of brushes and glue pots and drawings. Picks and spades and probes and every imaginable archaeologist's tool filled the corners. The rain drummed so hard on the corrugated iron roof that Span motioned to Wally to return with him to the main house, where they could hear each other.

After a lunch of baked sea bass, roasted sweet corn, hot tortillas, squash, and beer, Wally requested directions to the bathroom. That morning he had recalled ruefully that in his drunkenness the night before he had forgotten his long-standing rule and had let the proprietor of the *fonda* put ice in his drink. Now, he had the inevitable result: ants in his stomach. He shook his plastic bottle of Kaopectate and drank several gulps of it. It would put the ants to sleep for the time being.

When he returned to the main room Span and Yovi had moved to the living-room area among the statuary, and Huauchi was serving brandy and coffee and a large tray of desserts—flan, guava jelly, coconut meat, mangoes, papayas, cookies. Wally paused on the way to joining them to look out on the now-bright world. They were high—at least four thousand feet, he guessed—above the Gulf of Mexico, which was spread out—half glowering gray and half sunstruck—before him as far as he could see. He remarked on the unexpected drama of it.

"Yes," Span said, "a view like that, into infinity, you might say, tends to keep everything in perspective."

The shadow of the mountain stretched out over the Bahia de Campeche. Yovi called the children and the servants to say good-bye to the guest. Huauchi offered him a flower. The children behaved decorously, except for the youngest, who ran in naked and screaming with glee.

"He tried to piss over the cliff again," the blond boy said, "and it blew back on him."

"*Bruto!*" Yovi squeaked at him through her musical laughter. She smacked him on his bare behind as he ran past.

The miscreant ran out, vastly pleased with himself.

"Will Daddy be back in time to tell us a Skook story?" the blond boy asked.

"Of course he will," Yovi said.

"The circle of life," Wally said, not knowing precisely what he meant. "I do believe, dear friends, that you have managed to bring me to the edge of inebriation."

The following day at the new Olmec excavation the judge's illness came on him full force. He was taken to the hospital in Vera Cruz, where it was soon discovered that he was not suffering from a simple case of *turista* but a serious intestinal disorder. He developed pneumonia and was in intensive care for five days. His disappointment over having had to abort his participation in the expedition—a lifetime dream—was as nothing compared to the intense joy his discovery of Yovi and Span had engendered. To himself he acknowledged a secret truth: Even if he had not become ill, he would have left the dig early, so impatient was he to tell his story to his friends at The Swan.

The trip home exhausted him. It was a full week before he

felt strong enough to walk down the hill to The Swan. During that week of wandering around his cavernous house, he began to tell his story to the close friends who came to bring food and run errands. As a result, by the time he was able to leave the house, the tale—exaggerated and distorted by many tongues—had preceded him, and his reception at The Swan was not quite what he expected. His early visitors, sympathetic as they were to their dear friend Wally, could not help noticing that he had got suddenly old—whether because of his illness or his ever-increasing recourse to the bottle, they could not say—and his narrative tended to treat with equal earnestness the existence of Span and Yovi Barrman under new names somewhere in the wilds of Mexico—certainly a possibility, at least, to open minds—and the existence of Barrman's Cave and blind cave-sea bears two stories tall.

The old judge, they judged, had started to slip his moorings. He was still treated with great respect—perhaps even greater than ever—by his friends and the old guard at The Swan, but with barely disguised contumely and some open mockery by the young, the tangential, the bystanders who had been drawn into awareness of him by the widely circulated warped versions of his claims.

He had resolved not to mention The Skook. He concurred with Span's judgment that believers in The Skook had better keep their beliefs to themselves in the interest of community acceptance. He knew, therefore, that he had committed a grave error when, carried away one evening with his zeal and his Barrilito and soda, he told a few friends about The Skook. He knew immediately, but pretended not to know, that he had destroyed the last vestige of his credibility.

Still, he did not surrender. He went about the tasks he had set himself with dedication in spite of his limited strength. He tried to raise money to drill above some possible locations of Barrman's Cave, or to bring in oil-exploration equipment and make sophisticated soundings. He made himself available to the press, knowing they had come to ridicule him, but hoping his story would fall on one sympathetic scientific ear and find some support for the possibility of the existence of an inland sea under the hills of Hunterdon. The media gave him tongue-in-cheek coverage, placing him on a scale of veracity somewhere beneath Baron Munchausen.

The judge refused to accept himself as the new Don Quixote. He walked proudly, though at times unsteadily, meeting the world's eye. The world, more often than not, did not meet his. He sent out the messages he had promised Span and Yovi he would send: to the last-known addresses of Span's two daughters, putting as a return address "Bulletin Board, Swan Hotel, Lambertville, New Jersey." The messages were identical: "Your father is alive and well, but cannot make his whereabouts known. He sends you his love." Both letters were returned to The Swan marked NOT AT THIS ADDRESS. A similar message to Yovi's parents in Trieste was not returned and not acknowledged.

Wally's audience at The Swan dwindled. Most people are uncomfortable in the presence of mental derangement, no matter how benevolent or amusing it may be. Only one of the regulars continued to come faithfully to drink with Wally and listen to him night after night. This was probably due less to loyalty than to habit, or to lack of something better to do. This old pal felt himself disintegrating along with Wally and living in the same world of suspect reality. He recognized, with a shock of self-doubt, that he, of all the listeners, was the one who believed the judge's yarn. He began to ask for more detail. Wally, if he could, complied. If not, he would say, "Golly, I didn't ask" or "I don't recall."

One evening when Wally arrived to take his reserved seat on the old church bench, one of the partners, Jim, was waiting for him with a stricken face. Jim had never ceased for one moment treating him with respect. Now he intercepted him before he could get to the back of the bar, and told him with great regret that his bronze plaque, with the words *Reserved for Judge Walter Youngford,* had been pried loose and stolen by a souvenir hunter the night before. He assured Wally it would be replaced— an identical plaque was at the engravers at that moment. It was still Wally's seat, Jim said, *in saecula saeculorum.*

That night Wally drank more than usual. He rambled. His one remaining listener stayed with him drink for drink, then walked him home to his empty house on the hill and continued to drink with him till he fell asleep in his stuffed high-backed chair like an old bear with honey on his face. Somehow the loyal—or indiscriminate—listener found his way to his own house and bed. The next day at noon he was told that Wally had been found by his housekeeper, dead in his chair.

This was a signal to the sole believer to save himself and to honor his departed friend at the same time. He flew to Vera Cruz and drove from there to Villahermosa, and from there, using what clues he could remember, into the eastern mountains, where finally, after months of searching, he found the thriving expatriates and with their help committed to paper the story of Span and Yovi and The Skook.

The End